*Praise for*

# AWAY with the PENGUINS

'This year's *Eleanor Oliphant* . . . Funny,
bittersweet and wholly original.'
*DAILY EXPRESS*

'A glorious, life-affirming story. I read it in a day.'
CLARE MACKINTOSH

'This adorable tale will put a smile on your face.'
*GOOD HOUSEKEEPING*

'A warm-hearted and life-affirming tale about
ageing, human kindness, old-fashioned values
and protecting our planet.'
*CULTUREFLY*

'A touching, uplifting tale.'
JO WHILEY, RADIO 2 BOOK CLUB

'Veronica McCreedy will
capture your heart.'
TRISHA ASHLEY

*Praise for*

# CALL of the PENGUINS

'Sparkles with wit,
courage and kindness.'
**CELIA ANDERSON**

'A wonderful story, full of twists
and turns. Outstanding.'
**SAMANTHA TONGE**

'Just what the doctor ordered . . .
Funny, wise, touching. I loved it.'
**TRACY REES**

'So many readers are set to fall in love
with this charming story.'
*PRIMA*

'This gorgeous book has everything! Mysteries,
misunderstandings, arguments, reconciliations,
kindness, love, and lots of PENGUINS!'
**CLARE POOLEY**

'Beautifully written
by a born storyteller.'
**LORRAINE KELLY**

# GONE
## *with the*
# PENGUINS

# Hazel Prior

PENGUIN BOOKS

TRANSWORLD PUBLISHERS
Penguin Random House, One Embassy Gardens,
8 Viaduct Gardens, London SW11 7BW
www.penguin.co.uk

Transworld is part of the Penguin Random House group of companies
whose addresses can be found at global.penguinrandomhouse.com

Penguin
Random House
UK

First published in Great Britain in 2024 by Penguin Books
an imprint of Transworld Publishers

Text illustrations by Global Creative Learning.

A CIP catalogue record for this book
is available from the British Library.

ISBN 9781804993330

Typeset in 11/14.5pt Sabon LT Pro by Jouve (UK), Milton Keynes.
Printed and bound in Great Britain by Clays Ltd, Elcograf S.p.A.

The authorized representative in the EEA is Penguin Random House Ireland,
Morrison Chambers, 32 Nassau Street, Dublin D02 YH68.

'It is never too late to be what you might have been.'

George Eliot

# 1

# Veronica

*The Ballahays, Ayrshire*
*Late August 2014*

I HAVE ASKED Eileen to refrain from humming. In order
to read the article in the *Scots Times*, I require absolute
peace and quiet. Now silenced, she continues to busy herself flicking dust around the mantelpiece.

I was out on my litter-picking walk when the paper
arrived with the post an hour ago. Eileen has only resisted
looking at it so far because the package was sealed and
addressed to me, but she is loitering with intent. It is
impossible to ignore her presence, but at least I am comfortably settled in the Queen Anne armchair. My handbag
is tucked in beside me. My spectacles are on my nose. The
essential cup of Darjeeling tea is close to hand.

I peruse the words, taking my time.

Eileen drifts closer and I catch a whiff of her distinctive eau de bleach, Pears soap and furniture polish. She has abandoned her duster and is watching me impatiently.

'It's a lovely picture of you,' she comments, peering over at the page.

'Thank you, Eileen. It is quite acceptable. And they have included the salient points. But I do wish they wouldn't keep harping on about my age. It would be nice to be recognized simply for what one does rather than constantly reminded of one's state of decay. And the word "pensioner" is so very belittling.'

'Oh now, Mrs McCreedy.' She tuts. 'Why don't you just enjoy it?'

I am, in fact, enjoying it. I have become used to my name appearing in the press, not always in a way that covers me in glory. I will confess to being rather pleased this time, however. I am careful not to let this explosion of smugness register on my face. Although vanity flows through my veins, I am aware it is not my best attribute.

'Do they mention Pip?' Eileen asks.

'They do indeed.'

'And do they mention Sir Robert?'

'Absolutely.'

'And all about what you'll be doing next?'

'Yes, yes, Eileen.'

'And do they . . .' She takes a little gulp, and I perceive we have been leading up to this. '. . . I don't suppose they mentioned me, by any chance? No, of course they didn't. They wouldn't, would they? I mean, why on earth would they?'

I hold out the paper to her. 'You may as well read it for yourself.'

She homes in on it, simultaneously untying her apron and plunging her posterior into the chair opposite. It is the fastest I've seen her move in months. She bends her head to devour the article. Her unkempt curls, I notice, are threaded with grey these days and the effect resembles wire wool. She reads aloud, one plump finger following the lines as she does so.

I savour the words once more.

## PENGUIN HONOURS FOR LOCAL PENSIONER

Veronica McCreedy, 87, of Ayrshire, is to become the first ever person to receive the official title of Penguin Ambassador. The determined octogenarian attracted much public admiration when she rescued an orphaned baby penguin in Antarctica two years ago. Mrs McCreedy was featured in blogs written by Antarctic researchers which included photographs of herself with Pip, the penguin chick, gaining her a following of penguin fans throughout the world. She has since become known as a vibrant on-screen presence with Sir Robert Saddlebow, as co-presenter of his BBC wildlife documentary *Who Cares About Seabirds?*. In the programme she ably reported on several different species of penguin. She also spoke out about the potential damage of plastics to penguins and other wildlife. Mrs McCreedy has now been recognized for this and for her generous financial support of the Locket Island Penguin Project.

The new honour of Penguin Ambassador has been created by the Anglo-Antarctic Research Council in acknowledgement of Mrs McCreedy's contributions towards penguin awareness. She is to travel to the Galápagos Islands, escorted by Sir Robert, to present a minor part in his next documentary, before heading further south to receive her award in the AARC headquarters in the Falkland Islands.

Mrs McCreedy says: 'This is a great and unforeseen honour. I am immensely proud and shall endeavour to do all that I can in my new role as Penguin Ambassador.'

Eileen Thompson, Mrs McCreedy's housekeeper, says: 'Who would have thought it? Mrs McCreedy really has a way with the penguins. She's tickled pink about the award. I'm over the moon for her, and just so glad she's got another chance to follow the call of the penguins.'

Eileen looks up at me, her eyes a-glitter. Then flaps a little cool air at herself with the paper.

'It's beautiful,' she says. 'And they did put in what I said – almost the exact words! Gosh, it's quite a thing, isn't it? And what a time you're going to have!'

'Indeed I am.'

Sparks of anticipation fly about my stomach at the thought of all that lies ahead.

I don't know which pleases me more: the prospect of an exotic expedition with Sir Robert, courtesy of the BBC, or the fact that I am to become the first and only Penguin Ambassador in the world.

Sir Robert is not only my dear friend but also a television celebrity of great standing. His wildlife documentaries are the one thing of any value on television. He is (quite rightly) worshipped by the public for his longevity, his vast knowledge, his pleasing demeanour and his attractive Scottish voice that has a way of creeping into your system and warming you like a fine whisky.

Some would say I am obscenely privileged to have not only such a friend but also wealth, health and a fine Jacobean mansion on the Ayrshire coast. Yet I doubt that many would choose to be in my shoes. Awful things happen to rich people as well as poor people. I would give up every antique and every designer handbag in a heartbeat if it meant I could change the past. I have spent decade upon decade grieving. Or sulking, if you will.

Now, however, I am driven by an intense need to make up for lost time. At my age one is not expected to have dreams. They are supposed to be consigned to the dustbin along with one's pride, mobility and zest for life. But when have I ever heeded the expectations of society?

My chief focus these days is penguins. I am fonder of penguins than most people. And yes, that sentence can be read in two ways. I have now met many thousands of penguins and there has not been a single one that I've disliked. The same cannot be said for my own species. Eileen tells me that most people have photographs of their family all over the place, and I really must ask my grandson to send me a decent one of himself, perhaps together with his lovely girlfriend. Aside from a grainy old image that sits on the mantelpiece, the closest thing to a portrait I have here is the photograph of Pip that hangs in the hall. What a heart-wrenching pity that he lives so far away. If one is to see penguins at all, one must travel right across the globe, unless it is to see them in captivity, and I have mixed feelings about that.

From time to time my passion for penguins takes me to the Lochnamorghy Sea Life Centre, but it saddens me to witness these wild, wonderful birds cooped up in such cramped conditions. They seem cheerful, but that is not saying much, since a penguin's natural disposition is good cheer. And can they really enjoy an existence purely aimed at pleasing tourists?

Seeing them in the wild is a different thing altogether. I am so very grateful that this last opportunity has been granted to me. There is much to anticipate. The Falklands, as I know from previous experience, will be breathtaking. The Galápagos Islands intrigue and entice me. Flying across the world so soon after my last escapade might seem self-indulgent and far from environmentally friendly, but I console myself with the fact that, prior to 2012, I had not taken a single flight in half a century. Consequently, my average is a good deal less than that of a typical, holiday-greedy European.

When I first told Eileen about the filming expedition, she displayed a rare amalgam of delight and befuddlement.

'So remind me where the Galápagos is, exactly?'

'It is an archipelago in the Pacific Ocean, to the west of Ecuador,' I informed her. 'The islands are located around the equator.'

'And there's a penguin that lives there?'

'Several, I believe.'

Her brow furrowed.

'Not all penguins need ice and snow, as you well know, Eileen.'

'Yes, but the equator? Surely not. Sir Robert must've made a mistake.'

'Sir Robert does not make mistakes,' I told her severely. 'And certainly not about any matter pertaining to wildlife.'

'Well, you must've misheard, then. Was your hearing aid switched on?'

'Eileen, I do wonder sometimes if you take me for a complete idiot?'

'Oh no, Mrs McCreedy' – and her hands flew up. 'Never that. I just thought. Well ... Penguins, on the equator? It seems so ...'

'Improbable?' I suggested.

She nodded.

'Improbable, yes, but true,' I assured her. 'That is the whole point of Sir Robert's programme. It is about how nature adapts against all odds to survive in the most extreme circumstances. The Galápagos penguins have evolved to live in the heat of the equator, just as the Emperor and Adélie penguins have evolved to live in the sub-zero climes of the Antarctic. That is why Sir Robert is filming in Antarctica afterwards, to illustrate the extremes.'

I sniff involuntarily. I have not been invited to the Antarctic part of the trip. Whether this is the BBC's decision or Sir Robert's, I do not know. I suspect there is a feeling that Antarctica is too much for an eighty-seven-year-old. Sir Robert is not so very far behind me at seventy-nine and a half, yet I have noticed no protestations about *him* going there. But Sir Robert is God as far as the BBC are concerned.

*

My surroundings glitter and gleam. I am striding through a castle of ice. Glassy pillars rise to a vaulted white ceiling above my head. A carpet of snow squeaks under my feet. Warm in my robe, I walk through a sculpted ballroom and a vast library containing floor-to-ceiling bookshelves fringed with icicles. I push open the door at the end of the room. Before me is a hall, twinkling with crystal. An assembly of penguins is gathered around a marble table. Multiple beaked faces turn to look at me as I enter. One of the dignitaries solemnly indicates an empty seat with his flipper. I step forward. I am about to address them when my head drops forward and I wake up.

I am not in the ice castle after all, but in my Ayrshire home, The Ballahays. The window, flanked by velvet curtains, looks out on to the green sweep of summer lawn. The herbaceous border is a blaze of roses, gladioli and geraniums. Lavender spills from the two stone urns on the terrace. By my side, the teacup is empty. Eileen has gone.

The grandfather clock chimes in the hall. It is already midday. I rise stiffly to my feet. The newspaper is lying on the chair opposite. I glance over at it and catch myself smiling. I shall relish any challenge my new position demands of me.

Now that it is all official, it would be wise to ascertain exactly what my ambassadorial role entails.

I discover Eileen contemplating her reflection in the hall mirror, her arms folded over her capacious bosom. She unfolds them and pinches her chin between two fingers, fretting and sighing.

'I'm beginning to get a wattle, aren't I, Mrs McCreedy?'

I hesitate. Possible answers leap through my head:

'What do you mean, *beginning to get* a wattle? You've always had a wattle, Eileen.'

And: 'Many turkeys would be extremely proud of that wattle.'

And even, for reasons that altogether elude me: 'Gotta lotta wattle.'

I am too polite to say any of these out loud. Proud as I am of my own well-defined jawline, I must be mindful of her feelings. Distraction is always a good tool, so I reply: 'Wattle or not, I would be grateful if you could dust the chandelier, Eileen. I can see at least one cobweb suspended in it.'

After all, I don't pay her all that money so that she can stand there gawking at herself in the mirror.

'Of course,' she replies, deserting her reflection to burrow in the cupboard under the stairs for the long-handled feather duster.

I consult the mirror briefly myself and am glad to note that my lipstick is immaculate. These days I do not apply make-up to beautify, rather to de-uglify. My skin is like scrunched-up tissue paper despite the layers of cosmetic paste. I scowl at myself and then transfer my gaze to the photograph of Pip. His upward-pointing flipper seems to be waving at me, which cheers me considerably.

I return the teacup to the kitchen. It is one from my Royal Worcester set, a tasteful powder-blue design with the rim and handle finely picked out in gold.

Now, what was I about to do? My feet have taken me back to the drawing room, and I am sure there was a good reason for this.

Ah yes, I was going to seek out the original written communication from the Anglo-Antarctic Research Council. I would ask Eileen where she has put it, but as she is now balancing precariously on a stepladder, the feather duster tinkling away in the Waterford crystal, I am reluctant to trouble her further. I search my handbag, the dresser drawers and the walnut cabinet beside the pianola, and eventually find the letter hidden in the top of the bureau. It is scant on details, but there is a telephone number.

I make a call to the AARC's London office.

Despite my hearing aid, I can't make out very well what the young man at the other end is saying. Why must people always mumble these days? When I ask him to repeat himself, his manner becomes surly. The role of Penguin Ambassador is, he informs me, a mere gesture of thanks from the AARC and it bears with it no expectation. It is a promotional tool, a meaningless token, a hollow label. He does not say this in so many words, but he implies as much. I will be required to make a five-minute acceptance speech – no more, no less – in which I am to glorify the work of the AARC. I will be presented with a sash (I was not expecting a coronet or golden chain, but a mere *sash*!), given a handshake and put in front of cameras to be photographed. Then my work is done.

After further probing, it emerges that the original idea was to summon me only as far as London to receive my honour. Then it was argued that the media photographs would be more impressive if I were to pose with actual penguins in their natural habitat. Besides, most of the organization's bigwigs, who are eager to appear in the photographs too, are based in the Falklands. It seems I am to travel to the other side of the world for no greater purpose than a cheap publicity gimmick. And it will be far from cheap in a literal sense, as I am expected to pay for the flight from the Galápagos myself. Money, of course, is no issue for me, and the AARC knows this, but I am left with the distinctly unsavoury feeling of being used.

The telephone receiver lands with a bang. It is impossible to hold the wretched thing with clenched fists. My temples are throbbing. I may have raised my voice at the lad; I am not sure.

If there is one thing I detest in life, it is the feeling of being enfeebled by the attitude of others. The McCreedy spirit rises within me, undaunted, irrepressible. I am very, very far from feeble.

And I shall prove it.

# 2

# Eileen

*Kilmarnock*

'HAVE YOU SEEN the . . . ?'

I wave my hand in the direction of the *Scots Times* that's lying on the kitchen table. I came back from The Ballahays via Kilmarnock so that I could get my own copy, and I've folded down the page with the article so Doug can't miss it.

'Yes, Eileen. I have.'

I've told him all about the article and I've been aching for him to pick it up and read it. Finally, now he does. In my excitement I brush against the dancing sunflower that's by the kettle and set it off. Mrs McCreedy wouldn't approve because it's made of plastic and she's very anti-plastic these days, but it always cheers me to see it jiggling away. Our kitchen is cosy, cluttered and Formica'd, not like her grand one, with its huge pine dresser and regiments of china teacups.

I switch off the sunflower so as to watch Doug. His chin is a mat of fine, grey stubble. His face doesn't move apart from his eyes skimming the words. I know from the way his brow is clenched that I'm not to speak until he's finished.

Now a slight twitch pulls at the corner of his mouth. He doesn't look up but gives a little nod, which is his way of saying he approves.

It's hard to contain myself, I'm that pleased. 'Isn't it fantastic? The *Scots Times*, too! I'll have to snip it out and add it to my cuttings folder.' I dollop some porridge in his bowl and scatter salt over it, the way he likes it. I add sugar on mine. 'But still, I do worry about Mrs McCreedy.'

He doesn't respond so I repeat myself as I pour tea into his 'I heart cookies' mug and thrust his breakfast towards him. 'I do worry.'

He blows on the porridge and attacks it with a spoon. 'You worry too much.'

I plonk myself down opposite him and tuck in, too. 'On the one hand, I'm happy for her, because she was so miserable for ages and never really spoke to anyone except me and that was hardly . . . well . . . it was mainly instructions.' I pull a face, remembering. 'But ever since the penguin thing she's been like a new person. Travel must be good for her. And people. And penguins. On the other hand, she's eighty-seven now, and if you ask me, that's too old for all this "gallivanting", as she calls it.'

Doug frowns. 'Did you put any salt on this porridge?' he asks.

'Of course I did.' I automatically push the salt pot towards him before remembering the doctor said he should cut down. It's bad for his blood pressure. I'm sure all the salt over the years has done funny things to his taste buds, too. He seems to prefer takeaway haggis and chips to my home cooking these days.

He leafs through the rest of the *Scots Times* as he eats.

'Fuel prices going up again,' he mutters. 'And a shortage of diesel.'

My mind slips back to Mrs McCreedy. 'It's not that she's what you'd call doddery, not in the least. She's still so brisk and upright! I envy her posture, actually. But she will throw herself into risky situations. And she *will* have her own way. Always has done, always will do. "Eileen," she said to me the other day, "I only feel alive when there is an adventure on the cards. It's just as well I have this filming trip to look forward to, or I might as well be dead." "Don't speak like that, Mrs McCreedy," I said. But she carried on speaking like that. Even being a Penguin Ambassador doesn't seem to be enough for her now.'

I pause. Doug is still scanning the headlines whilst listening to me.

'Sir Robert is away such a lot, and with her grandson, Patrick, across the other side of the world, she's still so alone, really. I do wish she could just be happy, like we are.'

Doug sighs and rattles the paper. 'That McCreedy woman has no right to be unhappy, with all that money and waited on hand and foot by you.'

I don't like the way he called her 'that McCreedy woman', but I continue along my track, trying to make it

14

out. 'She got into one of her grumpies after that phone call to the research council people. She thinks they're not giving her enough to do. Isn't it crazy? Most people like to relax a bit in their old age, but not Mrs McCreedy. She's the opposite. The older she gets, the more she pushes herself. There's something almost desperate about her. I've got this feeling, right here' – I pat my chest – 'this worry that she's going to do something eccentric and noble and dangerous. You have to admire her, but I get so bothered wondering what she might do next. And if it, whatever it is, might just kill her.'

Suddenly – *woomph* – I'm dripping with heat. I consider splashing my face with cold water but that would mean getting up.

'Stop fretting, will you? The woman is like the Queen. She'll go on for ever.'

'Thank goodness she's got Sir Robert. Well, when I say "got", I don't mean there's anything like that in it. Just that he is a great friend to her, is Sir Robert.'

I pause again. Doug doesn't like to show it, but he is very impressed that I personally know Sir Robert Saddlebow (yes, not any old Robert Saddlebow. The famous one off the telly). And that Mrs McCreedy and he are special friends.

Doug licks his spoon slowly. 'Well, I guess Sir Robert will keep cooking up interesting things for her to do. She always gets her way.'

My husband is a clever man.

'You're quite right there, Dougie. She does. Always. Anyway, I'm glad we've got Daisy coming to visit. It's nice for Mrs McCreedy to have a child in her life. Such a

15

dear one, too. Oh Lorks, look at the time! I'd best be getting along to fetch her.'

'I'd best be getting along, too,' he says, swallowing the last mouthful and brushing the back of his hand against his lips.

Doug works in an oatcake factory, which is funny because he hates oatcakes. They're one of the things that Doug says are plain *wrong*, along with students, the government, Volvo drivers, English film stars being cast in Scottish roles and dachshund dogs wearing coats. 'Oats are for porridge, and porridge only,' he always says. 'Squash them into flat, hard discs and even a slab of cheese, ham and pickle can't take away the sensation of chipboard in your mouth.'

He does make me laugh.

Mrs M took Daisy under her wing (or should I say 'flipper', haha) when she came back from Antarctica with a new zest and zim and the need for a fresh project. Daisy is the daughter of Gav who is the friend of Patrick who is Mrs McCreedy's grandson, you see, and Daisy was seriously ill at the time. Mrs M helped the family by way of little injections of money for private treatments, not to mention a shower of gifts and holidays at The Ballahays whenever they wanted. When Daisy was well enough, she even took her, together with her mum, along to the Falklands, where she was presenting that documentary with Sir Robert. Daisy was hooked on penguins, too, what with all Mrs M's talk about them. That trip was a huge boost after the years of dreadful pain for the poor wee girl.

I pick her up from the service station where her parents

and I arranged to meet. It's midway between here and Bolton, where they live. I'm used to the drive by now.

She's grown bigger since I last saw her and the freckles on her nose are darker, too. She must have been out in the garden a lot in Bolton. It's lovely that she has so much thick nut-brown hair these days, gathered up with pink and yellow butterfly clips. It's the last week of her school holidays and we chat about all sorts of things – bicycles and spiders and the nicest flavours of ice cream and her best friend who is called Aurora – and the time flies by.

When we pull up, Mrs McCreedy is stood waiting in the grand porch of The Ballahays like a statue in a scarlet shawl.

Daisy jumps out of the car, pelts up the gravel drive and flings herself at Mrs M so hard that she has to put an arm out to the wall to steady herself.

'Let go, young lady. You are crumpling my blouse,' Mrs M tells her severely. She rummages in her handbag for a hanky and dabs her eyes. 'Eileen, would you put the kettle on, please? We need to get Daisy settled in.'

I've bought a treat for Daisy: some cupcakes with thick icing and multicoloured sprinkles. Like me, she loves anything sugary.

Mrs M has already arranged cups and saucers from one of her fancy tea sets on the table.

'What would you like to drink, Daisy?' I ask.

'Oh, I should like a Darjeeling, thank you, Eileen,' she answers, putting on a posh voice.

Then she bursts into giggles, giving away the fact that her answer was supposed to be an imitation of Mrs M. It was quite good, actually.

17

'Tee hee hee, not really! Have you got any squash?'

'Yes.' I put a bottle in front of her. 'Help yourself, dear.'

'Can I have it in a teacup, though?' Daisy asks, looking from me to Mrs M and back again.

Mrs M agrees to it, but I see her wince as Daisy pours a large amount of the squash into a cup, making it wobble as she rests the bottle on its fine edge. She then overfills it from the tap and has to slurp quickly to avoid spilling any.

We settle around the table. Daisy grabs a cupcake, spiking her fingers in glee, and I take one, too. Mrs McCreedy delicately accepts one of her favourite ginger thins that I've also laid out on a plate. (It took me a while, but I've managed to source some that aren't sold in plastic packaging. Mrs McCreedy is so pernickety about it.)

'And how are your dear parents and your brother?' Mrs M asks. She pauses then adds his name. 'Noah.'

I'm glad she got it right. She's not normally very good at names.

Daisy peels the icing off her cupcake, folds it in half and posts it into her mouth before answering. 'OK, I suppose.'

When I met them at the service station, her dad – the ever so nice, smiley Gav – told me his bicycle shop is doing really well now; so well he's looking into setting up another shop in the Scottish Borders. He's hunting for somewhere with a flat above it, he said.

Mrs McCreedy is pleased when I tell her because it means we'll get to see even more of Daisy. I also learned that her mum (a slim, quiet, sweet lady called Beth) is about to set off as supervisor on a school trip that Noah is going on. That's one of the reasons Daisy is staying with us. I tell that to Mrs McCreedy, too, and she fiddles with her hearing aid to turn it up, interested.

'Where are they going?' she asks.

'Switzerland,' Daisy answers. 'Dad's been so crazy busy he hasn't gone anywhere this summer. Nor me, neither, until now. But Noah gets to go abroad.' Her nose wrinkles. She puts her teacup down on the saucer with a crash that makes Mrs McCreedy shudder. 'Mum says it's because I've had a big holiday with you and the penguins and now it's Noah's turn.'

Mrs M surveys her. 'Don't be despondent,' she says. 'We will do our utmost to ensure you have an equally enjoyable time here.'

I've been instructed not to say anything about her trip across the world. At least, not yet. We'll pick our time carefully. I've been bursting to tell her, but I do understand. Daisy is likely to be jealous, and we don't want that.

Daisy adores her visits to The Ballahays. Still, looking after her is a lot for Mrs McCreedy to deal with on her own, so I always stay in one of the spare rooms when she's here. Doug is very good about it, and manages to microwave the ready meals I leave for him. I'll call him later and see how he got on with the cauliflower cheese.

'How are things at school?' Mrs McCreedy asks.

'All right. I'm doing a sponsored walk.' Daisy is very proactive (the word her mum used) at school as a fundraiser for cancer charities and conservation charities. Mrs McCreedy has been a good influence, I think.

'That is very commendable,' Mrs M comments.

'I should be delighted to sponsor you. Where will you be walking, and how far?'

Daisy shrugs. 'No idea. Somewhere around home, I suppose. I don't know yet how far. But a looooong way, I expect.' She opens up her arms to show us the long way.

'Sponsored walks are all the rage now,' I comment. 'Did you see that thing in the *Scots Times*? An old man is doing the Forth and Clyde Canal walk for charity. It's quite wonderful.'

Mrs McCreedy gives a little snort. She's not as impressed as I am, but then she is such an able walker herself.

'How old is he?' she asks.

'Oh, I don't remember. About your age, I think. I can check if you like.' I lean round because from here I can reach the kitchen dresser drawer. I pull it open and nab the paper. Just as I remembered, the article is on the front page, accompanied by a photo of the old man with his sweet, gappy smile and his Zimmer frame. 'Oh no, I'm wrong,' I mutter as I run through the paragraph. 'He's even older than you are, Mrs McCreedy. Quite a lot older, actually. He is ninety-three! Unbelievable. Ninety-three! He doesn't look it, though.'

'Let's see,' Daisy clamours, grabbing the paper from me.

'I think he looks tonnes older than Veronica,' she says, examining the photo. 'But then, *he*'s not wearing lipstick and eyeshadow, is he?' she adds.

'Don't be cheeky, little miss,' I scold.

But Mrs McCreedy doesn't seem to have noticed. 'What he is doing is laudable,' she says. 'Yet the Forth and Clyde Canal walk is not such an impossible achievement. Especially as he is only doing it a little at a time, and with the help of a Zimmer frame.'

Daisy swallows down the sponge of her cupcake with a swig of squash. I have just remembered she is not to see the article about Mrs McCreedy when she turns the page. Her eyes stretch wide.

'Hey, that's you, Veronica!'

I look at Mrs M, whose face is a picture of put-outness, then I look at Daisy and then I look at the newspaper. I squint at the picture and feign surprise. 'Oh, is it? Well I never! So it is!'

I try to reclaim the paper and there's a brief wrestling match, but Daisy wins. She reads the article, bleating out certain words louder than the others; words like 'Penguin Ambassador' and 'Sir Robert Saddlebow' and 'Galápagos' and 'Falklands', and with every bleat I feel more like a criminal.

'Why didn't you tell me?' she caterwauls.

Mrs M seems to be leaving the job of explaining to me. I blabber something about how we are just getting used to the news ourselves and how we were going to tell her soon, once she'd settled in, and how lovely it is, isn't it, and how proud we are of our Mrs McCreedy, aren't we? My face feels like a furnace.

Daisy has been well brought-up, so she congratulates Mrs M politely. She has taken the news better than we thought she might, but she's not what you'd call thrilled.

It's just as well we have a treat lined up for her tomorrow.

# 3

# Veronica

*Lochnamorghy*

Mac views us with beady eyes from atop his favourite stone. He hops down, stretches out both flippers and tilts his head a little to one side, as if in recognition. Mac is our favourite Scottish penguin; Scottish in the sense that he was born and bred here, at the Lochnamorghy Sea Life Centre. Daisy, Eileen and I are all enamoured of him. He possesses the usual black and white attributes that all penguins are famed for and, in addition, since he is a Macaroni penguin, he sports a superbly flamboyant golden crest that begins behind his beak and flows back on either side of his head.

The other penguins hang back but Mac is fascinated by the public. He waddles towards us over the mini zebra crossing on the concrete walkway. As he shakes his head from side to side, his glorious head feathers wave like streamers.

Daisy is carrying my shiny red handbag, which makes her resemble a little cartoon Queen Elizabeth. I feel somewhat naked without it. I was reluctant to let it into her rather sticky grasp, but she was clamorous and I was unwilling to cause any friction, emotions already being somewhat delicate.

Now, to my relief, she passes it back to me in order to crouch down and greet Mac. She maintains her distance, knowing she isn't allowed to touch him.

Eileen's driving has become a little erratic recently and my blood pressure has only just settled. Mac's presence helps. Whilst I am somewhat riled by the whole Penguin Ambassador debacle, the actual proximity of penguins is always therapeutic. It is also a pleasure to see Daisy's solemn face light up as she talks to her avian friend.

A boy – slight, serious-looking, a little younger than Daisy – is standing apart from the other tourists, hands in his pockets, staring. Daisy takes it upon herself to introduce him to the penguin.

'His name is Mac. Mac because he's a Macaroni,' she explains. 'That's one of the eighteen species of penguins. Isn't he cute? Those ones over there, with the black bands around their fronts, are African penguins. But Mac's the best. I'm Daisy and I live in Bolton, but I've travelled across the world and seen penguins in the wild, too. Did you know they have five different species in the Falklands? That's where I've been.'

The boy looks suitably impressed, so she continues.

'I met so many penguins you wouldn't believe it. And I know Sir Robert Saddlebow.'

'Seriously?' The boy's eyes are as round as saucers. The tips of his ears are tinged with red.

Daisy nods her vigorous affirmation. 'Yup, I actually do. He's really nice. And I'm here with that lady there, Veronica McCreedy, who I stay with sometimes.' She points at me and he darts a look in my direction. I produce a thin smile, which seems to terrify him because he immediately looks away again. 'She's got this mansion by the sea, called The Ballahays,' Daisy continues. 'It's huge, with, like, *eleven* fireplaces and *five* staircases, and full of really cool things like an old ship's bell and a globe on legs. And that's Eileen who helps look after it, and she helps look after Veronica, and me too sometimes, and she lives in Kilmarnock and likes cake.'

I glance at Eileen. She has her eyes fixed on Mac and is pretending not to be listening.

Daisy is in full flow. 'Me and Veronica and Sir Robert have been on TV. Hang on a mo, I'll show you.'

She pulls out her phone and swipes through images. The boy is lost for words. He is probably wondering why Daisy has no hair in the photos but now a thick crop of it tumbles around her cheeks. His eyes drink up the pictures, then veer back to Mac, then back to the pictures.

Eventually tiring of his silent admiration, Daisy tucks her phone away. A young couple, evidently his parents, usher the boy away in the direction of the cafe.

'What a sweet, shy little boy!' Eileen declares. 'You have a new fan there, Daisy.'

'I am aware that oversharing is the current trend,' I remark, 'but you need not have revealed every last detail of our lives within the first two seconds of meeting him.'

Daisy is unabashed. 'I was going to tell him about my cancer, too, but then I went off the idea.'

I put a hand on her shoulder. 'That is just as well. It is indelicate to refer to one's physical complaints in public, no matter how grievous they may be.'

Thankfully, Daisy has made a full recovery, although cancer is such a devious creature you never can altogether trust that it has gone away for good. I remove my gloves and unclip my handbag, assailed by a sudden urgent need for a pocket handkerchief. As I pull one out, I realize too late that a glove has dropped to the ground and Mac is aiming himself at it with unbridled zeal. I try for a save but am just too late. It has been snatched up by an eager beak and is now being experimentally chewed.

Daisy yelps with laughter. The gloves are beaded tulle and great favourites of mine, yet I, too, am amused. The fingers poke from either side of Mac's beak, the beads clicking slightly as he samples the taste and texture.

A vivacious young woman in wellington boots is striding towards us carrying a bucket. Her ponytail flows in the wind. She is one of the penguin patrollers here and we know her quite well due to our frequent visits. Her name is Tilly or Milly or some such thing.

She leaps in and wrests the glove from Mac. He retaliates by giving her kneecap an indignant peck.

'Oy, Mac. I've known you since you were an egg. Don't get cheeky with me,' she cries.

I accept the glove back with grace, concealing my chagrin. It is filthy and mangled, the intricate beading decimated.

The patroller, relieved at my equanimity, turns to Daisy. 'Hello, Daisy. Lovely to see you.'

'Hi, Molly. Is it feeding time?'

'It sure is. We need to get Mac back on his proper diet quickly, before he tries to eat anything else.'

She puts the bucket on the ground and starts dipping into it, withdrawing smelly, slithery fish and tossing them at the penguins. Daisy has helped her on a few occasions, but today prefers to watch and take photos. Mac has become particularly adept at catching fish in his beak. Tilly aims with precision and he snatches them, sometimes even leaping up and grabbing them in mid-air, to the delight of the onlookers.

'He's awfully good at it, isn't he?' Eileen exclaims.

'Yes, but he has an advantage since he is willing to come closer than the other penguins,' I point out. 'And Tilly is good at throwing.'

'Veronica, it's not Tilly, it's Molly!' Daisy crows.

I fix her with a stern look. 'One-upmanship is extremely unappealing in the young.'

Daisy chooses to ignore this. As Molly delivers the last fish, she babbles on about how she adores Mac and how brilliant he is.

'He's a star, isn't he? I love that one over there, too.' Molly indicates an African penguin who is snoozing standing up, his head slightly drooped. 'His name's Pablo. He's twenty-two years old now, same as me.'

'Cripes!' cries Eileen.

'He's more than double me!' declares Daisy, who has reached the noble age of ten.

'Penguins in captivity can live to a good old age, but he is exceptional. We're so proud of him.'

As we admire Pablo, he opens one eye. The pink patch of skin visible above it is completely unwrinkled and I briefly wonder what face cream he uses before remembering he is only a penguin.

'How do you recognize them all?' Daisy asks.

'Oh, you get to know the subtleties in their markings. That one who's having a shake by the railing is Florence, for example. She's got dark speckles like a constellation on her neck. And of course they each have their funny little habits, too. They're a lovely bunch of personalities. I'll be so sad to say goodbye to them.' She claps her hand over her mouth.

'Why will you say goodbye?' asks Daisy, quick to sniff out something amiss. 'Are you going somewhere?'

'Well . . .' The penguin patroller is reluctant to say anything. 'I am looking for a new job,' she admits finally.

'Don't you like this one?'

'It's not that I *want* to leave,' she murmurs, a distinctly furtive look on her face.

'Why are you going, then?' demands Daisy.

'I'm not supposed to say.'

'Tell us!'

I am just as eager as Daisy to know what this is about. 'We have been loyal visitors for several years, have we not?' I point out. 'We have a right to know what is going on.'

The woman takes us aside, deposits her bucket in a small outhouse and confides in a low voice.

27

'Lochnamorghy Sea Life Centre is to close down permanently in two months' time, due to financial problems. Eleven of us face losing our jobs.'

I should not be surprised at this. The place is not well run. The penguins, in my opinion, have insufficient space to waddle around. There is a distinct dearth of information for the visitors, and all the buildings have a shabby and decrepit air. The toilet facilities reek of mildew and the tea shop window frames are a warped disgrace. But still, I am appalled. We all are.

'What will happen to the site?' I enquire.

She shrugs. 'It'll be put on the market, I suppose.'

'And what about the birds and animals?' asks Eileen. Apart from twenty-four penguins, there are a few exotic species of fish in tanks, some rare ducks, seals and otters.

'We'll do our best to rehome them at zoos, aquariums and wildlife parks, but it's problematic. They'll be split up, for sure. They're nearly all marine species, so they need specialist facilities. They have to have the right habitat, the right social grouping and experienced staff working with them. So far, homes have only been found for the fish and the seals. And there's a place down on Exmoor that might take the otters. No luck with the penguins yet.'

Daisy pulls a face. 'Can't they be set free? It's nice countryside around here. And Scotland could do with more penguins.'

Molly smiles mournfully. 'That's not an option, I'm afraid. Most of them hatched out here in the centre. They don't naturally occur in the Scottish landscape, Daisy, so they wouldn't cope with life in the wild.'

Molly addresses me now and lowers her voice further. 'It's so difficult. There's all sorts of legislation we have to comply with: rules about the size of animal carrier, a tonne of permits and health certificates needed before they can travel . . . It's endless. We're all desperately worried. It's looking more and more likely that our penguins may have to be' – here her voice sinks to a whisper – 'euthanized.'

My heart drops in my chest. My grip tightens around my handbag straps. Eileen lets out a gasp.

'What's "euthanized"?' asks Daisy.

Nobody answers.

# 4

# Veronica

*The Ballahays*

DAISY REFUSES TO COME.

Her parents expressly said that she was to accompany
me on my daily constitutional, since she needs to build up
resilience for her school sponsored walk. However, Daisy
is distraught. And the weather outside the bay windows
is looking decidedly inclement.

'Don't be lazy, Daisy,' Eileen says, prodding her in the
ribs.

Daisy pouts. 'I'm not lazy. I'm just . . . Tell you what.
I'll play the pianola the whole time you're out, Veronica,
and all the pedalling can be today's exercise.'

I succumb. 'Very well.'

I am willing to let her off this time. On the way home
from Lochnamorghy she looked up 'euthanized' on her

phone and made a discovery that caused a great deal of distress. Her eyes are red-rimmed and swollen this morning. She has suffered a nasty shock.

I reasoned with her that thousands of penguins die every day in the wild, either by becoming a seal's dinner or perishing from the cold.

'But those Lochnamorghy penguins are special. And we love them. Especially Mac,' she wailed, bundling fists into her eyes. 'He's much too young to die. I thought that about myself, too, once. I *hate* death.'

'Me too,' I admitted gloomily.

I ready myself to go outside. In fact, an hour of solitude is welcome this morning. I need time to tidy up the maelstrom in my brain. I am fraught with concerns, what with running The Ballahays and taking care of Eileen and my doddery gardener, Mr Perkins, and keeping track of my pertinacious grandson, Patrick, and his girlfriend, Terry, in Antarctica, and Sir Robert as he makes multitudinous voyages around the world, and Daisy with all her wild whims. And now this Lochnamorghy issue.

I wrap myself in my macintosh and put on stout boots but I do not bring an umbrella. It is too much for me, what with the handbag, tongs and refuse sack, and, in any case, the cheeky coastal blasts would doubtless yank it from my grasp and whisk it up into the clouds.

I enjoy the vigorous challenge of a cold wind, but I am not fond of rain. It makes my knees creak and my bones moulder. The Ayrshire weather likes to bully me, but I will not give in to it. I have taken a walk every day (barring a couple of unavoidable interludes) since I took my very first tottering steps, and it is this habit that has kept me so very fit in mind and body. Eileen does not like my going out alone, but she knows better than to argue.

I am able not only to make lengthy perambulations, but, with the help of the tongs, to bend and pick up any offending article of litter as I go. My mind is equally proficient. On any given day I can complete most of the *Telegraph* cryptic crossword within two hours. And I still recall many quotations from the Shakespeare I studied at school.

' "So foul and fair a day I have not seen," ' I mutter to myself as I step through the gates of The Ballahays and sally forth on to the cliff path.

The wind pulls my hair and tussles with my handbag. Grasses bend close to the ground. Gulls skim the air. Surf jigs along the frayed edges of the sea, whilst its surface rolls out endless wrinkles and twinkles. Clouds dash manically across the sky, blotting out the sun and then releasing it again at irregular intervals. The mood keeps changing from dazzle to dark and back again.

The rhythm of the walk is punctuated only by a couple of stops to manoeuvre a squashed Coke can and a damp triangular sandwich packet into the sack. My thought processes are rapidly leading me to certain conclusions.

Something has to be done about the sea life centre. Mac, although he is a felonious glove thief, is very dear to me. He and the other Scottish penguins must be saved. I, Veronica McCreedy, am about to become the world's first Penguin Ambassador. Surely, Fate has decreed that I am the chosen one to act in this case. But how to do it?

Waves crash like cymbals; pebbles pound and clatter against the rocks. I draw up my hood and the fine patter of raindrops amplifies in my ears.

My thoughts seesaw between the past and the present these days, and now my mind flutters back to the email that arrived from Terry last night. It cheered me considerably after the upset of the day.

(I used to be dependent on Eileen when it came to communications via the ether, but I am proficient at email these days. Whilst I like the digital world no better than I ever did, and sense that it threatens our very humanity in subtle and underhand ways, it is admittedly a useful tool for communication. I have therefore invested in a computer. Most of the wretched machine's workings are a mystery to me. I fail to understand why it has been designed in such a way as to befuddle and confound one at every turn, often pinging incomprehensible messages before one's eyes, such as 'your cookie functionality has been turned off'. But Eileen advises I ignore them and use it for the emails, so that is what I do. I also follow Terry's penguin blogs from Antarctica, scouring them avidly for news of Pip.)

Last night's email was full of enthusiasm and detail. I don't know where that girl finds her energy. She heads the Locket Island team, but now she also spends weeks at the vast new research station on the Antarctic Peninsula, often taking my grandson with her. I never thought he would find his *raison d'être* as a penguin researcher, but then I never really thought Patrick would find his *raison d'être* at all. My heart lifts when I think about the young love between those two, although I miss them both sorely.

I scanned the email quickly, but there was no mention of Pip. Terry used to be all about the Adélie penguins, but now she seems to have switched allegiance to the

Emperors. No, perhaps I do her a disservice. She still adores the Adélies. It is just that they, having dispersed to sea for the cold season, are not yet returned to Locket Island, so instead she is at the mainland research station, focusing on the Emperors. Illogical creatures that they are, Emperors breed in the depths of the Antarctic winter.

*The satellite tracking equipment lets us know what they're up to,* Terry wrote. *Our penguins have an exceptionally long trek across the ice to their breeding grounds – nearly 100 miles. But they've done it and got through the tough, perilous egg-sitting stage, too. Emperors must be the most resilient of any animal or bird in existence. I'm still in awe of them.*

*So . . . You know we 'have to' name some of the penguins so I can blog about individuals? Well, guess what? We've decided to call one of the Emperors (or should I say 'Empresses') Veronica, after you!*

On reading those words, an exclamation of surprise escaped me.

Daisy looked up from her colouring book. 'What?'

I would normally have pointed out the rudeness of that word and insist that she say 'I beg your pardon' instead, but as she'd been so very quiet since our return from Lochnamorghy, I was just glad that she had said *something*.

I told her about Veronica Penguin.

'Wow! You're so lucky! I wish they'd name one after me.'

'You can always put in a request,' I suggested.

'I will! I'll ask them. Daisy's a good name for a penguin, isn't it?'

I assured her that indeed it was. Which went some way towards lifting her mood.

The clouds have lowered now and the rain is harder, heavier. I attempt to channel my thoughts back to the matter in question.

I skid on a patch of mud and nearly fall, saved only by my stick. My hood has slipped. I tug it back over my brow. My hair will be a disgrace by the time I get back home.

Yet without doubt the fresh air is stimulating my thought waves. An idea has washed up inside my head.

I decide not to take the path back along the coast, since the views are no longer visible. I stride through wet shades of grey and turn into the small road, barely more than a track, to take the shortcut back home.

A car is parked just off the road; a rather battered variety, one wheel a little higher than the others due to the slope. Caught in the grass beside the wheel, I spot a tattered polythene bag. There are so many selfish, ignorant morons in this world who would rather uglify the landscape than bother themselves for one second to bin their disgusting detritus. They abuse not only our wildlife but our future generations as well.

Enraged, I head for the offending article and grasp it with the tongs, skirting round the edge of the car. The bag is sopping wet.

As I straighten, a movement in the car catches my eye. Clearly visible in the front, a man and a woman are fumbling around with each other. She is in a puffy jacket and her suspiciously blonde hair is all over the place. What is the name of that shade? *Pesticide blonde?* No, that's not it. How exasperating it is when words slip from your brain. The man's hair is peppered with grey, so he must be a middle-aged specimen. I would have given the car a wide berth had I known about these shenanigans, but I have been so preoccupied that I didn't notice anyone was inside until I was quite close.

Just as I am about to move on, the man lifts his head. I realize at once it is a head that I recognize. Where on earth have I seen the wretched man before? Ruddy cheeks, a set jaw, patchy stubble . . . I know I've met him on several occasions.

I cast about in my mind, and in a moment I have it, with an icy shock of certainty.

The man is Eileen's husband.

And the woman most certainly isn't Eileen.

# 5

# Veronica

*The Ballahays*

EVEN AT THE senior age of eighty-seven, one sometimes finds oneself plunged into a new and unwelcome situation. I now have a dilemma on my hands. To tell or not to tell – that is the question.

I thrust the tongs and refuse sack towards Eileen, whose familiar rounded figure is waiting in the porch. She dumps them on the floor and helps me off with my coat.

'Goodness, Mrs McCreedy, you're soaking!'

She has brewed a pot of tea, in the imperial blue Denby china, as I requested before I set out.

'Did you get much today?' she enquires as I sink into a chair. I will see to my hair later. My need for tea is urgent, bordering on the obsessive. I do not answer Eileen immediately. I am still endeavouring to regain my compos mentis.

She repeats the question, assuming I have not heard her.

'A fair amount, Eileen.' I manage to summon up a few details. 'A squashed can, a sandwich packet, a few bits of random plastic and other sundry items.'

'I'll see to them straight away, then.' She struggles into her pink-checked overall.

I am the daily collector of Ayrshire coastline rubbish and Eileen is the sorter of it into different categories for recycling. It is a little routine we have maintained for at least a decade.

Eileen has been my staunch helper at The Ballahays for so many years now I have lost count. For most of those years I was distinctly stand-offish towards her, and it is only since my voyage to the Antarctic two years ago, when she was particularly helpful, that I have fully warmed to her. She is a mediocre cleaner and a purveyor of endless small talk and, for her, nosiness is an art form; but always, always, I have trusted her. I have in her not only a loyal paid household assistant but – when occasion demands – even a friend.

I view her now as she turns to pick up the sack: her well-upholstered barrel of a body, her head that sits on a neck that is too broad, her manic curls, her soft eyes set in a powdered expanse of face.

Once more, anger strobes through me. For Eileen does not have an unkind bone in her body. She certainly deserves better than a cheating husband.

When I saw the wretched oaf with that tart, rage flamed in me like a furnace. I wanted to rap at the car window with my tongs, use them to drag him out by the ears and thrash him there and then. Sadly, my physical trappings do not manifest as a youthful avenging hero but as an ancient crone, so this course of action was out of the question. The cad was so busy rifling inside the blonde's blouse that he did not even notice my presence.

I wish I could recall the name of the cad in question. Eileen mentions him almost daily. Derek, is it? I have only met him personally on a handful of occasions, and he was far from talkative. As a couple, they are not blessed with children, but there is a whole clan of relations who came to Christmas at The Ballahays once, when I had a rare fit of munificence. Eileen's husband, I seem to remember, consumed an inordinately large quantity of roast potatoes and then ensconced himself in a corner and remained stationary for the rest of the proceedings. Eileen compensated for his insipid presence by bustling about and chattering even more than usual.

'Eileen, remind me of the name of your husband.' I try to keep my voice light and casual.

'Why, it's Doug, Mrs McCreedy, you know it is. And it's funny you should mention him. Do you know what – when I popped home this morning, he gave me a lovely wee giftie! I was so pleased, so touched. It's a pretty beaded coral necklace. I don't know when I'm going to wear it, but it's not like my Dougie to go and spend money on decorative stuff like that, and it's just charming. I'd show it to you, Mrs McCreedy, but I put it straight away into my crocheted bag, where I keep all my treasures.'

I give a little grunt, which she may interpret as she chooses. There is no doubt in my own mind that the gift merely indicates guilt, given to her by the rat to appease his conscience. Despicable behaviour!

Should I disclose his infidelity? I know little of the affairs of the heart, for there was only one man I ever loved romantically, and that ended in tears. My ex-husband I do not count, for that was not love – it was a marriage built on flattery, flirtation and finance . . . I did not like him enough to be hurt by his serial infidelities. But Eileen? This revelation would eat up her happiness in one quick gulp, like a frog swallowing a fly. Yet it surely isn't right to conceal a truth such as this? I must consider carefully how to proceed.

Perhaps I should consult Sir Robert, my most trusted friend, on the subject. If so, I must broach it with subtlety, without giving away that it is Eileen to whom I am referring. Sir Robert is nothing if not perspicacious.

'Daisy! Snack time!' Eileen calls.

'Coming!' squeaks a voice from above.

Eileen wheels the cups, saucers and other accoutrements through to the drawing room on the trolley. Her chosen sweetmeats today are marshmallow biscuits, but I have no appetite whatsoever.

My thoughts flit about like bats.

It is only when Daisy trundles into the room with her face full of unhappiness that I remember there was something I was supposed to remember.

'She stopped pedalling at the pianola just five minutes before you got back,' Eileen hastens to explain, rubbing her hands on her overall with a guilty air and ushering Daisy forward. 'She's had today's practice for her walk, I promise you.'

Ah yes, that was it.

The Emperor penguins take a long walk every year. Some old codger with a Zimmer frame is going on a sponsored walk and Daisy will soon likewise be embarking on a walk for charity. And I, Veronica McCreedy, the first Penguin Ambassador in the world, will also be going on a sponsored walk. To raise funds for the Lochnamorghy Sea Life Centre. To save the penguins.

I make Eileen and Daisy sit down opposite me at the drawing-room table and I outline my idea.

Eileen lets out an 'Oh, Mrs McCreedy! That's so noble, so wonderful. Dear little Mac . . .' She drags her overall cuff across her eyes. 'Sorry. I've come over all . . . Gosh.'

Daisy is electrified. 'This is the best news!' she cries. She leaps to her feet so fast that the chair topples backwards, and she dashes round to my side of the table and hugs me tightly. 'I love you, Veronica.'

It is decades since I have heard those words and they fill me with delight, like a bath filling with warm water and bubbles.

I am rather choked and momentarily tongue-tied, so it is just as well Daisy is now gushing.

'I know! I've got it!' She claps her hands. 'I'll walk with you. I hadn't totally decided it was a cancer charity I was going to be fundraising for, and now it's definitely, definitely going to be for Lochnamorghy and Mac and Pablo and Florence and all the other penguins. You and me, we can walk together!'

This had not occurred to me.

Daisy's squeals are like drills inside my hearing aid.

'And I can raise money with my friends and you can

raise money with your friends and then it will be double. We can raise *thousands*.'

This is, I sense, optimism of a dangerous kind. As yet the idea is embryonic and I haven't a clue how much money is required to keep Lochnamorghy open. She has also highlighted a significant flaw in my logic. There are few people I can call upon in the name of friendship. I now realize I can think of nobody who will sponsor me other than Eileen – who has little money except what I give her – and Mr Perkins, my gardener, for whom the same can be said. Patrick and Terry would gladly do it, of course, except that all their spare money goes towards penguins anyway. Sir Robert? For some reason I would feel conflicted about even asking him.

Daisy, however, would doubtless receive support from not only her school friends but their parents as well. Word would spread quickly.

To walk together might be feasible. Yet she is based in Bolton, and I had not envisaged walking anywhere other than Scotland.

I sip my tea, gaining another moment's thought before I answer. 'We had better consult with your parents before you go making any drastic decisions. Apart from everything else, there is your schooling to consider.'

Daisy's parents always assume that I know when the various school terms and holidays fall, but in fact I haven't the faintest idea. 'Do you want to ask Gavin and Beth about it via Wotsit?'

She rolls her eyes. 'It's not Wotsit, Veronica. It's Whats-App; I've told you before. But Mum and Dad will be fine about it. Where are we going to walk?'

'It would be rather complicated to organize a continuous walk from A to B, say from Lands End to John O'Groats,' I answer. 'A more feasible approach would be to build up a set distance by covering ground every day. It should not pose a problem. Why, I do it already!'

'And how far shall we go?' asks Daisy, again assuming she will be accompanying me.

'Aha!' I reply. 'Terry mentioned the Emperor penguins in her email, and how they do a long march to their breeding grounds every year. Her colony have all walked a hundred miles. I thought I might do the same.'

'How long do the penguins take?'

'We'll have to ask Terry.'

'No, I'll google it,' Daisy says, getting out her phone.

I grimace. 'Are you unable to subsist for five minutes without that tiresome contraption?'

'Nope.'

Phones nowadays aren't content to be merely phones; they pompously insist on being cameras, encyclopaedias, calculators, personal trainers, news reporters, gossip-mongers and much else besides. In fact, with such a receptacle containing one's entire life, one scarcely needs a brain at all. I have chosen not to possess such a machine. My brain has always worked perfectly well, and should it require a little boost, all I need to do is to consult Eileen.

Daisy grins and taps away at the screen. ' "Emperor penguins take about a month to complete their long march," ' she reads out. 'We could do the hundred miles in one month, just like the Emperors.'

'That's an awful lot of walking,' Eileen observes, worry

knotting her brow once again. 'Why, it's . . .' Her eyes cross slightly with the strain of mental calculation before she gives up. 'It's quite a few miles per day.'

'Indeed, it is over three miles daily,' I reply. 'But I am blessed with a good internal engine and this battered old body still works pretty well. Daisy is keen enough to push herself, too. If it is not a challenge, there is no point in doing it. Moreover, we will not raise much attention or a significant sum if it is an easy feat. We need to make this big.'

Daisy whoops and performs a little jiggly dance on the Persian rug. 'We could get a titbit,' she suggests.

I look at her. 'A titbit?'

'No, I said FITBIT!' she yells.

'What in heaven's name is that?'

'It counts your steps and tells you how far you've gone.'

I am suspicious. It sounds very much like another of those unwelcome Big Brother-type mechanisms that maintain a voyeuristic and judgemental eye on one at all times. Still, we need to keep track of our daily mileage somehow.

'How about a pedometer?' Eileen suggests.

That sounds a more distinguished and attractive option, although I am not entirely sure of the difference.

After further debate, it is decided that I will invest in one such pedometer. Daisy wants one, too, and insists on ordering them immediately from her phone.

As she swipes and googles, I am swilling with a veritable cocktail of emotions. The ingredients consist largely of passion and determination. The elements of worry are just beginning to settle to the bottom like a dark sediment when Eileen – poor, downtrodden Eileen, whose husband is callously betraying her – speaks up.

'I'll do it too.'

Daisy and I both look at her, incredulous.

'Please, Mrs McCreedy. I really think it's sensible. I'd worry about you two walking so much, whether it's separately or together. You are ten years old and nearly ninety years old. You're both healthy now, but who knows what could happen? Walking so much, you'll get exhausted. What if you fell, Mrs McCreedy? What if you got sick again, Daisy? I admire you both, I really do, but I'd never forgive myself if something awful happened.' Her distraught expression is shot through with resolve. 'Besides, I need something like this. I know I'm not the world's fittest person. Goodness me, my thighs are like tree trunks and even going up the Ballahays stairs makes me wheeze, but you two put me to shame. I'm the one who should be doing this. And actually, I could do with losing a bit of weight. And I'd like to help save the penguins, of course. So, please, will you let me join you?'

I had envisaged doing this alone and claiming all the glory for myself. I had imagined beating Zimmer-frame Man at his own game and producing at the very least a double-page spread in all the Scottish newspapers. Still, there are practical advantages of having both Eileen and Daisy along. The mission is likely to raise greater funds if there are three of us. So I bury my doubts, such as they are, and say: 'Of course. Of course, Eileen. It would be a pleasure to have you walking with us.'

Daisy runs over and throws herself at Eileen.

Eileen has her choir and numerous friends and relations who will doubtless sponsor her. I repress a brief twinge of resentment that I, the Penguin Ambassador, will be the least effective out of the three of us. Still, this is not a competition. It is an altruistic undertaking to save the lives of twenty-four penguins.

The more I think about it, the more I realize this could work. 'We shall be a walking trio solely consisting of females, and females of very different ages. There is a certain poetry in that.'

'Girl power,' says Daisy, hands on hips.

We discuss a few further practicalities. We will need to put our plan into action as soon as possible, because it looks as if Mac and his friends have little time before their fate is sealed. We decide the whole thing must be done during the calendar month of October. Daisy will have to do her walking after school in Bolton with her parents or friends, but can join us for her half-term holiday towards the end of the month and perhaps take a second week off afterwards to complete the walk with us, since it's for such a good cause.

We will cover between two and five miles a day, depending on the weather. We shall gather as much sponsorship as we can possibly manage in the next few weeks, and hope to collect more as we go. The plan is shaping up nicely when Eileen, in a sudden flurry, gasps and throws her hands up to her face. 'Oh gosh, Mrs McCreedy, I'm sorry, but I've just realized there's a big problem.'

# 6

# Veronica

*The Ballahays and the Cloverleaf Cafe, Edinburgh*

WITH ALL THE kerfuffle about Eileen and this Lochna-morghy crisis, I had somehow failed to factor in the imminence of my voyage to the Galápagos and the Falklands.

Eileen's expression is tragic. 'I can't see any way it can work out. Not with Daisy back at school next week and the centre due to close so soon. We can't possibly get the walk done in time. We're doomed to failure before we begin.'

'Eileen,' I tell her severely, 'please do not use the F-word in my presence.'

'The F-word? I didn't . . . I would never . . .'

'I am referring to the F-word that rhymes with "dahlia".'

A minuscule pause, then Daisy erupts into hysterical laughter which I can only put down to an excess of yoyoing emotions.

I explain that I shall categorically continue with the mission, although I shall have to walk alone (which, despite Eileen's fears, is no problem at all) and in an unknown terrain (which might be). And it will be tricky negotiating around flights, filming duties and award ceremonies. But when has Veronica McCreedy ever failed to rise to a challenge?

Eileen and Daisy also assert their commitment to the walk. However, we will be split up, on opposite sides of the world and unable to progress together as a dynamic trio. Working around Daisy's school times was already going to be difficult, but now we shall hardly be together at all.

I telephone the Lochnamorghy Sea Life Centre and, after some botheration, succeed in speaking to the manager, a Mr Tector. I can glean little about the man from his voice, apart from the fact that he does not hail from Scotland himself. His accent seems more Birmingham. I inform him that I intend to raise sufficient funds to keep the business open and they are by no means to give up or sell up.

He sounds decidedly sceptical. He tells me Lochnamorghy has been running at a loss for some time. To save the centre, get it back on its feet and keep it going for just a year, our donation would need to be something in the order of £2 million.

'Two million pounds!'

'I'm afraid so.'

I will confess to blenching at such a sum.

'We'd need to have some indication within the next couple of weeks if you can achieve it, too. The property agent already has the details and will be putting the site on the market shortly. And we'd need to have the funds in well before our closing date, which is now set for November thirteenth.'

'Very well,' I reply, my voice mustering a fierce degree of confidence. 'You will be hearing from me.'

I replace the receiver firmly then make my way upstairs to see Daisy, who is bashing out words on the computer. She shuts down the screen the minute I enter the room.

'Daisy, how much do your charity fundraisers usually make?' I enquire with an air of nonchalance.

'I made sixty-seven pounds by selling home-made cakes in the school tuck shop. And a whole two hundred and thirty-three pounds when I did last year's sponsored read.'

'Tremendous,' I answer, conjuring a smile.

With the help of high-profile media coverage, our joint efforts might stretch to thousands ... but two million? Even if I dig deep into my own savings to supplement it, is such an amount remotely attainable?

Still, I cannot just stand by and let the lives of twenty-four penguins be snuffed out, here in Scotland, under my very nose.

I shall save those penguins or die in the attempt.

Sir Robert is already at the Cloverleaf Cafe, seated very upright in the plush reception area, when I arrive. I have managed to claim his company over lunch, spiriting myself to Edinburgh by taxi and leaving Daisy and Eileen to entertain each other in the comfort of The Ballahays.

He rises to his feet as soon as I enter and plants a kiss on my cheek. He is as sprightly as ever, his hair a silver whirl, his face animated, his eyebrows performing an arcing dance like an amorous pair of fluffy caterpillars.

'How wonderful to see you, Veronica, and how well you look!'

I may have spent a little extra time attempting to bouffant my thin strands of hair this morning and applying lavish make-up. My choice of lip colour is my favourite ruby, and a matching silk scarf is artistically knotted around my neck. It fulfils the dual purpose of covering some unsightly folds of sagging skin and offsetting my outfit.

Sir Robert escorts me to a table by the window, from where we can look out on the pleasant comings and goings along the Royal Mile. We order lunch: a warm salad of scallops with capers and fresh parsley, followed by lemon meringue pie.

We have met ostensibly to discuss my forthcoming trip.

'I will be off to the Arctic in two days,' he informs me, 'and from there I fly straight on to the Galápagos. I wanted to check you are happy with all the arrangements, since this is our last chance to discuss the trip together in person.'

He folds his hands neatly, which is something he often does whilst talking, whereas I gesticulate expansively.

I do so now. 'The Arctic! Gracious me!'

'Yes. Since the programme is all about adapting to extreme conditions, I'll be covering both polar regions,' he comments, as if this is an everyday occurrence.

'And people talk of your retiring soon!'

'No, I shan't do that. Not for a while yet. We all age at different rates and I am in no hurry. In years I may be pushing eighty, but my body has not been counting and seems to think I am a mere sixty or so.'

I smile. 'It is the same with me. I have a long life to look back on, and I cannot truthfully say, as Edith Piaf would have it, "*Je ne regrette rien.*" But virtually all of my regrets are things I *haven't* done. That feeling of time running out (doubtless a given amongst the older generations) is particularly strong in my case, since for so many decades I did nothing. I lived tightly wrapped in sorrow as the years slid by, never pausing to quaff from the golden chalice of life's wonders. These days, inactivity annoys me. I would even go so far as to say it upsets me. Before this body gives out, I want to do as much as I can, for better, for worse . . .'

'For richer, for poorer, in sickness and in health?'

'Quite. I am wedded to action. If I remain inactive, I shall stagnate.'

'We cannot have that,' Sir Robert replies.

'I am indebted to you for ensuring it does not happen.'

'The pleasure is entirely mine.'

It is no wonder the general public adores Sir Robert. He broadcasts just enough of himself to inspire their hero-worship, whilst they actually know very little about him. I, however, know various details about which the public are wholly ignorant. I know, for example, that he keeps his watch permanently set fifteen minutes fast to counteract his natural propensity for lateness. I know of his fondness for treacle tart and for a fine single malt, and that he grows nostalgic at the sound of bagpipes. That his politics lean towards Green (and who can blame him?), that he has always wanted a dog but that his lifestyle will not allow it, that over the years there have been a few discreetly conducted romances but that the great love of his life perished many years ago. I know also that he had to fight with extreme shyness at the beginning of his career but became braver as he went along. Or rather, he learned to ignore the shyness. He has always been brave, for what is bravery if not feeling fear but forging ahead in spite of it?

I do not possess such a virtue, for I am naturally fearless, some would say foolhardy. I have never been afflicted with shyness, but I begin to appreciate what a handicap it must be.

We consume our scallops and exchange pleasantries about the seagulls scavenging outside the window, the progress of the Locket Island team, his Edinburgh neighbours and so forth, then progress to details of our Galápagos filming schedule. All the while my thoughts keep racing along other tracks.

To Sir Robert I have unfurled more of my feelings than to any other being alive. He understands better than anyone my need to leave some good in this crumbling world. Yet I feel strangely coy about the penguin-rescue plan.

I present, instead, the other issue that is weighing on me. 'Sir Robert, may I consult you on a delicate matter?'

'A delicate matter?'

'Yes, indeed,' I begin. 'It pertains to no person in particular but is a theoretical situation that has presented itself to my mind . . . quite randomly . . . for no reason. Not any specific reason at all.'

My native eloquence has been disarrayed somewhat by my anxiety.

He replies with a minimal twitch of his excellently shaggy left eyebrow. 'My dear Veronica, you have my attention. I am always interested in the workings of your mind.'

I thank him for what I presume is a compliment.

I try to focus. 'This is a completely hippopotamus situation. I mean, a hypothermic situation. I mean . . . aaargh . . .' To my extreme frustration, the right word is refusing to release itself from my lips.

'A hypothetical situation?' Sir Robert suggests.

'Yes. Quite. A hypothetical one. Which is, if a person should witness an act of marital infidelity that relates to an acquaintance, ought they to disclose the act to the aforementioned acquaintance? Or would they be wiser to remain silent and hope the matter resolves itself?'

He observes me with those discerning blue, blue eyes of his and smooths his napkin.

'Well, that would depend entirely on the circumstances. May I presume this is a husband who is being unfaithful to his wife?'

I incline my head. 'You may.'

He considers. 'This might be the cliché of a middle-aged man who has been taking his wife for granted for many years and now finds himself tempted by a younger model?'

I do not reply, for his assessment is worryingly accurate and I believe he has seen straight through my subterfuge – or rather, lack of it. His natural perspicacity knows no bounds. There are people to whom you must explain and explain over and over, and even then they scarcely understand you. Eileen can on occasion be one of these. But to Sir Robert you need only say three words and he will immediately grasp not only your meaning but also your every nuanced feeling about the subject; even how those feelings are shaped by your experiences, your past hurts, your hopes for the future.

He reflects.

'I am no expert, but the husband, I'm guessing, is flattered that the younger model shows interest in him. He is weak and can't resist the temptation, but he probably doesn't intend to leave his wife. I would think it's no more than a fling, and involves no real depth of feeling. Am I right?'

'I suspect you are.'

Sir Robert's distaste for the affair almost equals my own. 'He doesn't deserve his wife; we know that. But for her own sake ...' His brow furrows. 'I have always believed in honesty, yet to reveal this would be to shatter her world.'

'Very true.' I cannot imagine how Eileen would cope.

'Tricky.' A slight pause. 'Blissful ignorance is the kindest way, and the kindest way is the best way,' he decides eventually. 'Having said that, it's likely she'll find out of her own accord sooner or later. Frankly, there's not much you can do about that. Unless you can somehow bring them back together before that happens.'

I wonder if there might be something I can do along these lines.

I envisage Eileen's face wrought with agony as she discovers the truth. 'If only I could make him appreciate her . . . It is the appreciation that is lacking.' I sniff. 'He needs to understand what a wonderful woman he has married,' I hear myself saying.

I've surprised myself. But yes, indeed, although Eileen drives me to distraction on a regular basis, she is worth more than a thousand dirty Dougs.

The spurt of anger on her behalf brings on a second torrent of emotion for the Lochnamorghy penguins, and I blurt out the threat of death that hangs over them. Sir Robert, horrified, takes my hand over the table. So then, in a cracking voice, I finally tell him of our projected sponsored march to try to remedy the situation. I do not specify the vast sum we must raise, but I inform him that I must somehow make time between filming commitments to walk an average of three and a quarter miles a day whilst in the Galápagos.

I see his apprehension, see how he turns the idea over and over.

'You think this is ridiculous. Well, I would rather be ridiculous than complacent,' I declare loudly and somewhat defensively.

He shakes his head. 'I'm just trying to think how I can help. I could maybe pull a few strings once I'm back from the filming trip. I could mention the plight of Lochnamorghy next time I'm on the radio . . .'

'No,' I cut in, my hand leaping up to stop him. 'There's no time. You're about to set off for the Arctic and won't be back for weeks. And the site is about to be put on the market.'

By now the desserts have arrived. Sir Robert picks up his spoon then lays it down again. 'Your idea is wonderful, inspired, full of promise. But a hundred miles is quite an undertaking when you'll be so busy. Why not reduce the mileage to something a little less ambitious?'

I carve into my pie and tell him sharply: '"Promise" is a lovely word, but put the letters C-O-M in front and it just becomes dull. I am quite decided. It is to be a hundred miles or nothing.'

He smiles. The crow's feet and crinkles just seem to accentuate the extreme blueness of his eyes. 'Well, if I know you, it won't be nothing, Veronica. But I must warn you: the Galápagos is tricky terrain, with all that lumpy volcanic rock. A fall would be bad news, and would stymie the rest of your walk. Why not keep it to Scotland, or Scotland and the Falklands, if you must. Have a break in the middle for the Galápagos Islands.'

My heart clinches with a fresh certainty. If something is difficult, that is not a reason to avoid it. That is a reason to do it. The McCreedy recklessness rises, strong and undeniable, within me.

'Emperor penguins defy the odds, and I shall, too.'

I excavate a lemony blob from the depths of my dessert. The sculpted landscape of meringue and cream reminds me of frozen climes. I envisage penguins trekking steadily along the ice. 'How splendid it would be to see those indomitable Emperors. Especially since they are my inspiration for this walk.'

'But it's only possible to see Emperor penguins in Antarctica, Veronica. And in the coldest, most treacherous parts of Antarctica, too.'

'I know,' I reply. 'My grandson, Patrick, is out there, remember? And so is Terry. And so is Pip.'

'I think I can see where this is heading,' he murmurs, concern spreading across his face.

How marvellous it would be to revisit the research centre that contained so many epiphanies for me, and to meet dear Pip again, the hero penguin who once saved my life. And then to travel even further south, to the Emperors. Would not so extreme a destination attract masses of media attention for my mission? Would it not be a grand finale to my travels?

My life is my own; my decisions are my own.

'From the Falklands it is not, comparatively, such a long way to Antarctica,' I muse.

Sir Robert puts his head in his hands.

# Daisy's Penguin Blog

Welcome to my Penguin Blog.

DEATH THREAT FOR PENGUINS!!!

It's not a joke.

The penguins at Lochnamorghy Sea Life Centre are my friends. My favourite one is Mac, the Macaroni penguin. He's not shy, and his hobbies are waddling, jumping to catch fish and eating gloves (see photo 1. Super-cute or what?!). There are African penguins too, like Pablo who is 22 – reeeally old for a penguin (see photo 2) and Florence who loves swimming and has pretty spots (see photo 3).

24 penguins live at Lochnamorghy in total. But they are all in DANGER OF DEATH. ☹

It's true.

It's horrible.

The only reason they're going to be killed is because the sea life centre is short of money and must close down.

So I'm going on a sponsored walk with Veronica McCreedy who is 87 and is a Penguin Ambassador and

Eileen Thompson who is 50-something and has nothing to do with penguins but just wants to help. We are going to walk 100 miles and we're going to do it in a month, just like the Emperor penguins.

Will you sponsor us, please?

# 7

# Eileen

*The Ballahays*

SHE'S DUE BACK any minute, and if I know her, she'll want some tea first thing.

'You go and give Mr Perkins a hand cutting back the border, dear, whilst I get the kettle on. Mrs McCreedy is going to be so pleased about everything we've done.'

Daisy scampers off into the garden happily. But when I glance out of the kitchen window, she isn't helping Mr Perkins; she is sitting cross-legged in his wheelbarrow. Mr Perkins looks as if he is trying – and failing – to persuade her out of it.

It's just as well the taxi is pulling up on the driveway now. An elegant, stockinged leg pokes out of the taxi door, followed by a stick and a shiny red handbag. At once, Daisy is out of the wheelbarrow and hurtling across the lawn to meet Mrs M.

Mr Perkins mops his brow and tugs at a weed in the flower bed. He staggers backwards slightly when it comes out sooner than he was expecting.

Daisy is meanwhile chatting to Mrs M. She'll be desperate to tell her everything. I see Mrs M turn and make a questioning letter-T sign at Mr Perkins. He nods, parks the barrow under the chestnut tree and sinks on to the garden bench. Mr Perkins doesn't come inside much (he worries about mud from his wellies) but his wife sometimes pops in to tell us his arthritis is playing up again or to drop off a home-made tart or chat to me. A good sort is Mrs Perkins.

I fill the teapot and turn it around twice to help Mrs M's fragrant Darjeeling do its thing, then I mash a PG Tips teabag in a mug for Mr Perkins. Each to his (or her) own.

'Eileen and I have done *loads*,' I hear Daisy boast as she pulls Mrs McCreedy inside. 'We Skyped with Mum in Switzerland and Dad in Bolton and they're going to help. When I'm at home they'll take turns to walk with me because I'm not allowed to do it by myself; and maybe my friend Aurora and her parents can walk with me some of the time. They said we should tell my school ASAP, so we did that, too. That is, we couldn't get through to anyone except the bursar, Mrs Meeks, but she said *well done us* and maybe the penguin plan could be announced in assembly once term's started and we could put it in the school newsletter to ask all the parents for their support.'

They are in the kitchen now. I should ask after Sir Robert but I'm just as keen as Daisy to fill Mrs McCreedy in. 'We've set up an online form where people can sponsor us, and we've got some names already! My Auntie Mary and Fran and Callum and even wee Kevin. And Daisy's parents. And—'

'Don't say it, Eileen. Let *me* tell her!' Daisy cuts in, bursting with pride. 'You'll never guess what, Veronica. We've phoned the *Scots Times* and they're going to meet us at the Lochnamorghy centre the day after tomorrow for an interview!'

'And a photo shoot,' I add. 'They were very keen. Especially when I mentioned they'd already run that article on you being the Penguin Ambassador, Mrs McCreedy.'

Mrs McCreedy makes a huffing sound but I can tell she's impressed. 'How many people have signed up to sponsor us?' she asks.

'So far, six,' I reply. 'I'll just take that tea out to Mr Perkins, shall I?'

'No, Eileen, I will take it myself. I wish to have a quick word with him.'

As she takes the mug into the garden, Daisy and I beam at each other.

'She's pleased, isn't she?' Daisy says.

'Oh yes, she is that.'

From the window I see her presenting Mr Perkins with some wet wipes (biodegradable, of course) so as to be sure his hands are clean before taking the tea. Her face doesn't look that thrilled, though. She is talking earnestly with him.

Daisy gobbles up her scone and disappears upstairs to use the computer again. She's been at it a lot today.

'Eileen, do you have a moment?' Mrs M asks as she enters the hall again.

'Yes, Mrs McCreedy?'

'Permit me to present you with a little something.' She hands over a gift bag, prettily patterned in gold ferns. 'A small purchase from Edinburgh.'

What could she have got for me? I tear off the tissue paper eagerly and pull out a small bottle of perfume. 'Oh, Mrs McCreedy. This is too, too generous!'

'No, no, it is not,' she argues. 'I have given you very few gifts over the years, Eileen, and I wish to make up for my stinginess. It would please me greatly if you would wear this when you go out with your husband, Desmond, this evening.'

I gape. 'But I'll be here, won't I? And my husband is Doug and we've no plans to go out this evening.'

'Doug. That is what I meant to say. When you go out with Doug this evening.' Her lip curls. 'I wish you to have a delightful meal with your . . .' she frowns '. . . your good man. I have booked a table for you both at the Dainty Duck. My treat. The place is not swish enough to alarm you, but it is tasteful and . . .' she pauses '. . . romantic.'

Well, how lovely. I always knew she had a golden core of goodness, even though she hides it well. I haven't had a romantic evening out with Doug for years. I'm glowing at the thought of it. My heart is dancing a happy little jig.

Doug couldn't believe it either when I told him, back in our kitchen at home. He looked quite struck.

'But won't she want you to be there tonight, at The Ballahays, to cook for her and Daisy?'

63

'Mrs McCreedy has ordered in pizza,' I replied.

'What?' he said.

I repeated myself. 'Mrs McCreedy has ordered in pizza. I'm as surprised as you are, to be honest. She's never, ever done that before. When I asked her about it, she said she was "definitely not averse to Italian cuisine, Eileen". She doesn't eat much herself, which is probably how she keeps her lovely figure, but I'm guessing she did it for Daisy, who adores pizza. Mr and Mrs Perkins will be eating with them, so I don't need to worry. Mrs Perkins is going to bring a pudding, so they're all sorted. And it means you and me can go to the lovely restaurant, dearie.'

He looked at the begonia and then back at me. 'Well, no.'

'Why ever not?'

I'd popped home specially to tell him. The house reeked of air freshener and the sink was piled high with dirty plates and glasses, but Doug unexpectedly rushed to do the washing-up himself the minute I arrived. So sweet of him. He was in his nice, open-necked shirt but when he slumped into his chair I noticed the bagginess around his eyes. He looked exhausted, which was maybe why he couldn't take in what I was saying.

'Mrs McCreedy has booked the table for us and everything, and she said we must order whatever we want, she's paying.'

I would have thought he'd be over the moon, because he doesn't much like paying for things himself.

He tapped his teeth with his fingers. (It's a habit I used to think was funny. I find it a bit annoying now.) 'I didn't think you'd be around, Eileen, and I've arranged to meet Jim for a, er . . . meeting.'

Jim is one of the oatcake lads, but I didn't think they normally had meetings about it. I wouldn't have thought there was much you needed to discuss about oatcake manufacturing, but what do I know?

'Not just Jim. Some of the others, too. Sorry, but I can't get out of it.'

Doug's hours at the factory have got quite strange recently. The new rota is called flexitime, but it doesn't seem that flexible, if you ask me.

'Why don't you go to the restaurant with one of your choir friends instead?' he suggested.

So I did. I went with Fiona, who sings alto next to me. (I felt a bit guilty, mind, since Mrs M had said the meal was for me and Doug, but I'm sure she just wanted me to have a good evening.) We had a marvellous dinner, very posh, with starters and wine and everything. We giggled together over our pernickety choirmaster and the new soprano (a real prima donna with a voice so shrieky it makes my teeth hurt) and we chatted about our hobbies. Fiona goes circle dancing on a Tuesday.

'It's great fun,' she said. 'We do dances from lots of different countries, and it's just energetic enough but not too energetic, if you know what I mean.'

'Oh yes,' I said. 'I do. Too energetic isn't good.'

'And you don't need a partner, which is great if you're not part of a couple. My husband passed away six years ago and this has really helped to take me out of myself.'

'Oh my gosh! I didn't know.' I felt so, so sorry for her. I can't imagine what I'd do without my Doug.

'Anyway, do tell me about you, Eileen. You're a knitter, aren't you? What kinds of things do you knit?'

'Oh, little presents for my friends and relations. Scarves, cardies, soft toys. The last thing I knitted was a toilet roll cover for my Auntie Mary. I do like to cherish people.'

'How lovely! Now there's a word you don't hear very often. "Cherish",' said Fiona.

'Yes, I suppose it is an old-fashioned idea, but I like a bit of cherishing. Mrs McCreedy won't let me cherish her. She lets me help her with the practical things, cleaning and cooking and arranging the dentist, et cetera, but that's very different from cherishing, isn't it? And Doug isn't really into being cherished, being a man. Maybe that's one of the reasons I like it so much when Daisy comes. I can cherish her all I like.'

Fiona gave me a knowing look. 'Perhaps you should cherish yourself more.'

Then she asked about Daisy and I told her how we are walking for the penguins. She said how amazing that was; all three of us were amazing. (Fiona is much more interested in the penguins than Doug is, but then she's interested in everything. She's always asking questions when we meet at choir practice, but women *are* more chatty than men, aren't they? Doug only livens up if you're talking about cars or fishing or complaining about the government.)

All in all, we had a very good time together. I was able to tell Mrs McCreedy over breakfast the next morning quite honestly that I'd had a lovely evening. I even wore a squirt of the expensive perfume she gave me, which made me feel quite special.

'And how did your husband enjoy it?' she asked.

I pulled at my collar, which was suddenly too tight. I

could feel a flush coming on. I flapped air at my hot cheeks, tried to ignore the dampness gathering under my nylons.

'Eileen, did you hear my question?'

'Yes, yes, Mrs McCreedy. Doug had a very good evening indeed,' I said, hoping it was true. In fact, he arrived home after I was already asleep, so the meeting must've gone on and on. I feel a bit bad for having enjoyed myself so much without him.

'Did he notice the perfume?'

'I'm not sure. I . . . I think he did.'

She surveyed me in a way that would have made me feel quite chilly if I hadn't been feeling so hot.

'Eileen, you are an abysmal liar. Please look me in the eye and tell me you did take your husband with you.'

I had to confess then that it was Fiona that I went with, but what great company Fiona was and what a fantastic opportunity it had been to get to know her better. I thanked Mrs McCreedy again for her kind thought. She seemed put out, though.

I felt strangely out of sorts after that. When I was washing up after the mid-morning cuppa we usually have together, I somehow managed to break one of her beautiful bone china saucers. It made a loud crash as it shattered in the sink.

Then I burst into tears, which is not like me at all. It's just as well Mrs McCreedy was out in the garden and Daisy was upstairs, doing something on the computer. I felt so foolish crying over a little thing like that. I wouldn't have wanted them to see me.

# 8

## Eileen

'THIS WALKING,' SAYS Doug. 'You're not really serious about it, are you? I mean, come on. *A hundred miles*. All that effort, just for a few penguins?'

'I do know it's not the most sensible thing in the world,' I admit.

'It's crazy, if you ask me. Impractical. Stupid.'

'Well, I wasn't asking you. And yes, I know it's maybe eccentric, but what else could I do, with Mrs McCreedy and Daisy so keen? It's useless trying to stop Mrs M doing something once she's made up her mind. And I couldn't let them do it on their own, could I? An eighty-seven-year-old lady and a ten-year-old child? What kind of a person would I be if I just left them to it? A not very nice one, that's what. And I'll tell you what else. Yes, it may be crazy, impractical, stupid even. But sometimes stupid can be rather lovely.'

My husband holds up his hands. 'Whoa, Eileen. OK, OK. Point taken.'

Am I overreacting? Doug seems to think I am. Come to think of it, I *was* speaking rather louder than usual.

'Do you think I'd be a nicer person if I was on HRT?' I ask.

'How should I know?'

'I asked Fiona about it because she's at the same stage as me, and she said maybe it might help but it's just not worth it. Her sister got breast cancer, you see, and she blames it on that. But I keep seeing different things about it on telly, and it's so blooming confusing.'

If you can be nicer, more energetic, less achy, less moody, cleverer, healthier and happier, and the NHS is prepared to foot the bill, well, how tempting is that? Very, very tempting.

Doug pulls his face into a funny shape. 'Please don't go on about women's issues, Eileen. Makes me squirm.'

Well, I do think a little squirm isn't nearly as bad as what I'm going through. But I don't say so.

So much preparation! I spent hours yesterday in Kilmarnock with Daisy, traipsing round and ticking things off the shopping list: flasks, plasters, wipes, a lightweight rug, a canvas groundsheet, a fold-up camping chair, an inflatable cushion, waterproof trousers, soup ingredients, Kendal mint cake . . . you name it.

Mrs McCreedy stayed at home, resting and planning, but she has treated me to a brand-new pair of walking boots. I can't believe how generous she's being at the moment. I've never needed walking boots before, since most of my walking has been around The Ballahays and I wear flats for that.

'Have a careful look in the shops,' Mrs McCreedy instructed, 'and choose yourself a pair you like, but please ensure they are good quality. Do not scrimp. You must spend seventy pounds as an absolute minimum, preferably more.'

'Shouldn't all that money be going towards the sea life centre?' I said.

'Trust me on this, Eileen. I used to be a businesswoman. As you well know, I once committed matrimony with a disagreeable tycoon, ran his property letting business and earned him a great deal of money, hence my own supply of not insubstantial savings. Indeed, I also raked in large profits from the divorce settlement. (I feel no guilt whatsoever on this count. It is compensation for Hugh's multiple infidelities, about which he was glibly remorseless.) And I can tell you, Eileen, the old maxim is true: You have to speculate to accumulate. I am not having you suffering from blisters. That would be unpleasant for you and do our fundraising effort no good at all.'

It wasn't easy but, in the end, with Daisy's help, I found a pair of comfy boots that fit my wide feet and they were £72.99, so Mrs McCreedy couldn't complain. We bought some thick, snuggly socks for Daisy, too.

'We will need to practise walking together before October, when we start the challenge properly,' Mrs M said. So today we'll take our first practice walk.

According to the helpful lady at the tourist information centre, there's a very pretty three-and-a-bit-mile route just up the road from the sea life centre. The first ten minutes is on tarmac, but after that there's a scenic path beside the loch. Since we are meeting the journalist from the *Scots Times* (whose name is Marvin Bishop) in the morning, we can have a cuppa at the Lochnamorghy cafe then get walking straight afterwards.

After much discussion about what to wear for the photo shoot, we agreed our walking gear would be best – or a slightly dolled-up version of it. Daisy is cute in a pink sweatshirt with her jeans, hair held back in an Alice band. I am wearing my hand-knitted penguin jumper, thick leggings and the new boots. Mrs McCreedy looks very stylish in tweeds with a smart Burberry hat, a stick and her tartan handbag.

When we arrive at the sea life centre we're dismayed to see a new sign on the door announcing the closure on 13 November. It does look as if they've given up. I march straight up to the receptionist, a chubby-cheeked lad with his hair gelled into a tuft at the top.

Swelling with pride, I tell him we are the walking team who are going to save the centre.

'OK.'

It's a very slow 'O' followed by a very slow 'K', and I'm not sure whether that's a smile or a smirk on his face.

'Have the press arrived yet?' Mrs McCreedy asks.

They haven't.

'Oh well,' I bluster, 'we can go and check out the penguins first.'

We stride down the corridor. Odd, frilly fish drift listlessly around their tanks or goggle at us as we pass, but some of the tanks are already empty.

We're the only visitors today. The penguin area is packed with black-and-white waddly life, though; lovely to see, even if rather on the smelly side. Daisy scuttles ahead to find Mac. He is basking on his front, feet stretched on the ground behind him, but he scrambles up and waddles towards us when she calls his name. He cocks his head sideways to survey us then lets out a satisfied squawk. I could swear he recognizes us. Such a friendly little penguin!

Daisy murmurs sweet nothings, assuring him again and again that we're going to save him. She adores that bird. I do, too, I have to admit.

Amongst the posse of African penguins we can make out the elderly one, Pablo, who is gazing at the pond as if thinking of going for a swim but not quite convinced about the idea. Then we see the speckled one, Florence, who barges in front of him and actually does go for a swim, quite splashily.

'I do believe my watch must be running fast,' says Mrs McCreedy after a while. 'What time do you make it, Eileen?'

'It's . . . Oh, it's already ten twenty-five. The journalist should be here by now.' I'm struck with a terrible worry that, what with all the preparations, I've gone and got the timings wrong. I ring the *Scots Times* office on my mobile and ask what's happened to Marvin Bishop. I can't get hold of him, though, only one of his colleagues, who says Marvin did set off this morning for an interview but he doesn't know anything more.

I hurtle back to the reception desk. Mr Chubby Cheeks is still there, fiddling with his phone, but no other staff are around, not even Molly. It's her day off, he tells me when I ask. And no, he knows nothing about any interviews or photo shoots. I would have thought the manager (Mr Tector) would have passed it on, but it seems he didn't.

'Well, let us give this Martin a little longer,' suggests Mrs McCreedy once I'm back. I don't bother to correct her on the name. I'm still thinking I must've got in a muddle over timings. That does seem to be happening these days. Stupid me. Stupid menopause.

I'm glad of the cafe, the cuppa, the snack. Every few minutes Daisy runs out to see if there's any sign of a journalist, but there never is. After the third time she tells us she just went out and called: 'Marvin!' And only the penguins turned around to look. I somehow don't think any of them is called Marvin.

After the fifth time she looks as if she is about to cry in spite of having eaten two chocolate brownies. 'I can't believe he didn't come.'

Mrs McCreedy finishes the last mouthful of her date slice. 'Remember the penguins, Daisy.' (Mrs M always tells her to 'remember the penguins' when things get tough and she wants her to be strong.) 'Penguins refuse to give up, no matter what happens. And at least we are fortified for our walk, now. We should be getting on. Let's take a few photographs ourselves quickly first. We can send them to the *Scots Times* later.'

Daisy's mouth is a drooping line of disappointment. I feel awful: I'm clammy hot, then clammy cold, and then just weirdly scratchy. I wish I could scratch my guilt away. This is all my fault.

We hurriedly take some shots of Daisy and Mac together with Daisy's phone, which takes better pictures than mine. I dash back to reception and try to get Mr Chubby Cheeks to leave his desk for a moment to photograph the three of us together with the penguins, but he won't. Not until Mrs McCreedy herself goes to persuade him. I don't know how she does it, but a few moments later he comes trotting after her. We pose together. With the penguins. On the zebra crossing. At the entrance. Beside a sign at the edge of the car park that says 'Footpath'.

Then we really must be off.

It's a hard uphill slog on top of all that dashing to and fro. I'm panting and wheezing after the first ten minutes on the road. I'm lugging the picnic, rug, folding chair and first aid kit in my backpack, which doesn't help. Daisy scoots on ahead, not bothered by her smaller backpack. Mrs McCreedy keeps a steady pace, helped by her stick. It's hard to know what she's thinking, but she must be cross with me about the Marvin mix-up.

When we reach the off-road track, I'm glad to see the land levels out, but my new boots are already chafing and my lungs feel like they're full of treacle. I have to stop. 'How far have we been?' I gasp.

Daisy consults her machine. 'Only a quarter of a mile.'

Three and a bit miles is a horrible thought, I must say. And a whole month's worth of three-and-a-bit-mileses seems completely impossible.

I slump against the gate. 'Is it OK to take a wee breather?'

'Yes, Eileen,' Mrs M says, to my relief. 'For a few

minutes we may. And when we reach the loch we can have a proper break. It's important we learn to pace ourselves.'

Daisy has perked up. She points to the grass at our feet. 'Hey, there's some litter. Did you bring the tongs?'

Mrs McCreedy looks at me. I shake my head. Another thing I've forgotten.

Daisy insists on picking up the crisp packet anyway. She is very keen – a bit too keen, if you ask me. Luckily I have wet wipes. I wouldn't want her to go catching something nasty.

The walk beside the loch is very pretty, and easier going, thank heavens. Soothing greens surround us, and reflections of the sky and hills wobble on the silvery water. A few midges zizz about but they don't hassle us much. The path is well worn and level, and we're covering ground faster now. I chatter on about choir and Doug and Fiona, and Daisy talks about her schoolmates and her teachers and her brother and the pet guinea pigs they used to have.

Mrs McCreedy hardly talks at all. She is very wrapped up in thought these days. We have some difficulty getting her over a stile, but manage it in the end with a bit of pushing and shoving.

At last it's picnic time. We spread the rug on a bank in a mossy little glen. Silver birches sprout from the crevices in the rocks and young rowans stoop with the weight of berries. Daisy enjoys unfolding the camping chair and Mrs McCreedy settles on it quite comfortably. With views, hot pumpkin soup, sandwiches and a growing sense of achievement, things are turning out pretty well after all.

We march on. Leaves flutter in our faces, and Daisy jumps about, snatching at them.

'You can have a wish if you catch one,' she pants, between leaps.

At last she manages it, and I see her scrunch her eyes up tight as she makes her wish. I think I know what she is wishing.

It speckles with rain on the way back. My ankles are swollen, my calves ache and my lungs burn. Still, the downhill is a lot easier than the uphill and I'm proud of myself. Proud of us all.

'We don't have an article in the paper, but we've done a very good practice walk,' I tell Doug on the phone after we've got back to The Ballahays and recovered. 'I am beginning to think we can do this. And you know, seventeen more people have signed the petition and pledged to sponsor us.'

'Great. That's really great,' he says. I may be imagining it, but I think he's just a teeny bit impressed.

# 9

# Veronica

*The Ballahays*

SHE THROWS UP her hands. 'Oh no, Mrs McCreedy! I couldn't possibly. Please don't ask it of me.'

'But why ever not, Eileen?'

Normally she is as pliable as plasticine.

She is wearing the penguin jumper she knitted herself. Although charming in its way, it increases her girth rather than flattering her curves. And her hair, also charming in its way, is sticking out in wild corkscrews from her face. Alas, that men are so susceptible to these superficialities, but her husband's eyes are evidently diverted by a more streamlined figure and sleeker appearance. It is not for me to offer advice on her garb or her hairstyle, however.

I selected that perfume with much deliberation. Affection is more likely to materialize when the olfactory senses are pleasantly stimulated, so I was hoping the heady scent of Coco by Chanel – sweet amber with a touch of musk rose – when dabbed liberally upon her neck, would awaken in her husband replenished feelings of love. But my plans for a resuscitation of romance at the Dainty Duck have gone sadly awry.

Much as I would prefer to see the man publicly whipped, I am striving to save their marriage. I must put my own feelings aside, for Eileen's happiness is the greater goal; as Sir Robert warned, any marital rift would cause her utter devastation. If she knew of Doug's infidelity, she would quite possibly even blame herself.

It occurred to me in the middle of the night that Eileen's conversation might be one of the relevant factors in the demise of her relationship. She loves to talk, but her subject matter tends towards trivia, since her life is rather small. Small in terms of her daily routine, at least. If she were to lead a more adventurous life, her conversation would surely take a more scintillating turn. Eileen, I feel, has never stretched herself much. If she did, she might unearth all manner of hidden potential and reap great rewards.

As I mulled this over, the idea slipped into my brain. The more I thought about it, the more certain I became. Eileen is set in her ways, but if anyone can persuade her to do something new, that person is me.

Daisy is currently engaged upstairs on the computer, so I've seized this opportunity for a little confabulation with Eileen in the snug.

'Come on, Eileen,' I say.

'But I haven't been travelling in years, Mrs McCreedy,'

she protests. 'Even going to Inverness in the car gives my tummy terrible wobbles. Ships and planes are even worse. I'd be no good to you at all, Mrs McCreedy.'

'Oh, tosh!' I retort. 'You are unaware of how much medicine has advanced since you last travelled. You can now obtain all sorts of drugs that reliably rid you of motion sickness. I will not accept that as a valid reason. And naturally I will pay all your expenses.'

'It's not just that,' she responds, tugging at one of her curls and making it even more unruly. 'It's Doug.'

I was wondering when his name would come up. I batten down the rage and try to focus.

By putting some distance between Eileen and her husband, my aim is to (a) make her realize she can do perfectly well without him and (b) make *him* realize he is quite incapable of doing without her. He may relish his freedom for the first couple of days and indulge in his detestable affair all the more. However, once the cat has got his fill of the cream, he will doubtless sicken and crave a wholesome diet again. Three weeks may well be sufficient time for Doug to come to his senses. Failing that, I can only hope he will confess to Eileen, leaving her with some grace and dignity. And, of course, a good divorce settlement. She may reside here at The Ballahays if there are problems over their house. She lives here much of the time anyway.

Before inviting Eileen to be my travelling companion, it was imperative that I consult Sir Robert. My email managed to reach him at Oslo airport, whilst he was waiting for his flight to Svalbard. He replied at once. With typical generosity, he was quite willing to have Eileen along to the Galápagos Islands and said accommodation could be provided there, although he added that it might prove difficult to get her a last-minute flight. Then there would be the onward journey to the Falklands to organize as well. *And Antarctica, if you really are set on that, too.*

I am.

Eileen mutters something.

'Speak up, will you?' I adjust the volume of my hearing aid.

'I was saying how I can't leave Doug for three weeks. He'd never cope. He'd have no idea what to do. Food-wise and everything.'

'He could learn. It would be an important lesson for him,' I say with force.

She shakes her head emphatically. 'Sorry, Mrs McCreedy. I'm going to stick to my guns on this one. I'm sure there are lots of younger, more able helpers who'd be glad to come along if you need company on your trip.'

'No, Eileen, it is you who I need. Who else knows the intricacies of my medications? Who else knows which compartments of my assorted handbags contain my eyebrow pencils, lipsticks and hearing aid batteries? Who else knows of my preferences for dark chocolate over milk, for lemon curd over jam, for Stilton over Camembert? Or my tastes in tea? Who else can iron handkerchiefs into neat triangles the way I like them? Besides all that, you are my signed-up companion in the walk for the penguins.'

She frowns, unconvinced. But I am not above wheedling and flattery. 'You are an angel, Eileen. You are the only one who can put up with my little ways, and I have become quite reliant on you.' It occurs to me that the frail-little-old-woman card might come in handy. It is a card I seldom play, but it can have its uses at times. I hunch a little into myself and screw my face into a paradigm of pathetic ineptitude. 'I will be so very lost, coping for so long without you.'

She nibbles her lip. 'Well, it's true I don't like to think of you going all that way on your own,' she admits. 'I know you did Antarctica before, but that was a couple of years ago and—'

'Yes, yes, I'm not getting any younger, I know,' I cut in sharply before remembering I'm supposed to be acting feeble. I heave a tragic, quivering sigh. 'I really don't see how I can manage at all without your help.'

'I'll talk to Doug about it and see what he says,' she concedes with the air of a hunted animal who is finally cornered. 'But if he's not happy, I really can't do it . . . And I'm sure he won't be happy.'

I, however, am not so sure.

How will it all pan out? I wonder, with a pang of concern. It seemed such a brilliant idea at the outset, but daily I become more tormented by thoughts of the vast magnitude of money we must raise. Failure isn't an option. Yet, even if we do manage to gain proper press coverage, can this be done? Can it really be done? I fear I shall have to top up our donation by emptying all my personal savings accounts, and these still won't stretch far enough. Much of my money is already siphoned off in a monthly standing order for the Locket Island research project.

I am finding it hard, also, to see beyond the first week

of our mission. At the outset I had envisaged a strenuous bout of solitary hiking in Ayrshire. Sir Robert's warning about the terrain in the Galápagos has not discouraged me, but walking there, in the Falklands and in the snowscapes of Antarctica will be an altogether different experience. The global aspect lends a beautiful drama and frisson to the venture (I can see the article now: *'Courageous Penguin Ambassador Treks From Equator To Pole'*), but is not the whole effect diluted by the well-intentioned but logistically complex additions of Eileen and Daisy? (*Accompanied, or rather not accompanied, by a small girl who will simultaneously be walking in Bolton* – Bolton, of all places! So unpoetic! – *and a middle-aged woman who* ... Well, who knows about Eileen? It all seems rather random.)

Still, the online petition is up, Lochnamorghy have been informed, the press have been contacted and October approaches, when our walk officially begins. We must muddle on as best we can.

My grandson, Patrick, was astonished when he heard about the plan. At least, his email came across as astonished. I was unable to see his face, which is a pity. He and Terry, together with their fellow scientists, will be putting me up at the study centre on Locket Island, where I stayed before. I gave them no choice, which I have found is always the best way to operate. I cannot wait to feast my eyes on the colonies of Adélie penguins once more. If I can only meet Pip again, I hardly care what else happens. To see the Emperor penguins, I must travel yet further south. I shall stay at the new research centre on the Antarctic Peninsula (again, employing my usual modus operandi). No ordinary tourist would be permitted to do this, but I am no ordinary tourist. I am Veronica McCreedy, the first Penguin Ambassador, and it is only right that I should meet the Emperors.

Taking my broad hint, Terry and Patrick have now named two other penguins Daisy and Eileen, so now we all have namesakes in the Emperor world.

Eileen and Daisy were thrilled to see the photos of Veronica Penguin, Eileen Penguin and Daisy Penguin, which Terry has posted in her blog.

My own namesake stands tall in her glorious gold-and-white plumage, beak pointing outwards, looking out over her mountainous snowy empire. Eileen's is a stouter character with short flippers and a winning expression. Daisy's a cute little fluffball. How proud we are of them!

Daisy is wildly jealous that I shall be meeting them in person. It is just as well we have been diverted by the arrival of the pedometers in this morning's post.

At first I was irritated by the outrageously finicky setting-up process and the minuscule printed instructions that only a gnat could read. Luckily, Daisy's eyesight is as good as any gnat's. She was happy to read them out again and again. Before anything was possible, we had to enter our weight and our stride length. This involved a tussle with the bathroom scales and a long hunt for a tape measure, then an argument about footwear, and then repeated sets of strides on the Ballahays driveway performed with markers and measurements. But with Daisy's help I believe we cracked it in the end. The machines gave us the option of metric or imperial.

'What's imperial?' Daisy asked.

When I explained that it meant inches rather than centimetres, she was dubious; but when I added that 'imperial' means pertaining to emperors, I won my case. Imperial it is.

Eileen assures me that she has forwarded the photos to that journalist fellow, and we worked together on a carefully worded press release. We have had no response, though. What is the man playing at? What other Scottish news item could be more important?

There is good news, however. Not only has Eileen persuaded most of her choir to sponsor us and sign the petition, but her misguided husband is quite happy for her to travel with me across the globe.

'I never would've thought it,' she declared, 'not in a month of Sundays. Us not having been apart, hardly, since we got married – only when I come and stay here, and that's not exactly far away, is it? But he was fine about it. More than fine. He was even quite encouraging. He said it would do me good to have a change and a break. Not that it will exactly be a break, what with all the walking.' She produced a taut, hollow sound that wasn't quite a laugh. 'He won't find it easy. But I promised I'd stack the freezer with ready meals and leave instructions for heating them. He's quite partial to a takeaway in any case, is Doug. And he can always get a pork pie from the corner shop. Oh, Mrs McCreedy, I can't quite believe I'll be doing that huge long voyage and exploring places so far away. And seeing you filming with Sir Robert himself. And actually being there when you receive your Penguin Ambassador award. And seeing wild penguins!' She paused for a quick breath, almost a gulp. 'And it's so soon. I can't take it in at all. I hope I won't be a burden to you.'

'I shall be delighted to have your company, Eileen,' I reply with an attempt at sincerity.

I hope it will be a useful exercise for her, in more ways than one.

We broke the news to Daisy in the snug, during tiddly-winks (by good fortune, Eileen discovered the ancient game at the back of one of my wardrobes and Daisy has taken to it).

'Oh,' she cried as a tiddlywink shot through the air and landed alarmingly close to the crystal decanter.

'Only because Mrs McCreedy simply can't do without me,' said Eileen, a little purr in her voice. She pinged the wink back at Daisy.

It hit the child lightly on the neck and started sliding down her T-shirt. She grappled for it and retrieved it just before it sank beyond reach. I observed that she was wearing the locket that I gave her, which is similar to mine. Seeing me notice, she grasped the locket tightly in her fist for a moment. Emotion flashed across her face but she said nothing more.

She has been very up and down over the last few days. Children, unlike us tough old birds, abandon themselves freely to both laughter and tears. They need to be handled with care. We must ensure Daisy returns to Bolton with sufficient enthusiasm to embark upon her walking task, especially now that she will be left so much to her own devices. Daisy is determined but she is young, and it is hard for the young to keep up a long-term daily commitment. I have spoken to her mother, Beth, on the phone regarding this. It was particularly difficult to hear what Beth was saying, the line to Switzerland being scratchy, so I did most of the talking, but she made noises that sounded understanding and supportive.

With help from her parents and friends, I believe Daisy will stick to the target, provided we all keep up contact via email and encourage, encourage, encourage. As I suspected, due to the support from her school (who approve of all her fundraising schemes), she is the one who has so far gained us the most sponsorship. We already have seventy-six signed-up sponsors and £540 committed to our cause.

I tell her this as we are in the porch, preparing for what she calls a 'training exercise', although it is no more than my usual litter-picking excursion.

'You are a vital member of the . . .' What is the word now? 'A vital part of the doo-dahs.'

'Am I? Am I a vital part of the doo-dahs? You mean the three of us? The team?'

The concept of 'team' is not very familiar to me, but I suppose that must be what I mean.

'We should have a team name,' Eileen asserts as she pulls on her boots. 'Like the Famous Five . . . only not five, of course.'

'If we are to have a name, it should be related to our walk. The Striders, the Marchers . . . the Penguin Pilgrims?'

Daisy frowns. 'No, that sounds too religious.' Her parents are churchgoers but she has recently rebelled against it and identifies as an atheist.

'Maybe we could use Mac's name.'

Eileen grins. 'The Mac Pack?'

Daisy shouts out: 'The Three Mackateers!'

I am not convinced. 'We can refer to ourselves as that if you like, Daisy dear, but for the online petition I was thinking of something with more gravitas and urgency, like a military operation.'

'Like SOS?' she asks.

I nod, although this is not quite what I meant. 'An acronym would work well, if we can find something appropriate.'

We discuss several options as we tramp along the road – Save Our Penguins (SOP – rejected on the grounds that it is insufficiently suggestive of strength and stamina), Save the Ayrshire Penguins (SAP – marginally worse), Save Lochnamorghy's Ayrshire Penguins (SLAP – punchier, admittedly), Saving Mac, which would be abbreviated to SMAC (also possessing a certain, although not wholly positive, vigour) – then fall into a lull. The only sounds are the distant gulls and our footsteps and my stick as it taps a steady rhythm on the weathered tarmac.

'I believe I have it,' I declare at last. 'We shall call it "Penguins In Peril". Otherwise known as Operation PIP.'

# Daisy's Penguin Blog

## KINDNESS AND THE PENGUINS

Mac has a special message for you. He says THANK YOU SO MUCH, all you lovely people who are sponsoring Daisy and Veronica and Eileen. He says please tell your friends. He says per-leeease give as much as you can for Operation PIP (Penguins In Peril) because he really, really wants to live . . . Maybe until he's as old as Pablo, or even more.

We're calling ourselves the Three Mackateers to support him. And we're doing loads of training for our 100-mile walk.

Veronica's grandson works with penguins in Antarctica, and the research team there have actually named three Emperor penguins after us. Here's a picture of them. The baby one is Daisy!! Just look at that little face. Look at all the fluff. Look at those teeny flippers. Have you ever seen anything sooo cute?

Emperors are the biggest species of penguins, up to 120 cm tall, which is almost as tall as my brother. They're also amazingly strong – and kind. Daisy Penguin only exists because of the humungous efforts of her parents.

Can you imagine waddling a whole 100 miles in the dark, in a great long procession across the ice? After the mum had laid an egg, the dad looked after it, keeping it warm in a 'brood pouch' on his feet. He had to be so careful and he couldn't eat a thing for nearly 4 months. No snacks even. Plus it was horribly cold, with temperatures dropping to −60°C. Brrrr!!! Meanwhile the mum was doing the long trek all over again to reach the sea and find food . . . and then all over AGAIN to get it back to the chick! She must have been so relieved to arrive and find Daisy Penguin out of the egg, alive and well. I bet the dad was relieved too.

See how kind they were?

I WISH I could meet Veronica, Eileen and Daisy Penguins, but I have to do my own walking in boring old Scotland and Bolton.

I just hope we can save Mac.

# 10

# Veronica

*The Ballahays*

'VERONICA, IS IT OK to do something naughty if . . . well, if . . .?'

'Do you mean tormenting poor Mr Perkins?'

'No, not that. A different thing, more important. Is it OK to do something naughty if it leads to something good? Because I think it is. If the naughty thing isn't really *that* naughty, and it's just being honest, and if tonnes of good – very, very good stuff – might come out of it.'

'We'd call that the end justifying the means,' I answer. Now, where did Eileen put the sugar tongs?

'So it's fine, then?'

I consider. I have been known to bend my own upright morals for the greater good. I am also rather impressed by the maturity of Daisy's argument, her ability to see that solutions are not always straightforward. Evidently she is angling for something she wants very much. I am curious, but no doubt we shall learn all about it soon enough.

' "Naughty" is a very subjective word. Where is Eileen?'

'Here I am.' Eileen emerges from the back room with a dishcloth and cleaning spray. She gives the marble work-top a few spritzes and rubs it frenetically, as if to demonstrate how very thorough she is. I indicate the Wedgwood tea set and cake tin. She promptly resigns her cleaning duties to join us.

Once our tea ceremony has been performed, Daisy can contain herself no longer. 'I've got something to show you. Can you both come upstairs, please?'

She leads us up to the study and points to the chairs in front of the computer. We sit. The air is charged with the frisson of a red-carpet film premiere.

Eileen is bubbling over. 'Oooh, so exciting!'

Daisy fusses with the keyboard, then turns to face us. 'I've prepared a seventeen-slide PowerPoint presentation and I'd like you to watch it.'

She moves aside to reveal a sentence in gaudy script and huge letters, surrounded by bouncing cartoon penguins. It reads: *Why Daisy Should Travel To The Galápagos And The Falklands And Antarctica With Veronica And Eileen.*

Rather flabbergasted, we watch as pictures and words blink across the screen. The presentation is a well-organized and illustrated set of arguments.

It includes such sentences as:

- *It's not fair that you two get to go and I don't. We are a TEAM.* (This accompanied by photos of each of us arranged in an equilateral triangle with the words 'Operation PIP' in the centre.)

- *Mum and Dad are busy busy with trying to buy a new bicycle shop and school runs and Noah and it will give them a break.* (A photo of Gavin and Beth outside the bicycle shop in Bolton.)
- *I love Mac!* (And now she's used the very photo that was used to coax us into letting her come to the Falklands: herself – smaller, balder, paler – standing with me and her favourite Scottish penguin. Red hearts, cleverly added to the image, float between herself and Mac.)
- *I've had cancer and proved how brave I can be.* (A photograph of herself in hospital with tubes coming out of her nose.)
- *I'm doing a penguin blog like Terry's and if I get to travel with you it will be SO MUCH BETTER. And that will get us lots more £££.* (On the computer screen is another computer screen with the words 'Daisy's Penguin Blog' written across it.)
- *Euthanasia is murder. We have to stop it.* (Blood dripping down the letters.)

The slideshow concluded, Eileen claps loudly. Daisy takes a bow.

I view her with awe and pride. Such persuasive arguments. Such powers of manipulation!

Apparently she has already shown the presentation to her parents, who promptly made her promise not to show it to me. 'But only because they're embarrassed. Mum said you'd already been too kind and it wasn't right to ask for another holiday with you, and Dad said they can't afford it. But this isn't a holiday, is it? It's a *mission*.'

She is quoting my own words back at me.

Because she has been severely ill, moreover with the big C, Daisy thinks she has an automatic right to anything and everything. She does not realize how huge this is.

'You have made a very good case, Daisy. This is complicated, though. We are already pressed trying to find last-minute flights for Eileen, and it would be rude to inflict yet another person on Sir Robert during his filming work, even a very small person.'

'I asked him already,' she retorts. 'Without telling Mum and Dad. His email address is on your computer. I emailed him this presentation and he emailed back and said it was a superb set of arguments and very well done me. And he said it's OK with him so long as you and my parents agree.'

I wonder if those were his exact words or if she has bent the truth somewhat. 'Well, that is all very lovely. Sir Robert is kindness personified. But much as I would wish to have your company, you would have to miss weeks of school, Daisy, which would be regrettable.'

She has already got her answer prepared for this, too. One of the weeks we'd be away is the half-term holiday. She has missed so much school anyway over the last few years due to her illness that missing three more won't make much difference. She is used to catching up. She is part home-educated anyway (Beth teaches languages and is surprisingly capable).

I am so very tempted to throw caution to the four winds and simply say yes to Daisy, but I warn myself not to commit before I have given this all due consideration. I cannot afford to build up false hopes.

'Listen, Daisy. If I were to fund your journey, I would be spending even more money on our travels, money that could go towards saving Lochnamorghy instead.'

She screws up her face.

'However,' I muse, 'one has to speculate to accumulate. And the mission would certainly have more dramatic impact with the three of us walking every step together rather than separately. Which would gain greater publicity . . .'

As would her prettiness. As would the pathos of her cancer-ridden history, although I do not say this.

Eileen has sided emphatically with Daisy. 'And wouldn't it be just so perfect to have her at your ambassador ceremony, Mrs McCreedy? Only imagine!' She almost knocks me off my chair as she leaps to her feet. 'I'll look into those flights, shall I?'

'Is that Lochnamorghy Sea Life Centre? It is? Good. I wish to speak to Tilly.'

The voice at the other end, who I suspect is the lackadaisical man on reception we saw during our last visit, informs me that there is no Tilly at Lochnamorghy.

I sigh. 'Milly, then. Or Molly, or Mandy. The penguin patroller.'

'Ah, Molly,' he says. 'Just a minute, I'll see if she's available. Who is speaking, please?'

'Veronica McCreedy. The, ahem, the first Penguin Ambassador.'

There is a noise like a harrumph.

A moment later, a lighter voice speaks to me down the line. 'Hello, Mrs McCreedy.'

She already knows about our walking plan. I explain that we were hoping to have a large spread in the *Scots Times* to gain publicity, but that Marvin the journalist let us down. I then update her with recent developments: by some miracle, we have managed to book flights for both Eileen and Daisy, and we shall be trekking our hundred miles together in varied landscapes across the planet. I have accepted that, although more expensive and inconvenient for me personally, the addition of my two fellow marchers will make a phenomenal difference. With the project so much bigger, it is likely to attract far more attention nationwide, if not worldwide. Everything is falling into place. This was meant to be.

'Lochnamorghy will become famous,' I declare. 'It will be known far and wide as The Sea Life Centre That Was Saved.'

I am expecting a rapturous response. But what comes is a quiet sigh. I am informed that, despite countless enquiries, no new homes have been found for the penguins (nor for the elderly octopus). Moreover, a property developer has already put in a bid for the site; a bid that is about to be accepted.

I struggle to take this in. There's a short pause. A crackle on the line. When she speaks again, Molly sounds close to tears. 'It's wonderful that the three of you are so keen to help, Mrs McCreedy . . . Truly amazing . . . But I'm afraid you're too late.'

# 11

# Veronica

*The Ballahays*

I slam down the phone. My fingers and my heart are quivering with rage. After numerous recorded messages which instructed me to press first 4, then 7, then 8, I finally spoke to an actual human being, but to no avail. My brain is a boiling vat of frustration. I am possessed by a strong desire to scream and break something. The Dutch Delft vase would do, but I know I would only be cross with myself afterwards and it would make extra work for Eileen clearing up the pieces.

I would, of course, consult with my dear friend Sir Robert, but he is currently circumventing the North Pole on an icebreaker ship, amidst narwhals and polar bears.

Daisy has returned to Bolton. With the support of her school and Eileen's choir, our campaign is steadily growing, with sponsorship money of nearly £2,000. But that is a long way from two million, and hardly significant in any case now. I have not yet told Daisy what I learned about Lochnamorghy. I have been reviewing ways that we might yet save the penguins.

Eileen bumbles into the room, a duster in one hand.

She apologizes and is about to withdraw, but I point to a chair and she obediently sits. Unaccustomed as I am to laying out my intentions or my woes, I vent some of my grievances into her eager ears.

When I have finished, Eileen blows out her lips. 'I don't know about these things, Mrs McCreedy. I can do hoovering and arrange flights for you and I'm happy to try and look things up, but I've never been good with money. My Doug deals with all of that.' She hesitates. 'I could ask him, if you like?'

'Do not dream of such a thing, Eileen.' It is all I can do to stop myself from spitting. 'I am far from incompetent myself. In the past I was very much prized for my financial acumen. But everything has changed since those days. Banks are not what they were, accounting is not what it was, and everything has grown absurdly complicated.'

It seems, indeed, that nothing can be achieved without filling in five hundred forms and setting up online portals with passwords that need to be certified with other passwords that can only be sent by text and lapse within five minutes. One needs nimble fingers, a mobile phone, the patience of a saint and the technical know-how that only a child of the computer age can muster – none of which attributes I am fortunate enough to have.

Moreover, I have no wish to spend what remains of my

life banging my head on such stress-inducing walls. Time is too precious. After so many lost years, I mourn the loss of every moment that flits by purposelessly.

Yes, I have money, gathered in stocks, shares and accounts of various kinds. Most of these, however, are stuck for one, two or three years in high-interest investments. To release that money, I am told, would involve losses that make no sense at all. With absurd penalties, I can access £150,000. The rest of my funds have been tied up by financial sharks.

'You don't look very happy, Mrs McCreedy.'

'I am not very happy, Eileen. I am most disgruntled. It would not be an exaggeration to say I have never in my entire life been less gruntled.'

She clucks sympathetically. 'I get annoyed with that sort of thing, too. It's always so much easier if you can see somebody face to face.'

The crisply ironed young lady in the bank ushers me to a chair.

'Why do you wish for a loan?' she asks.

I am somewhat evasive, unwilling to be cast in the role of batty old woman. I have carefully power-dressed in a dark, sleek suit that can out-crisp any bank clerk, but nevertheless my age is against me.

I look her firmly in the eye. 'This is for an investment in a local business that I wish to support. It is merely a short-term bridging loan until we have raised sufficient money to top up their funds and ensure the aforementioned business survives. But it will take a couple of months to do that and speed is of the essence.'

The bank clerk clicks away at her keyboard, asking

various questions which I answer promptly. When I tell her my date of birth, a slight wrinkle appears in her brow. When I tell her that the business is Lochnamorghy Sea Life Centre, her lips curve upwards and a spark of interest kindles in her eyes, although she does not comment. When she asks how I am intending to repay the loan, I take the *Scots Times* article from my handbag with a flourish.

'A Penguin Ambassador! Well, that's the first time we've had one of those in.'

I explain the sponsored walk. She is looking a little out of her depth now.

Due to the sizeable amount of money I wish to borrow, any loan would, she advises, have to be a mortgage against the value of my home. Since The Ballahays is worth some £3 million, I tell her that should not pose too great a problem. The property has grown shabby in places since I bought it in 1956, but nobody can deny it is a magnificent building. It manifests unique Jacobean charm and its three acres of land have, over the years, been beautifully tended by Mr Perkins.

The wrinkle appears again. 'There might be a small issue due to your . . .' she pauses '. . . seniority.'

There is little I can do about my seniority, so I glare at her and wait for a solution.

'A lifetime mortgage may be possible,' she suggests with sudden brightness. 'Certainly I can make an appointment with the mortgage expert for you.'

Dismayed at the prospect of another appointment, I am yet more dismayed to learn that the next available one is four weeks on Thursday.

Four weeks on Thursday I shall be in the Galápagos.

'Is there no alternative?' I ask.

After more clicking on the keys, the woman tells me that in fact a telephone call should be sufficient. 'Our expert will ring you later this week,' she says with a pink and perfect smile.

I call Lochnamorghy again. I speak to Milly-Molly-Mandy, who is very chatty and has revelations to impart. There is a reason why Marvin the journalist fellow never got back to us. Apparently, he is friendly with Molly's cousin's boyfriend, and this boyfriend, over a pint at their local pub, extracted the information that a certain amount of money was passed over to Marvin by the property developer who is bidding for the sea life centre. In exchange, Marvin promised not to run our story.

Outrage sizzles in my stomach. I have no doubt that backhanders are regularly given and received by people in positions of power. But bribery such as this, under-mining a brave act undertaken by three females to save a group of innocent penguins? How could Marvin Bishop stoop so low? How dare he?

Be that as it may, there is more than one journalist who works for the *Scots Times*.

'Anyway, the sale documents haven't been signed yet,' says Milly. 'As far as I can gather, there's been some delay.'

I am relieved to hear it, bearing in mind the imbecility of the bank with regard to my monies.

'I'll see if I can find out any more. I'll let you know when I do,' Milly promises.

I ought to have a word with Lochnamorghy's manager, rather than just talking to her, but apparently he is out.

'Tell me, what is your manager like?' I ask her.

'Oh, Mr Tector – Simon – isn't particularly hands-on. Sits in his office all day feeling sorry for himself because he's going through a divorce. I think he might have had enough of running this place, to be honest. But that's no reason to . . .' Her voice has become brittle and sharp. 'Anyway, I will be rooting for you, the three of you. Let me know if I can do anything to help. At the very least, we can offer free entry tickets for yourself, Eileen and Daisy for as long as we stay open. I'll persuade him.'

When the mortgage expert finally rings, he is full of verve and bluster. He blabs on about credit checks and household expenses and seems to require a vast quantity of documentation that will have to be scanned and emailed. The questions resemble the Spanish Inquisition, and I part with all sorts of intimate information about my finances. The line is appalling and I constantly have to ask him to repeat himself. My hearing aid shrieks at me every time I adjust it, which is trying in the extreme.

When he asks what the loan will be for, and I reply, 'To save Lochnamorghy Sea Life Centre,' there is a long pause and then it is his turn to ask me to repeat myself. Clearly he has no idea which box to tick. I am then put on hold and a noise that scarcely resembles music assaults my ears, on loop, for what seems like infinity. I can feel my life ticking away.

I make tea and sit by the phone, sipping it and furiously quoting *Hamlet* in my head to stop myself from dropping off.

When he comes back, he runs through the possibility

of equity release, a permanent arrangement which means interest adds up at an extortionate rate and they will take pretty much all of Patrick's inheritance after I am dead. This is not what I wish for.

I explain again that I want the loan to be only short term, to be repaid as soon as I've had a chance to pool all my resources, including whatever money will be raised from our walk (currently we are still stuck around the £2,000 mark, but I do not tell him this).

'It's not looking as if any short-term loan would be possible.'

I almost explode at him.

'Well, what do you expect me to do, then?'

I am put on hold again. I grind my teeth. My blood pressure is mounting. This whole rigmarole is sapping the very life out of me. It makes me feel so impotent, so fragile. I am not used to this. And I do not like it one bit. The Dutch Delft vase catches my eye. A moment longer and I shall hurl it to the ground and shatter it to a million smithereens.

A second irritating man comes on, his voice a dreary monotone. I can pick up little of what he says.

We go round and round in circles for a while but no loan is forthcoming. Common sense is overruled by the system, and it is rapidly becoming apparent that not a single human being is capable of overriding that system. My eyes prickle. Blood pounds in my ears.

After the conversation has finished, an automated voice has the audacity to ask if I would complete a short survey about how satisfactory my experience was with the bank today.

I shout down the phone: 'It was unutterably hellish!'

# 12

# Veronica

*The Ballahays*

I UNCLASP MY silver locket. I always wear it, for it contains memories of those I love. I tend to contemplate them whenever I am in need of fortitude. Amongst the specimens of human hair lying in my hand is a tiny tuft from a baby penguin. It was once a part of Pip.

'Remember the penguins,' I mutter to myself.

I fought for the life of Pip and he would want me to fight for the lives of the Lochnamorghy penguins. Mac, Pablo, Florence and the others absolutely must not perish. I could not bear Daisy's distress – or my own – were this to happen. And having got this far, I feel personally responsible. Those twenty-four little lives must be pulled back from the brink. For them, for Daisy, for myself, for common decency's sake. There must be a way.

If only I could buy more time . . .

If only I could control the situation . . .

If only I myself owned Lochnamorghy . . .

What a vision!

If I owned Lochnamorghy, I would surely find some means of restoring it, of keeping it on its feet. I know I would.

No sooner has the thought occurred to me than it burgeons and expands to fill every atom of my being. Yes! One way or another, Lochnamorghy must be mine. It is destiny. I feel it in my bones.

The idea does not at first seem steeped in rationality, since I currently have no access to any funds . . . but then again, the agents do not know this.

I gaze down at Pip's feather, then gently replace it and close the locket again, rehanging it around my neck. I think and I think.

Of course, the plan will throw up a plethora of problems for me – a veritable swarm of complications – but it appears my mind has already made itself up. My imagination has joined in and painted me a splendid, spectacularly penguin-centric future. I could – nay, I *will* – transform the place into a bastion of ecological hope in Scotland.

It is vital that I act fast, before the housing developers get their grubby hands on it.

I telephone the sea life centre and I am pleased to receive another update from our favourite penguin patroller. She is proving to be an excellent source of information.

'Apparently, there's only been the one bid for the centre

so far, and it's a low one. Negotiations are going on but it's dragging out a bit. Don't let on that I told you. I shouldn't actually know this myself . . . but I do.' She gives a strange little tinkle of a laugh.

'Excellent. Thank you so much, Mandy.'

'It's Molly, actually, to rhyme with "jolly" – but you're welcome,' says she.

'May I speak to your manager, Mr . . . ?'

'Tector. Simon Tector. Yes, he's just come in. He's . . . ooh!' Her 'ooh' is a blushy little sound, as if somebody has just tickled her in the ribs. If I didn't know better, I would presume something was going on between those two. 'He is right here. I'll pass you over.'

Mr Tector is interested to hear about my new plan, although not as enthusiastic as I would have wished. He evidently does not care for the penguins as much as his staff do.

'You are very lucky to have Holly,' I tell him, to which there is a distinct lack of any reply.

Still, I manage to extract from him the details of the commercial agents who are dealing with the sale of the centre.

I promptly ring them to register my expression of interest.

'If I were to purchase the sea life centre, would we be talking thousands or millions?' I ask.

Apparently, as yet it is thousands. Well, this is wonderful news. To keep the centre running would cost £2 million, but to buy it outright will be a mere few hundred thousand. Such is the irony of business life. I can put in my bid, save the penguins and work out how to manage running costs in my own sweet time. With sound decision-making, this failing institution and its flippered inmates might thrive again.

With a jumping heart, and before any doubts have the chance to sneak in, I put in my offer. I am thanked and told I will hear from them shortly.

I have scarcely drawn breath when Eileen crashes in, tangled up in the vacuum cleaner.

'You haven't really? Did I hear right? You haven't actually bought Lochnamorghy, have you, Mrs McCreedy?'

I must try to curb her terrible habit of listening at doors. I am too excited to be angry, though.

'I believe I have, Eileen.'

'Woohoo!'

For all her faults, Eileen seldom argues when I put forward a plan which others might find far-fetched. She accepts everything blithely. Indeed, her whole face is lit up at the idea.

She waves her hands about as if wanting to hug me but not quite daring to, which is just as well. One must maintain a dignified distance between oneself and one's paid staff, even if one is fond of them. Her enthusiasm has already dislodged one of the Hoover attachments, which clatters noisily across the polished oak floor.

'Do we tell Daisy?'

Eileen, like me, would love to see Daisy's reaction to the news.

'We had better not say anything until it is all signed and sealed, Eileen. But I am feeling quietly confident.'

'How will you run it when you have it?' she enquires.

'Fear not, Eileen. You will not have to clean out the

penguins daily on top of your Ballahays chores. I will retain the staff that are currently working at Lochnamorghy, assuming they are willing to stay. And improvements will be made so that conditions are enhanced not only for the penguins, but for the public, too. Even for the elderly octopus, if he is still in residence. I know I can turn this business around. We will need to set up a trust and a committee. I am aware I do not have all the requisite skills and the thing must continue after I am no longer here. I shall consult with Terry, with Patrick and with Sir Robert in due course.'

As I say the words, I promise myself there will be no doubt about who is to be boss of proceedings. 'Everything will be sorted satisfactorily once I own the place.'

My relief and elation are so great that immediate celebration is called for. I ask Eileen if she would be kind enough to open the bottle of champagne that is chilling in the fridge. Unfortunately, the cork is too stiff for her to manage. So we toast the success of the new McCreedy Sea Life Centre with Darjeeling tea, sipped from Royal Doulton porcelain.

What has happened to time? These last few weeks have accelerated at an unapologetically absurd rate. Like an anxious hedgehog, September scuttled away far faster than I was expecting, yet its overexcited follower is welcome. October is here.

Daisy has joined us once more. Her buoyant presence lights up The Ballahays. I have outbid the bidder for Lochnamorghy, but we shall still need as much money as we can possibly garner to keep the centre going.

The *Scots Times* has finally run that article about our walk, complete with our photographs. It was not written by the corrupt Marvin, but some other very capable journalist, and we are delighted with the results. The piece is brief, but effective. It was a feat accomplished only after I had spoken to the editor himself on the phone, having gone through numerous secretaries, answerphones and other assorted stumbling blocks. One must go to such enormous lengths if one is to get anything done, anything at all. I do feel sometimes that life is a battle of attrition.

Our charity fundraiser has already gained a mountain of support from the general public, who all seem to adore penguins, heaven be praised! The sponsorship money is now totalling £6,000.

Daisy was a shrieking bundle of excitement when I revealed all this to her. I explained also, since I believe it to be a valuable lesson, that getting to this point has cost me a great deal of effort.

'Few things in life can be achieved without tenacity, Daisy. The key is to continue pushing forward even in the face of multiple setbacks.'

'Like the penguins,' Daisy reminded me once she had calmed down a little. 'You remembered the penguins, didn't you, Veronica?'

'I did indeed, Daisy.'

Eileen, meanwhile, has been baking vigorously and I sense a new determination in her. All three of us are thrilled to be on the cusp of a new adventure.

We start our hundred-mile trek today. We have received many good wishes from our supporters. A card from Mr and Mrs Perkins. An email from Terry and Patrick.

Another from Sir Robert, written in advance and sent by one of his colleagues since he is currently out of signal in the Arctic. A phone call this morning from Daisy's parents, Gav and Beth, and her brother, Noah. A message from Eileen's friend Fiona, complete with a donation. Even despicable Doug has sent us a good luck message via Eileen.

We will be trying different variations, sometimes completing our daily distance all in one go, sometimes in two separate walks, one in the morning, one in the afternoon. The plan is to get ahead whilst we are in easy walking terrain, so we are aiming for at least four miles a day in Scotland. Today, the weather being fine, we shall do a single long walk, and we shall start at Lochnamorghy.

Eileen has prepared us an autumn picnic.

Her morning's baking, accompanied by delicious smells, was performed with much out-of-tune but triumphant humming of some church anthem that I do not recognize. The anthem emerges again at various times during the drive, but I do not silence her. We all deal with our excitement in different ways. Daisy expresses hers mainly by shrieking and giggling.

I have channelled mine into equipping myself, physically and mentally, for all that lies ahead. No challenge should be faced without great hope, bold lipstick and a smart, good-quality handbag.

When we arrive, Lochnamorghy is looking dowdy and run-down rather than resplendent in the morning sunlight. I survey the stained breeze blocks and peeling paint with dismay. My first task, once I am owner, will be to repair and redecorate.

Still, this occasion is very different from our last visit. A cheer rises as soon as we enter. All the staff are gathered to applaud us, and several journalists are present as well.

Molly introduces us to Simon Tector. He is a colourless excuse for a man with a wispy beard that fails to disguise the fact that his chin is virtually non-existent. He shakes our hands, thanks us and wishes us well in a manner that can only be described as limp. How he ever landed this job in the first place I cannot imagine.

I shall run the sea life centre infinitely better than he does.

As if to make up for his lack of it, the penguins are full of vivacity. Florence is running round in circles with one of her friends, dear old Pablo is rearranging his tail feathers, and Mac comes waddling up as soon as we call his name. Daisy takes innumerable selfies with him. She even makes Eileen video a conversation between herself and the beloved penguin in which she tells him that he, his friends and his home are safe and all his dreams are going to come true. Quite what Mac dreams of, I do not know, but Daisy has her own ideas.

I cast a proud eye over the black-and-white throng. I am beginning to view these penguins as my people.

By the time we leave, the pedometers (we now have one each) tell us we have already walked a quarter of a mile.

We are headed for the woods. Daisy carries only her mobile phone. I carry nothing but my handbag and stick. Eileen has insisted on carrying the picnic, which she has stuffed into a lumpy little rucksack.

It is breezy, bright and chilly. The tufts of heather are no longer blazing but have mellowed to a soft purple-brown. My walking pace is not as fast as it used to be, but I am still brisk by many people's standards.

Daisy streaks past me as if her life depended on it.

'If you canter along like that, you will not get very far,' I tell her. 'The idea is persistence, not speed. Slow and steady.'

She slows a little. 'Like the tortoise, not the hare.'

'No, like the penguins,' Eileen says. She sticks her arms stiffly to her sides like flippers, hands flattened and stuck outwards, performing a perfect waddle.

Eileen can be quite amusing. Daisy is now in paroxysms of laughter.

We take the fork that leads us gently uphill and away from the sea. A group of old twisted birches arc above us, dropping dapples on the road. Tall, tawny willow herb, well past flowering, releases its fluffy seeds to the wind.

After a further twenty minutes we turn on to a track that leads us across a field and into a woodland. A green pathway stretches ahead. The wind rummages in the trees, plucks fragments of leaf and twig and scatters them down on us. Soft light pours through the chinks in the canopy and settles in pools across the mossy woodland floor.

I am a little on the cold side but Eileen is sweating profusely. Every ten minutes or so she stops, panting, and asks Daisy and me if we are all right. We assure her that we are. We consult the pedometers often. When the first mile is complete, we let out a cheer.

We stoop under jutting holly boughs, tread carefully over boot-hooking brambles, dodge tangled ropes of ivy. Daisy crows with delight at every little thing: fungi clinging saucer-like to a tree trunk, a feather lying on the path, a procession of ants, a fallen log festooned with woolly lichens that resemble a fairy forest.

We break for elevenses, and an hour further on we find a glade that is a suitable spot for lunch. Eileen unfolds the camping chair for me and spreads the rug with sandwiches, cheesy pasties, tomatoes, a flask of hot soup and another of tea, plus the gingerbread she made this morning. She and Daisy sit on the rug, whilst I look over them from my chair, which (despite a slight worry that it might spontaneously fold up with me inside it) feels like a throne. Eileen has tucked me in with a lightweight fleecy blanket. I am quite comfortable.

As we feast amongst the greens and tarnished golds, Daisy reaches for her phone again.

'It will be better when we're abroad, then I can get pics of us walking with penguins. But for now . . .' She photographs the pedometer readings and the gingerbread men. 'These will get me *so* many likes.'

A 'like' is apparently a mark of approval from your peers. Young people collect and count them to measure their own self-worth.

'Life is not a popularity contest, Daisy,' I remind her, for I abhor such vain inanities. Daisy gives me a look that says I could not possibly understand.

'Mum and Dad are getting Noah a drum kit for his birthday,' she says, somewhat randomly.

'How lovely!' Eileen exclaims.

('Lovely' is not the word I would have used. In fact, I deeply question the wisdom of this parental decision. It was bad enough when, on a previous visit to The

112

Ballahays, Daisy brought her recorder, an object that has no right to call itself a musical instrument – it is more akin to an instrument of torture, if you ask me. Thankfully, Daisy has not pursued her musical career. At this rate, she is more likely to become a naturalist.)

The afternoon is wreathed in pine-scented air as we head deeper into the conifers. The trunks are towering grey pillars. Thousands of pine needles blanket under our feet in thick layers of tan, fawn and yellow. Fir cones lie scattered across the path, scales stuck outwards as if doggedly defending their brittle little bodies.

The sound of our three sets of footsteps, soft on the vegetation, finally hardens as we reach tarmac again.

We have completed four miles and it was easy. No falls, no twisted ankles, no arguments. Our inaugural walk of Operation PIP is done: the first in a month of triumphs.

# 13

# Veronica

*The Ballahays*

I PICK UP the stapled sheets of paper, a slight tremor in my fingers.

### The Ballahays

A stately country residence oozing charm and enjoying fine sea views. Category A listed building dating from late Jacobean times, boasting many period features, set in extensive, beautifully maintained walled grounds of approximately three acres.

My beloved home, reduced to a few lines of banal estate agent gibberish. The Ballahays, the dear, dear Ballahays, up for sale. But what else could I do?

My offer for Lochnamorghy has been accepted in theory, upon my submission of a document outlining my plans for the centre (I may have happened to mention Sir Robert Saddlebow's name, as a potential trustee). Yet the sellers, it would appear, care little about the future of the penguins, so long as they receive money for the crumbling old site. The savings I have scraped together do not cover it. I had assumed the finances could be arranged once the transaction was complete, which would take at least a month. I was wrong. It has now been stipulated that I must supply proof that I can make my offer good, along with various guarantees. Nothing is done on trust these days. Which is sad, but perhaps inevitable. My counter-bidder has proved himself to be unscrupulous, what with the bribery of certain journalists, and it is the likes of him that make life so much more difficult for the rest of us.

The Ballahays is my best asset. I know this as a fact, even if cretinous mortgage companies do not acknowledge it. As a property it may not be flawless, but I have persuaded the Lochnamorghy agents that some wealthy member of the aristocracy is bound to fall for its charms, as I did back in the 1950s. And they said my offer would stand if I immediately put my home on the market. So that is what I have done.

I broke the news to Eileen first. She was beside herself, gave a little shriek, uttered a horrified 'No!'

She has still not come to terms with it.

Daisy is upstairs at the computer, selecting photos and putting her latest blog post together. I have not told her of this recent development and shall have to do so carefully.

Eileen picks up the property details now and heaves a woeful sigh. 'Such a sad, sad thing! Have you told Patrick yet? And Terry?'

I inform her I have not.

'What if somebody puts in an offer for The Ballahays this week? What will you do? And where are you going to live? You can't live at the sea life centre. It's only got accommodation for penguins. How could you fit in all those handbags and tea sets around the buckets of smelly fish? And how can you keep up with what's going on when you're abroad so much of the month? It's all so impossible.'

'Too many questions, Eileen. But trust me, it is not impossible. "There are more things in heaven and earth, Horatio, than are dreamt of in your philosophy."'

A little quotation from Shakespeare is usually sufficient to silence her. Eileen is spectacularly bad at keeping anything to herself, so I have not enlightened her regarding my true intentions in the matter.

To be honest, this is not something I do lightly. It would be unthinkable to actually part with The Ballahays. But by the time the paperwork has gone through, we will have finished our walk and gathered the proceeds. We are already at £7,980 and word is spreading. By the time I have reaped further fame at my Penguin Ambassador ceremony and reached the Antarctic finishing line, we will be swimming in money. I shall then promptly take The Ballahays off the market again. For now, I just need to *appear* to be selling it.

The timing, however, could hardly be worse, committed as I am to all this travel. And Eileen, my right-hand woman, will be away, too, unable to keep an eye on things. But I must – literally – take one step at a time.

I have engaged the help of Wallace and Bell estate agents, who I am assured are the best in Scotland. I have entrusted them with a key so they can show people around in my absence. Mr and Mrs Perkins will regularly check that all is in order. Eileen's friend Fiona has also promised to come in. She has even said she'll bring fresh flowers and make coffee so that the aroma in the house will be suitably enticing. I dare not tell her that entice-ment is not, in truth, what I desire. Walls, as they say, have ears.

I gaze out of the window at the herbaceous border, now past its best, and the sweep of lawn where Mr Per-kins is trundling around behind a mower. The chestnut tree bows low. A couple of scrawny squirrels streak across the green swathe and dash up into its boughs.

The sales particulars for The Ballahays are still in my hand. My fingers clench, scrunching the detested sheet of paper into a tight ball. A sharp pain twinges in my rib-cage, my knees wobble and I have to sit down quickly.

Everything has grown so complicated. How I wish I could guarantee an extra decade on this planet to sort it all out. Much as I fight to claim control, the situation keeps escalating and forcing my hand. I resent this rotten ruin of a body that I must inhabit, that makes every action so much more difficult. How frustrating it is to be old. To have your abilities and strength stolen away on the final stretch, when you at last have the experience and insight to know what you want out of life. Doubtless I should accept it with grace, but I don't. I won't. I can't.

My reverie is interrupted by a squawk from Eileen. 'You're not thinking of going into a care home or anything, are you, Mrs McCreedy?'

'No, Eileen, I am not – categorically not – thinking of going into a care home.' My voice has become a bellow. 'Never, never. I respect such places, of course I do. But, despite your insinuations, I am nowhere near that stage. I am absolutely able to look after myself on every level. I have no use for so-called "care". Even you . . . You may think that you are indispensable to me, Eileen, but in fact I merely employ you for matters of convenience. I could do perfectly well without you.'

Her chins start to wobble. She reddens and begins murmuring an apology. With a sharp gesture, I stop her.

'Forgive me, Eileen. That was uncalled for. I am under a lot of pressure at the moment. Please bear with me.'

'Of course. Of course, Mrs McCreedy.'

# 14

# Eileen

*Kilmarnock*

'WHERE WILL IT end?'

Doug lifts his dumbbells, up and down, up and down. He is sitting on the edge of the bed, legs apart, arms busy. I'm back at home to cook him his tea and have just popped up to the bedroom to fetch my knitting whilst the stew's simmering.

'Where will what end?' he grunts between ups and downs.

'This whole thing. The Travelling Across the World. The Buying of Lochnamorghy. The Putting Her Home on the Market. The whole caboodle. It's quite wonderful – really, it is – but scary, too. Where will it end?'

'Well, if you don't know, I certainly don't.'

'I mean, do you think it could be a form of . . . a sign of . . . you know . . .'

'Dementia? I wouldn't be surprised.' He pinches his left bicep to see how it's doing. He frowns at it, does three more lifts of the dumbbells, then dumps them next to him on the duvet. He has only got them out recently. They were sitting in the back of the wardrobe for years. I suppose, like me, he must have realized his body is in need of a bit of attention these days.

Doug and I were childhood sweethearts, but I first fell for him properly when I saw him toss the caber at the Argyllshire Gathering. We were both different then. I was smaller, slighter, shyer than now. He was bigger, brawnier, noisier than now. Funny, what time does to you.

Now he does some neck stretches, eyes half closed.

I feel disturbed at the sight of his neck sinews bending. I don't know why. I ignore the strange feeling and go back to my train of thought. 'I guess I just can't help wondering about the future. She jumped down my throat when I mentioned a care home, but when you think about it, what's the alternative when she gets really bad? It's not as if her grandson, Patrick, can look after her, not if he wants to stay in Antarctica with Terry and the penguins. I'm here, of course, but I just don't know if I can cope if this is the beginning of the end. She's been such a huge part of my life for so long.'

'You're not kidding,' he says. He is always so understanding.

'Anyway' – I sniff – 'I'm very honoured she wants me there abroad with her. Very surprised and very lucky. So's Daisy. Her parents were cross and terribly shamefaced that she showed us that PowerPoint presentation. I don't think they quite know how to deal with Mrs McCreedy. Not many people do, to be honest. But isn't it just so lovely of her to pay for us both? Especially when she has to fork out to buy Lochnamorghy now, too.'

'Well, she's rolling in it, isn't she? It won't even dent her pockets.'

I swallow down my unexpected prickle of anger. 'It's ever so generous of her, all the same.'

He's stopped with the neck stretching but something in his face – maybe a slight movement of the eyeballs – makes me wonder if I've said all this before. I lose track sometimes of what I've said and what I haven't.

'I can't believe she's put The Ballahays on the market. I wonder if I should let Patrick know? I mean, she said *don't* let him know, but he should, shouldn't he? Know.'

'Yup.'

Doug seems very sure. I debate with myself. Patrick is a bit rough round the edges but a nice lad with a good heart.

I pick up my wool basket from the chest of drawers. I've nearly finished the scarf I'm making for Daisy – thick-knit, candy-pink with white dots on it. It's for her to wear in Antarctica. I'd never forgive myself if she caught a cold. It's a lovely scarf, though I say so myself.

I think I *will* send Patrick a quick email. He's Mrs McCreedy's only family, after all. He oughtn't to be kept in the dark.

Doug stands and wipes a trickle of sweat from his brow with his sleeve. He reaches for the dumbbells again. Up and down they go.

121

I should let him get on with it but I'm not ready to leave the room yet. Exhaustion hits me. I sit down on the bed, on the warm patch where Doug was sitting before. 'Mrs M has asked me to keep a logbook of our daily distances so we can keep track,' I tell him. 'And I have to upload all our pedometer data on to the sponsorship page so everyone can follow us. A hundred miles is an awful lot. Still, we've done three walks and covered twelve already.'

It feels like so much more. I'm not sure how I can keep up at this rate.

I look down at my stomach gloomily and pull my cardie tighter around it. It's the worst of both worlds: I'm simultaneously expanding and becoming invisible. I can't help feeling I've passed my sell-by date, like a tub of mousse left forgotten at the back of the fridge.

'I wish I wasn't so lardy. I'm determined to eat better things, so that I'm healthy enough to keep going all month.'

Doug heaves out loud breaths. 'I noticed there wasn't the usual deep-fried haggis and chips on Friday night.'

'Yes. From now on, any haggis I get in will be fresh from the butcher's, with nice, healthy neeps and tatties on the side. I'm going to include more salads in my diet, too.'

But even the word 'salad' only makes me want more cream cakes. And now heat is roaring over my skin. 'All this walking has to be good for me, doesn't it? Fiona says exercise is better than HRT.'

He doesn't answer. I wonder whether to remind him what HRT is but decide not to. I feel I should say something appreciative. 'And look at you, making an effort, straining away with your arms all muscly and firm. Look at us both!'

I'm not actually doing anything physical as I say it, but he knows what I mean.

'That reminds me, would you mind teaching me how to bake a potato, for whilst you're away?' he pants.

'Yes, of course, dearie. It's very simple. You'll pick it up in no time. The main thing is to stab it all over with a fork to avoid explosions.' I mime stabbing the potato using a knitting needle and ball of wool, probably more ferociously than I need to. I'm making myself hotter and hotter.

Then, as quickly as it came, all the heat drains away again and I feel like a limp rag.

'It's a huge responsibility, going all that way with Mrs M and Daisy,' I mutter. 'Thank heavens we'll be with a film crew in the Galápagos, and then in the Falklands Terry and Patrick are flying over to join us. And they'll be with us in Antarctica, too. It'll be marvellous to see those two again, but I do hope I can keep up with everyone.'

I like to have lots of people around me. I've always wanted a big family, and that's what I've got if you count Auntie Mary and my cousins Fran and Callum and wee Kevin. But it would have been extra lovely if Doug and I had our own children . . . a little daughter like Daisy or a cutie of a son like her brother, Noah. Years ago I did get pregnant, but I lost it in the first few months. It was the hardest thing. Doug was really upset, too. I don't know if it did something to my insides, but I never got pregnant again, even though we tried a lot.

For some reason, I seem to be thinking about that more

and more these days. It's too late now, of course. Even if it wasn't, I don't quite fancy Doug in the way I used to. Not as in wanting-to-do-the-act-with-him-day-and-night, anyway. I do like a good snuggle with him, though. We're not one of these couples who say 'I love you' every five minutes, but we are what I like to call 'comfy in love' with each other.

I look at him now, as he gives up on the weights and slumps down next to me. I take in his flint-grey eyes and the hairs sprouting on his chest above the neck of his vest top, at his belly that's become a bit of a beer belly over the years, at his soft cheeks and stubbly chin.

'You are going to miss me when I'm away, aren't you?' I ask, trying not to sound desperate.

'Of course I'll miss you, Eilee.'

I open my arms. 'Can I have a Dougle-snuggle?'

We nestle into each other, like we have done for decades, and I breathe in his manly, salty tang.

Then he edges away slightly. 'How about you show me how to bake that potato, now?'

I used to check and print out all Mrs McCreedy's emails for her, and sometimes I forget I don't have to do it any more. So I accidentally happened to read Patrick's response when it pinged into her inbox.

*Dear Granny,*

*What are you playing at? I know I'm hopeless at writing emails and this is not a great start, but seriously, WHAT ARE YOU PLAYING AT? Eileen has let on (even*

*though you told her not to, but she did it out of the*
*goodness of her heart so please don't kill her) that*
*you've put The Ballahays on the market.*

*Not wanting to question your wisdom or anything,*
*but nobody will think any the less of you if you take it off*
*again. You've always scoffed at the idea of downsizing*
*and sworn you'd stay in The B for ever. I know you, and*
*I can't believe you really want to sell up. And buying*
*Lochnamorghy??? Sure, you want to save your beaky*
*buddies, but there's got to be a simpler way. Couldn't*
*you get a loan off the bank or something?*

I can't help having a little chortle at this, which is
unkind of me, but it's just the image I have of Mrs
McCreedy's face when she reads those words!

*Loving the idea of the walk, though. Terry and I both*
*think it's ace. Rooting for you every step of the way,*
*here. We are majorly looking forward to seeing you in*
*the Falklands – all three of you! Been reading Daisy's*
*blog. What a great kid.*

*Can't believe you've persuaded Eileen to come.*

Is he going to say something bad about me? I hurry on.

*Glad you did, though. Terry says she's an angel and I*
*totes agree.*

An angel! I'd so love to read that bit out to Doug,
but mustn't. I'm not actually supposed to be reading it
at all.

125

*News here: all fine, but there's still no sign of Pip. His tracking device seems to be on the blink, too, so we've no idea where he is, just that he was last registered heading south from Locket Island. He's a sturdy little guy now and we're confident he'll be OK.*

*The Emperors are doing well, including our own waddly versions of Veronica, Daisy and Eileen. They all managed an epic march, and so can you three.*

*My scientist chums send love. Well, Dietrich and Terry do, and Mike sends his stiff, caustic best regards, which I bet you'll return with equal enthusiasm.*

*Terry is as busy as ever. She's going to put a feature about you on her blog, which should get you some more sponsorship money.*

*Please don't fricking sell The Ballahays. I know us McCreedys are stubborn mules but this is insane. Still, I guess we'll talk about it when I see you. Must stop now. Not used to so much keyboard stuff. Totally desperate to get out and wrestle with malfunctioning equipment in sub-zero temperatures among a load of smelly, over-excited birds. (Yup, really!)*

*Big hugs,*
*Patrick*

It's sweet of him to write to her, but he won't be able to change her mind about anything. There's only one person who can change Mrs McCreedy's mind, and that's Mrs McCreedy.

# 15

# Eileen

*The Ballahays*

'DID YOU HEAR from Patrick?' I ask, knowing full well that she did.

'Yes, Eileen, and thank you for removing from me the worry of how and when to inform my grandson of the recent developments,' she replies, her voice stinging rather than sweet.

'I only meant for the best, Mrs McCreedy.'

She snorts. 'You feel I should not be selling my home, Eileen?'

'Well, it does seem sort of drastic.'

She strides to the window to look out, as she often does. The tulip tree has turned a beautiful shade of yellow and leaves are fluttering in the wind.

'"Though this be madness, yet there is method in't."'

'You said that before, Mrs McCreedy, and it doesn't make any more sense to me now than it did last time.'

Daisy was horrified when the 'For Sale' sign went up. She loves The Ballahays like she'd love a giant playground.

Mrs M had a word in her ear, and she seemed better after that, though.

Walking, I've realized, must be good for the mind as well as the body. Stresses always seem less big when I'm busy putting one step in front of another. Thoughts stop swarming around so wildly and seem to settle down. But sometimes when I'm walking all I can think is: I want to stop. Three or four miles a day isn't much for most people, but most people are fitter than I am. My calves ache and every breath feels like brambles being dragged through my ribcage. I try to picture those Emperor penguins, like in the film we saw. Onwards they march, like the 'Christian soldiers' in the hymn, ever onwards through the storms of life. Even if they slip over in the snow, even if blizzards fly around them, they keep trudging on no matter what. They are not going to be beaten, and I won't be beaten either.

Thank heavens I'm with Mrs McCreedy and Daisy. I don't think any of us could do it on our own, to be honest. Well, Mrs McCreedy probably could, but she might have a fall or something. Daisy wouldn't have the self-discipline to keep at it, and I'd just be too busy to see it as a priority. It's good that Mrs McCreedy makes us do it.

This morning the grass is wet underfoot, but the air is clear. Even a thin strand of sunshine pokes through the clouds from time to time. Apart from the coast path, there are several other scenic walks we can take from the front gates of The Ballahays. The gulls' shrieks fade as we head for an open bridleway, flanked with bracken, bramble and mighty thistles. Mrs McCreedy manages really well with her stick going over the rough ground. I pause to look back at the view – rolling hills, bilberries and gorse, grouse scooting across the rutted land, a chink of harebell-blue sea.

We plod on. We discuss how Lochnamorghy is going to change when Mrs McCreedy is in charge, and how the twenty-four penguins will live in luxury.

Daisy grabs up fistfuls of grass and tosses them away again as she walks. 'Mac is my favourite penguin in the whole universe.'

'Mine too,' I reply.

'Who is your favourite penguin in the universe?' Daisy asks Mrs M.

'Mac is lovely, of course, but you must remember that I have a very special relationship with a certain Pip.'

'Oh, of course. Pip.'

Daisy often admires the large, framed photo of Pip in the hall at The Ballahays. 'Do you think we'll meet Pip when we go to Locket Island?' she asks.

'I think we might,' says Mrs McCreedy. I can tell she's hoping for that more than she lets on.

'My friend Aurora can make a penguin out of the inside of a toilet roll,' Daisy boasts.

'Really?' Mrs McCreedy does not look impressed.

'Yes. She's so clever.' She turns to me. 'I'm hungry. Have you got any of those pick 'n' mix, Eileen?'

I rummage for the bag of sweeties, which is a good excuse to stop for breath. I hand them over. Mrs M doesn't like them but I pop a couple in my own mouth. I wouldn't want Daisy to feel greedy.

Just then we spot a stag, standing proudly at the forest's edge, antlers branching, steam pouring from his nostrils into the cold air.

'What a magnificent beast!' Mrs M declares.

He eyes us for a moment before bounding away into the greenery.

I squint at my pedometer. We're doing well (3.6 miles so far today, and twenty-three in total) but I'm out of breath again.

A big black cloud is hovering just above us. Every day we check the weather forecast to try to work out the best time of day to take our walk, but the weather is always naughtily changing its mind.

Now the cloud starts chucking rain down on us.

Mrs McCreedy already has her scarlet macintosh on just in case, and Daisy has a cagoule with a hood, but I've completely forgotten to bring my rain cape.

I make a run for cover and crouch under the thicket for a moment, but there's no let-up and water is dripping through the leaves anyway, and Mrs McCreedy is keen to press on. So on we go, squelching through the mud and puddles, trying to console ourselves with the prospect of Galápagos sunshine. I'm sopping wet by the time we reach the road again.

We underestimated the time as well, so now we're running late. It wouldn't normally matter except that there is the first viewing of The Ballahays today, and Mrs McCreedy wants to be there for it.

We stumble through the sheets of rain and reach the gates. The Ballahays looks its best in the sunshine, the tall chimneys and crow-step gables reaching for the sky, the stonework shining, the garden so welcoming with its play of light and shade. But today, wrapped in a shawl of wet mist, the place looks sad.

Mrs McCreedy has kept amazingly dry and only needs to change her shoes. Daisy's top half has been protected by her cagoule but her trousers are sodden. My own clothes are all weighed down with icy water, clinging to my legs, trickling on to my skin. I'm bone-tired, shivering and smelling like a wet dog.

Daisy has lots of stuff with her, since she packed for the whole month back in Bolton, but I don't have much here. 'You'd better go back home and get into some dry things, Eileen,' Mrs McCreedy advises.

'I'll just pop the kettle on first.'

As it reaches the boil, the house agent, Mr Wallace, arrives with the people for the viewing.

Mr Wallace is a snazzy type in a blazer, not like the *Wallace and Gromit* Wallace at all. Mrs McCreedy greets them in the porch and I can see it in her eyes: she's reluctant to let anyone round her house. But she's going to have to whilst we're away, isn't she? The people are a couple in their sixties from London, and I hear them telling Mr Wallace they only recently got married and want a romantic fairy-tale place to live in, and Scotland is cheaper than England. He is a leadership consultant of some sort and she is an ex-ballerina who now runs her own business making candles.

They seem to like The Ballahays, although I can't help noticing as I pause in the porch that Mrs McCreedy is pointing out all the bad things, like the mould in the cellar and the mouse holes in the skirting. Sometimes I don't understand her at all.

# Daisy's Penguin Blog

## TEAMWORK AND THE MACKATEERS

Mac says thank you for your generosity and he'd give you all a big bucket of fish (his favourite food) if he could.

We can do this.

Veronica, Eileen and me are (all of us) now going to be trekking in not just Scotland, but in the Galápagos, the Falklands and (OMG!) in Antarctica. Yay yay yay for the Three Mackateers!!!

We'll be seeing at least 8 species of penguins in the wild and we'll even get to see those fantabulous Emperors who inspired our long walk.

Veronica says layers are the secret to keeping warm so we'll need to pack our thickest fleeces and woolly jumpers . . . but penguins don't have any clothes. How on earth do they manage to survive in Antarctica? I'll tell you.

Emperors have layers too: a thick layer of fat, TWO layers of feathers and even fluffy little feathers all over their legs – penguin socks! They also have smaller beaks and flippers than other penguin species to prevent heat loss. Most amazingly, they have a way of packing themselves tightly together in a great big huddle to stay toasty, maybe 5,000 penguins all jammed together. They're shuffling around all the time, taking turns on the outside where it's cold, then shuffling back to the middle to warm up. Teamwork is everything, the difference between life and death.

Teamwork is important for us, too. We Mackateers have now finished the Scottish walking. 29 miles down, 71 to go! See photos.

Best Wildlife Spotted So Far: A stag (a ginormous slug came a very close second).

Funniest Thing So Far: Eileen's imitation penguin waddle.

Worst Moment So Far: Getting caught out in the rain. And saying goodbye to Mac. But I've told him that when we return there'll be good news for him and his friends. We love you, Mac!

# 16

# Veronica

*In transit*

SIR ROBERT HAS managed to get an email through to me. *Don't forget high-factor sun cream, sunglasses and your swimming costume. I don't think I have to remind you about walking boots.*

Because my own flights have been booked for months, and Eileen's and Daisy's have been somewhat last-minute, we have not been able to marry them up. I shall travel before them and we'll not meet again until we are all assembled along with Sir Robert and the film crew on Xavier Island in the Galápagos. We must individually build up our distances as much as possible at the airports and compare notes at the other end. I fly in the morning via Edinburgh, and Eileen and Daisy fly the next afternoon via Heathrow. All of us will stop over in

Quito, the capital of Ecuador, a city set high up in the Andes.

Daisy has googled. She reads out to us: ' "Quito is located approximately two thousand, eight hundred and fifty metres above sea level and visitors may experience some altitude sickness." '

Eileen assumes an expression of horror and starts rocking to and fro in her chair. 'Oh gosh, oh no. How will we cope?'

I sigh. Isn't it obvious? The answer to these things is always the same. 'Grit, determination and medication, Eileen. Grit, determination and medication.'

If she is wobbly now, however are we going to get her through?

My own travel companion for the flight out is a certain Miriam, who is part of our filming team in the Galápagos. The others in the crew travel directly from the Arctic with Sir Robert. I met Miriam in the Falklands last year, and remember she is a bright girl of immense technical knowledge. When I say 'girl', she is probably in her forties, but all of Sir Robert's entourage come across as younger than their years. They are a remarkably fit and enthusiastic team. It must be the effect of working with nature so much.

I am relieved to find that Miriam is there waiting for me at the airport, and relieved also that I recognize her. Her face is pleasant in an unremarkable way, but she has trademark raven-black hair that she wears in a thick plait over one shoulder.

'I'm so happy to meet you,' Eileen exclaims as they shake hands. She has kindly transported me here.

'Me too,' chirps Daisy, who was also keen to see me off.

Miriam smiles. 'And I'll be seeing you two again in the Galápagos, I believe?'

Eileen pulls Daisy close. 'Yes. Yes, you will. We're all so thrilled. And I'm so glad Mrs McCreedy will be travelling with you, especially through Quito.' She gives a small shudder. 'I can breathe knowing you'll be there with her . . .' She throws a sideways look in my direction. 'Not that she wouldn't be completely fine anyway.'

Having said our goodbyes, Miriam and I check in speedily. Being rather a fitness fanatic, she is happy to march innumerable laps around the lounge with me during the wait. Eileen and Daisy have promised they'll achieve their daily perambulation, but I am determined mine will be longer. The pedometer is a fiddly creature for arthritic hands, but once I have managed to unclip it from my belt and scrutinize it, it assures me I have already covered 0.85 miles.

During our conversation, I learn a little about Miriam ('crazy about sea life, especially whales' but 'terrible boyfriend problems because I'm away so often') and she asks questions about our penguin walk. We also discuss Sir Robert. She raves about him and I wonder if it's possible to have a crush on a man who is over thirty years your senior. I suppose it is.

I am interested to learn of a few incidents in Sir Robert's history that he has not shared with me: the time he saved Miriam's sunhat from being eaten by a crocodile; the time he was repeatedly kicked in the stomach by a teenage kangaroo and reacted with typical stoicism; the time he coaxed a particularly shy armadillo out of its hole . . . He talks to the animals in between filming, which is something I was not aware of on our Falklands trip last winter. I was busy filming myself – although, come to think of it, I do remember him having a few exchanges with Petra the rockhopper penguin and with the Macaroni who we called Tony. Kindness to animals (and birds) is always and unequivocally the sign of a good soul.

In my head I am also going over my short script for filming in the Galápagos, but it may change when we are on the spot. Preparation is my friend, but inflexibility is my enemy. So I have learned my facts, but I will not let them mar my spontaneity. Improvisation, I have learned, can be most effective. As for my ambassadorial speech in the Falklands . . . Well, we shall see.

Thirteen hours is far too long for a flight. I have been painfully reminded how inadvisable it is to sleep in an upright posture. The shaped neck pillow must have helped, but it certainly does not feel like it.

Although I staggered up and down the aisle as much as possible, my muscles feel like concrete as Miriam escorts me from the plane, easily shouldering my hand luggage as well as her own. Slowly, my legs remember how to work. It is just as well I have been literally putting them through their paces so much of late.

We have reached the equator. Like any city, Quito is a jumble of traffic and clamour, but from the taxi I can appreciate the array of modern and historic Spanish-style architecture. Beyond are glimpses of mountain peaks; proud and mighty, their heads encircled by pearly coronets of clouds.

At the hotel we dine on deep-fried plantains (an

Ecuadorian speciality), but I scarcely notice the meal, nor Miriam's talk of Incas, condors and Winged Madonnas, due to an imperative urge to lie down.

The next morning we are off on a much shorter flight.

Now anticipation ripples through me. I twist and crane my neck to look out of the tiny plane window.

The sky and the Pacific Ocean are matching shades of satiny blue. Little white huddles of cloud hang above their own shadows in the sea.

As we come in to land, my first sight of the Galápagos is a flat plain dotted with grassy clumps and stubby trees. Miriam points out what she says is an iguana, but it could be a long brown rock as far as I'm concerned.

'I hope you have sun cream with you?' she asks.

'Factor fifty,' I assure her.

Seymour airport, on the island of Baltra, is the world's first green airport. The site, Miriam informs me, was a US military base during World War II, and was given to Ecuador after the war. I note with approval that the new airport was designed to create a minimal impact on the ecosystem.

My companion kindly carries my luggage during the transfers. We are borne by boat across a choppy stretch of water past a series of baked, volcanic islands to our destination: Xavier Island.

Several arms are proffered to help me out of the boat but I make sure I do not lose hold of my handbag. When I lift my head, my heart lifts also.

Sir Robert is there, standing on the jetty, welcoming me with a wide smile and open arms. Beneath his elegant straw panama hat, his skin is tanned, his eyes burn bright and he has a fresh, zingy air, presumably derived from his recent Arctic visit.

I fear I am pasty in comparison, although I lavishly applied make-up in the Quito hotel this morning. (Incidentally, despite Eileen's fears, I did not suffer from altitude sickness in Quito. Grit, determination and medication, as I have previously mentioned, are all that is required to deal with that sort of thing.)

Sir Robert and I embrace, and I shake hands and exchange pleasantries with the other members of the film crew who are with him.

Sir Robert ushers me forward, all smiles. 'We have so much to talk about, Veronica, but first come and see where we're staying. No doubt you'll need a day to recover from jet lag, but the filming itself won't take long and I hope you can just enjoy being here. I think you're going to love it.'

Warm air washes around me. Scotland was getting cooler by the day, so it is very agreeable being clad in cotton again.

We trundle along a rough track and are helped into a minibus by a local young married couple. Sir Robert introduces us.

'This is my dear friend Veronica McCreedy, who is here by my request to help with the documentary, and who is shortly to become the first official Penguin Ambassador. Veronica, this is José and this is Gabriela, who run the nature reserve.'

They are both slim, and have skin like polished mahogany. José wears an orange bandanna and walks with a swagger.

Gabriela's eyes flash as she flicks back her wing of luscious, dark hair. 'It's a pleasure to meet you, Mrs McCreedy,' she says in perfect but heavily accented English.

'This whole island is owned by a group of ecologists, which includes us two,' José is keen to inform me.

'We are very privileged to be here,' says Sir Robert.

Judging by our hosts' expressions, they are the ones who feel privileged to be receiving a visit from the great Sir Robert Saddlebow. I flatter myself that they are also rather pleased to be visited by the very first Penguin Ambassador.

During the drive they rattle on with pride about the archipelago, which apparently a young Charles Darwin called 'a little world within itself'.

Sir Robert also chats as we go, filling me in on various facts about Xavier Island. It was apparently chosen for filming because it is one of the most diverse and prettiest of the islands, whilst being off the tourist trail. 'Normally, only certified scientists can set foot here. Lava plains, sandy beaches and cacti forests – it's all ours to explore. We are staying in an eco-lodge close to a sunken volcanic crater. It's within walking distance of both a tortoise reserve and the Galápagos penguins site.'

Light streams through the minibus window and I admire the colour palette. Whilst the Scottish landscape is pure watercolour, the Galápagos appears lavishly daubed in bright poster paints.

We pull up in a grove of spindly, sinuous trees.

'Scalesia trees, endemic to the islands,' José says.

The lodge is a series of adjoining buildings, made up of smooth surfaces: glass, wood, steel, stone. It is too modern for my taste, but comfortable, nonetheless. The main rooms all have overhead fans, as does my bedroom, which I visit only briefly. Miriam deposits my luggage there. The others fuss around me, asking if I'd like to lie down.

'I desire nothing more than a good cup of tea and a little tête-à-tête with my friend,' I assure them, indicating Sir Robert.

I have brought my own tea, for fragrant leaf Darjeeling is one of life's indispensable pleasures. Once it is has been located, they kindly disperse.

Sir Robert and I settle in the lounge, sipping and smiling. I ask first about his Arctic expedition.

'It was bitterly cold and relentlessly bleak. Conditions were tough and the work was painstaking and repetitive. And it was utterly wonderful.' His eyes sparkle as he tells me of virgin snows, of the magical sightings of Arctic hares, polar bears, Arctic foxes and narwhals. 'And I can't say how delighted I am to be sharing the next bit of the adventure with you, Veronica.'

I am pleased to hear it.

'How is Eileen?' he asks.

'She is well, very well, but struggling with unassuageable fears about travelling.' I do not mention the matter of her traitorous husband, although I perceive that was also implied in the question.

'I'm so glad she'll be joining us. Daisy, too!' He is very fond of the girl.

'She is one very fortunate little madam. She is over the moon to be part of this venture, and is particularly looking forward to Antarctica. Like me, she is desperate to see Pip.'

'Any news of the little fellow?'

'No, alas. I dearly hope he will have returned by the time we get there, but as yet he is still missing.'

Concern leaps up in my friend's eyes. He is one of the few people who know what Pip means to me.

'I have the unfortunate habit of losing those whom I love,' I state baldly.

'Oh, Veronica, you have lived a hard life.' He says it as much to himself as to me. 'I wish . . .'

His voice fades, the wish remains unexpressed, he lapses into silence.

'And how is Operation PIP going?' he enquires eventually, after our cups have been drained.

'We have now exceeded thirty miles, so are slightly ahead of schedule. We also seem to have charmed the public.'

I am deliberately evasive regarding money. I have not told Sir Robert about my intention to purchase Lochnamorghy, nor that I have put The Ballahays on the market. It is essential, though, that I do so before Eileen goes blabbing it out.

I have been disappointed with everyone's reactions so far (especially my grandson's) but I am quite willing to ignore them. With Sir Robert it is a different matter. He is a man who will always find the best in me, who knows I tend to be impetuous and does not hold this against me. Yet his respect is something I treasure, and I would be loath to lose it.

I regret nothing . . . yet in spite of the equatorial brilliance of our location, I can't fight off this feeling of foreboding, this sense of darkness beginning to gather.

# 17

# Veronica

*Xavier Island, The Galápagos*

I HAVE YET to see the Galápagos penguins but soon I will. Even the thought of them reminds me of their counterparts in captivity, those poor Lochnamorghy penguins whose lives may be cut short because of human shortsightedness and idiocy. Not, however, if I have anything to do with it.

Due to the failings of my ageing body, I have spent much of today resting, but this afternoon Sir Robert and I decide to take the short trek from the lodge as far as the giant tortoises. I ensure my pedometer is set. We are accompanied by José and Gabriela.

The sun sits in the sky like a great, drippy blob of butter. Under our feet, the ground is scratched and parched. The trail takes us across scrubby brown swells of land and through spouting tunnels of emerald vegetation.

Ahead is a fenced enclosure full of humps and domes. José opens the gate and lets us in.

We edge round a tortoise. Such an extraordinary creature! It is as if somebody has squashed up a dinosaur and tried to pack it into a shell, leaving various appendages sticking out.

'The Spanish word for tortoise is *galápago*, so you can see how these islands were named,' Sir Robert informs me.

José is keen to tell me more. 'By 1835, when Charles Darwin arrived on these islands, the tortoises had already evolved into many distinct species. They helped him come up with his theory of natural selection.'

Gabriela points to another giant, armour-shelled being with club-like feet and an ugly, friendly face. 'This is Agata. She is a hundred and nine years old.'

I blink. 'Makes me feel quite youthful.'

Agata tears up a tuft of grass then cranes forward, her neck even more wrinkled than mine, grass blades poking from her mouth.

'I expect you've heard of Lonesome George?' José enquires.

'Remind me.'

'He was the very last of his species, a Pinta Island tortoise. He was over a hundred years old when he died in 2012. He became a symbol of our need to protect endangered species.'

'Poor Lonesome George,' sighs Sir Robert.

'Poor Lonesome George,' I echo.

Gabriela is scrutinizing Sir Robert and me, as if we, too, are the very last of a dying breed.

In addition to the cumbersome adults, five or six baby tortoises are clambering around too, scone-sized, very sweet.

I wonder what the future holds for them.

Eileen and Daisy have messaged from Quito, ready to depart on their onward flight. Eileen has been queasy, despite consuming innumerable tablets. Daisy, thankfully, is fine.

José, Gabriela, Miriam and the rest of the film crew join us for supper: tortillas jewelled with red and green peppers, followed by a lime sorbet with fresh bananas.

Two small, wild boys appear sporadically during the meal, scampering around the tables, causing havoc and then disappearing again. Gabriela shouts at them in Spanish.

'I have monkeys for sons,' she says apologetically, clearing the dishes.

I wonder what Daisy will make of them when she arrives. They are younger than her, but possibly their company will provide a little respite from us adults.

I have learned that José and Gabriela own a panga, a small metal fishing boat with which they take the children to school, do shopping and conduct some sort of social life. Other conservationists also stay here at different times, apparently, travelling in by boat.

I ask about the distance to the tortoise enclosure, and the couple debate together for a while. After a heated discussion about kilometres and miles, it is decided that my walk today must be in excess of two miles, which correlates to my pedometer reading. It is sufficient, but I should like to do more.

So whilst the others are washing up, I head out again.

An unfortunate truth: any activity you thoroughly enjoy – as I do walking – loses much of its appeal as soon as it becomes compulsory.

Now I am pacing, pacing, pacing. Up and down in front of the lodge, the only place where the ground is smooth. I stride briskly and the pedometer is racking up the distance. I glance down at my lightweight walking boots, which are very different from the mukluks, the every-terrain boots I purchased for Antarctica two years ago and which I shall be wearing next week. Nevertheless, they are too hot, as is the rest of me. They are gathering a felty grey covering of dirt.

I walk and I walk. Huge birds flap overhead but I do not heed them. Proper sightseeing will be tomorrow, when we are all together again. Now, not a moment must be wasted.

I am beginning to flag when the front door of the lodge opens and Sir Robert steps out.

'Do not laugh,' I warn him as I turn sharply and pace back the way I came.

'I am not laughing,' he replies, watching me. 'This is a very serious undertaking. I can see that.'

'More serious that even you know.'

I continue walking, always walking.

'Are you allowed to stop for a little break?' he asks. 'Maybe some tea? The kettle has just boiled.'

I consult the pedometer. I believe I can allow myself a short rest.

It is also an opportunity to divulge what must be divulged.

The others have gone; the kitchen is wiped clean. As soon as we are seated and I have recovered my breath a little, I blurt it out.

'I am intending to buy Lochnamorghy outright. To that end, I have placed The Ballahays on the market.'

His eyes widen and, for a moment, I am engulfed by their blueness.

'Dear Veronica! Wow, well I never. That is so extremely generous of you.'

I wince at the word 'extremely'. Everyone thinks my actions are extreme.

'Putting my home up for sale is merely as a safeguard,' I add quickly, 'a gesture to show I can pay. Operation PIP will bring in enough funds to enable the Lochnamorghy purchase, so I will not need to go through with it.'

Transferring his gaze from me to his mug of tea, Sir Robert now seems a little lost for words.

I wait.

He knows I am waiting.

'It's hard to express how much I admire your spirit.'

My face begins to smile. Yet the compliment is about to be spoilt. A 'but' is on its way. Yes, here it comes, prefaced with a small sigh.

'Don't take this the wrong way. But it really isn't up to you personally to solve every penguin problem on the planet.'

'Not every penguin problem on the planet,' I acquiesce. 'But this problem is right on my doorstep, in Ayrshire. Those Lochnamorghy penguins need me. And if not me, the first Penguin Ambassador, then who else?'

'Point taken. But even though you're a Penguin Ambassador—'

'—*The* Penguin Ambassador,' I correct him.

He reconsiders. 'The title wasn't created to burden you with extra responsibilities, Veronica. It was a thank-you. It was designed to acknowledge your immense achievements with regard to Locket Island and environmental awareness.'

'You seem to know an awful lot about it,' I answer, suddenly suspicious.

He flinches slightly, clears his throat, sips his tea.

'Why, Sir Robert, I do believe you are hiding something from me. Did you have something to do with my ambassadorship?'

I eyeball him until he spreads his hands in resignation. 'Well, yes, in a way. I can't take any of the credit, though. It was down to Terry, really.'

'Terry?'

'It was her idea. When we met at The Ballahays last summer, I jokingly called you a Penguin Ambassador. She and Patrick latched on to the idea, and we agreed you had received hardly any recognition for all the money you've ploughed into the Locket Island project. It was such a shame and you deserved more. So Terry put forward the suggestion of the award to the Anglo-Antarctic Research Council. Unfortunately, they ignored her request. That was when she came to me.'

'I see.'

'I merely backed her up.'

'But you are a television presence, and much more influential, so they suddenly sat up and took notice.' My words are short jabs. It is a shock to discover that my friends have been conspiring behind my back.

'Please don't be angry.'

'I'm not angry with you, Sir Robert, or with Terry or Patrick, for your intentions were kind. However, I am disappointed that this matter was swung by my friends. I had thought that the AARC deemed me worthy; that they were keen to give me this honour.'

'And indeed they were, once it was suggested.'

'Yet it had to be suggested, and by a notable celebrity.' He knows I do not mean it as a compliment.

'Well, let's not fall out over this.'

'No, indeed,' I reply tersely.

'I just wanted to assure you that you need feel no pressure in your post as Penguin Ambassador. It is not a call to action but a token of appreciation for all you've done.'

'All you've *done*,' I echo, chewing over those words. His assessment is very much and very disappointingly in the past tense.

He leans forward. 'I only wish I could be there in the Falklands to applaud you. But . . .'

I see where his mind is going. If he were there, he would steal all my thunder, because the press and everyone else present would be entirely focused on him rather than me.

'. . . But my schedule simply will not allow it,' he continues. 'I need to go straight from here to Antarctica.'

'Poor old you,' I comment dryly.

'At any rate, I shall accompany you with your walking whilst we are here in the Galápagos together, if you will permit me?'

'So long as Eileen and Daisy don't object.' My response contains more crabbiness than I intended. There is no way Eileen and Daisy are going to object.

A small but tense silence inserts itself between us.

Sir Robert grapples for something positive to say. 'At least you can focus on the wildlife here, rather than having to put up with people poking their noses around The Ballahays.'

'That is very true.'

Grateful as I am for these exotic surroundings, the thought of people poking their noses around The Ballahays makes me utterly miserable.

To dispel the wretched image, I tell Sir Robert how everything will be run at the sea life centre when I am the owner. He mentions he has various contacts who will be able to assist me in my endeavours.

'I do not need any help from you, or from anyone,' I find myself saying ungraciously, even though I had been intending to consult him. I don't know why I am being so prickly.

'Oh, Veronica,' he cries.

The way he utters those words makes my heart flip. It has been troubled much of late and is in a delicate state.

'Veronica, it is all right to ask for help from other people sometimes. It really is. Especially when they *want* to help.'

'I would rather do things my own way,' I respond tartly.

'Even sacrificing your beloved home for a handful of birds?'

'As I said, I shan't be sacrificing it. And it isn't just a handful of birds, is it? It's a handful of birds plus an elderly octopus, plus eleven members of staff, plus Daisy's mental health, plus my own self-respect.'

'And if somebody puts in an immediate offer for The Ballahays?'

Those Lochnamorghy agents have their eye upon me. 'If there is a spectacularly good offer, I shall have to accept it,' I snap, and the realization that this could happen is like a brick being hurled into the pit of my stomach. 'And I shall be homeless.'

His mouth twitches. His eyes kindle with that twinkle I know so well. He thinks I am being a drama queen.

'I'm sure you won't be homeless, Veronica. And if ever that does happen, you can always come and live with me.'

Sir Robert lives in a modest townhouse on the outskirts of Edinburgh that he inherited from his parents. I would have thought he earned a great deal of money from his work, but I suspect he gives most of it away. I know he is a patron of various charities.

'I beg your pardon,' I say, twiddling my hearing aid. I can't have heard him right.

'You can always come and live with me.'

I stretch my eyes. 'Sir Robert, I have been on a particularly long journey, not to mention intervals of intense walking; and much hard work and anxiety lie ahead, I have no doubt. Do not jest with me.'

A look of apology flashes across his face. 'My house isn't as splendid as The Ballahays, but it is large enough that we wouldn't get in each other's way. And if you do not approve of us living together singly under one roof' – he pauses, picks up a brochure entitled *The Giant Tortoise* that is lying on the table and turns a few pages – 'if it made you happy and if it made things easier legally, you and I could always get married.'

Whilst I am thinking about what might be an appropriate reaction, and trying to quell my actual reactions of anger, stress and a strange, sneaky pleasure, I take a sip of tea.

Unfortunately, I don't quite aim the mug right and the tea dribbles down my chin.

I rise stiffly from my chair to seek out some kitchen paper. There is a roll of it on the sideboard. I tear off a piece and blot myself, furious at my stupid lack of co-ordination. But Sir Robert has doubtless regretted voicing his absurd notion, for when I turn round I find I am alone in the room. He has vanished.

# 18

# Veronica

*Xavier Island*

EILEEN'S FACE IS a picture, her mouth constantly dropping open, her eyes popping with surprise. 'Honestly, Mrs McCreedy, I just don't believe it. I don't believe it at all. I'm sure I'm going to wake up any minute.'

'Pinch yourself,' suggests Daisy.

Eileen takes a soft mass of her own forearm flesh between her thumb and forefinger and squeezes. 'Ouch! Well, I still seem to be here, don't I?'

'Yup, you definitely are.'

Daisy is likewise enchanted with Xavier Island, as I knew she would be. Unlike Eileen, though, she has mastered the art of taking everything in her stride.

I confess to feeling an ambivalence regarding the presence of my two walking companions. Fond as I am of them

153

both and glad of their safe arrival, a dark thread of resentment twines amongst my better feelings. With a forceful child and a menopausal woman in tow, I can no longer do things wholly my own way. Moreover, I must now share Sir Robert and the Galápagos experience with them. Spread between three of us, the delight, like the last spoonful from a jar of fine marmalade, will doubtless be thinner.

Daisy has told me in confidence that Eileen spent much of their journey flapping and swallowing pills. Eileen told me in confidence that Daisy never stopped wriggling or asking for sweets. They survived and look well, however. Eileen sports a yellow cloth sunhat pulled over her curls, Daisy is in a baseball cap, T-shirt and shorts. They are as keen as ever and, like me, they have been walking at every possible opportunity. 'Eileen didn't want to in Quito but I made her,' Daisy mentions proudly.

'And Daisy didn't want to in Baltra airport but *I* made *her*,' Eileen returns.

They have evidently been badgering each other on. Despite my best efforts at beating them by many miles, I am only 0.7 miles ahead of them and they will easily make that up whilst I am filming tomorrow.

We have spent most of the morning crooning over giant tortoises but now we embark on our first proper walk here together. Sir Robert walks with us. Eileen is awestruck by his presence, but I am not so easily impressed. Indeed, I was hardly bowled over by the romance of his offhand proposal last night. Although he has apologized for his abrupt disappearance (something to do with a Skype appointment with the BBC), my annoyance lingers. My own marriage was nothing to shout about, but

I still respect the institution as a whole, and his flippancy was ill judged.

I also keep questioning if he was pouring ridicule on my action regarding The Ballahays and Lochnamorghy. I replay his reaction over and over in my head, but in truth I cannot be sure what he made of it. Most of my acquaintances seem appalled at what I have done, convinced that I will never be able to implement such an outlandish plan. This just makes me more determined to prove them all wrong, to make a success of both purchasing and running the sea life centre. I know I can do it. I must work on staying alive well into my nineties to ensure that my ambitions come to fruition.

As we walk, the others chatter.

Sir Robert was not exaggerating when he said the land was lumpy and unwelcoming. We are currently making slow progress across a lava field. The ground is black, crinkled, crusted; unkind to old limbs and unsteady legs. I've had to surrender my handbag to Daisy because it is impossible to keep holding it whilst manoeuvring two walking poles, which I find I need. Sir Robert has offered his arm several times. I have declined.

I must be careful, though. The ground gets harder as one ages, and although one's metaphorical skin thickens, one's physical skin does the opposite. Were I to fall, this particular ground would not hesitate to puncture and bruise.

The heat and humidity are also tiresome. Eileen glows like a beacon and shifts her backpack uncomfortably.

Despite all this, the walk is curious and stimulating. Spoon-shaped cacti sprout from clefts in the rock. We have covered barely a mile but already have seen an army of land iguanas and a scuttling turtle, not to mention all manner of peculiar birds. The sky is milling with them. Sir Robert is able to identify most of them (we have so far had various finches, storm petrels, short-eared owls and Galápagos hawks). Daisy soaks it all in, to be regurgitated into her blog later. She likes testing him.

'What's that one that looks like a pterodactyl?' she asks, pointing out a silhouette perched high up in a spindly tree.

He answers without hesitation. 'That is a frigatebird. They're known as pirates of the Galápagos. They have terrible manners. They're always plundering other birds' nests. They've been known to grab another bird by the tail and shake it until its dinner has been regurgitated, and then they eat that.'

'Urgh!' She shields her eyes to scrutinize the bird. 'Hey, it looks like he's got a great big red handbag, like Veronica's.'

'It's actually a throat pouch. It expands like a big balloon. He's swelling it up with air to show off to the females.'

'Boys are always show-offs, aren't they?'

Sir Robert chuckles. 'I can't deny it. Nature has ordained it: males strut about bragging, whilst females get on with the important things like caring and nurturing.'

'You don't strut about bragging, though, Sir Robert.'

'That's kind of you to say so, Daisy.'

'You're the least strutty and braggy person I've ever met, Sir Robert,' agrees Eileen.

She looks at me; it's clearly my turn to offer an opinion. I offer nothing. But, perhaps due to his sweetness to

Daisy, I reach the decision to put my awkwardness with Sir Robert behind me. I owe him a huge debt of gratitude, after all, and despite my concerns, I am thrilled to be here.

We scramble through a patch of scrubby undergrowth and come to a halt again to admire the view. Ahead of us lies a great lagoon. The water is thick and green and shimmery.

'Take a look to your left,' Sir Robert tells us, pointing.

Daisy gasps. On improbably thin pink legs, with an improbably thin pink neck, is the improbably pinkest bird you could imagine. He – or maybe she – stands on the edge of the lake, feet submerged, beak dipped. An upside-down bird of equal pinkness is attached, legs leaning conversely. As a ripple rolls over the surface, the second bird wobbles and becomes a series of pink streaks.

'Oh my God!' cries Daisy. 'Look at his knobbly knees. Look at his beautiful feathers. I love, love, love flamingos. They're my top favourite bird.'

I put a hand up to my ear. 'Sorry. Did you say flamingos are your top favourite bird?'

'Yes.'

I give her a look. Sir Robert, who has cottoned on, smirks silently.

I shake my head forlornly. 'My hearing aid is evidently not functioning today. You're going to have to speak up.'

Eileen is about to reiterate Daisy's sentiment, when she too cottons on. At last Daisy realizes and bursts into a fit of giggles, which promptly gives her hiccups.

'I meant to say my – hic! – *second* favourite bird. Ooops! My second favourite, of course. After penguins.'

The flamingo raises a black-tipped beak out of the water and surveys us.

'Oh, I – hic! – hope he didn't hear me.'

Sir Robert lowers his voice. 'You've gone and made him blush.'

Daisy spurts more laughter. She makes us all pose in front of the flamingo so she can take a photo, then makes Sir Robert take a photo of the Three Mackateers.

I am slightly concerned that, with all this abundance of vivid wildlife, the poor old Lochnamorghy penguins will be forgotten. It is just as well Daisy is writing a blog, which should help keep her focused on them.

We are headed for the penguin colony where I and the film crew will be working tomorrow. Thankfully we are now on a proper path, and staying upright is no longer quite such a challenge. The trees thin and straggle to nothingness. We find ourselves in a rockscape that towers, juts and jags all around us. And right in front of us, perched on a guano-splattered stone, is our first Galápagos penguin.

She (I have decided it's a she) is a young one, much tinier than I was expecting. Camouflaged against the dark crags, her plumage is brownish black, her belly a soft mist-white rather than the snowy white of adults. She waggles her head from side to side and gives her tail a vigorous shake.

'Cute, cute, cute!' mutters Daisy, enthralled. 'Cuteness overload.'

Eileen is mopping her eyes. 'Sorry, Mrs McCreedy. I don't know what's come over me.'

I am reminded of the first time I myself saw penguins in the wild. It is a strangely emotive experience.

Our penguin responds by leaning forward and shattering the air with a rude and raucous noise like a donkey braying.

'Will you take our picture with the penguin, Sir Robert?' Daisy asks, thrusting her phone at him.

Sir Robert does his duty as cameraman again, humble for one who is so used to the limelight. I am glad Daisy has learned to say 'thank you' nicely.

Soon after, we arrive at the colony itself. Serried ranks of birds gather in the crannies of gnarled rocks. The adults are more demarcated than the juvenile we saw just now. Each has a thin white line encircling the chest and tummy area, with black spots straying over a white chest. They hunch close to the ground as they waddle.

These penguins breed all year round, and we spy two little chicks peeping out of a nook. A parent hops to the entrance protectively and they disappear inside again. Another adult nuzzles the first, and the two of them spend some time tapping their bills together and gently preening each other.

I turn to Daisy for an instant and I'm struck by her expression. Her mouth twists downward; her eyes are tight little knots. Her lips are pulled over clenched teeth.

Eileen distracts us all by dropping her water bottle, and when I look at Daisy again her face is covered in smiles. I must have imagined what went before.

The chicks have emerged again. A stream of pink sludge squirts from the parent's beak and, as one of the chicks tries to push the other out of the way, splatters them both.

'Gross or what?' Daisy is at her phone again.

On the way back, she is still fiddling with the wretched contraption. Thank goodness I grew up in a time when I didn't have to be continually tethered to such a tyrannical object.

'How do you spell "Humboldt"?' she asks.

Eileen looks at me, panic in her eyes. I spell out the word to Daisy, who duly transcribes it into her machine. It is tiresome to talk, think of spellings and navigate the terrain simultaneously.

'What have you written about hum-bolds?' asks Eileen, all encouragement.

'This,' Daisy answers and puts on a news reporter voice. 'Only the islands on the west of the Galápagos are home to penguins, because that's where you get the cold Humboldt Current.' How she manages to read from her phone and walk on this bumpy surface at the same time, I have no idea.

'You are very informed,' I note, with approval.

'Google,' she answers. 'And should it be "sunburnt" or "sunburned"?'

I am tiring of all these questions. My ankles ache and the nape of my neck is tickling uncomfortably.

I indicate the patterned shade under one of the trees. 'I think Eileen would like a rest.'

Eileen comes to an immediate and grateful halt. 'Ah, ah yes, Mrs McCreedy. That would be nice.'

'And whilst you are at it, Eileen, did you happen to bring that folding chair?'

Eileen has sent an email to our helpful penguin patroller, Molly, to inform her of our progress. Thanks to the article in the *Scots Times*, we now have hundreds of sponsors and have raised £11,355. This should increase manyfold by the time we have completed our stint in the Falklands and have all that extra attention from the press. In the meantime, I continue to correspond with the agents for Lochnamorghy. They tell me the other bidder is considering increasing their offer. They also enquire if I am anywhere near selling my house yet.

My own agent has informed me that there have been another two viewings. Mr Perkins does not communicate by email, but Mrs Perkins has given me to understand that they were city types and Mr Perkins couldn't rightly tell if they were interested or not. Eileen informs me that her friend Fiona went in both times and made coffee and put fresh flowers in the drawing room, dining room, kitchen and master bedroom. She sat in the snug and did a jigsaw whilst they were there.

I have also received an email from Terry in Antarctica. The Emperors are doing all right, but she doesn't mention Pip. I know she would have done if he had turned up. Most of her email is backing up Patrick's plea for me not to sell The Ballahays. They know how much my home means to me. They also do not believe a pensioner is capable of managing a sea life centre.

My head is so full of flamingos, tortoises and penguins that I am finding it hard to discern a way forward when I return to Scotland. My life is about to undergo a metamorphosis, but what strange new thing will it become? Am I too fragile now to negotiate the maze of complications that lies ahead? Am I leaping headlong into a chasm? My companions here are outwardly supportive, but I do wonder if they think this is the last desperate act of a madwoman.

# Daisy's Penguin Blog

## HOT STUFF

Whoa! What would Mac think if he could see us now?

We are here, in the Galápagos!! We are staying in this cool conservation place with SIR ROBERT SADDLE-BOW and THE BBC! Woohoo! Every time we step outside we're in giant tortoise heaven, and flamingo heaven, and iguana heaven . . . and, get this, penguin heaven too!

Sad thing: Galápagos penguins are totally endangered, the most endangered of all penguins.

Random thing: They're 'banded penguins', related to African penguins (*waves to Pablo and Florence*) and also the Humboldt and Magellanic penguins.

Interesting thing: They live the furthest north of any penguins. You can even get a few north of the equator.

How did penguins get here?

A few thousand years ago, a group of penguins were swept all this way up here from Antarctica on the cold Humboldt Current. This current still washes around the western Galápagos and is the coolest place to be around here, so the penguins like it. They've had to adapt to completely different conditions, though.

How do Galápagos penguins stay cool?

Sir Robert says that if you're little it's easier to lose heat. That's why the Emperor penguins in the Antarctic are so big but these ones are so small. People sweat when they're hot, but penguins can't do that. So Galápagos penguins pant like dogs! They'll stand with their white bellies facing the sun, because white reflects the heat away. Or sometimes they hunch over to shade their feet because nobody likes to get sunburnt toes.

Veronica says: To survive, one must constantly adapt to changing circumstances.

Eileen says: Clever little poppets, aren't they?

# 19

# Veronica

*Xavier Island*

I AM WOKEN by screams. They are not the bloodcurdling variety, but unnerving nonetheless; desperate, jolting yelps, loud enough to wake me and shock me out of bed. Once I've realized it is not my bed at home, I reason with myself that it must be some strange creature of this island, perhaps an endemic species of bird. I reach for my slippers and wrap my negligee around my shoulders. I pad across the room, draw back the curtain and glance out. I can see nothing but the silhouette of Scalesia trees against a spattering of stars. The noises come again, pitiful little howls. I realize they are emanating from inside the building, from the next-door bedroom. Daisy's.

Pulling my negligee tighter around myself, I go to her. Her door is slightly ajar. Her small form lies untidily on top of the covers, one hand flung across the pillow. I stroke her hair, speaking softly, soothing her back into this reality.

'Sshh, Daisy. Shhh, child. It was just a dream. Just a bad dream.'

Her eyes snap open and look straight into mine. They pool with tears.

She sits up in bed and wraps her arms around me, clinging tight. I feel her little heart thumping against mine. My instinct to protect her rises like a fire within me, as if she were my own daughter.

I ask what she was dreaming about, but she won't say. I hope she wasn't imagining the death of Mac and those beloved penguins at Lochnamorghy.

I am required to do only one short piece of presenting, and I do wonder if Sir Robert really needs me at all for this programme. Still, he was insistent, and I was atypically compliant. When penguins are on the agenda I need very little persuasion.

Positioned with some artistry against a cliffy backdrop, penguins popping in and out of their holes behind me, I focus my mind in readiness. My outfit is pristine: a cream cotton blouse with lacy collar and a light mulberry-red jacket with matching skirt. An elegant straw hat completes the ensemble. I brought two handbags with me today, since I couldn't decide which was better: silky cream or silver-trimmed maroon. The consensus was the cream, hence my asking Eileen to look after the maroon.

I face the cameras and enunciate my words with care. 'Greetings, dear viewers, from the Galápagos Islands, the only place in the world where you can find this exceptional species of penguin.' I indicate a bird who is conveniently basking on a rock close to my left knee. 'Galápagos penguins are severely endangered and have suffered much in recent years. As well as the fishing industry that robs them of food, they must contend with another powerful enemy: El Niño. This warm current heats up the coastal waters, making them uninhabitable for fish such as anchovies and sardines. El Niño events spell out wholesale famine for the poor penguins. In 1982 their complete population was down to a mere four thousand and sixty-three.'

'Stop, Veronica, stop!' calls Miriam, holding up a hand. 'It's only four hundred and sixty-three, not four thousand and sixty-three. And a penguin honked at the wrong time so we missed a bit. Can you do another take, please?'

Daisy likes to watch me present, but there are only so many repetitions of the same information that a child can take. She starts stabbing at her phone with a finger.

'Oh no, I can't post anything. There's no phone signal,' she moans between takes.

'Well, you'll just have to do it later, dear,' Eileen tells her, proffering a boiled sweet. Daisy accepts it eagerly.

My three-minute piece takes over three hours to film, what with adjusting the lighting and sound levels, ensuring I deliver the correct words and, most importantly, obtaining suitable footage of penguins behind me.

Some voiceover will be tacked on at the end, but this will be recorded later in the studio in Scotland.

Once we are done, Sir Robert kisses me on both cheeks.

'Excellent, Veronica. Your passion for your subject does you credit.'

I put my lips together. He has been his usual cheerful self, and yet there is something not quite right between us and I don't know if the fault lies with him or with me. Still, my heart is gladdened by his words. Few people become a wildlife documentary presenter in their late eighties.

The sandwiches prepared by our hosts contain a fishy kind of paste I do not recognize. As we eat, we are entertained by the penguins. On the other side we observe a marine iguana, a pitted, scaly black creature sunning itself on a pitted, scaly black rock. Fine spikes like bristles extend along the length of its spine. An enormously long tail hangs down the edge of the rock, as do four muscular legs.

'Funny fellow, isn't he?' Sir Robert says.

'He wouldn't win any prizes in a beauty contest, for sure,' Eileen chuckles.

The iguana turns a warty face towards us and blinks slowly.

'Don't listen to her, Iggy!' cries Daisy. 'You're beautiful.'

We head back to the lodge for a siesta, monitoring our steps all the way. We will only need a short walk this afternoon. I am sapped of energy and, at the moment, all I can think about is tea.

As soon as we are back, Eileen puts the kettle on. What a relief to hear water bubbling, to receive a steaming mug (even though a porcelain cup would have been preferable), to savour fine Darjeeling tantalizing one's taste buds and sliding blissfully down one's throat.

Daisy, glad to be back within phone signal, loftily ignores the two little boys who have crept in to watch her. She reports that her friend Aurora, her brother Noah and her parents have all left comments on her blog. I see her flinch as she scrolls, though. According to Eileen, she has had a few issues with an online troll, which is apparently every bit as wicked as the fairy-tale type. How sad, that some people can only manage to make themselves feel bigger by making others feel smaller.

'It is a million times easier to destroy than to create,' I point out. 'This world contains many, many destroyers ... but you are a creator, Daisy, which is infinitely better.'

She nods, abstractedly. At least she has now found a way of deleting the troll's unsavoury messages.

'Dad has found a property he likes,' she informs us, having evidently moved on to her emails. 'It is a "sweet little shop in Jedburgh"' – she pronounces it 'Jed-bug' – '"with a flat above it". He's put in an offer, he says.'

Eileen claps her hands. 'That's brilliant, Daisy. You'll be able to visit us so much more often from there.'

'I guess.'

I feel she is not as thrilled as she should be about this. I begin to wonder if I am not so much liked for myself as for my fairy-godmother-like ability to bestow penguin adventures and my glorious, romantic mansion by the Scottish sea. Perhaps if I no longer live at The Ballahays, Daisy will be less keen to visit. I rebuke myself for the thought but its unpleasant flavour lingers like sour milk on the tongue.

*

Every Galápagos guidebook harps on about Darwin, his expedition to these islands on the HMS *Beagle* and his theory about the survival of the fittest.

'I'm definitely not the fittest,' Eileen moans, fanning herself as we set out on our afternoon perambulation.

'Eileen, it doesn't mean "fit" like that,' Daisy explains earnestly. 'It means like . . . like giraffes who grow long necks so they can eat the leaves on very tall trees. But the giraffes with short, stumpy necks can't reach the leaves even if they stretch and stand on tiptoe. So they can't eat and they starve and they're dead and it's impossible for them to marry other short-necked giraffes now, and that means no short-necked giraffe babies get born . . . and eventually there's no short-necked giraffes left at all. There's only long-necked ones.'

Eileen smiles sweetly. 'Oh. Oh, I see.'

If Darwin himself explained it, she couldn't be more deferential.

I tread this uncooperative ground with care, since I wish to reach Antarctica in one piece. With the giddiness of youth, Daisy scoots ahead. Soon we come across an outcrop where iguanas galore are languidly heaped over the stones and each other.

Eyes fixed upon them, Daisy reaches for her phone and I hear a sharp cry as she stumbles and falls headlong. The iguanas untangle speedily and shoot off in different directions.

Daisy pulls herself up, rubbing her elbow. Her skin is grazed and speckled with blood. Eileen roots about for the first aid kit, dabs the sore spot with TCP and sticks a plaster over it.

'It's not too bad,' Daisy assures us. 'Even penguins fall over sometimes,' she adds.

Sir Robert pats her on the head. 'If you were a penguin, you wouldn't be hurt at all, though, because you'd have so much natural padding.'

She grins as we walk on. 'If I had to live here for ever, in the Galápagos, I'd adapt, for sure. I'd grow lots of padding, like the penguins, and I'd grow a beak for opening shellfish. And a long neck, like the giraffes we were talking about, so I could reach treetops. Or flappy wings so I could fly up and get bananas and papayas. But . . .' she frowns '. . . actually, I don't like shellfish or papayas that much . . . Oh, I know! I'd have a *converter* in my tongue that made every single thing taste of toffee!'

'That's an awful lot of adapting,' I remark.

'I'd also grow a "stop pain" button in my tummy that I could press so nothing could ever, ever hurt.'

Eileen looks at Daisy, then down at herself. 'I'd grow a "stop fat" button, so I could eat whatever I wanted and never ever put on any weight.'

'And I'd grow a "stop wrinkle" button,' I say glumly.

'Oh no, that would be a shame,' Sir Robert protests. 'Wrinkles are good. Wrinkles are fascinating. Every wrinkle tells a story.'

If I try very hard, I almost feel complimented.

Daisy has become thoughtful. 'Humans are totally useless, aren't they? I mean, I know the press-button ideas are silly, but animals do adapt loads better than us, don't they?'

'Quite true,' Sir Robert answers. 'But we manage, in a terribly complicated way: clothes instead of fur or feathers, tools instead of claws and beaks. Medicine and surgery rather than natural resilience. A strange way of surviving, but it sort of works.'

'We've also devised some highly efficient killing machines,' I point out. It is my prerogative to make scathing comments about the human race. Indeed, my companions would be disappointed if I failed to do so. 'And we are killing ourselves by polluting our own environment. Extreme cleverness alongside a complete absence of wisdom – a fatal combination.'

'We have music, though,' Eileen puts in. 'And all sorts of hobbies. Did Darwin explain that? I don't suppose tiddlywinks or knitting or singing help me survive, but they do make life so much nicer.'

I squint at her in the sunlight. A philosophical Eileen? She is looking to Sir Robert for an answer. He ruminates. 'Good point,' he says. 'Most of our favourite activities don't actively contribute to our survival. Darwin's explanations were to do with the evolution of social instincts and how we select a mate.'

I speed up a little, taking a risk with the crusted lava underfoot.

'Mum and Dad believe in God,' Daisy tells us, with a pout, 'but I don't. I'm an atheist. I believe in Darwin.'

'*I* believe in God,' Eileen counters staunchly.

'What do you believe, Sir Robert?' Daisy asks.

He removes his hat and stirs his hair until it resembles a dandelion puff. 'Scientists tend to think they have all the answers, but really they've only begun to scratch the surface. I believe in evolution, yes, but much else besides.' Seeing we are all waiting for more, he goes on. 'I believe in the evolution of each person throughout their life.

I believe we each have a purpose. And I believe there is truth – God, if you like – in all life, right inside it; a kernel of God in everything. I believe in Arctic foxes and duck-billed platypuses and trees and rainbows and volcanoes and eagles bursting into flight. I believe in people, too – some of them, at least. I believe . . . I believe in you!' he claims passionately, and I think for a second that his eyes swivel towards me. '. . . In you three Mackateers,' he concludes with a sweep of his arm.

This is all rather unexpected.

'And *I* believe we've found the beach.' I point, glad to diffuse the sudden intensity, suppressing my own odd bubble of emotion.

Sir Robert replaces his hat and pulls it firmly over his brow.

We step forward. The sand is an intriguing mottle of colour; red-gold here, green-grey there. A gang of penguins waddles along the shore just ahead of us. In the distant blue, whales are lunging and breaching. Closer at hand, Daisy discovers a cluster of stones with thousands of tiny red crabs clinging to their sides.

The beach is tricky in a different way from the lava field. It is so soft that we keep sinking in, up to the ankles. The slightly wet, compacted grains make for easier walking than powdery dry sand, although too wet and you are sucked down with every step. Still, we are doing well, and have reached our target distance for today.

The tide retreats, leaving a series of wet wiggles, pearly shells and ribbons of seaweed. We examine the patterns of imprinted marks: the delicate motifs of birds' feet, a flurried trail left by a turtle.

Sir Robert has escorted us this far, but now he needs to continue his own work, filming the Galápagos finches and iguanas. He leaves us to relax for a while in this glorious setting. José and Gabriela have promised to pick us up from here in their jeep later.

Daisy and Eileen are wearing their swimsuits under their shorts and T-shirts. They peel off their clothes. Already their skin is two-toned: shrimpy-pink arms and legs, white further in.

It is slightly alarming to see Eileen so scantily clad. She looks alarmed at her own state of dishabille as well, and seems to be sucking herself in as she treads the sand. Daisy runs full tilt at the sea, whereas Eileen steps in gingerly. They splash each other, sending up gauzy wings of water.

'Come on, Veronica, come in with us!' calls Daisy. 'It's delicious!' She scoops up handfuls of water and chucks them into the air, creating a kaleidoscope of diamonds.

My legs feel stiff, but I manage to rid myself of the walking boots and socks. What a joy it is to let my feet breathe. I sink my soles into the sand, then into the cooling water. Relief laps around my toes.

Swimming would be too much, but I willingly paddle. Eileen is floating on her back, a trio of rounded islets. Daisy is diving and surfacing repeatedly, holding her nose. When she sees me, she points to a streak of penguins who porpoise in and out around her.

I wade in a little further, up to my knees. The water is crystal clear. Shoals of striped fish flick by in the deep. I see the shapes of penguins, like little torpedoes. Their black backs swoop just below the surface.

Without warning, a strong current swirls around my knees and threatens to sweep me sideways. I head back for the line where the sea meets the sand. To my delight, the penguins follow me. Their heads pop up before they ground in the shallows, sticking out their flippers to regain their balance. They gather around me in a little flock.

I paddle with the penguins, and it is beautiful.

# 20

# Veronica

*Xavier Island*

MY FINGERS STUMBLE over the keys in my haste. It is a message from the Lochnamorghy agents. My eyes skim the words. Bad news: my opponent buyer for the sea life centre has upped his game and put in a higher bid than mine. I reply, typing slowly and firmly, that I shall up my game as well and I will instruct them further within a week. I add the link to Daisy's blog to demonstrate our commitment to Lochnamorghy, then change my mind and delete it. The blog is mainly photographs, and the words of a child will do little to further my cause. It might have the opposite effect, for all I know. I need to ensure that I am being taken seriously or my bid will count for nothing. To attain a big spread in the press and attract sufficient funds, I must wait for the Falklands ceremony.

I'm about to sign out from the lodge computer when an email from Molly pops up.

*I hope you're enjoying your time in the sun. I'm sorry to be the bearer of bad tidings but a date has been fixed for the vet to come in and euthanize all the penguins here, and it's much earlier than we thought. It's to be on 14 Nov, the day after we close.*

God, no!

*Needless to say, I and the other staff here are devastated. Unless you can sell your house soon or get masses more sponsorship money (I've been following your progress online) it does look as if we're doomed. The developer guy is really keen to get the place and management here know he can pay, so they favour him.*

Doubtless they think my property will not sell in time. Probably they do not trust me with the future of Lochnamorghy. Certainly they have no faith in Operation PIP.

*You three Mackateers are our only hope. So sorry again, but I had to let you know. All my very best and with fingers firmly crossed, Molly.*
*P.S. Don't let on that I've told you, please. The info about the penguins' euthanasia is strictly confidential.*

I can only hope the next week will bring better news. My own agent, Mr Wallace, has informed me of multiple viewings of my home, but nobody has shown significant interest. A flurry of panic is gathering in my chest. I have been so definitive about everything, so sure it would all work out, and if it didn't, I would make it. Now I am beset with dark misgivings. In my eyes, The Ballahays is a grand old palace of delights, but I am starting to wonder if, in most people's opinions, it is not so. My home, like myself, has become unattractive. Redundant. A fusty, musty, mouldery burden.

And twenty-four penguins are closer to their deaths than ever.

The others are already at breakfast in the open-plan dining room.

Their voices jangle in my hearing aid. I help myself to breakfast, and sit a little apart from them all, hunching over my egg and toast. I picture the little round bodies of twenty-four penguins, limp and lifeless, carted off in a wheelbarrow.

At least the rest of this week will be devoted simply to walking and admiring the wildlife of Xavier Island. There will be much business at our next stop, the Falklands, what with the award ceremony, catching up with Terry and Patrick, sticking to the walking schedule and dealing with any developments at home. The Falklands will be a turning point. I must use this time to gather mental and physical strength. I need to keep a clear head.

Miriam steps over to me as I am helping myself to a second cup of tea.

'So, today it's been decided, since the light is more vivid, to do a few further takes of your spiel in front of the Galápagos penguins, assuming that's OK with you?'

It is very much not OK with me. My thoughts are bungee-jumping about so much I feel quite dizzy. I am hardly in the mood for flaunting myself in front of cameras.

Still, I have been telling Daisy that our moods are not always our friends, that we must walk even if we are not in the mood for walking, so I suppose I must present even if I'm not in the mood for presenting. After all, the wretched TV documentary is the reason that I am actually here.

I catch Sir Robert's eye as I am heading back to my bedroom to don my more glamorous outfit. His mouth curls up on one side apologetically, and I frown. I resent the fact that it was Miriam who delivered the unwelcome news, and not himself.

But what do I care? He has plenty of friends here apart from me, I tell myself as I fasten my crimson skirt. He is not obliged to talk to me, I remind myself as I paint my downturned lips a deeper shade of red.

I must remember the penguins. An image of Pip appears in my head, as he was when I found him: a tiny chick, bedraggled, weakened by hunger, so very unlikely to survive that Terry talked of putting him out of his misery. I remember how I wouldn't let her, how I went against the group of scientists and insisted we should hand-rear him, and how, against all the odds, we did it. *He* did it, rather, by sheer will-power and determination. The thought of him both strengthens and saddens me. How I long to see him again!

Once again I am put in front of a display of Galápagos penguins. Once again Miriam and Dave fuss over the light, the sound, the angles. Once again I reel off my words. Today the air is suffocating and the sun feels like a hot weight pressing down on my shoulders.

I explain how these penguins nest in the rocks for

protection. Some species of penguins migrate, some don't, but all of them have a fixed place that they view as home. As I stress the importance of home for penguins, a great lump rises in my throat.

I swallow hard, but my sentences tangle and snag. My lips can't seem to fit around the word 'adaptation' and I keep saying 'allegation' instead. The cameraman instructs me to smile more, but I can't manage it. Sir Robert suggests a break. I hate it when he does that, and so I insist on carrying on until the official break time, although Daisy complains she is hungry. She is already dipping into the lunch pack that Gabriela has prepared.

'Oh no, guava. Yuck.' She wrinkles her nose and flings the fruit away, muttering the word 'biodegradable' before it hits the rocks.

She bites into her sandwich. 'Ugh. It's got something lumpy and hot in it. Can I give it to the penguins?'

'I'm afraid not,' says Sir Robert. 'It's not like feeding the ducks at home. We're conservationists here, and we mustn't interfere with their lives.'

She leaves most of her lunch and then whines about wanting ice cream.

Having lived through a war, I am appalled at such wanton wastage. Young people today are incapable of recognizing how obscenely lucky they are.

I try a few more takes. They do not go well.

I am in dire need of a break and something to eat now.

No sooner have I sat down than a young sea lion lumbers into the vicinity and Daisy shrieks, 'Oooh, photo opportunity! Stand up, Veronica, and look this way.'

I do not stand up and I do not look that way.

'Veronica, quick!' she urges.

'Enough, Daisy,' I snap. 'That's quite enough of your rudeness. I am not your slave.'

She thrusts the phone back into her bag and glares at me. 'I know, but that picture would've been so perfect and now the sea lion's gone away.' She spits out the words: 'Why are you so horrible?'

I catch a glimpse of Eileen's face, which is aghast. I will not sit here and be called horrible by a child to whom I have given so much.

'How dare you? If you speak to me like that again, you will be sent straight home.'

'No!' she screeches.

'Well then, stop acting like a spoilt brat.'

She shrinks back, shocked at my acerbity, then her face twists in fury.

'You wouldn't understand. You don't understand anything!'

Miriam steps forward. 'Perhaps you and Eileen would like to take a little walk, Daisy, whilst we get on?' she suggests. 'There's another path that leads to the beach that way.'

Eileen looks panicked, but Daisy sticks out her chin. 'OK,' she says, reaching for Eileen's hand. 'Let's do that. Galápagos penguins are really boring, anyway.' Words chosen to wound me.

'*Boring?*'

As the first Penguin Ambassador, I am personally affronted.

She will not back down. 'Yes. They're totally dull compared with the Kings or rockhoppers or Gentoos.' She glances sideways at Sir Robert, keen to show off her knowledge of the Falklands penguins.

Sir Robert, with a sad half-smile, stoops a little to be on her level. 'They're not as striking and they are shyer, yes, but their shyness is their strength. You'd be shy if your whole species was so endangered.'

'I suppose.'

A brief look of apology flits across her face, but it is aimed at Sir Robert, not me. Nonetheless I am grateful to him for defending these particular penguins. Having spent so much time with them, I am grown fond of the retiring little creatures. I take a deep breath to steady my nerves, and gaze around at the beaked faces, a pang of concern in my heart for their future. My own hassles suddenly seem trite in comparison.

Eileen's and Daisy's backs are retreating into the shimmery air. Sir Robert turns to me. His expression startles me. His brows are drawn together, his eyes fierce with rebuke.

'Why so unkind to Daisy? Was it really necessary, Veronica? When she has come so far and is trying so hard to help you in your mission? You really upset her. I know you're stressed, and none of the rest of us would have minded if you'd channelled your anger at us, but at Daisy? She's a *child*.'

My heart plummets.

'And perhaps we need to think about who is the "spoilt brat" here,' he adds, sotto voce.

I am speechless. Mortified. He is right, of course. And Daisy was quite accurate in her assessment of me. Indeed I am horrible. I am a mean, ungrateful, despicable old hag. I have crashed in Sir Robert's estimation, and in my own.

# 21

# Eileen

*Xavier Island*

I DO BELIEVE I might be developing some hard muscle in my thighs. My lungs are coping better today, too. Maybe that's the swimming we did yesterday. Fiona from choir does wild swimming every morning and swears by it. She says there's something about cold salty water that's incredibly good for your health. Mrs M mentioned that her corns were feeling better after paddling in the sea, so I'm thinking Fiona must be right, although *she* does her swimming off the west coast of Scotland. Brrr. I could never do that.

It's just Daisy and me at the moment, trundling along together whilst Mrs McCreedy is busy with her filming. Daisy has gone very quiet, so I'm just letting my thoughts run on. We are on a scorched, sandy pathway. I've said we'll go back in twenty minutes to see how the film crew are getting on. I do hope Mrs McCreedy will calm down and get her words right. She looked so miserable when we left.

The path winds past a jumble of prickly pear cacti then takes us into a band of greener vegetation.

One of the anthems we sing in the choir is going round and round in my head. I may have hummed it out loud because Daisy side-eyes me and says: 'You're funny, Eileen.'

She's not laughing, though. I've never thought of myself as funny, but would rather that than be dull. She even called the penguins dull, so what must she think of me? Recently, I've been worried about my levels of dull. I've felt duller than Mrs Dull from Dullhampton in Dullshire.

Would HRT help with the dullness, I wonder?

Mind you, look where I am! I was saying to Doug – well, not saying to him, because I couldn't get FaceTime to work, but emailing to him – how proud I was to have got here despite my fear of the plane crashing and a gippy tummy in Quito and seasickness on the boat. And how well we were all doing with the walking, and how Daisy and I had now covered more miles than Mrs McCreedy and she'd be the one having to catch up.

Doug's email back was very short, but then men don't like writing much, do they? Or talking. They are more into things like car chases and fishing and complaining about the Tories. Doug would laugh if he could see me. It's as if I've been whisked out of my own life and I'm naughtily trespassing in somebody else's. It makes me giddy, the realness of it. No cooking or cleaning at all, not for Doug, not for Mrs McCreedy. It does feel wrong to be out walking and looking at funny birds instead of wrestling with the Hoover but, as I said to Doug just before we left, you never know where life is going to take you, do you? I mean, one minute you're scrubbing at a spot of mould on the windowsill at The Ballahays, and the next you're splashing about in the sea with penguins across the other side of the world. Or being asked to pose with a flamingo.

That flamingo reminded me of the pink ballet dress I had to wear at school. I adored that dress but I never was any good at ballet. I didn't have the feet for it, according to Miss Pickroach, my teacher. She didn't let me dance in the end-of-year show, even though I wanted to, very much. I cried when she said no. At least I was allowed to join the school choir.

I find myself humming the anthem again . . . It may be the alto line, I don't know. I'll have some catching-up to do on choir music when I get back, but I expect Fiona will help me. Fiona was so surprised when I told her I hadn't had a holiday in fifteen years, and she said it's high time I did. I said I felt massively guilty about travelling to exotic places and leaving Doug all on his own, and she said I shouldn't.

I wonder if Doug is managing all right with the jacket potatoes?

Maybe now I'm more used to travel I'll suggest that the two of us can go somewhere together when I get back. Stockport, perhaps? Auntie Mary says it has a brewery and some lovely parks.

Daisy is lagging. In between pointing out all the funny birds, she's hardly said a word. Mrs McCreedy was quite terse with her and I hope it didn't upset her too much. How can I cheer her up?

I know.

My flat feet are no good for ballet but they're brilliant at waddling. I squat a little, planting them outwards one after the other, and make a loud penguiny squawk. That makes her laugh. Phew.

She's probably just tired, like me. When we first knew Daisy she was having chemotherapy and needed masses of rest, but not so much these days.

'Are you all right, dear?' I ask, just to check. She nods lots of times.

'Shall we play a game or something to help us along?'

'Yes.'

'What game would you like to play? I Spy?'

'No. I don't like that much. How about Lists? I suggest a thing – like birds – and we take it in turns to list different birds but we mustn't stop. If one of us stops, the other gets a point, and they have to suggest a new list and we start again.'

I'm guessing Daisy has played this game before with her parents and brother.

'So I'll start, and we can do birds,' she says. 'Penguins.'

'Flamingos,' I return.

'Frigatebirds,' she says.

'Chickens,' say I.

'Robins.'

'Partridges.'

'Ducks.'

185

'Wrens.'

'Um . . . Oh no, I stopped.' She shakes a little fist in the air, furious with herself. 'So you get a point. And you get to choose what's next.'

'Cleaning products,' I suggest. 'I start, do I? Washing-up liquid.'

'Soap.'

'Dettol.'

We carry on listing things. After we're done with cleaning products, Daisy chooses cartoon characters, then I choose objects you can find in The Ballahays and that one goes on for so long that I'm bursting for a wee by the time we've finished.

'Just wait here for a minute,' I tell Daisy. 'I'm going to pop behind this rock.' She crosses her arms and stands in the shade of one of those scaly trees. I wish my bladder worked better. I don't like having to relieve myself outside, especially in a foreign country, because you never know what creepy-crawlies might start climbing up your legs. The thought of it gives me the heebie-jeebies. It's times like this that I'd like to be back with my three-ply loo paper and the reassuring scent of bathroom air freshener. Still, I do what I have to do.

When I come out from behind the rock, Daisy isn't standing under the scaly tree any more. It's so bright I have to squint, even through my sunglasses. She's not up the path or down the path or anywhere, as far as I can see.

'Daisy?'

She must be playing tricks on me. Hiding behind a bush or one of those slabs of rock, maybe.

'Daisy! Where are you?'

After I've called and called, I'm not seeing the funny side any more. And I wonder if she could have got herself lost. The temperature suddenly seems to have shot up. Heat rampages through my bloodstream. I long to crawl into a freezer and sit pressed up against a stack of choc ices, but there's no freezer here, only parched earth and stones and scrubby vegetation. My feet are swollen and my scalp is prickling. I'm sticky all over. I flap air desperately up my T-shirt. Run a little further up the path and call Daisy again. There's still no answer.

The sun lolls in the sky like a poached egg in a big blue dish. I think I might melt.

I knew this trip was risky. It's all very well looking after Daisy at The Ballahays, but everything is different here. I was supposed to take care of that dear child. What was I thinking, taking my eyes off her for even a moment?

I haven't had much sleep recently, and my brain has gone fuzzy and I'm doing the stupidest things.

Should I go on or back? What on earth could have happened to her? Perhaps she went back to see the filming. But surely she would have told me?

Could she have been attacked by some giant reptile? Or have raced onwards to the beach and been swept up by a huge wave?

Now I remember there was something in the guidebook about sharks. Oh God oh God oh God.

'Daisy, please come here. Dais-ee!' My voice is hoarse, screechy.

There's still no answer.

# 22

# Veronica

*Xavier Island*

'WHERE ARE EILEEN and Daisy?' Sir Robert asks as the crew are picking up their things and humping them into the minibus.

'They should be back by now. They said they'd be gone twenty minutes.' I examine my watch. How long exactly has it been? I am finding it hard to gauge but it must have been well over an hour.

I am disorientated, dismal, hot, and more weary than I'm prepared to admit. Today's filming session has been dire, due to my severe lack of concentration. I seem to have spent most of the morning cursing myself, and now I have lost my companions.

'Which way did they go?' I ask.

He points past me to the pathway which weaves out of

sight where a clump of sunlit vegetation creeps over the hill.

Sir Robert calls to the crew to hold on and starts striding off in that direction.

'Wait!' I cry.

He obeys, perusing the distance with his eyes as I struggle out of my smart shoes and back into my walking boots. We continue together, propelled forward by anxiety.

We have scarcely left the penguin colony when Eileen comes tumbling towards us. As she approaches, I see that her hat is off, her hair is frothing wildly, and her eyes are showing too much white. She is panting hard.

'Is she . . . Is Daisy here?' she gasps, frantically struggling to take in enough air as she scans the group of adult figures for a smaller one.

Alarm jumps up in my ribcage like a jack-in-the-box. 'No. What do you mean? She went off with *you*.'

Tears spring from Eileen's eyes. 'She was right by my side all the way, but I popped behind a rock just for a minute, a tiny little minute, and she said she'd wait but the next thing I knew she was gone.'

The tears are spurting now.

'Take us back to the exact spot where you last saw her,' Sir Robert commands, gentle but firm. He calls the others for help.

'No, wait,' I exhort him, struck with an idea. 'Daisy will have her phone on her, for she never will let go of the wretched contraption. Why don't we simply ring her?'

I am pleased with my stroke of genius but I notice one of the cameramen roll his eyes and Eileen huffs with frustration. 'I've already tried that, Mrs McCreedy, but there's no phone signal here, nothing. And I've been calling. Calling and calling.'

'Right,' says Sir Robert. 'Let's split up.' He directs the film crew to the left and right whilst we take the easiest route straight back to the point where Daisy went missing. We agree to meet back here in fifteen minutes.

'Whatever could have possessed her?' mutters Sir Robert.

I am mindful that his career will be ruined if anything happens to Daisy. And if she is hurt, her parents will never forgive me. I will never forgive myself, either. Was she devastated by my harsh words? Why couldn't I rein in my scolding tongue?

Daisy is a sensible girl and will not have wandered far. At least, that is what I keep telling myself as we walk briskly down the path, under the beating sun. But the more I repeat this to myself, the more worried I am that something awful has happened, otherwise she would have turned up by now.

The ground thumps under our feet as we pound on. Sir Robert speeds along, his strides swift and steady. The throbbing in my chest hampers my progress. Eileen trails behind us, hardly able to keep up, since she hasn't yet recovered from running to meet us.

'Daisy! Daisy!' she yells. The sob in her voice is hard to bear.

'Are we nearly back at the spot where you lost her?' asks Sir Robert.

She looks around wildly. 'Yes. I think so, anyway, but my head is such a jumble of panic, I can't be sure.'

The three of us come to a halt, scan the landscape, call again. Then stop and listen.

The sounds of the wild are all around us. The crash of waves, the calls of birds, something croaking, something whispering, something rustling. A dry kind of squawk.

And then, very faintly, a human cry.

# 23

# Veronica

*Xavier Island*

DAISY COMES GALLOPING towards us, tripping over her own feet, her hair streaming behind her.

No sooner has she arrived than she grabs Eileen by the hand and starts dragging her forward. Then she lets go again, circles back and starts physically pushing me so that I can hardly stay upright.

'Daisy, stop that at once! What on earth are you doing? Where have you been? What's all this about?' shrieks Eileen as I lurch and totter.

Daisy puts both her arms around me to steady me. Words tumble out of her.

'You have to come and look! I think they're still there, but you have to be *quick*. It's the most amazing thing I've ever seen. Come *on*!'

'What . . . what are you talking about, Daisy?'

She slips her fingers into mine. Her hand is small and sticky.

'Boobies!' she cries.

Eileen frowns, all confusion.

Sir Robert looks at me, his alarm immediately melting into that sheer, boyish twinkle for which he is so famed.

'Can you manage to go a little further, Veronica,' he enquires, 'if maybe I take your arm?'

I acquiesce at once, for this intense level of activity has jolted my bones so much that I am quite wobbly. I am also keen to see Daisy's discovery.

Only Eileen remains confounded. 'What did you say? What do you mean, Daisy? That is not the kind of word I expect you to use in front of Sir Robert and Mrs McCreedy. It's not on, not on at all. Say you're sorry or I will send you back to Bolton without any dinner.'

I would laugh at her absurdity if she weren't so upset.

'And as for going missing,' she continues, louder. 'Have you any idea? We've been desperately worried, worried sick about you.'

Spittle shoots from her mouth. Her face is a deep shade of puce. She is as angry as ever I've seen her.

'Sorry,' Daisy says quickly. As Sir Robert takes my arm she relinquishes her hold on me and starts dragging Eileen along.

'You have to see the boobies, though. They are sooooo big and beautiful, and the blue is just bluer than I thought could ever be possible.'

She hustles us along the path until the silhouettes of two birds are visible ahead of us. Their long necks are straight, as are their long beaks. Their plumage is downy, grey and white, with darker, pointed tail feathers. They are elegantly planting one webbed foot after the other on to the sand. With each step the foot is splayed in a synchronized, slow dance. And as we come closer we see that Daisy has just cause to enthuse. Those feet are massive great paddles. And they are a stunning, shocking shade of cerulean blue.

'Blue-footed boobies,' Sir Robert is explaining to Eileen. 'Endemic to the Galápagos. They are courting. They're known for this ritual of showing off their amazing feet to each other.'

The two birds seem very conscious of how splendid they are. Every so often they point a proud beak in the air. But it is the feet that keep drawing attention to themselves.

Daisy is splitting her sides with suppressed laughter. 'I got some videos on my phone,' she whispers. 'They were doing it even better before. I'd have shouted, Eileen, but I couldn't because it would have scared them away. But after I finished filming, I came back to find you, and you'd gone, so I followed them again because I really couldn't miss it, could I? And I didn't know where you were anyway, and aren't they just beautiful?'

Eileen is so tickled by the birds and so relieved that she lets out a loud, unladylike grunt of a laugh. The boobies stop and turn startled faces towards us, uncertain whether to freeze or fly.

'Shhh!' Daisy hisses, finger on lips.

Deciding we are not worth bothering about, the birds resume their impressive foot display.

Even Sir Robert, who has seen blue-footed boobies before, is entranced.

'Well,' he says after we have gazed a little longer, 'I'm afraid we need to get back to the penguins now, and the film crew. But maybe we can find the boobies again tomorrow, Daisy.'

'Oooh, I do hope so!'

Sir Robert has to dash off again for more filming this afternoon, but our bond seems to have re-established itself. At any rate, we chat together for a while in the front seats of the minibus as it bumps us back to base. I'm reluctant to confide my worries about The Ballahays lest we should have another humiliating fake marriage proposal, but I quietly voice my concerns about the success of our walking mission. After the dramas with Daisy and Eileen today, I question whether I should have brought them with me at all. They are, both of them, a liability. Sir Robert listens, his head a little to one side as he considers.

'I know you like to be independent, but despite today's little blip, I feel that both Daisy and Eileen are indispensable to Operation PIP.'

He may, I suppose, be right.

'We are ahead with our mileage and our sponsorship money has reached some twelve thousand pounds. However, the sale price of Lochnamorghy is being driven up and now we need at least four hundred and fifty thousand to rescue those penguins. Not to mention ongoing running costs.'

Gravity and compassion shine out at me from the depths of those eyes.

'I know very little about fundraising matters, but you might need to step things up if you're really intending to raise enough money.'

'Step things up? And how on earth do you suggest I do that?'

He sighs, surveys the trees flitting by the window as if trying to gain another perspective, then turns back to me. His hand touches mine. 'I wish you'd let me help you, Veronica.'

At this point a phone is thrust in our faces from the seat behind us. 'Look at my vids!' cries Daisy. 'Blue-footed boobies are my top favourite bird. I mean' – and she looks at me – 'my second favourite bird, after penguins.'

'I thought that was the flamingo?'

'Oh yes, it was. But now I'm not sure. Boobies. No, flamingos. No, boobies. No, flamingos.' She keeps arguing with herself about it all the way back. She is so amused by the whole episode that she seems to have forgotten her grievance against me, for which I am sincerely grateful.

Daisy is on Skype with her parents whilst Eileen and I recoup over tea. Eileen is apologizing repeatedly, manically. She is normally dependable, stolid and not given to such tantrums. I don't know what has come over her.

'Eileen, would you kindly refrain from all this self-flagellation?'

She pulls her chin in, brows knotted.

I rephrase. 'Would you please stop beating yourself up?'

'But I can't help it, Mrs McCreedy,' she replies, still teary.

'Yes, you can if you make the effort, Eileen. You cannot

be held responsible for the limitations imposed on you by your body. And it was your modesty that took you behind a rock. And modesty is a commendable virtue, is it not?'

'Well, when you put it like that . . .'

'What you *are* in control of is your thoughts, so please marshal them in a more self-forgiving and productive direction.'

'I still feel it's my fault, though.'

'Balderdash! It was nobody's fault. You were merely obeying your physical needs. As for Daisy, she was led astray by her natural delight at the exceptional birds, and we must not criticize her for that, either. Nobody is culpable; nobody is to blame. Circumstances just conspire against us at times. In this case, all turned out well and we must be grateful.'

I have delivered quite a sermon, but Eileen is significantly brighter and her smile has returned.

'I shouldn't keep blaming myself for everything, should I?'

'You should not,' I reply. 'You must remember that you are in my employment, and I expressly forbid it.'

She rubs her nose, which is sunburnt and beginning to peel, then gives a little nod. She has understood, perhaps more than she usually does.

An unwelcome image of dastardly Doug in the car with the harlot flashes across my mind. Is he missing Eileen at all? Has he ended the affair? Is he tortured by bitter regrets? I do hope so.

Daisy clatters in. She comes to a standstill in front of us.

'I was thinking,' she says.

I look at her over my spectacles. 'And?'

'I told Mum about how you were cross with me and I was cross with you. And about the boobies and then Eileen being cross, too. And how cross we've all been today. And Mum said that was a shame because we should be working as a team. And she reminded me that the Three Musketeers' motto is "All for one and one for all." And the Three Mackateers should have that motto, too.'

All for one and one for all. Whatever does she mean by it?

'Are you suggesting we try to support each other more, Daisy?'

'Yes. That's it. Like the penguins do. And by the way, the Galápagos penguins aren't boring *at all*.'

I reach out my arms to her. She walks into them and, to my surprise, Eileen is suddenly on her feet and walking into them, too. The three of us share a little hug.

'All for one and one for all,' we chant together.

# 24

# Veronica

*Xavier Island*

DAISY POSTED THE blue-footed booby antics on her blog, to the wholehearted approval of her school friends, who left comments, hearts and smiley emojis galore. Many also shared it with their friends and families. Word is spreading.

She came in beaming. 'I've got three hundred and ninety-two followers now!'

Unfortunately, she let slip to her parents that she had followed the boobies alone. Now they have both emailed me. (Gavin: *She's a good kid. God was looking after her. But do keep an eye on her, won't you?* Beth: *Could you please ensure that in the future Daisy is accompanied at all times by a responsible adult.*)

After some debate it is arranged that José will

transport Daisy and Eileen to one of the islands where they can take a kayaking trip this morning. For excursions of this sort, the presence of a certified tour guide is mandatory, which allays my fears. Besides, Daisy has solemnly promised she will not go scampering off without telling anyone.

After a third day's presenting (because my performance yesterday was so dreadful) my energy levels have plummeted. In contrast, Daisy and Eileen return refreshed and invigorated. Eileen's hair is a frightful mess, but her skin glows and there's a new swing to her gait.

'Mrs McCreedy, I never thought I had it in me! I never thought in a million years that I'd do such things.'

Daisy bounces around, equally enthusiastic. 'Eileen got soaked in the kayak, but she went *so* fast. Look.'

She waves her phone under my nose. I watch Eileen in a blur of white water, shrieking, whirling down the currents and disappearing off the edges of the screen many times, whooping when the video catches up with her again.

'We saw fishermen on the beach – look!' Images of brightly coloured boats and locals hauling nets flash up as Daisy swipes. 'And there were sea turtles and *sharks* – look.' On the tiny screen sinister shapes glide indistinctly beyond a shoreline clump of mangroves.

'Not dangerous sharks, though,' Eileen adds quickly. 'Our guide swore on his life they weren't the dangerous sort.'

Daisy carries on. 'Whitetip reef sharks, he said. Then we went to a market.'

She scrolls through images of stalls heaped high with fish, fruit, coffee beans, sarongs, basketwork.

'I got this.' She lifts her wrist to display a black, beaded bracelet. 'It's made of lava. And we bought you a present.'

She dumps a paper bag in my hands.

'How kind.'

I peep inside. She seems to have given me a selection of dusty brown pebbles.

'They're sweeties, made with real cacao.'

'Thank you.'

Touched, I sample one, grateful for a sugar rush. With it comes a flash of awareness that these are precious memories indeed. The bittersweet flavour of dark chocolate will henceforth always remind me of this moment, this place, Daisy's eager, much-loved face.

'We still have more walking to do today,' I remind them, offering the packet around.

Sir Robert joins us, and we make a vivacious group as we set out again. All this sunshine, the searingly beautiful colours and the anticipation of seeing curious wildlife around every bend must be doing us good.

The only certainty in life is change, and my own moods are as changeable as traffic lights. Now, despite my lurking fears, I'm feeling very much lifted and newly hopeful.

The Galápagos filming is over. Miriam and Dave slap their hands together in what I believe is known as a high-five. Sir Robert, more dignified, comments that this is a very important documentary and he believes it will be effective.

Our party will soon be split three ways. Sir Robert departs from here directly to Antarctica, along with Miriam. Dave, who was with Sir Robert in the Arctic, returns home and will be replaced in the frozen south by another cameraman. And I fly Falkland-wards with Eileen and Daisy. Although we shall be sad to bid the Galápagos adieu, this feels like a marker, a significant turning point, for it is 15 October and timing-wise we are halfway through our month-long walk. And we have walked sixty-six miles, which is well over half, but that is as it should be, bearing in mind the long flights to come and the challenges of walking in Antarctica.

Because it's our last day here, the film crew, myself, Eileen and Daisy have a treat in store. We are to go on a snorkelling expedition. Snorkelling is something I have never tried, and I question whether it is a fitting activity for a woman of my advanced years, robust though she may be. Sir Robert, who has snorkelled many times, reassures me.

'We've picked a place where the waters are calm as a millpond. We'll see coral reefs and a huge variety of benign sea life. It would be such a shame for you to miss the experience. And we shall all be keeping an eye on you, Veronica.'

'That will be unnecessary,' I retort. 'I am up for anything. It is just that I am mindful that I need to preserve a tip-top state of health if I am to see Operation PIP through to its end. What good will I be to anybody if I drown?'

'I will take it upon myself to ensure that you do not,' he replies. 'We shall only be in shallow waters, where it is quite safe. And anyway, in addition to all her other skills, Gabriela is a trained medical officer.'

Eileen is blinking a lot. 'I'm really not happy front-wards. I only ever swim on my back.'

'You're good at keeping afloat, though,' I remark.

'Yes, true. I don't know how that works, to be honest, because there's quite a lot of me. I must be hollow or something. But I'm worried about water getting down the snorkel air pipe and into *my* air pipe.'

'That may happen at some point, but it's easy to clear. Trust me,' Sir Robert answers.

Eileen's face relaxes. She does trust him, so that is that.

We bob around the island's coast in two small boats, then offload into a sandy cove. Miriam is laden with a full wetsuit and underwater cameras, since she will be heading for the deeper waters. 'It's not part of the remit, but I can never pass over a cool filming opportunity.'

There is quite some palaver fitting on all our snorkels and goggles, pulling straps tight, donning high-visibility buoyancy vests and big yellow fins for our feet. When all is done I feel like an alien from a different planet. Despite slight fears that my face will be permanently disfigured by the imprint of the snorkelling mask, it is a thrill to embark on something I have never done before.

Gabriela teaches us how to exhale quickly into the snorkel to clear out any water. Daisy, who cannot wait to get in, promises, a little grudgingly, that she will not splash.

Alongside the others, I wade in. Sparkles dance around me. I launch flat on to my stomach and give my weight to the wibbly-wobbly waters. Head and body submerged, I concentrate on taking slow, deep breaths through the tube, as instructed. The cries of birds become muted, and the jangles of my mind are quietened, too. My breath comes in and out with a soft gurgle. Through the mask, I see the yellow fins of my companions, I see intricate feathers of seaweed fluttering in the ebb and flow, I see translucent blobs of algae in pastels and bright pinks, shoals of neon fish jetting past. Corals spring into focus; fingers and florets in rainbow colours festoon the rocks. I float across a landscape of meadows lush with strangely tentacled blooms, stones furred with growths in vermilion and orange, cyan and minty green. Two giant rays flap past in slow motion like great winged birds.

Beneath me a penguin performs aerobics, a Milky Way of bubbles streaking in its wake. I dip my head to watch, taste salt and feel a trickle of water sliding down my throat. With a forceful exhalation I manage to expel it from the airway, as I have been instructed.

My legs are drifting apart from each other. I try to pull them together again. They scissor wildly for a moment then curl under me. I seem to be tying myself in knots. Stubby dark shapes are swooping around, above, below. They have beaks and flippers.

A cheeky current of water tugs at me, turns me.

My mind is a jumble. Oscillating images of Daisy in tears, Eileen in a panic, her horrible husband in flagrante, Mac waiting for his death sentence, Pip lost somewhere in an Antarctic sea, Terry and Patrick against a backdrop of ice and snow, Sir Robert rebuking me for my unkindness, the problem of plastics, the crisis of climate change, the 'For Sale' notice at The Ballahays, blue-footed boobies, giant tortoises, flamingos, iguanas, emails, blogs, banks, agents, ambassadorship, walking, walking, walking . . .

But I am not walking now, I am . . .

I have no idea which way is up and which way is down. I flail out with my arms. I am spinning round and round.

A hand grips mine. I am gently steered to the surface. The clasp is firm, gentle, kind. The hand is knotted and gnarled; scoured all over like my own, but larger, warmer. Sir Robert's.

Our palms kiss, our fingers tie together. He keeps holding on until I am steady and straightened out again, but even then he does not let go. We float together in the swaying, dazzling blue-green, suspended in time and space, gazing down on an underwater realm, surrounded by penguins.

# Daisy's Penguin Blog

MOVING ON

My favourite memory from the Galápagos: Blue-Footed Boobies.

Eileen's favourite memory from the Galápagos: Kayaking (even though she says it was scary).

Veronica's favourite memory from the Galápagos: Snorkelling with the penguins.

We have done SO MUCH walking, too, because we never forget why we are here: to save the Lochnamorghy penguins. We're now at 66 miles!

But next we have another looooong flight.

Like us, most penguins travel huge distances. This is because seasonal temperature changes make it harder to find fish or a suitable breeding ground. Galápagos penguins don't need to migrate because on the equator the temperature is more constant, but many species swim for hundreds of miles. And of course, the Emperors do the long march.

If Emperor penguins had a top tip for travel, it would be this: Stuff yourself with loads and loads and loads of fish before you set out.

My top tip for travel is this: <u>DO NOT</u> forget your phone charger.

Next stop: The Falklands!

# 25

# Veronica

*Bolder Island, The Falklands*

LINEN AND COTTON have been replaced by thermals and woollens. I loop my scarf firmly around my neck and stretch to look out of the window. With a soft thump, the eight-seater plane touches down and careers along the tiny, grassed runway of Bolder Island, The Falklands. It is the end of another lengthy journey but adrenalin ensures I stay wide awake.

I maintain a calm presence, but internally I am jumping with joy to be here again. In the seat behind me, Daisy is babbling with excitement, pointing everything out to Eileen.

The pilot walks round and helps us out. A couple of white geese stalk off, disturbed by the noise of the plane. I cast my eyes around and see the tilted Vs of gulls blown on the wind, a knobbled moorland, a congregation of grey rocks gathered in front of a silvery sea. As our bags are unloaded, we trundle towards the microscopic but well-equipped hut that calls itself an airport. A Land Rover has just pulled up beside it.

Out leaps Terry, her smile as sweet as ever, her hair in two messy bundles, her pallid beauty twinkling behind thick-rimmed glasses. Despite Terry's lack of style and finesse, it is impossible not to like her. She is the kindest person I have ever met, devastatingly selfless and conscientious to a fault. Exposed to her constant good influence, even my grandson has become vaguely likeable.

And here he is, heading straight for me with hearty, swinging strides. Last time I saw Patrick he was bearded, but now he is clean-shaven (his antipathy towards his own facial hair is matched only by his dislike of shaving in Antarctic conditions, so his beard comes and goes). I am swept up in his muscular embrace.

'Granny!'

I used to flinch whenever he said that word. I used to find it sickeningly puerile, presumptive and provocative. For most of his life I did not even know that Patrick existed, and when we met for the first time neither of us took to the other; and that is perhaps the understatement of the century. But life has changed seismically for both of us since then. Now I have taken the word 'Granny' into my heart, and it sits there, purring.

I inhale deeply into his jacket as if I am sniffing one of the Albertine roses from the walled garden at home. But this is a very different scent. 'Ah, I can smell Antarctica on you.'

209

'That'll be the penguin poo,' he answers glibly.

I extract myself to receive a gentler but equally enthusiastic hug from Terry. It is then Eileen's and Daisy's turn, and after cries, laughter, cuddles and exclamations of delight have been shared all round, I take a moment to survey my grandson and his girlfriend. They only arrived here from Locket Island yesterday. Seeing them makes my heart ache with happiness and sadness and longing.

I wobble slightly and Terry takes my arm. 'Keith is waiting for us at the lodge. He said he'd get the kettle on, you'll be glad to hear, Veronica.'

I am.

We agree to take the short walk together whilst one of the helpers drives our luggage there in the Land Rover. Every opportunity to walk must be taken. I had forgotten how the Falklands wind tries to knock one off one's feet. I keep hold of Terry and tread gingerly, whilst Eileen walks on my other side and Patrick gallops on ahead with Daisy.

The big presentation ceremony takes place in the capital, Stanley, but we will be spending the first part of our Falklands visit on Bolder Island. Daisy and I are familiar with the landscape and we also have excellent accommodation here.

A crowd of small waddling figures comes into view, and memories flock back. That is the Gentoo penguin colony where I did my first piece of filming here for Sir Robert. And that is the cluster of rocks where Terry sat, full of news, waiting for Patrick. And that is the pathway to the beach which we walked so many times, a younger Daisy tugging her kite along. And that is the little hill with its small mound and a home-made cross, where we sang and wept. And now I see the lodge itself with its corrugated red roof and wind turbines and there is the wide veranda on which Sir Robert and I sat and discussed so many things.

The lodge door opens and out comes a burly beaming man who stretches his arms wide for Daisy. She runs into them and he enfolds her, then I see him turn to Patrick and shake hands. As we catch up, he greets us all warmly.

I do the only necessary introduction. 'Keith, this is Eileen, my helper in Scotland and the other third of the penguin walking team. Eileen, this is Keith, who runs this lodge and most of Bolder Island.'

'I've heard a lot about you,' they both say at once.

An 'ooops' comes from Eileen.

'Sorry for interrupting,' says Keith. 'Oh damn, I did it again.'

They laugh. He ushers us in. 'You must be tired, Mrs McCreedy.'

I frown at him. 'Tired?'

Patrick guffaws. 'Not the right thing to say, Keith. Granny doesn't *do* tired.'

'No, indeed. I do not,' I confirm. 'But I should dearly love some tea, if you would be so kind.'

'Of course, of course.'

He shows us into the front room and brings in a tray of mugs and the hugest teapot I've ever seen. As we are taking our seats round the table, he proudly displays the tatty friendship bracelet that Daisy made for him. Daisy has long since passed her friendship-bracelet phase (I 'accidentally' lost the one she made for me) but Keith's gesture is a kind one. Daisy is now pestering him about a penguin whom we befriended last year.

'Is Tony-the-Macaroni still here? Please, *please* say yes! I'm dying to see him again.'

Keith's face is wrapped in a grin. 'Yes, Daisy. Tony is still around. He's been asking after you.'

'Really?'

'Yes. You know, very few people understand penguin language, but—'

'—You do!' she proclaims, bouncing herself backwards into one of the easy chairs. 'Can we go and see Tony after tea, Veronica?'

'Yes, in a little while.'

Daisy is ecstatic. 'Do you know, Keith, Eileen can do the best penguin waddle in the whole world, ever. Eileen, show Keith your waddle.'

But Eileen is busy. She has taken proprietorship of the teapot and is assiduously pouring.

Keith tries to stop her. 'Hey, nobody but Keith pours out the tea on this island.'

I had forgotten his tiresome habit of referring to himself in the third person, but Eileen seems to find it amusing. They argue over the teapot for an irritatingly long time before deciding to divide the duty equally between them.

Our wander down to the sea is scenic, chilly and delightfully familiar. Waves slap the beach. Gulls, ducks, oystercatchers and several species of penguin potter about the shoreline. However, it is a disappointment that Daisy's second favourite Macaroni penguin (after Mac) is nowhere to be seen.

How exquisite, though, to behold the wonderment on Eileen's face as she witnesses the abundance of penguin life here. The gregarious, chaotic, orange-footed Gentoos are dynamos compared with the coy Galápagos penguins she has seen hitherto. They mill about everywhere, squawking and squabbling together.

'Wow, look at that chubby one!' she cries, admiring a stocky character waddle towards a clump of silver-leafed sea cabbage and plump himself there as if it is his own private garden.

She is even more thrilled than Daisy, who, excited as she is to be back, is now a little blasé about the actual penguins. She regales Eileen with penguin facts, whilst taking endless photos and videos with her phone.

'It's important for when we're famous,' she chants. 'We're the Three Mackateers, aren't we?'

'More like the three little piggies,' Patrick teases.

He has such an easy way with the girl. He hoists her up, charges towards the sea with her and threatens to throw her in, much to her screeching delight. She wriggles free and they prance about on the sand like a big lollopy Labrador and a playful puppy. The penguins give them a wide berth.

'Did you know that penguins were once used as kindling at whaling stations?' he tells her once their breath has returned.

'What's kindling?'

'Stuff you use when you light a fire, to help it burn.'

'So, you mean, they actually put them on the fire?'

''Fraid so. A penguin is full of fat, you see. Sizzles nicely.'

Eileen cringes and makes a face at Patrick, indicating he should cut out the gory details, but Daisy is fascinated.

'Is that why they're called wailing stations, because the

penguins were so upset about being burned they were wailing?'

'Er . . .'

He throws a look at Terry, a look that says: *How do I explain this one?* She shrugs.

He clears his throat. 'The whales were quite likely wailing, too.'

Daisy takes a moment to consider this. 'Are there any wailing whales in Wales? You don't have to answer that,' she adds, spouting laughter. It's just as well she isn't squeamish.

Another beat. 'People can be *so* horrible, can't they?' She's serious now.

Patrick grimaces. 'Too fricking right.'

Eileen is helping Keith cook dinner, despite his protestations. Daisy is upstairs engaged with her blog. I am settled in the common room with a glass of sherry. ('Keith got it in specially,' said Keith. 'He remembered how much you like it.') Terry and Patrick have said no to sherry in favour of beer. There is no accounting for some people's tastes.

I am eager to catch up with every aspect of Locket Island news, but one in particular.

'Everyone's well,' Terry assures me. 'Dietrich is forever juggling penguin business with trips back to Austria to see his family, but he manages.'

'And Mike is as cantankerous as ever,' Patrick says with a grin.

'We've all visited Centaurus, the new research station on the Antarctic Peninsula where you'll end your mission.'

214

'It's kinda space-age.' His voice is charged with enthusiasm. 'Tonnes of new technological developments. I've been setting up these time-lapse cameras all over the place. They're dead cool. The images go up online, then the general public all over the world can help us – a citizen science thing. All people have to do is click on the penguins they see in each photo. The system records the numbers counted in different colonies.' He goes on explaining in interminable detail before he registers my expression. 'Sorry, Granny. I'd better switch out of geek mode.'

He mimes flicking an invisible switch at his ear.

'It is great, though,' Terry says, casting him a fond glance. 'We're able to collect so much more information about the movements of the colonies, and the survival rate of chicks.'

'And are they surviving?' I ask, thinking of one that nearly didn't.

They both hesitate. Terry leans forward, her mouth on a slant. 'It's been a difficult year, much warmer than the last few, which is bad news for the penguins. They need the sea ice to survive, as you well know, Veronica. And there's no getting away from the fact that it's melting. Still, the Emperors are through the worst. Most of the chicks are big and robust now. As for the Locket Island Adélies, they're doing fine.'

I am about to enquire after Pip when Patrick leaps in and asks about The Ballahays.

I sigh. 'We have had several viewings—'

'Fricking hell!'

'—but no interest yet.'

He utters some words under his breath which I can't catch, then speaks up. '. . . bad idea. Think, Granny. It's great that you're still so ambitious,' he urges, emphasizing the word 'still' as if I really should be packing my bags for the afterlife by now. 'But to buy a sea life centre and try to run it . . . at your age? It's not exactly the most realistic plan, is it? I mean, to be honest, I've seen more realistic stuff on *Star Trek*. And as for The Ballahays . . .' Now his vocabulary sinks to a level so base that I regret adjusting my hearing aid. 'And what if you don't manage to find a house near Lochnamorghy? You can't run a place like that from afar.'

Sweet that he cares. Insufferable that he will not accept my choices.

Terry joins in. 'You've already raised so much money to help them, anyway. How much is it now?'

'Eileen will update us soon, but I believe we are at nearly thirteen thousand pounds.'

'It's a fabulous achievement,' she says warmly. 'Surely it's enough to help them over the hump? You don't need to do anything more.'

'Oh yes I do,' I answer, like a pantomime dame.

'Oh no you don't,' Patrick returns, shaking his head wildly.

I suck my cheeks in. 'Really, you two.' I sigh. 'This is tantamount to bullying.' A statement which in itself is tantamount to slander. 'If you must know, I put The Ballahays on the market as a ruse, to buy time. The Lochnamorghy agents wouldn't accept my offer otherwise.'

I do not mention that, although £13,000 isn't bad, my savings cannot cover the shortfall. Operation PIP will need to raise thirty times that amount for the purchase to go ahead.

It shall, it must go ahead.

How can I explain to them this fire that burns within me? They see me with myopic eyes; they see me as too old. They do not realize that every old person contains a young person, one who remains wide open to change, to hope, to possibility.

I steer the conversation back to Locket Island, still hungry for news. The tone lightens once more.

Terry is keen to tell me about the extraordinary Heath Robinson-like contraption that Patrick rigged up at the Adélie colony for her birthday.

'We walked out there together and he gave me a disgusting piece of raw fish,' she giggles. 'At first I thought *that* was my birthday present! But then he made me place it on a platform. As we watched, one of the penguins stepped on to the platform to grab it, setting off a series of pullies and cogs, then a banner flopped down in front of my eyes. It was painted with the words: "Happy Birthday Terry! And thank you for helping us. You are the best. Love from the penguins. PS. Patrick would like a kiss."'

My grandson leans in and gives Terry a kiss now.

Touching. But all this while I have been waiting eager-eared for a news bulletin about my dearest little feathered friend. No information is forthcoming.

The elephant in the room is . . . is, in fact, a penguin.

# 26

# Veronica

WE ARE A sizeable group today. Patrick and Daisy are just ahead of me on the creamy-white sweep of sand, whilst Keith walks with Eileen and Terry just behind me. I feel the lack of Sir Robert, though, who brings a distinguished quality to any gathering. Goodness, he will be nearing the South Pole now.

I pause and gaze out to sea. It shines blue, the purest blue, the blue of the heaven in medieval frescoes. Agapanthus blue. And I find my thoughts drifting off to the agapanthuses in the herbaceous border at The Ballahays.

I only stop briefly to admire it, though. Patrick and Daisy have stopped, too. The group behind me accelerates and we all bundle together.

No sooner have we joined forces than a huge bird sweeps down, skimming our shoulders. Terry whips out her binoculars to examine it. 'Handsome, but vicious. It's a caracara, isn't it?'

Keith nods. 'You need to watch that one,' he warns us. 'It's known to us at the lodge. It likes to steal people's hats.'

Most of us are wearing hats. Eileen is in a knitted bobble hat, Terry has her unattractive woollen creation with dangling tassels, Patrick has a padded cap with ear flaps, and I am muffled up in a scarlet scarf and matching beret. Only Keith and Daisy are bare-headed. I imagine Daisy is glad of so much hair these days.

I check my distance today, always a fiddly process. 'I do get so cross with my Parmesan . . . my pepperpot . . .'

Because vocabulary sometimes eludes me, people assume I haven't a clue what I'm talking about. I know precisely what I'm talking about. They are the ones who haven't a clue.

'Your pedometer?' Terry suggests eventually.

'Of course my pedometer,' I answer tersely.

Patrick examines it. 'Not bad, as they go. But in the next few years, pedometers will become way more accurate. They'll be based on GPS, and you'll be able to track your distance from your mobile phone.'

'Come on,' I urge, pounding onwards, unimpressed.

Terry's remark trails behind me on the wind. 'She's like a woman possessed.'

Daisy runs to catch up with me. She trots by my side, kicking up sand. Every so often she stops to pick up a shell. She reports to me on everything: the gulls glissading in the clouds, the sheep in the distance, the stranded seaweed, the wandering penguins.

She walks backwards for a moment, eyes alight. 'Veronica! Terry and Patrick are holding hands.'

'Ah.'

'I know exactly what bridesmaid dress I'll wear at their wedding.'

'Isn't that a little previous, Daisy?'

A quick glance confirms that my grandson and his girlfriend are indeed holding hands, looking very much like an advertisement for some exotic holiday as they stroll down the windswept beach. Eileen and Keith have dropped back to allow them some space. Or is it to give themselves some space? No doubt the man is starved of female company. A few staff help out at the lodge, but they are here on a seasonal basis and change regularly.

I transfer my gaze back to my grandson, who now tucks his arm around Terry's waist. 'Daisy, I must inform you that, devoted as they are to each other, Terry and Patrick are showing no signs of getting married. They are modern young people who will insist on doing things their own way.'

'That's no good,' she grumbles. 'They're getting *old*. If they leave it too much longer, it'll be too late.'

Patrick is only thirty, Terry in her late twenties.

'Too late for what?'

'You know. Proper romance.'

I sigh. What is proper romance anyway? My mind drifts back. To him. My first love. How different I was – how different *everything* was – then.

When you are sixteen and know you are beautiful, it is inevitable that you romanticize yourself. And if you are bored and sad and far from home and a gallant young man strides into your life, what you do is you fall in love. If you are open-hearted you do, anyway – and I undoubtedly was, albeit proud and headstrong, too. And so was he. Such passion we shared! Such adoration, such tenderness, such dreams.

When you are young, you never believe you'll grow old. When you're old, you don't believe it either. Yet I cannot envy my younger self. I doubt that youth is really as delicious as we imagine when we look back. For me it was a time brimming with pain, anxiety and the constant weight of hopes crushed and, no sooner had they resprouted, crushed again. At the time I fancied myself a tragic heroine, a kind of Scarlett O'Hara in *Gone with the Wind*. These days I would rather be Gone with the Penguins.

'Veronica, did you hear me?'

Daisy, cutting through my reverie. 'It's a Macaroni, look.'

The penguin washes in from the sea in front of us, finds his feet and waddles up the beach. He is different from the Gentoos, smaller, stubbier. The light falls on his sunflower-yellow crest.

Daisy shrieks and runs at him. 'Tony!'

Taking fright, he scoots off. She realizes her mistake and slows down immediately. He slows, too, peers back at her with his head slightly ducked. She crouches down and stretches a hand out to him, crooning gently. He half turns his body towards her, curious. They are a few feet apart, and he senses now that she means no harm. He even waddles a little closer.

I stand and watch. I haven't a clue if this is the real Tony who we met last year, but it is certainly a Macaroni penguin, and the only one on this beach at present. He will do nicely.

In the evening Eileen takes Daisy up the hill at her earnest behest. Satisfied with today's augmented mileage, I elect to stay at the lodge. I make use of the computer here and, with some help from Keith, manage to conjure my emails on to the screen. Or, rather, my email, for there is only one. I am disappointed to see it is not from Sir Robert until I remember he is on an icebreaker in the Antarctic and would not be able to communicate with me even if he wanted to.

The email is from my agent, Mr Wallace. I click it open, prepared for the usual lack of progress and dearth of interest in The Ballahays.

I need to read the email twice, once without my spectacles and once with them, just to be sure.

Somebody has put in an offer. He wants to progress with the sale as soon as is humanly possible. He sounds very much like my late ex-husband in his I-want-so-I-will-get attitude, heedless of inconvenience to anyone else. But he is offering the asking price.

I reflect.

I believe we shall complete Operation PIP with, if not a blaze of glory, then at least a sense of satisfaction, and we shall raise a substantial amount ... yet even with phenomenal publicity from my ambassadorial speech, it is unlikely to total more than a hundred thousand: not enough. Given time, I might conjure more funds, but time is a luxury we do not have. The death sentence of those twenty-four penguins looms ever closer. Then there will be the actual running costs of the centre ... at least £2 million yearly, if I am to believe what I've been told. It is time I grasped that reality.

The Ballahays is my fortress and has been my true love this last half-century. The vision of leaving it hits hard, like a punch to my heart. Yet that selfsame heart is set on buying Lochnamorghy, on saving those penguins.

Do I, an eighty-seven-and-a-half-year-old, really need to live in a twelve-bedroom mansion?

My thoughts, which have been whirling like snow-flakes these past three months, crystallize at last.

I read through the email one last time. Would I like to go ahead and accept the offer, my agent asks?

I punch out a reply before anyone can try to stop me. Only two words.

*Absolutely yes.*

# 27

# Eileen

*Bolder Island*

DOUG SAYS HE never believed I'd get all this way. But I
did.

'I was sick on the plane,' I admit as we FaceTime. 'Just
as I always am. I survived, though (thank you, dear pills!),
and during the flight I even looked out of the window at
the clouds this time. Fiona from choir talks about feeling
the fear and doing it anyway and says that's true courage,
so I do feel chuffed that I've managed it.'

'Good,' Doug says. 'Good for you.' His face looks different to how it normally looks, and I wonder if it's the
fact he's proud of me or just because the image on the
phone is blurry.

'So here I am! Look.' I angle the phone so he can see.
'This is the view from our – Daisy's and my – bedroom at

the lodge on Bolder Island. And can you see the sea in the distance?'

He says he can. 'But we have sea here in Scotland,' he adds.

'That's very true, Doug,' I answer. 'And come to think of it, the coast here isn't that different from Ayrshire. All ragged and rugged and cliffy but with plenty of sandy beaches, too, and nobody on them. But there you're in autumn and here we're in springtime. Lovely bright, breezy mornings and nature doing its thing. Lots of the birds are sitting on eggs. But otherwise it's really quite like Scotland. Only with penguins.'

'Just as well you have the penguins,' he says, implying it would be silly travelling all that way otherwise; maybe that it's silly anyway. He can think what he likes, though. I'm the one who's here and I like it, far more than I thought I would.

I should ask him all about life at home and the oatcakes but I'm so excited about the penguins that I don't.

'So many different penguins, too. Not just your plain black-and-white, but the ones with big orange feet and little white bonnets (they're the Gentoos) and the ones with yellow tufts behind their ears (they're the rockhoppers and Macaronis) and the ones with a band of black round the belly and a pink patch round the eyes (they're the Magellanics) and the ones with egg-yolk yellow on their cheeks and chests (they're the Kings).' Doug's eyes are glazing over. 'I'm not showing off,' I tell him, 'but I've learned it all recently and it's good for me to keep repeating it because Mrs McCreedy gets cross if I muddle which is which. She's very particular about penguins.'

'She's very particular about everything.'

'Haha, yes, I suppose so. I had no idea how to pronounce "Magellanic" when I read it in the guidebook but she told me it's "maj", like "majestic".'

'Talking of which, how is Her Majesty?'

He thinks he's being funny, calling Mrs McCreedy that. I don't laugh. 'She's doing marvellously well. All that walking and travelling doesn't seem to have worn her out at all. I've never known anyone so driven about anything. There's that gleam in her eye, too, and I know she's looking forward to being made Penguin Ambassador, even though she might grumble.'

'That Sir What's-His-Face not with you now, then?'

'No, his filming schedule said he had to go straight from the Galápagos to Antarctica, and you can't argue with the BBC, even if you are Sir Robert Saddlebow.'

'I hope the bairn isn't giving you too much hassle?'

'Oh, Daisy's a good girl, a dream. She's so happy to be back here, and to find her special penguin called Tony. Tony-the-Macaroni, you see? And she's over the moon to meet up with Patrick and Terry, too. She's really fond of them both. And she adores Keith.'

'Keith?'

I've told him before that we'd be staying with Keith but he's forgotten. 'He's the man who runs the lodge. He's ever so generous and brilliant with Daisy and such a good cook!' Saying it makes me feel guilty about leaving Dougie to cook all by himself for so long when he isn't used to it. I can see from the background (my dancing sunflower is just visible behind him, in the corner of the screen, only it isn't dancing) that he's in the kitchen. I can see a load of dirty plates piled up by the sink, too. I am itching to scrub them clean but it's no good. You can't do that sort of thing over FaceTime.

I tell him about what I learned from Keith. 'The Falklands were first discovered by the French, but they didn't hang about here. I suppose they missed their petits fours and their haute couture and their fried snails so they went away again. Then the Brits arrived and I suppose they thought, hey, it's got nice beaches and we like a nice beach, and sheep would do well here. So they stayed. And the sheep *did* do well, and so did the Brits. But then one day Argentina, in a tizzy about its own problems, thought it would come and take over. So all of a sudden the quiet Falklanders were overrun with guns and violence. That was back in the eighties. Do you remember it happening, Doug? I was at school at the time and I knitted a balaclava for one of our brave soldiers. But I didn't really think about it much until now. Those soldiers were so young and they travelled all the way round the world to defend these people. And quite a lot of them (the soldiers) never came back.' I stop there for a moment, thinking of the rusty bit of aeroplane we've seen and the shipwrecks and the memorials. 'What a terrible thing,' I say.

'Bloody Tories,' he says.

I look at him again, and realize what's different about him. It's the fact that he's clean-shaven. He's not one for shaving often, so I'm surprised. Maybe he took the trouble because he knew we'd be FaceTiming. My heart gives a little quiver inside my chest.

'Are you managing all right?' I ask. I want him to be missing me as much as I'm missing him. More, even. 'Tell me about everything going on there. How's work? How are the oatcakes?' But the image has frozen. I shake my phone and try slanting it different ways but I can't get him back.

Dougie has his faults but I do feel horribly cut adrift when we can't chat. I'm glad there is so much here to keep me busy, and people who stop me thinking dark thoughts.

Patrick and Terry are one of the loveliest couples I know. You'd hardly know Patrick is Mrs McCreedy's grandson; he's not like her at all, except that the two of them share a habit of acting on whims. Terry is a sweet girl and knows everything there is to know about penguins. She's lived out in the Antarctic for years. She's a real scientist and I'm a bit in awe of how she can be so young and so clever. She even runs the whole Locket Island operation – in charge of three men. Can you imagine?

Mrs McCreedy adores both Patrick and Terry, even though she'd never say it out loud. They adore her, too, otherwise they'd never bother coming all the way to the Falklands to see her. Still, I suppose it's easier than travelling from Antarctica to Scotland (my geography is a lot better than it used to be).

I'm wondering whether it's worth trying to call Doug again when there's a rumpus from the next room, like a small series of thuds, and Mrs McCreedy is calling my name.

'Mrs McCreedy, what is it?' I head for the open door of her room and peep in. She is on her hands and knees on the floor.

'Eileen, would you be so kind as to assist me?'

I rush to help her up. 'Whatever happened, Mrs McCreedy?'

'It is most infuriating,' she snaps. 'I simply cannot find

my pedometer. I have been searching for it under the bed, but to no avail. Did you take it out of my handbag and put it somewhere?'

'No, no, I didn't.'

'Well, somebody must have done, because I've searched high and low and it's nowhere to be found.'

'I'll go and ask Daisy if she's taken it, shall I?'

Daisy is chatting with Keith in the kitchen. I trundle down and ask them, but neither of them has seen the pedometer recently. I trundle up again and report back to Mrs McCreedy. I assure her I'll do a thorough search.

I start by looking up and down the corridor, scanning every inch of the carpet. I wonder if the pedometer could have got itself hoovered up. It's small enough, if you were using a Hoover without the nozzle, which I sometimes do to get into corners, but it would make quite a clatter on its way down the pipe. You'd notice. I think it's Keith who does the hoovering here as well as most of the cooking. What a practical man he is! I will ask him.

I'm just passing Terry and Patrick's room when I hear Patrick's voice inside.

'Are you still feeling sad?' he asks.

'Yes and no,' Terry's voice answers. I wonder why Terry would be feeling sad, and I hope she isn't ailing, so I put my ear closer to the door and listen some more. I don't like people feeling sad, and if there's anything I can do to help, I'd like to do it.

'At least Veronica and Daisy and Eileen are OK,' Patrick says.

I nod to myself. We are all three OK, apart from the small matter of the pedometer.

'Yes, such a relief,' Terry answers. 'I wasn't sure they'd make it.'

'There's a long way to go yet.'

'True. But they've got through the worst stage.'

Have we? I'm not so sure.

'They just need plenty of fish and they should be fine.'

Plenty of fish? I didn't realize that was the recipe for success. Fish are rich in vitamins, though, so I suppose it makes sense.

'What do we do if one of them dies?'

'Not much we can do.'

He sounds horribly resigned about it. As if it's the sort of thing that might happen quite easily. I press my ear closer to the door.

'It would be awful if they got eaten by seals. Daisy's especially vulnerable. She's only little.'

My blood runs cold. I am paralysed. How can they talk about this so coolly? If I'd realized we were in such dire danger I would never have come. I would have persuaded Mrs McCreedy and Daisy to stay at home somehow, even if it meant tying them up. I had no idea you got man-eating seals on this side of the world. Why did nobody tell me? And do Daisy's parents know? Surely not. I'm imagining all sorts of ghastly, grisly things now. I jump as Patrick speaks again.

'Veronica and Eileen will guard her fiercely, any way they can.'

Of course we will.

'Of course they will. Feet, beaks, flippers . . .'

All of a sudden, I get it. They're not talking about us but about the three Emperor penguins who share our

230

names. It is such a relief I let go of all my breath at once and it makes a kind of hissing *aaaah* noise.

'What was that?' Terry asks.

'Dunno. Dodgy plumbing?' He pauses for a second, then carries on. 'So if one of them *does* die, do we tell?'

'I believe in honesty,' Terry's voice answers.

'But not at the expense of Granny's happiness. Or the others', dammit.'

There's a brief pause, then Terry again. 'All right. It would be too demoralizing for them at this stage. I'll agree with you, just this once . . . But don't expect it to ever happen again.'

I think they're kissing next because it's that sort of silence that follows. I'm about to tiptoe away when Patrick speaks again, and it's with sadness.

'I truly am sorry about Pip,' he says. 'We'd better not tell them about that, either.'

'No,' she agrees. 'Definitely not.'

'You never know. He may be OK.' Patrick's voice is thoughtful. 'It could just be that he's staying very, very still.'

'Come on, Patrick. I'm not that naive. Neither are you. There's no way his tracker device could have come off and it shows he's been stationary at the bottom of the ocean for three days. Penguins are good at holding their breath underwater, but not that good. He's dead, for sure.'

I let out a gasp and realize it's quite loud again, so I scoot away from the door and start polishing the banister with my sleeve. I'm just in time because the next moment Terry comes out of the room, Patrick in her wake.

My 'Oh, hello!' isn't as cheery as I'd like it to be.

231

# 28

# Veronica

*Bolder Island*

KEITH'S LAND ROVER swooshes along the empty road. I travel in the passenger seat beside him whilst the others are all wedged into the back. We are headed west, to a colony of Kings.

Moorland flies past. Bolder Island is bereft of trees but vastly generous when it comes to sea and sky. Inland, it features grey rivers of rock and shale and countless knobs of the tightly packed plant known as 'diddle-dee'. Upland geese hunker down in its contours and an occasional bedraggled sheep wanders in the wilderness.

The day is overcast. Clouds scud about over the hills, pewter-dark and surly. All is amicable within the vehicle, however.

Behind me, Patrick chats with Daisy about her parents, who are great friends of his.

'I miss them, y'know. They both helped me out through some godawful times. Beth talking through stuff with me right here in the Falklands. And, going back to my Bolton days, all Gav's nuggets of wisdom over a pint down at the Dragon's Flagon.'

Daisy chuckles. 'Oh yes, Dad likes that pub. He still goes there sometimes.'

'Gav and me used to have endless geek-outs at the bicycle shop, too, discussing the aerodynamics of bike helmets and the ideal number of spokes in a wheel. That shop was a bit of a refuge for me back then. Funnily enough, I got an email from Gav just yesterday. He told me about buying that pad in Jedburgh for branch two of the bike biz. And about the new guy he's got in at the Bolton shop. Big changes, all steaming ahead.'

Patrick has no idea how very fast my own business is steaming ahead. The documents have been forwarded by email, and I have both electronically signed for the sale of The Ballahays and upped my bid for Lochnamorghy. I will have to sign in person and wade through additional paperwork as soon as I arrive back in Scotland, but my buyer has already arranged for a survey and things are moving on apace.

I have bundled all this to the back of my mind and I hope it will stay there for the time being. It would be nice to enjoy this day, this place, this company.

Keith swings the steering wheel and we veer off track, launching on to open moorland. He clearly knows where he is going, but the Land Rover lurches violently over non-stop humps and bumps and we are jolted in every possible direction.

'Bloody hell!' Patrick exclaims.

'It's like being on a bucking bronco,' Terry laughs.

I am immune to such things and Daisy is laughing too, but Eileen is suffering. At least, her exclamations of 'Oh, I left my tummy behind', 'Cripes, that was a big one' and 'Flipping Nora!' shorten to 'Eek', 'Whaa', 'Ug' and other senseless monosyllables before melting away altogether. When we finally stop and tumble out, her skin is blotchy and tinged with green. She totters towards a large rock and bobs down behind it.

When she emerges ten minutes later, it seems the fresh air has restored her somewhat, for the natural rosiness has returned to her cheeks.

By this time our attention is fastened on the Kings, who strut about the countryside as if they owned it. They flaunt perfectly polished plumage; yellow around the neck area softening to pure white, with sleek backs of silver-grey. They waddle in twos and threes, pausing every so often to strike elegant poses, like a beakier genre of Florentine statues.

I turn to Daisy. 'Whenever life becomes unpleasant, remember this, Daisy: you have fraternized with Kings.'

'Such handsome birds,' Eileen declares. 'I'm loving the yellow.'

'Aren't they gorgeous?' Terry agrees. 'They're the most colourful of all the eighteen species of penguin.'

'And they're related to the Emperors, aren't they?' says Daisy, ever keen to file more facts in her head.

'Yes, but not quite as big. The Emperors are the biggest of the lot.'

The grassy swell of land is streaked with white guano and scattered with feathers. Several Gentoos patter about, looking small next to their larger cousins.

A brown bird with a cruel curved beak is jabbing and tugging at a carcass. Only a few ribbons of flesh and the telltale rubbery orange Gentoo feet remain.

'Is that a skua?' I ask.

'Yes,' Patrick confirms. 'Not the gentlest of birds. Don't look, Daisy.'

If one thing is guaranteed to make Daisy look, it is to tell her not to look.

Thankfully my pedometer has turned up again (it was in my handbag all along) and it monitors my steps as we wander up to the colony, where a bustling symposium of Kings is assembled. Due to their complicated breeding cycle, we're able to see them at every stage in their development. The juveniles are clad in woolly brown coats, not unlike the coats of Highland cattle. They seem an entirely different species from their parents; it is hard to believe they will turn into such immaculate fashion icons. Several have begun to shed their wool and wear a mismatched collage of different textures. They look self-conscious and scruffy.

Keith whistles us over. 'There's a newborn,' he says, indicating a minute, ugly black chick squeezed between the feet of an adult. The parent bends its head down to regurgitate food into the baby's gaping beak. We watch for a while, enthralled.

Eileen stands there, legs a little apart, hands on hips,

admiring the scene, and I think how much better she looks than she has done in a long time. She will never be a lithe person, but she has lost that certain puffiness of face from spending too long indoors. She seems more muscular, more defined. Stronger. Brighter.

'Why did you never have children, Eileen?' Daisy asks suddenly.

A wrinkle appears on Eileen's brow. It's a question I have never asked her, nor even thought about. Her eyes fix ahead and shadows move across her face, subtle shifts reflecting memories, no doubt.

Her mouth readjusts to a smile.

'Well, the fact is, Daisy, I *did* want to have children. I wanted them very much. Doug and I tried for years. But sometimes things just don't happen the way you want them to, and you have to accept it.'

'Too true,' mutters Patrick.

The topic of parenthood is a sensitive issue for at least three of us here.

I automatically put my hand up to the locket which hangs around my neck at all times. It is a very beautiful silver locket engraved with a V, given to me by my dear father.

Eileen starts gabbling, oblivious to the fact that Daisy, too busy filming penguins on her phone, isn't listening any more.

'. . . But I've got plenty of children in my family, like my nephew, wee Kevin, who I'm very fond of. And, of course, not having children has meant I've got to know you, too, Daisy. And, you see, it was probably all for the best, because if I'd had children I'd be so busy looking after them I wouldn't have been able to look after Mrs McCreedy for all these years—'

She notices my expression and quickly alters her vocabulary. 'I don't mean *look after* Mrs McCreedy, of course; I mean help her out with little jobs, like arranging window cleaners and optician's appointments and dusting The Ballahays.'

One mention of The Ballahays and my thoughts snap back there again. I'd hoped and believed it would be my home until my life's end. Those sturdy old walls have been my sanctuary for so long. The wrench in my gut is so painful I don't know what to do with it. I grip my stick and focus all my inner thoughts on dear Pip, on the strange love that was born in me the minute I first set eyes on him. And I remind myself that flesh and blood – and feathers and flippers – are more important than stones and mortar.

Keith wishes us a pleasant day and drives off. He has work to do at the lodge and will pick us up at a fixed point later.

We picnic amongst the Kings, I on the folding chair that Eileen brings everywhere, and the others perched on stones. Terry and Patrick squeeze together on the smallest stone available and feed each other sandwiches, ridiculously lovey-dovey. Perhaps, after all, Daisy is right and we shall hear wedding bells before too long.

My mind flashes back to Sir Robert's ludicrous marriage proposal to me. Whatever would he have done if I had taken him seriously and said yes? He would have run a mile. In fact, that is pretty much what he did . . . and that was before I'd even had a chance to respond.

A podgy chick toddles into view and starts pestering

one of the adults for food, presumably its parent. The adult, evidently exhausted, pushes it away. The chick returns and clamours for attention, twittering incessantly. It stretches its neck and shoves itself up against the bigger barrel of a body, ever hopeful. Weary with the argy-bargy, the adult gives it a quick peck. The chick, deterred but unharmed, finally gives up, tucks its beak backwards into its plumage and starts preening.

The doorstep sandwiches Keith has prepared are tooth-some and nicely peppery, but Daisy seems to be choking on hers. She splutters and coughs. I pat her on the back, to no avail. Her eyes are streaming.

'Did your mouthful go down the wrong way?' asks Eileen.

Daisy shakes her head.

To my shock I see that she is crying, silently but jerkily. She balls her fists into her eyes and dashes the tears away.

For a moment she gains control, but then bursts into a fit of sobbing. Eileen tries to hug her but she won't have it.

I am baffled. 'Whatever is the matter, dear girl?'

She cannot speak for crying. We stop eating, dismayed, and try to comfort her.

Once her emotion has ebbed a little, I ask: 'Are you homesick, dear Daisy?'

The child shakes her head again, mute.

'Please don't worry about Mac. We are doing all we can, and I'm sure we'll be able to save him.' (More sure than she knows. Should I tell her? I want to, but I am not yet ready to divulge the sale of The Ballahays to another soul.)

Daisy nods, trying for a smile, not managing it.

'What is it, then? You're not hurting anywhere, are you?'

Fear lurches through me. Could it be that her cancer is returning? Might it already be invading her delicate young body again? And here am I, forcing her into physical exertion every day, far from home and family. Yet until now she has seemed so fit and well.

She darts a look up at me, her eyelashes beaded with tears. 'No, not hurting. I'm OK.'

She struggles to her feet and walks away.

We exchange questioning glances.

Eileen shrugs her shoulders. 'What was that all about? Was she upset at the skua eating the dead penguin?'

I ponder. 'It didn't seem to affect her at the time. It might be . . . certain memories coming back? Being here might have accentuated them, possibly?'

'Yes, maybe. It's not like her, though, is it? She's normally so cheerful.'

This is true; she is a remarkably buoyant girl and seldom inclined to sulkiness. I would worry less if she were willing to share the problem with us. She is pacing up and down on the grass, a short distance away. Every so often she pulls her sleeve across her face. The penguins eye her curiously.

'Shall I go to her?' Terry offers.

Without waiting for an answer, she shoots off, and I see her walking at Daisy's side, the two of them conversing. It seems to be Terry who is doing most of the talking. We pack up the remains of the picnic. Patrick offers his arm and I reach for my stick and handbag. We must be getting on.

Patrick strides ahead and takes Terry's place at Daisy's side. Terry loops back towards us.

'She seems a little better. I was telling her all about the three Emperor penguins who are named after you three.

Distraction tactics. She wouldn't say what was troubling her, though. Maybe it's worth contacting her parents.'

I am reluctant. Gavin and Beth have put their trust in us, and I do not wish to imply that we are doing a less-than-perfect job of looking after their daughter. Especially after the booby shenanigans in the Galápagos.

'I could WhatsApp them once we're back?' Eileen suggests.

'That might be an idea,' I concede.

We make our way along the path. Daisy has calmed down, but speaks very little. All the ingredients are there for a perfect walk. We have our backs to the wind, which blasts us along. The sun has edged out and the clouds are putting on a pageant of ever-changing gold-trimmed glory. The land slopes down to rumpled dunes and a sparkling sea, pigments of green and lilac-blue, fronted by a pale streak of bay. Penguins, ducks and geese populate our route. Yet today we don't seem to fall into our usual rhythm of walking. Our steps are haphazard, wavering, out of kilter with one another.

As soon as we are back at the lodge we contact Beth and Gav via Eileen's Wotsit. We word the message carefully, mentioning that Daisy seems to be struggling but we cannot determine what ails her.

Beth replies at once. She is not able to tell us what's up at all, only suggesting what has already occurred to us. Her concern much in evidence, she informs us she will ask Daisy directly if she's all right. If she wishes to go home, we will do our utmost to arrange it. Eileen promises she will travel back with Daisy if need be. It will spell the end of our walking together, but so be it. The mission would not exist without Daisy's desperate desire to save Mac, and if that is now subsumed by other concerns, what can we do? If this happens, however, I, Veronica McCreedy, first Penguin Ambassador, shall complete Operation PIP alone.

Somewhat surprisingly, I do not relish this prospect. I have become accustomed to – nay, enamoured of – the idea of completing the task as a trio.

A few hours later there is a ping from Eileen's doo-dahs. It is Beth, letting us know that she has FaceTimed with her daughter. Daisy is adamant she wants to continue with Operation PIP. She apparently denied being upset at all.

Beth points out that her turmoil might merely be a matter of emotional overwhelm, since sometimes a mix of many things (fears for Mac, a grand undertaking, foreign travel, removal from one's normal comfort zone) can mount. Gavin has also Wotsitted Daisy separately. He cannot fathom it either, but puts her behaviour down to tiredness.

It is unaccountable, but if she wants to continue, then that is what will happen. All we can do is to keep a careful eye on her and hope that, whatever it is, the issue will resolve itself.

We do not see Daisy until supper, and then she stomps in, scowling at us. Betrayal is written all over her face.

'How dare you?' she rages. 'How dare you tell Mum and Dad I'm "struggling"? I'm not struggling at all. The walking is easy-peasy, and you know – you *know* – how much I'm wanting to save Mac and Pablo and Florence and the others. How *could* you go behind my back? How could you even *think* I want to go home?'

Eileen blurts out an apology. I try to explain that we were merely trying to help. Daisy is still mutinous. Her eyes smoulder; her forehead is clenched and contorted.

Keith marches in at this point with a tray of sausage rolls and steaming vegetables. 'Miss Daisy is looking as if she needs extra sausage power today. And if she needs anything else, she just needs to come to Keith. Keith is always here if she needs him; I hope she knows that. In fact, Keith has a little job to do, because Tony-the-Macaroni has asked for help.'

Despite herself, Daisy is curious. 'Why does Tony need help?'

'Penguins aren't much good at writing, you see.'

'Writing?'

'Yes, writing. Which is why Tony has asked Keith to write a postcard on his behalf.'

A sneaky smile is spreading across Daisy's face. 'A postcard? To who?'

'To his fellow Macaroni penguin in Scotland, to cheer him on.'

'Tony wants to write a postcard to Mac?'

'Yup.' Keith gives a quick glance in our direction, accompanied by a scarcely detectable wink. 'Keith is going to do the actual writing, but it would be great if you'd contribute because your spelling has got to be better than mine.'

Daisy's anger has all melted away.

She stuffs her mouth with sausage rolls in her hurry to be done with supper so that she can get on with assisting Keith in the important matter of penguin postcard writing.

# Daisy's Penguin Blog

POSTCARD FROM A PENGUIN

Dear Mac,

I'm a Macaroni penguin, like you. I've never been to Scotland but I hear it's beautiful, with delicious fish, like here. The weather is good in the Falklands but it's always so windy. Sometimes I get sand in my eyes.

I hope you and the Lochnamorghy penguins are well? Please don't worry. Your human friends are walking every day to save your home and your life.

Sincerely,

Your penpal penguin, Tony

PS. Daisy sends her love.
PPS. So do Veronica and Eileen.
P.PPS. Keith says hello. He'd really love to meet you one day.

Talking of walking (haha, I rhymed!) did you know about penguins' knees? Penguins don't seem to have any, only little legs with waddlery feet on the ends ... but Terry says all birds have knees, just backwards ones!

243

Flamingos' knees are really obvious but you can't see penguins' knees because they're deep inside the penguin under layers of flesh, fat and feathers. Penguins don't really use their knees to get around like we do. Instead, they swing from side to side like a pendulum. It looks like it's a lot of effort but actually isn't. Patrick (our useful bird nerd) says: 'Their to-ing and fro-ing converts to kinetic energy. The penguin wacky walking style is actually more efficient than ours.'

Maybe we should be waddling the 100 miles, not walking? Eileen would be good at that. I suggested we should all do it but Veronica said no.

# 29

# Veronica

*Bolder Island*

WE ARE ON a clifftop. Cormorants soar above, waves churn below. A lone Magellanic penguin waddles just ahead of us, his stumpy back view silhouetted against the azure strip of sea. My limbs are working slowly today. My knee joints grind and my calves ache, unhappy that they have been pushed so much of late. I coax them onwards.

Daisy stops frequently to take photographs, and I worry that she is treading too close to the edge. In this buffeting wind it is surely not safe. Terry and Patrick are hand in hand again and too involved in each other to notice. Luckily Keith and Eileen are keeping track of her.

Before long we encounter a community of rockhoppers. Their sprouting yellow crest-feathers wave in the wind, their white bellies gleam. They are busy nest-building, hefting unwieldy sticks in their beaks, prodding at pebbles. I see several pinch sticks from each other's nests. Others bounce up and down a rickety, steep incline to and from the sea. Their shenanigans are a joy to watch.

A sudden high-pitched shriek pierces the air.

Daisy.

I turn. She is teetering on the clifftop, waving her arms around in distress.

Simultaneously Eileen and Keith hurtle towards her and almost collide. Eileen pulls her in and crushes her in a hug whilst Keith crouches down to her level to check that she is all right. I wend my way hastily towards them to find out what is happening.

'My phone!' Daisy wails.

Apparently a strong gust plucked it right out of her hand and hurled it on to the rocks way below us. We look down, craning our necks at different angles, trying to spot it. I can make out nothing, but Keith points. 'I think that's it.'

Terry and Patrick have caught up with us.

'I'll go get it for you,' Terry volunteers without a moment's hesitation.

'No you don't,' Patrick protests.

'Watch me,' she cries, and starts shimmying down the rock face, completely unfazed by the dizzying height.

'Fricking hellstones,' says Patrick, and starts to clamber after her. They are both young and fit, but my heart is like a piston as I watch them manoeuvring downwards amidst the jags. For a while I can just see the tops of their heads, then Terry disappears altogether. My grip tightens on my handbag. If anything should happen to that girl . . .

Now Patrick has vanished out of sight, too. My blood pressure is skyrocketing. How dare they risk their lives for a stupid mobile phone?

A moment later they both reappear, further down.

Terry reaches the spot first, and I see her leap, goat-like, on to a narrow ledge, pick something up and place it in her pocket. Patrick arrives beside her, and they share an impassioned kiss before climbing upwards again.

Eileen, Keith, Daisy and I watch, all breaths bated.

The moments draw out. I catch sight of a moving elbow, a corner of woolly hat. Then two flushed faces. They have made it safely to the top.

'Never, *ever* do that again!' I bark, clutching at the locket that hangs against my heart.

Terry delves into her pocket and returns the phone to Daisy. 'I'm afraid the screen is smashed, so it's probably not much good to you any more.'

'Thank you,' says Daisy in a very small voice. She fiddles with the machine, trying different things.

'Let me have a go,' Patrick offers.

If he cannot get it going, nobody can. Alas, it is useless. The wretched gizmo is beyond repair.

Daisy is grief-stricken. The sort of grief that only a ten-year-old with a broken phone can invoke, i.e. complete histrionics. She bawls like a baby. She is wholly unable to exist for twenty-four hours without her toy.

At Terry's suggestion she has tried writing a blog post on the computer at the lodge but declares she hates it.

'And anyway, I can't carry the stupid computer out with me on walks and take photos with it, can I?'

Daisy's dark mood has spread through all of us. I don't know how to remedy the situation. There is not a single shop on this island. Food and supplies are normally flown in by the tiny local aeroplanes, but if Daisy and Eileen fly to Stanley tomorrow in search of a new phone, they will not be back until the next day at the earliest and precious time will be lost.

Eileen has, of course, offered up her own phone for Daisy's use, but that won't do, either.

'It takes rubbish photos and it's just soooo old,' she whines.

I am getting fed up of all this.

'In three days we shall be in Stanley anyway, for the ambassadorship ceremony,' I tell her with a degree of acidity. 'Can you not wait until then?'

No, it appears she cannot. At any rate, she erupts into yet another tempest of tears.

Now, big softy that he is, Keith steps in and offers to take Daisy to East Falkland in his motorboat tomorrow morning. She nearly bites his hand off in her urgency to say yes.

'Goodness knows how much a new phone will cost,' Eileen mutters.

Daisy has her comeback ready. 'You have to speculate to accumulate.'

I need to watch what I say in her company. She listens to everything, and she is sharp, is that one. And I am under no illusion about who will be footing the bill. In my childhood I would never have expected such indulgence, but nowadays attitudes are vastly different. Tempted as I am to utter the words 'spoilt brat', I hold back, mindful of Sir Robert's reprimand. I, too, have a distinct habit of getting whatever I want and the label of 'hypocrite' is far from endearing.

'It can't be easy for her, so far away from home, and with nobody her own age around,' Eileen whispers.

So it is all arranged, and Eileen is to go with them. They will be keeping tabs on the steps they make whilst trawling around town in pursuit of a brand-new phone.

Whilst I appreciate that we are making a communal effort, their constant presence has become rather trying of late. I welcome some freedom from it and look forward to my day with Terry and Patrick. We have two coastline walks planned that will encompass three penguin colonies. In the presence of penguins I will reveal to my grandson that I shall indeed be selling my home and taking on proprietorship of Lochnamorghy Sea Life Centre, and that documents have been signed to that effect, whether he likes it or not.

As well as windswept beaches, headlands, heath and a plethora of birdlife, Bolder Island is home to several small war memorials. I avoided these last time I was here. I feared they would provoke painful memories, for as a girl I lived through wartime tragedy and great are the scars it left on my soul. However, this time I linger by the thin, sad white cross and the stone etched with the names of those who perished, and I pay my respects. So much courage has been spent, so much sacrifice. Behind each of these names was a living presence, a unique conundrum of experiences. Each one was a precious vessel of thoughts, wishes, hopes, fears, love. Each one, along with vast multitudes of people throughout history, destroyed by their fellow men.

I turn to face the wild sea.

'What a piece of work is man,' I quote softly to myself.

It feels both miraculous and unfair that I am still here, that I have withstood life's slings and arrows for a full eighty-seven years. And so many of those years I have wasted, stewing in privilege. In privileged despair, rather.

A cold blast scythes through my bones and my rickety body wobbles in the wind. On either side, Terry and Patrick step up and hold on to me.

Despite sobering thoughts, today is a rare treat. I drink in the moments with these two, relish having them to myself. As we hike over Bolder Island they point out many birds to me: dotterels, meadowlarks, cormorants, night herons, steamer ducks and, of course, penguins. Yet I cannot seem to find the right opportunity to tell them of The Ballahays' sale. I do not fear their judgement. No, it is more that I seem to have an allergy to saying the words out loud.

I scold myself once we are back at the lodge.

'The Ballahays has been sold,' I mouth to my reflection in the bathroom mirror, by way of a practice. My reflection looks startled.

I try again. This time my reflection looks completely furious with me.

Envy darkens every line of that face; envy of the man who is buying The Ballahays. With a bitter pang I envisage what he might do to 'improve' it. Rip out my beautiful oak panelling to make room for a colossal flat-screen TV? Install a computer console in the bread oven? Convert the dining room to a gym? Replace the bay windows with plastic Velux hideosities? Concrete over my rose garden? Cut down the trees in my gorgeous plum orchard? Build a complex of studio flats in my beloved walled garden? It does not bear thinking about. I shall never be able to go back and visit, just in case these things come to pass.

I think of Mac, and I harden my heart.

Loud exclamations downstairs inform me that Eileen, Keith and Daisy have returned from Stanley. I pull myself together and head to the hall to greet them. Daisy is triumphant with her new phone. She is trying out the video on Patrick, who is pulling the most extraordinarily ugly faces at her.

'We need to go and see Tony so I can video him, because he's much, much handsomer than Patrick,' Daisy trills.

Patrick makes a great show of pretending to be wounded to the core.

After which we set off together again. This will only be a short stroll, down to the Gentoo colony and the beach.

Light rain splatters in our faces, but we are brightened by Daisy's reborn enthusiasm.

'Veronica?'

'Yes, Daisy?'

'Would you like to live in the Falkland Islands?'

I consider. How wonderful, how uplifting it would be to live amongst penguins. And the coastline here is stunning, with its craggy cliffs and miles of untrammelled beaches. And yet . . .

'No, I think not, Daisy. I should miss too much the rowans and birches of the glens, the birdsong from our full-throated robins, larks, thrushes and blackbirds. I should miss hearing the sound of bagpipes wafting on the wind. The outline of ruined castles. The history.'

'OK. I just wondered. How about you, Eileen? Would you like to live here?'

Eileen giggles. 'I'm trying to imagine it, but I just can't. Let me see.' She closes her eyes for a moment, scrunches up her face in concentration. 'Nope. I can't see it at all. I can't see Doug here, either. Whatever would he do?'

Keith eyes her curiously but says nothing.

We have been walking for a mere ten minutes when a vast winged shape drops out of the sky. As it swings towards us, we bob down in an automatic response. The shape bounces off Eileen's head. She lets out a shriek. The caracara launches off again, her woolly hat in its talons.

Daisy has whipped out her phone and is tracking the bird with her lens, laughing and yelling, 'Stop, thief!'

Eileen isn't laughing, though. Her face is drained of colour. The curls on her head are in shocked disarray, as if they have been violently fighting amongst themselves. She puts her hands up to them slowly. Her fingers come away covered in blood.

# 30

# Eileen

*Bolder Island*

I TELL THEM I'm OK and I am, really. Well, I am and I'm not.

It's more shock than anything. The pain stings but I've known worse. And I'm a bit upset about that hat, which was one that took me a while to knit and was cosy and pretty colours. Maybe the wicked bird will drop it, but I don't think so. He's disappeared off into the sky. He'll be already feeding it to the other wicked birds, I expect.

I'm bleeding from my scalp but it must look worse than it is. A little trickle of blood keeps running down my forehead. I'm surrounded by anxious faces who help lower me on to a stone. I fumble in my backpack.

'The first aid kit's in here.'

I've been carrying it around with me everywhere in

case Mrs McCreedy has a fall, but now I can't find it. I pass the backpack to Terry but she can't find it either. Then I remember I didn't put the kit in this afternoon because this is just a local walk and I'd thought to myself, I don't need to lug all that around, but I should have known better. I should always, always have it with me. I never imagined I'd be the one in need of it.

The blood is beginning to clot in my hair.

'Oh, please, don't stop,' I tell the others. Daisy wants to find Tony and Mrs McCreedy is wanting to get in another mile. 'I'll just make my way slowly back to the lodge and find my TCP wipes and put my feet up for a bit.'

'Keith will come back, too,' says Keith in that funny way he's got of talking about himself as if he were somebody else. 'You shouldn't be on your own after a shock like that.' I laugh, slightly manically.

Terry and Patrick start saying they'll come back as well, but then they see Mrs McCreedy is keen to press onwards and so's Daisy, and they realize it might not be clever to leave her alone in the wilds with a young child and all these dangerous creatures around.

So it ends up being just Keith and me. He chats away about his life here, the sheep, the lodge, the seasons, the few social occasions, the vastness.

I tell him about Doug and how he never really liked that hat. I did, though, but what does it matter because I can always knit another once I'm home, and maybe Keith knows somewhere in the Falklands where I can buy one in the meantime because sunburn can be a menace and the Antarctic will be terribly cold and hats serve a lot of purposes, don't they, and what a shame the bird theft didn't happen before Daisy and I went to Stanley because that would've been an ideal opportunity to buy a new one. I am gabbling; I don't know why.

Then we get to the lodge and my head does feel rather sore, to be honest. Keith says I should sit down in the front room, so that's what I do. He says: 'Keith will have you fixed in no time.'

'Keith is very good at sorting out other people's problems, isn't he?' I mutter thoughtfully, but he has already gone in search of the first aid kit and doesn't hear me. He is back a moment later. He gently dabs the dried blood from my hair, and the pungent smell of TCP fills the room.

'This really needs a bandage or plaster. In order to get it on, I'd have to shave off a little patch of your hair, though.'

'Oh gosh, no, I don't want that.'

'It would be a shame,' he says, fingering a curl then letting go of it again quickly. It may be that it's stabbed him (my hair isn't softly ringleted like it used to be; it's become brittle and crunchy) ... or maybe he's worried about being forward, as if he hasn't just spent the last ten minutes in very close contact with the rest of the top of my head.

'Well, I expect it'll be fine,' he says. 'You look pretty healthy. I bet you're a good self-healer, Eileen.'

Somehow, the way he says my name triggers something. I'm coming over all peculiar. My emotions are clumped together in a tangled mess and whirling around like they're in a washing machine set on fast spin. That's

255

fine, so long as I keep the washing machine door firmly closed.

So I focus hard on grabbing random little rags of thoughts that come to me, and I end up chattering about the time I twisted my ankle in the rockery at The Ballahays and how it swelled up like a balloon and Mr Perkins had to take me to A & E, and how it was a problem because I couldn't stand up much and Doug would be wanting his dinner and I didn't think there was a ready-made in the fridge.

Keith is crouching on the floor beside my chair, listening. His eyes are fixed on mine, steady and chocolate-brown and full of kindness. I peter out.

Then (and I don't know how it happens because I thought I'd got a grip on myself) all of a sudden my face becomes an explosion of tears. I'm bawling just like Daisy was the other day. Heat surges up my neck, moisture gathers on my skin and I know I'm turning an awful shade of crimson.

Keith's face has gone wobbly. But his voice comes clear and kind.

'What's the matter? Oh, please tell me what it is, Eileen?'

I gulp, try to make sense of it. Squeeze my palms into my eyes. 'Ignore me. It's nothing. Nothing at all.'

He puts his hand on my knee. Even though I've got my waterproof trousers on over my thick leggings, I feel the comfort of that hand.

'It's clearly *not* nothing,' he says.

I try again, and the truth spills out in a strangled sob. 'It's because you're interested in me!' I take a gulp of air and look down at his hand, which is hairy at the knuckles. 'It makes me come over all panicky and emotional. You're interested in me, and I'm just not used to it. Nobody is ever interested in me.'

'I'm sure that's not true.'

'Oh, but it is. You've no idea. They wish me well, I know that, but it's not the same as being interested, is it? And I can't really blame them, that's the thing. I've never been magnificent and glamorous, like Mrs McCreedy, or sunny and cute like Daisy, or brave and clever like Terry, or bouncy and witty like Patrick. I've always been a nothing. A no one. A splodge of meaningless padding.'

'Stop right there, Eileen. You're spouting rubbish.'

'Am I? I don't think I am. Even my own husband finds me dull.' I'm wringing with tears again.

I clamp my eyes shut to try to stem the flow. I wish the ground would swallow me up. Wish I could behave like a sensible being. I feel so ridiculous. I can imagine Mrs McCreedy saying, 'Pull yourself together, Eileen. Don't be absurd.'

I drag in deep, long breaths, count to ten in my head, forwards and then backwards. I do the things that normally cheer me up, like imagining 'All Things Bright And Beautiful' played on the organ and my plastic sunflower jiggling away.

It's gone silent and the weight of Keith's hand isn't on my knee any more. I wonder if he's still there. He's probably gone off, because men don't like you saying how you feel, do they? And they really hate it if you cry.

I open one eye a crack, and see he's gone. But then his big form comes lumbering back towards me, dragging up

257

a chair. He plants himself beside me and presses a warm mug between my hands.

'Tea,' he says. 'And let's talk. Properly. You tell me what's going on in that good, good heart of yours.'

So I take a big gulp of tea and I do talk. He asked, so it's his fault. I'm blooming well going to take the opportunity.

I tell him how I keep fretting for Mrs McCreedy because I've found out that Pip is dead, and I know she adores, just *adores* that little penguin. She has known grief before (haven't we all?) and she's always so strong, but this is a different kind of relationship and it's sort of symbolic for her. Almost like that bird is her baby.

'It worries me, that's all,' I say.

'That's all?' he echoes.

So I tell him it isn't quite all. I've got this niggle deep down in my gut about Daisy. I do wonder if there's something wrong with her, even though she says there isn't, bless her. We've still got masses of walking and masses of travelling to go, and will she be OK? And what if she isn't?

Keith nods and seems to expect more. So I tell him about my life in Scotland, dashing from home to The Ballahays and back again like a ping-pong ball. At The Ballahays writing things down in Mrs McCreedy's diary, making appointments, mopping floors, polishing silver, dusting tea sets, topping up the stocks of ginger thins, putting out the recycling, and then at home making sure there's always a fridge full of food, too, and some clean laundry. I tell him how, between looking after Doug and looking after Mrs McCreedy, I always feel pulled about. Even here, even on this mission, I feel pulled about, only now it's between Daisy and Mrs McCreedy. And I say how nobody ever really notices me except perhaps for Fiona.

'She's my friend from choir,' I explain.

'So you sing in a choir? How fabulous!'

And I look at Keith, awestruck. 'You see? Interested!'

'Only interested because you are interesting, Eileen. Yes, you are,' he insists, before I can deny it. 'Others don't see it, by the sounds of things, but you really are.'

'If you say so.'

'I do say so. You're kind and true and funny and brave. Yes, you *are* brave,' he insists, before I can deny it. 'And if anyone treats you badly or judges you wrongly, that's their problem not yours.'

'Oh, you mustn't get me wrong. They're always very lovely to me. I shouldn't grumble, I really shouldn't. It's just that I feel . . .' How do I feel? I'm not even sure any more. I gulp down another swig of tea.

I'm surprised that Keith hasn't started reading a paper or something.

He seems to be thinking. I'm not looking at him, I'm looking hard at my mug, but from the corner of my eye I see him pushing up his sleeves as if he's decided on something and means business.

'You mustn't take it personally when people take you for granted and don't appreciate everything that you do, everything that you are, Eileen. People are all about themselves. Fighting their own battles. Wrapped up with their own issues. I suspect Mrs McCreedy is brimming with them. And no doubt Daisy has hers, too. That's why the two of them aren't so sensitive towards you at the moment. It's a compliment in a way, because it shows they trust you. They know you're there for them. You are rock solid. They can depend on you, and that is the one thing they don't ever need to worry about.'

I certainly never saw it like that before. 'Gosh. Thank you.'

I venture to look at Keith again, at his weather-beaten skin, his gentle chocolatey eyes, his eyebrows that are crooking upwards.

'As for your husband. Well, I don't know about that, but I'd say he was a . . .'

'A what?' I ask quickly. I'm curious as to what he was about to say. Hoping it might be 'lucky man'.

But Keith doesn't answer.

# 31
# Veronica

*Stanley, East Falkland*

I AM NOT in velvet robes, alas. But I am elegant in a skirt-and-jacket suit, in the plush reds of the McCreedy tartan. I add the finishing touches at the hotel in Stanley where we are now staying; my red woollen wrap, my shiniest hand-bag and my most striking ruby lipstick.

This is a proud day indeed. What would my dear father have thought if he saw me now, about to be awarded this high honour? He would have taken a thoughtful puff on his Woodbine and said, 'Well, I never! Look what has become of our little Very.'

I hope he would have acknowledged that I have, in my way, contributed towards making the world a better place. And my mother (who always said I would be an

261

explorer when I grew up) – she would have laughed that joyous, tinkling laugh of hers.

And my son? If we had not been torn apart, if he had lived long enough to see this day?

I allow myself a sigh for all that might have been.

Still, there are some left who are dear to me, who are here to support me, who even manage to love me . . . and I could never have said that three years ago.

My grandson walks at my side, head high, shortening his strides to match mine.

'All right there, soon-to-be First Penguin Lady?'

I nod.

Pride emanates from him. I am fiercely proud of him, too, of how he dragged himself out of the deprived mire of his childhood, took risks, made mistakes but finally made something of himself.

'Nervous?' he asks.

'Not in the least.'

However, there is adrenalin aplenty, and anticipation. My only concern about the event is that, under pressure, my words may evaporate or – worse – mutate into other words that convey a completely different meaning. Still, I have practised repeatedly in my head and before the mirror, and I know that presenting an issue I am passionate about is one of my fortes. One could call it a fortissimo.

Daisy squeezes my hand and reaches up to whisper in my ear. 'One day I'm going to be a Penguin Ambassador too.'

I squeeze her hand back.

'That's my girl.'

Today three huge cruise ships loom in the harbour. They have disgorged a host of tourists into the normally tranquil streets. Heads turn to look at me as I stride forward with my entourage.

The grand ceremony does not take place at the Anglo-Antarctic Research Council headquarters itself, but in a substantial hall in one of the government buildings. A flock of people is gathered outside, and the room itself is jam-packed. A couple of hassled-looking men are scrambling to put out extra chairs.

My fingers close around my handbag straps. Eileen and Daisy, Terry, Patrick and Keith take their places in the front row. I think of Sir Robert, who is not here, who will doubtless now be in a swirl of Antarctic snow, and I wonder if he is sparing a thought for me at this moment, too.

A chair has been put out for me in the wings and I wait. Preliminaries include a long-winded preamble by a tedious bearded man and a five-minute talk from Terry about scientific research on Locket Island. She is far too meek, if you ask me. It is a mistake I shall not make.

My name is called. I march on stage amidst thunderous clapping. I do not use my stick. With all this press coverage, image is important, and I wish to come across as empowered, not enfeebled.

Daisy is filming everything with her phone.

I smile graciously as I am presented with my sash (thankfully red) and the award. Terry and Patrick cheer, and Patrick gives a shrill whistle that zizzes through my hearing aid.

The award itself is a small wooden shield embossed with a silver penguin and some words I can't make out because I am not wearing my reading spectacles. I park it, along with my handbag, on the very useful small table that has been placed between the two chairs on the stage. I indicate to the bearded man, whose name I have not registered, to sit down. I remain standing.

I turn to the microphone, clear my throat. 'I am deeply honoured to accept this award. It would not be an exaggeration to say that I never expected my life to pan out this way. I would like to thank the Anglo-Antarctic Research Council for their commendable work preserving penguins and their environment.'

I pause, and gaze around the room at the upturned faces, the hands poised to clap again. They think I have finished, but no, oh no, there is plenty more to say.

'I would like to take this opportunity to announce the action I am taking in my new role as Penguin Ambassador. I am currently engaged in Operation PIP – Penguins In Peril. This comprises a sponsored walk to save a sea life centre that is local to me, in Scotland. Lochnamorghy is the home of two dozen penguins, whose lives are in the balance.'

If I had Daisy's technological abilities, I would have magicked up a series of endearing photographs here, but my only mode of persuasion is vocabulary and a certain stage presence.

'I do not walk alone,' I continue, 'but in the company of two exceptional human beings. Would you be kind enough to stand, Eileen and Daisy?'

Daisy springs to her feet, and Eileen stands up beside her, promptly pinkening as all eyes swivel towards them.

'As you see, we are a trio of feisty females of three

different generations. You may sit,' I add to Eileen and Daisy, who oblige. Daisy resumes filming.

'Our walk, within this calendar month, will total a hundred miles, as a tribute to the march of the Emperor penguins. Had we been three strong young lads, this would be no challenge at all. But we are disadvantaged by our bodies – too old, too young, too middle-aged; and altogether too female. Which only goes to prove that we are mentally far stronger. Aside from our ages, we three have numerous other disparities, and we have already overcome several challenges. However, we share much common ground – pun intended' – here there is a murmur of polite laughter –, 'and we also share a special quality. We are witnessing how penguins of different species have evolved to live in extremes, from the equator to the South Pole. We, too, have that vital ability to change as our environment changes, to adapt as circumstances demand.'

I sense approbation wafting up from the audience. But also doubt.

'You may think, looking at me, that I am incapable and deluded. You are wrong. You will, perhaps, appreciate my utter commitment when you learn that I have just sold my house, my own beloved home, in order to buy Lochnamorghy.'

I turn my eyes towards Terry and Patrick, who are spectacularly failing to hide their horror. They exchange glances in consternation, frown at me, but there is nothing they can do. It is, in its own way, quite entertaining.

'At this juncture you may conclude that I have gone doolally, dotty, bananas in pyjamas. You are wrong there, too,' I announce, addressing the audience as a whole. 'I absolutely must sell my home if I am to save those twenty-four penguins. I also need to complete this walk to guarantee their well-being and safety in the future. I have discussed exactly how to run the centre with my dear friend Sir Robert Saddlebow . . .' – this has the desired effect, as a murmur of admiration ripples through the room – 'and we are agreed on the basics. The other animals (apart from one elderly octopus, who may stay) have already been rehomed in various wildlife parks and zoos; this will leave more space for the penguins. In the future, Lochnamorghy will be solely devoted to penguins, but we will not operate alone. Following Terry's introduction, you will know I have close links with the penguin project of Locket Island in Antarctica. In addition, I have newer links with penguin conservationists in the Galápagos, and, from my former filming duties, with Ginty Island in Australia, where scientists are studying Little penguins. And, of course, I have links with you, here in the Falklands.' I motion towards Keith, who nods encouragingly. 'All of us will liaise and support each other. By forging more connections with penguin researchers worldwide, we can help each other ensure that penguins stay on our planet.

'I am proposing to make my Scottish penguin site not only a sanctuary for its flippered residents, but also a centre for citizen science, where members of the public can help monitor penguins in all these places. In my day, an apple was a fruit, a mouse was a small, furry creature, an iPad was something you wore if you had an ophthalmic condition and online was where you put your washing. These days everything is very different. Why, you can even hold all your memories in a stick.' I would bang my stick on the floor at this point but I have left it in the wings. 'I am not wildly enamoured with the digital age, it has to be said, but it has brought us this advantage: we can now sit in an armchair in Ayrshire whilst counting penguins in Antarctica. I have spent much of my life operating in isolation, but I am beginning to realize that as a team we are stronger.' Here I look at Daisy, who beams back at me, and at Eileen, who is fanning herself, a little dewy-eyed.

'Once more, I would like to thank the Anglo-Antarctic Research Council for the honour of this ambassadorship. Now, with your support, I can make it truly meaningful. We have so far raised thirteen thousand, six hundred and thirty-seven pounds, but we need so much more. Monies from my house sale will be enough to buy the centre, but not enough to sustain it for long. Will you assist us in this vital fundraising effort? Will you help us rescue the penguins?'

I view the sea of faces and see that I have caught their attention, caught their imagination. Possibly even caught their hearts.

The tedious bearded man stands and starts to rattle out thanks, in a hurry for his post-event drinks and nibbles. With a swift hand gesture, I silence him. He sits down again.

'We have already covered eighty-one miles,' I announce, 'and we shall not go back home. Not yet. We shall go on. The remainder of our long trek will take place in Antarctica.' I pause to allow this to sink in. There are several gasps.

'It has been hard, and it will be harder still. We have

already experienced the vicissitudes of diverse climes. We have walked in the beating sun and the drenching rain and the swirling winds. We have walked in our homeland, in the northern hills, beside the Scottish sea. We have walked the equatorial forests and volcanic plains of the Galápagos. We have walked the contours of your beautiful Falkland Islands. We have walked on the beaches, we have walked on the clifftops,' I proclaim, aware of a Churchillian bent to my phraseology which I hope adds weightiness. 'And soon we will walk the frozen wastelands of Antarctica, amidst icebergs and snowdrifts. We will walk amongst the penguins. And we will walk *for* the penguins.'

As if they are a single being, everyone in the room rises to their feet, their clapping a great roar. I beckon Daisy and Eileen up to the stage, and I wish Eileen had put on something glamorous, rather than her chunky jumper and unflattering leggings. But they stumble up and join me, one on either side, and stand there, facing the crowds.

'If anyone would like to sponsor us, Eileen will take your details. This is an unusual project but an important one, so any donation will be of immense value. Any questions?'

A hand shoots up. A skinny woman in a bright-blue anorak, one of the cruise ship contingent. 'We're so impressed by you and everything you are doing. But is it really sensible for you three to go walking in Antarctica? As you mentioned, you are' – she simpers – '*no spring chicken*. And the girl . . .' Her eyes veer towards Daisy.

'Do not fear for our safety,' I reply. 'We have all the necessary gear, plus experts on hand, and, what is more, we are – all three of us – equipped with unstinting deter-mination. The Emperors were the inspiration for this challenge and it is fitting that we finish it amongst them, in Antarctica. Any further questions?'

Another hand rises slowly.

'Yes, Terry?'

'As I understand it, you put your house on the market to secure your offer on the sea life centre, not actually intending to sell. With all the extra support you've gained today, surely you won't be needing this extra sacrifice of The . . . of your home?'

Her face is etched with worry. A shroud of doubt falls across my own heart. Is it conceivable that we might raise sufficient monies to maintain both The Ballahays and the sea life centre? But I have already accepted the offer on my home. And, although my faults are legion, I am a woman of my word. Besides, hundreds of people are watching for my reaction, and this is my moment to show them how deeply, how passionately, the very first Pen-guin Ambassador cares for penguins.

'It is indeed a vast sacrifice, and I am aggrieved to lose my beautiful home,' I acknowledge. 'But' – and I raise my voice, imbue it with as much force as I can muster – 'this is insignificant compared with the great penguin rescue.'

It is out there now, in the public, and there is no going back. Once again the crowd erupts into tumultuous applause. I take a bow, rather overwhelmed by my own magnanimity, fortitude and heroism. I ignore the dark shadow of the Ballahays-less future and bask in the glow of admiration that illuminates this present moment.

Terry doesn't say anything more. I suppose she's

digesting the new information. At her side, Patrick just looks shell-shocked.

The minute I step off the stage I am surrounded by a swarm of people wanting to sponsor us. I refer them to Eileen, who enters names into her database. She has to enlist the help of Terry, Patrick and Keith, who eventually get hold of a couple of clipboards so that people can leave their own names and details, with promises of money towards our cause.

'If you weren't famous already, Mrs McCreedy, you surely will be after this,' whispers Eileen.

# 32

# Veronica

*Stanley, East Falkland*

'NEVER BE AFRAID of growing old, Daisy. It is quite marvellous. You can get away with absolutely anything.'

'Uh-huh.' She is unconvinced.

I, however, am positively effervescing. It is most fortunate that my speech occurred on a day when Stanley was seething with tourists. They are perfect for our purposes; they adore travel, they love penguins, and they are not pecuniarily constrained. We now have thousands more sponsors. Some individuals have donated hundreds of pounds. Success at last feels within reach, and my thrill knows no bounds.

Together with the bigwigs of the Anglo-Antarctic Research Council, we pose and smile for the press until our jaws ache. After which we move on to a grand tea party, where small talk, fudge cake and finger sand-wiches circulate. The cacophony in my hearing aid makes such gatherings irksome, but I graciously put up with it. Daisy enjoys a great deal of attention. She is looking particularly endearing in a carnation-pink mini-dress, a glittery comb in her hair. Of course she is now perceived (quite correctly) as a little heroine in her own right. It is wonderful to see her looking so happy again. Eileen, too, possesses a new air of confidence that becomes her well.

What of her and Doug, I wonder? She still seems to be contacting him at every opportunity, which is ominous because it gives him no opportunity to miss her.

'Is your husband following Daisy's blogs?' I ask.

'Oh, of course he is. He will be, for sure, yes.'

I put in a request to Daisy: that she publish in her blog the photo of Keith and Eileen in cahoots together on the beach.

'But there's other much better ones,' she protests.

'All the same, I would be grateful if you could include that one,' I say, fixing her with a stare that will brook no further argument.

'Whatever,' she replies, with a shrug.

The only blight on the occasion is the attitude of my grandson. Patrick seems unable to forgive me for selling The Ballahays. In his opinion I have been rash and impul-sive. The McCreedy way has ever been to leap first, look later, and I would have thought Patrick would be the first to understand this. I suppose he'd assumed The Ballahays would pass down to him in time, which indeed was the plan before the emergence of Operation PIP. I overhear him discussing it with Terry, and the words 'fricking loony thing to do' filter through the cacophony, accompanied by a daggers look in my direction.

I elbow my way towards him, then declare pointedly: 'Well, that was a resounding success.'

However, congratulations are not flooding my way. He is the only one who refuses to acknowledge the brilliance of my speech.

'It always has to be so extreme with you, doesn't it?' he growls. And then, under his breath: 'You can't run a fricking sea life centre from a fricking care home.'

I am deeply affronted, but Terry leaps in to pour salve on the situation. She, at least, is unstinting in her praise of my speech. She does not refer to the house sale.

Refreshments finished, we are transported by bus, together with the aforementioned officials, to a local bay where a colony of Gentoos and a colony of Kings are both known to frequent the shoreline. I am escorted to the prime penguin area and we pose for yet more photographs, surrounded by penguins. The photographs and the news story, I am assured, will be distributed throughout the press both locally and in the United Kingdom. I hope that Sir Robert will see the coverage online at some point, or perhaps in print on his return to Britain.

The officials depart again via bus. Terry and Patrick go, too, in order to purchase various items of equipment for the Locket Island research station. Eileen, Daisy and I are left with Keith, who is keen to accompany us on our daily walk, for walk we must. It will be easier to cover miles now than in the bitter Antarctic conditions that lie ahead.

Keith, rather charmingly, presents Eileen with a new

hat (which would explain why he popped into one of the Stanley shops on his way to the ceremony). It is thick and woolly, in yellow and turquoise, with penguins marching round the edge and a pom-pom on top. Eileen receives it with astonished glee.

'Well, you'll need one for Antarctica,' he says, 'and I felt bad, seeing as it was my caracara that stole your old one.'

'*Your* caracara!' she chuckles, pulling the hat over her curls.

We use the local facilities – there is a small hut with conveniences beside the track – to change into more practical garb. Then we walk, drinking in the sparkly air and the glory of all that has occurred this morning.

The beach is spread with penguins and gulls, pottering on the sand amidst an assortment of rock formations. The fine views across the water to the other islands are marred only by the presence of the vast cruise ships. The passengers have been called back on board by now, however, so we have the site to ourselves. Keith and Eileen stroll on ahead, deep in conversation. They seem to have a lot to say to each other. It occurs to me that they are getting on like the proverbial house on fire. Evidently they share a mutual admiration. Attraction, even.

'Ha! Put that in your pipe and smoke it!' I bark to an imaginary Doug, who I wish was here to see it, although I do not, obviously, say the words out loud.

Daisy and I pause to view a pair of Gentoos who skid clumsily down from the dunes then waddle in circles around each other, their feet slapping the sand.

'Can I take a picture of you standing by that long rock,

Veronica?' Daisy asks. 'Please,' she adds, remembering the magic word before she has to be prompted.

I am in a good humour, and grateful to Daisy, whose charm has undoubtedly contributed to the success of the morning. The stone is very smooth, rounded and glazed with water. My scarlet attire will show up well against its mottled greys. I go and stand in front of it, holding my handbag and trusting that my hair and make-up are still impeccable.

I am aware, suddenly, of a yelp coming from Daisy. Simultaneously, from the corner of my eye, I catch a movement behind me.

I turn my head. The stone is moving, expanding, rearing up.

It is not a stone, but a gigantic monster, towering over me. From a bewhiskered face, a pair of bulbous eyes fixes on me. A huge orifice of a mouth stretches open, and for a second I look into a chasm edged with pointed, yellowing teeth. The oversized head then disappears upwards beyond a mass of slithering grey body. The sheer density of that body is impressive, enormous, appalling. And it is bearing down on top of me.

Time freezes. Thoughts rush through my brain:

- *I'm about to be entirely flattened, crushed, pulped, and nothing will remain of me but a Veronica-shaped stew pressed into the sand.*
- *It is not good for a child as young as Daisy to witness so violent a death of somebody close to her.*
- *How galling that our mission must come to this*

275

*premature and ignominious end, and before we
have even reached Antarctica.*

- *At least the press managed to get some excellent
photographs first.*
- *This will make an exceptionally shocking news
story, and it may be enough to save the penguins
of Lochnamorghy anyway.*
- *Still, I do not want to die just now because I have
actually begun to relish life.*
- *Just how grief-stricken will Sir Robert be about this?*
- *This is going to hurt and I won't like it.*
- *I should run but I am so shocked that I am completely unable to move.*

My eyes have become blurry. Nevertheless, certain
facts are lining up and I find myself observing them as if I
am a spectator:

. . . that this is the end . . .

. . . that something is shrieking . . .

. . . that there is a familiar blobby shape catapulting
towards me . . .

. . . that I am jolted out of the way just as the creature
plummets down and hits the ground with a *thunk* on to
the exact spot where I was standing a split second
earlier . . .

. . . that I am floundering in the damp sand . . .

. . . that a hot human body is pressed against me . . .

. . . that the giant sea lion is now galumphing into the
waves, moving at an alarming rate . . .

. . . that I have been saved from certain death . . .

. . . by Eileen.

All of this has happened too fast for my body to process, but now I start shaking violently. Eileen is gazing at me, the pupils of her eyes tiny dots in two white full moons. She starts spurting words.

'Oh my goodness, Mrs McCreedy. Oh wow. Oh Lorks. That was close. Thank the Lord I happened to look back at you when I did. Oh gosh, gosh, gosh. How are you? Are you all right? I think it's gone now. What a whopper! Oh, my heart.'

She lapses into heavy panting.

We are still entangled in a heap. I am sore and sandy but decidedly grateful to be alive. I am unable to get up, however.

Daisy comes pelting towards us. Her shrieking evolves into short, jagged words that no ten-year-old ought to know. She sinks to her knees, quite overcome.

I manage to pull myself into a semi-supine position and scrape the sand off my left cheek, where it has scratchily lodged itself. Alas, my very favourite handbag has been ruined by countless criss-cross abrasions.

Eileen has now sat up, too. Keith is here, stooping low, offering strong arms. Once the four of us are upright we still need to steady each other. Our embrace is heartfelt, grateful, intense ... and a little painful around the ribcage. Penguins look on.

Apparently, at this time of year the male sea lions tend to be bellicose, and possessive over their territory. This one, though, was doubtless just taken by surprise, as was I.

Luckily, the mobile signal on the beach was sufficient for Keith to arrange for us to be picked up, and we are now back at the hotel. Terry and Patrick are yet to return from the shops, Daisy is writing up her blog and Eileen is in the bath. She was anxious about me, but I refused to see a doctor. The left side of my body is a little bashed and purpling in places, but it is my foot that is the main cause for concern. Keith, who has studied first aid, has carefully checked it over, and assures me that it is not broken. My ankle has been twisted badly, though.

'You should keep it up and not walk on it for a day, Mrs McCreedy.'

I cannot afford to do this. Whilst the terrain is hospitable we must walk, walk, walk. I explain this to Keith, and he binds my ankle very tightly with bandages.

'What with Eileen's head and my foot and Daisy's phone, we have been a considerable trial to you, young man,' I comment.

He smiles at the 'young man', doubtless seeing himself as ancient. 'You have, all three of you, been a great change in an otherwise pretty samey life,' he replies. 'Try walking around the room now.'

I gently shift my weight on to my feet, start to hobble.

'No, wait,' he interjects. 'Pedometer. Every single step counts.'

'You are quite right. Would you be so kind as to pass me my scarlet handbag? I believe it is in there.'

He does so, and my tottering steps start to add up again, but it is painful.

'Is it cheating if you lean on somebody's arm?' he asks. 'Keith's arm is right here at your service.'

'Why, thank you, Keith's arm, and, indeed, Keith. I believe a little support is allowed, according to the rulebook.'

'Is there a rulebook?'

'No, not as such. But we must be transparent in all our actions, especially now that the paparazzi have seized upon the story and are sniffing around. They must be informed of what has happened, but also assured that we will absolutely continue with Operation PIP. The news is somewhat dramatic, and will possibly help our cause,' I muse. 'We should include the photograph that Daisy took before the sea lion struck. A press release will suffice, emailed out to as many papers as possible from the hotel. I shall ask Eileen to do it.'

The small pause that follows is tinged with accusation.

'Eileen does a lot for you, doesn't she? Maybe it would be kind to give her a break?'

It is my turn to insert a pause, and this one is packed with sly insinuation.

'Ah,' I say finally.

At this suggestive monosyllable he hastens on. 'Maybe Keith could send the press release? I'm not brilliant at that sort of thing, but I'm willing to give it a go and I'm sure Patrick would help me.' He tips his head to one side, having second thoughts about Patrick's eloquence. 'Or Terry.'

'By all means, do that. I'm sure Terry will cast her eye over it and supply expert advice. She is a blog-writer extraordinaire and has experience in publicizing scientific projects. But I very much doubt you will keep Eileen out of it, even if you wish to . . . And I'm not convinced that you do.'

What a rare and satisfying pleasure it is to provoke blushes in a middle-aged man.

279

# Daisy's Penguin Blog

## THE PENGUIN AWARDS . . . AND A SCARY THING

Veronica is now the first Penguin Ambassador! See link to her speech in full. See pictures.

But she nearly didn't last very long. See next pictures.

EILEEN IS A HERO!

The sea lion was so big you wouldn't believe it. His head was massive and he had a mane like a lion. Just. So. Scary.

Veronica has a new shiny sash and award.

If I was going to give my own awards to the Falklands penguins, they'd be like this:

Funniest penguin: Southern rockhoppers. Because they're hilariously bouncy.

Oddest penguin: Magellanics. Because they pop out of holes in the ground like rabbits and they make loud *eeyore* noises like donkeys.

Prettiest penguin: Kings. Because they have beautiful golden yellows on their head and neck.

Craziest penguin: Gentoos. Because the parents make the chicks chase them for food so they'll get strong.

And they run round and round and sometimes trip over, the sillies.

Bravest penguin: Macaronis. There aren't many here, apart from Tony, and they usually nest with their friends, the rockhoppers. They remind me of Mac, who is so unbelievably brave, not knowing if he's going to live or die. PLEASE SPONSOR US, EVERYONE!

More than a million penguins live on the Falkland Islands. I love it and I wish we had longer here . . . but one day I'll be back.

Next stop: Antarctica!

# 33

# Veronica

*In transit*

WE HAVE MADE our fond farewells. We have flown above
the islands one last time, waving goodbye to Keith and to
Tony-the-Macaroni, to the other people and penguins we
have met here, to the distant outline of Bolder Island, to
the rooftop mosaic of Stanley, to the ragged jigsaw of
land and sea that makes up the Falklands. We have
pointed south-west, towards the tip of the Americas. We
have shot through the sky, conquering another 413 miles
(precious few of them on foot) and descended upon
Ushuaia, the world's southernmost city.

From there we boarded a ship. Together with a gaggle
of intrepid tourists from far-flung places, we were presented with safety briefings and champagne. Eileen, quite
overcome with it all, accepted her champagne flute with

trembling hands. Daisy's eyes sparkled as she took her permitted small sip that turned into a rather large slurp. Standing on a chilly deck, we raised our glasses to the continued success of Operation PIP. Terry and Patrick joined us in the toast, although Patrick has continued to be surly with me since learning of The Ballahays' sale.

We now make our nests in assorted cabins. They are narrow nooks, each with a single porthole; far too confined for my tastes, but I must adapt (who knows where I will end up living? Cramped conditions might become my new normality). Eileen and Daisy share whilst I, thankfully, have one to myself. I potter about, checking the cleanliness of the bed linen, unpacking my negligee, corn plasters and tea, extracting a lavender sachet from between the neat folds of my smalls and wafting it around the room, for there is nothing that makes one feel at home like the scent of lavender.

Terry and Patrick, of course, have done this journey many times before. They are even now chatting with other researchers whom they have met on board. Daisy has rallied greatly after the resounding success of the ambassadorship ceremony and is thrilled to have reached this most marvellous leg of the journey. She has been clingy with me since the sea lion episode, though, wanting to support me everywhere, and I have had to be firm with her about needing my own space. Eileen seems well, too. She told me coyly that Keith promised to come and meet us in Ushuaia on our return journey, despite the scarcity of time available before our homeward flight. It shows an astonishing level of commitment and friendship. What if romance were to bloom between those two?

She could do a lot worse . . . but the distance! And I can imagine neither Keith adapting to life in Scotland nor Eileen adapting to life on Bolder Island. If she did, in some parallel universe, establish herself in the Falklands, whatever would I do without her? Independent as I am, I have become so accustomed to her being around that I baulk at the very idea.

Once I have settled my belongings to my satisfaction, I venture outside again. My ankle is mostly healed now, having been rested during the flights, and I am able to make good progress with the help of my stick, even if at a slower pace than usual. I set my pedometer and tread the distance from my cabin to the lower observation deck. I gaze back at South America's craggy, gradually diminishing mountains, then drag myself up the steps to the top deck. Stick tap-tapping on the boards, I walk until I am at the very front of the ship.

I face the future. It is glassy, silver-white and enormous.

The wind whips the sea. And now I can taste the sharpness of Antarctic air as it charges through my nostrils and into my lungs. And with that extra shiver of cold comes another shiver; one of longing, of excitement. It intensifies as I stand in the blast, and as we glide onwards, fragments of the past whirl around my mind like snowflakes: a harder, icier Veronica McCreedy – the Veronica of two years ago – staring out to Locket Island and taking in that jagged skyline for the first time. Two figures on the shore. The research station, a dark oblong in the white snowscape. The sting of not being wanted counterbalanced by the strong compulsion to stay. Penguins, five thousand Adélie penguins, spread over the valley like a rippling black-and-white quilt. Entering their ranks and wandering amongst them, Terry at my side. The emotion. The awe-inspiring vastness and the shock of my own minuteness. Then the close-knit trio of scientists, the arguments, the compromises. The finding – oh, the finding – of Pip, my dearest Pip, a mere wisp of a creature on the outskirts of the penguin city, abandoned and starving. His tiny flippers, tiny feet, tiny, fluffed, drooping head. My urge to save him. His will to live. *To live.*

It is Pip who has been inspiring me every day, ever since. It seems absurd that a human life should be transformed by the life of a single penguin chick a world's width away, but it is so.

I sniff. There it is, that Antarctic tang again, pouring into me.

Pip will surely return to Locket Island soon. I feel that all will be well if only I can see Pip again. He will give me the strength to go on, as he did before, no matter that I am losing my home, no matter if my indisputably ambitious plans are thwarted, no matter what else happens. Pip will ensure that I carry on.

Hours pass. The sea is a sequinned shawl. The ship drifts onwards, our course following in the historic wake of Charles Darwin and HMS *Beagle*. In the meantime we feast sumptuously, read and sleep. When night arrives it is crystalline and cloudless. We are able to make out the constellation of the Southern Cross suspended above us in the velvet darkness, spilt glitter in a sea of yet more glitter. Each speck seems so modest, refuting its real identity: that of a gigantic sun, fiercely spewing flames, separated by millions of light years.

'It's beautiful. Do you think my new phone can get it?' Daisy asks.

'You can try, dear,' Eileen replies.

But her gizmo, clever though it may be, is quite unequal to the task.

During daylight hours, lectures are provided. They are presented by scholarly types with name badges pinned to their chests and miniature microphones wrapped around their faces. I attend most of these, although I find my head lolling at times and I cannot guarantee that my eyes remain open during all of them. We learn about tectonic plates, marine mammalogy, Antarctic botany, evolutionary science and albatross populations. And, yes, there is a lecture on penguins, during which Daisy has her head bowed as she scribbles notes. Terry and Patrick do not attend much. They have heard these lectures before and seem more interested in chatting with the hard-working Filipino crew who skivvy below.

I like to rise early and take a brisk walk before breakfast. However, I have managed only 153 steps out on deck today, and they were more lurches than steps, since the boat was unsteady and made several attempts to tip me up entirely. I would gladly battle on despite the elements, only I am already somewhat battered and do not wish to dent or damage this flesh-and-bones walking machine any further.

I breakfast alone (where are they all?) and then, with

reluctance, I resign myself to my cabin and my copy of *Tess of the d'Urbervilles*.

No sooner have I put on my spectacles than I realize I haven't yet taken my blood pressure tablets. At least, I think I haven't. The blister pack is labelled by date, but I cannot for the life of me remember whether today is Tuesday or Wednesday. If I had one of those insufferable mobile phones, no doubt it would tell me, but I do not. Eileen normally fulfils the functions it would achieve (and how much better the world would be if we all had a pocket Eileen!). I make my way along the passage to her cabin to consult her.

My steps wend in a zigzag fashion. The walls tip one way and then the other; the floor plummets and rises alternately.

I knock on the cabin door and there is a muted moan from within. Eileen appears at the door.

'Oh, Mrs McCreedy, how are you?'

'Quite fine, Eileen, thank you, but I wish to know if today is Tuesday or Wednesday.'

She puts a hand up and wipes it over her face. 'Wednesday, I think,' she answers faintly. 'Is it Wednesday?' she asks Daisy, who is sprawled on her bunk.

Daisy reaches for her phone. 'Yes, Wednesday. But there's no signal,' she adds, sulkily.

'I just wished to check on account of my medication,' I explain. My eyes go from one of them to the other. They look in need of medication themselves. Daisy is drooped over a heap of pillows and Eileen's complexion is like curdled cream. She emits a low groan.

'Are you unwell?' I ask.

She can only nod.

'It's worse than chemo,' Daisy whimpers, clutching her stomach.

It is only then that I notice the smell, and retreat quickly back to my own cabin.

Very few people are at lunch, and I cannot spot any of my own party, so I take a table by myself.

I am joined soon after by an elderly gentleman who says, 'May I?', indicating the chair opposite me. I tend to eschew the company of strangers, but if you removed his fulsome grey beard, he might somewhat resemble Sir Robert. So I graciously smile and tell him that he may. I am a little tempted to reveal my acquaintance with Sir Robert, which would not fail to impress, and my own status as the first Penguin Ambassador. However, I simply cannot be bothered, so I concentrate instead on my steak au poivre and let him rattle on about his three ex-wives and his far-from-scintillating life in Denver.

However, when the cheesecake arrives, he takes one look at it, dabs his mouth with a serviette and rises to his feet. 'Excuse me, I think I'm going to have to leave.' And with that he weaves his way through the tables and out of the room.

I take up my fork and carve a small piece of cheesecake from the rest. I post it into my mouth. It is quite delectable, with a subtle vanilla flavour, flaked almonds and a drizzle of raspberry coulis. What a shame the others are missing it. I eat meditatively.

I am still dismayed about the bad atmosphere that persists between myself and my grandson. It eclipses all the pleasures of this trip. I regret now that I did not confide in him about The Ballahays before I announced it to the general public. It is imperative that we make our peace before we reach Locket Island.

Cheesecake consumed, I rise to my feet, handbag in hand, resolve in my heart.

My progress is slow due to the constantly bucking floor, but thankfully there are plenty of walls and banisters within reach.

An announcement over the tannoy informs me that this afternoon's lecture on whales is postponed. I arrive at Patrick and Terry's cabin and rap three times on the door with my stick.

At first I think that nobody is within. I'm about to turn and go back again when Patrick appears.

'Ug. Hello, Granny.'

Within a second he has stumbled off to one side and there are spluttering and heaving sounds from the ensuite.

I step into the room. Terry is sitting on the upright chair, but is herself distinctly non-upright. Her pale hair straggles over her shoulders and her body curls in on itself. She takes her head out of her hands to look up at me.ßßß

'Hi, Veronica.' Her voice is empty of its usual enthusiasm.

I perch on the side of the bed, since it is unlikely I will maintain my balance if I remain standing.

'I wish to make things right between me and yourselves,' I begin. 'I have, perhaps, been a little insensitive, and I think we need to discuss what has happened with regard to The Ballahays and my intentions for the future.'

A small gurgle issues from her throat, like rainwater in a distant drainpipe.

I am about to continue when I am interrupted by the roar of the flush being used several times in the ensuite, followed by the emergence of Patrick. He is clasping his sides. His brow is slicked with sweat and his face is a ghastly shade of custard.

'Veronica wants to talk about The Ballahays,' Terry murmurs.

Patrick sways drunkenly then sinks on to the bed beside me. 'Not now.'

'I feel that an apology is due. Not from you, from me,' I hasten to explain.

He says nothing, but paws my hand roughly. The contact is welcome, and I place my other hand over his.

'You were no doubt expecting to inherit the fine edifice of my much-loved home, instead of which you will now be inheriting a less physically attractive, but arguably more interesting tourist attraction housing marine life, to wit, twenty-four resident penguins and one elderly octopus.'

Patrick's head moves very slowly and very slightly to one side, as if he is trying to shake it but not managing very well.

'I am hoping – yes, I admit that I am hoping – that the Lochnamorghy centre will continue after I am no more. But I am not thereby trying to force you into an unwelcome situation. My aim is not to put you, as it were, in a tight spot. Plenty of alternative provisions can be made, and you may wish to pass the centre on to other wildlife experts rather than take on the responsibility yourself. Good solicitors can be found to deal with such things.'

I am not getting very much response out of my grandson, so I glance across at Terry. She wobbles to her feet, mumbles, 'Ooops, my turn,' and staggers to the bathroom, slapping a hand across her mouth.

I focus my attention on Patrick again. 'Have you heard what I'm saying?' I ask, expressing myself rather more loudly than usual in case he hasn't.

'Tomorrow,' he mutters, forcing the word out with a huge effort. 'We'll talk about it tomorrow.' His torso slumps into a horizontal position. He yanks his legs up so that he is lying on the bed. He is still wearing his shoes, I note with dismay.

The sea is admittedly choppy today, but I fail to see what is wrong with everybody. It seems I am surrounded by namby-pambies and weaklings. I reason with myself that these youngsters have not lived through a war, as I have.

I arise, disgruntled. The momentum of the ship flings me towards the door.

'Tomorrow, then,' I declare, before it slams shut behind me.

# 34

# Eileen

*In transit*

WE'RE OUT ON deck. My tummy has finally settled down again and so has everyone else's, heaven be praised. We've been pacing up and down because Mrs McCreedy is anxious about the walking schedule.

'I would easily have done three miles on deck yesterday if the wind had only permitted me to stay upright,' she growls.

'I wouldn't have,' Daisy admits. 'I was too ill.'

'You weren't the only one,' Patrick replies, grimacing. 'God, I hate the Drake Passage.'

The Drake Passage is the stretch of water we've just been through, apparently, which Mrs McCreedy calls 'rather choppy'. I'd say it was more than choppy. I'd say it was like riding a supermarket trolley with a missing wheel that's being pulled along by an overexcited kangaroo.

'It's notorious,' Terry explains. 'When it's bad, it's very bad.'

'Are there drakes on it?' Daisy asks.

'No,' Patrick tells her. 'It's named after Sir Francis Drake, the sixteenth-century explorer. But, funnily enough, he never actually sailed this bit. It's the shortest route to Antarctica, but he went via the Strait of Magellan instead – less dangerous, but way longer. But one of his ships drifted southwards and accidentally discovered it.'

I'm just glad that part of the journey is over. Today, the sea is behaving properly and the view is breath-taking. Again, I have that feeling I'm simply not me any more, because Eileen Thompson doesn't do things like this. Maybe she does now, though.

The first iceberg we saw was flat-topped, thick at one end and tapered towards the other. It was just sitting there on the sea like a slab of Brie on a china-blue plate. And now the water beneath the bows has become a white fleece, and the water behind the ship is cut through with a clear, dark line. Now, the icebergs are everywhere, great flocks of them, and so many shapes and sizes: giant towers, and caves and pillars and floating meringues. I'm quite mesmerized by them all. Daisy loves them, too. We have seen our first Antarctic penguins as well – small, beaky figures lined up on the top of one. And then another group, who gathered on the edge and plopped, one by one, into the sea.

'Adélies, they're Adélies, like Pip!' Daisy screamed.

I was excited, too, but at the same time riddled with anxiety because I could see from Mrs McCreedy's expression that she was hoping to meet Pip and I know he's dead and should I say anything? I probably shouldn't. It's for Terry and Patrick to tell her.

I look at them now, as they lean over the side, pointing out seabirds to each other. I wonder if I should mention it. But that would mean admitting I'd overheard the conversation and I don't want them thinking I'm a nosy parker.

The back of a whale breaches the surface of the sea, arcing out then in again. The cold slaps my cheeks, sets my teeth chattering, charges me with oxygen. I huddle in my thermals and woollens. I worry for Mrs McCreedy, but I have to say, she's looking well. She's never been one for smiling much, but when she does you notice it because of all that ruby lipstick.

She's aiming her smile at her grandson now. I'm glad because they've been frosty with each other recently. I'm keeping half an eye on Daisy, making sure she doesn't drop her phone in the sea, but at the same time I turn my ear towards them. Just in case they choose now to tell her about Pip. Her reaction might be quite extreme, so I need to be on hand.

I hear her say: '. . . but any kind of disempowerment is depressing. I am already disempowered by the physical forces of ageing, and I can do without being disempowered by the attitudes of my few friends as well. It would be nice to be able to make the wrong decisions for myself.'

I can't catch his reply, but I see the smile slide off her face as she makes another comment.

Now his voice rises enough for me to hear him. 'I never said "care home"!' She must have accused him of something because he's sounding defensive. 'Or if I did, I didn't mean it. I was just shocked, that's all. You do spring things on us, Granny.'

'I had intended to inform you of the sale earlier,' Mrs McCreedy admits. 'It was just impossible to do so until I'd accepted it myself. It has taken me a while, but now I believe I have done.' She sweeps a hand out towards the sea, the icebergs, the little figures of the penguins. 'This all helps so much to get things in proportion. It reminds me that I am the first Penguin Ambassador and I was put on this planet for a reason.' (Didn't Sir Robert say something about that?) 'But also that my home and my silly old life matter very little in the great scheme of things. And the more I think about Lochnamorghy, the more I realize I can make it bigger, better, more far-reaching. Liaising with other penguin conservationists around the world, we could make a significant difference, you know.'

Patrick nods thoughtfully. 'Well, you've certainly drawn attention to OPIP, in a big way. And of course I want you to succeed, and, to be honest, I think you will, after your amazing speech and with Sir Robert's help. I just wish you hadn't sold The Ballahays.' He holds up a hand, as if to stop her. 'And I don't give a bat's bollock about my inheritance, by the way.' She raises her brows at his fruity language but lets him carry on. 'I'd never cope with a mansion like that. It's totally you but it's just not me. I mean, can you imagine me living there?'

He puts on an expression like a schoolboy who's been promised a lollipop, but instead has received a hamper of champagne and caviar.

I snort with laughter. I can't help it. Terry, Mrs

McCreedy and Patrick are all chuckling too now. Then Patrick stops. 'But I do know how much you love that place. I just didn't want you to have to part with it.'

Their voices sink to murmurs again. It is a sad thing, certainly. I'm fond of The Ballahays myself. I know every little nook and cranny of it. I've been asking myself, what happens to me as well? Mrs McCreedy has said she'll still need my help wherever she ends up. She's mentioned buying a modest cottage near Lochnamorghy, but that's not such an easy travelling distance daily from Kilmarnock.

I told Keith all about it when we were walking on the beach after the ceremony. I've never confided in a man like that before.

That is, I *have*. I've plagued Doug with plenty of my personal worries. (Does this top look nice on me or do I look like mutton dressed as lamb? How am I going to hit the low G of this choir piece? What am I going to cook for my nephew, wee Kevin – who is so fussy about his food – when he comes to stay? And lots and lots of worries about Mrs McCreedy.) But I always have the impression my words are just fluff to Doug. For Keith, it seems like they're jewels. And he asks questions that make me dig deeper and work things out. Then I go and say more than I mean to.

On that beach walk I even told Keith about hot flushes, night sweats and desperate bladder urges; about chronic fatigue and odd, irrational bursts of anger; about everything feeling so much more difficult than it used to; about how I keep being walloped by emotions and sometimes all I want to do is to crawl under a thick duvet and munch my way through a bumper pack of marshmallows. It was women's stuff, but he didn't cringe once. How strange that was!

I'm beginning to realize that not all men are like my Doug.

'Middle age is a time for big changes,' Keith said. 'Physical changes happen without our permission, but maybe we should push for our own changes, the ones that we actually *want*. Especially now that we have the benefit of experience, so we've got a better idea about what that is.'

'Oh, Keith,' I cried, because I couldn't help it. 'You say it so well! I think you've got the nub of it there.'

He asked what I'd do next, if I was intending to help Mrs McCreedy out with the Scottish penguins or what? And I couldn't answer at all. Doug assumes we'll just carry on much the same, but I don't feel like it *can* be the same.

When you spend a lot of time with somebody like Mrs McCreedy, you do question things more. She's so strong when it comes to decisions, always so sure of herself. If she wants to do a thing, she just goes ahead and does it, no matter how difficult it is. In the future, when I'm in a tricky spot, I'll be asking myself: what would Mrs McCreedy do now?

I asked Keith what *he* wanted out of life. He sighed and told me that if you had inherited a sheep farm and a tourist centre on a small Falkland island, then sheep farming and tourist hosting is what you did. He'd never done anything else. But now he was wondering if there might be more to life.

'I wish we had longer to chat about it. I think we'd be able to work things out better with each other's support.' He was saying 'I' not 'Keith' like he normally does when he talks about himself, and I realized he says 'I' when he's being more serious. See how well I was getting to know him?

That's when he said about coming to Ushuaia to meet us when we're on our way back, and I said oh gosh, he couldn't, it was hundreds of miles for him, and he said he could and would, and he needed a change of scene anyway and a stay in South America would help stop him turning into a boring old fart. I said he could never be that, and he said thank you, Eileen. And said he'd be coming anyway. He was going to say more, but that was when I happened to turn round and saw Mrs McCreedy disappearing under a tonne of sea lion. There's not much else that could have made me move so fast.

'There it is!' Terry's voice soars like a gull. 'Locket Island.'

It's only a faint blob in the distance but we are all fixated on it as it gets larger. Mrs McCreedy keeps dabbing her eyes with a hanky and muttering about the wind.

Daisy keeps saying she can't believe she's here. Neither can I.

'Look, look,' she cries, pointing. 'I can see a building.'

'That's the research station. It's not pretty but it's home,' says Patrick. Then he glances uncertainly at Mrs McCreedy. The word 'home' has become a sensitive subject. She keeps her eyes on the shoreline.

Soon the small boats they call the Zodiacs are lowered into the sea and we are transported across billowy waters to the beach. It's not white sand, like on the Falkland beaches, or multicoloured like the Galápagos ones, but black. Not a grim black, though, because it's full of sleek rainbow-coloured streamers of seaweed, gullies of water reflecting the sky, smudges of snow, seabirds strutting about and what I now recognize as penguin poo, which is pink.

Two people are standing by the shore to greet us. I recognize them from the photos in Terry's blogs – her fellow scientists, Dietrich and Mike. Dietrich has a kindly, rounded face and whiskers like a wire brush, whilst Mike is made up of sharp angles. Not much meat on him at all.

'I've heard such a lot about you two,' I cry.

I am waiting for one of them to say he's heard such a lot about me, but neither of them does. Dietrich pulps my hand between his thick paws in a friendly way, though.

Mike gives a long-suffering smile. 'My God, I thought we'd got rid of you,' he says to Mrs McCreedy, which is just unbelievably rude. She doesn't seem to mind, though, and replies: 'I am glad to find you still here, Mike. One should always establish an appropriate target for one's vicious scorn.'

Barrels and boxes are being unloaded from the boats, the provisions needed by us and the scientists. The team stack them on to sledges, and Daisy jumps up and sits on a heap of them. Patrick tows her along, whilst Dietrich, Mike and Terry drag the other sledges. Walking is tricky and I never quite know where to put my feet, what with all the ice and rocks. Mrs M is managing well, although semi-supported between Terry and Dietrich.

I gawk at everything in awe. The mountains are draped in cotton-wool snow; super-pure, like it's been washed in Persil Pro Formula laundry liquid. Even the sky looks scrubbed clean.

'Whoa, it's so sparkly!' cries Daisy. She leaps off the sledge and kicks up a cloud of crystals before scampering onwards.

'What a lot of changes you've made,' Mrs McCreedy comments as we finally reach the building.

'Yup, we've extended,' Patrick replies. 'Now we have solar panels to supplement the wind turbines. There are more rooms, too, and – you'll be glad to hear – a proper loo.'

*I'm* certainly glad to hear this, although Mrs McCreedy looks a little insulted.

Tea is the first thing, of course, and Dietrich and the others are so very hospitable. The research centre is bigger than you'd think from the outside. As well as the new bathroom, there's a comfy central sitting room, a brightly painted kitchen packed with shelves and cupboards, a lab (so many machines I haven't the foggiest about), a computer room, storerooms and the bedrooms. I'll be sharing with Daisy again.

'Unless you'd like my room?' Terry offers. 'You'd be very welcome, but it does mean you'd have to share with Patrick.'

Patrick and I just look at each other and laugh.

I notice quite a few inked cartoons of penguins up on the walls. They're clever and cute and I happen to know they've been drawn by Dietrich. He's very humble about it when I compliment him, and even gives one to Daisy. It shows a bunch of penguins enjoying a snowball fight.

'You can chuck it in the bin later,' says Mike.

'Why would I do that? I *love* it!' cries Daisy.

I give Mike a hard stare.

'Don't mind him,' Dietrich tells me, giving him a friendly slap on the back. 'We're all used to his incredibly hurtful comments.'

'He's a good egg, really,' Terry adds, smiling.

'*Eggs-tremely* odious, you mean,' says Patrick.

'Ah, thank you, Patrick,' says Mike. 'Looking at your face has just reminded me I have penguin poo to analyse.'

Mrs M, Daisy and I can't wait to see the Adélies. Since we all slept well last night, we set out with Terry and Patrick as soon as tea is finished. Mrs McCreedy struggles with the slope and declares it has got steeper and slipperier since last time she was here. Daisy holds her handbag for her with one hand and pulls her along with the other. I'm not sure it's helping, to be honest. We make it to the top all right, though.

The views are unbelievable. Glaciers and great capes of snow and, in between the glowing whites, sudden splashes of colour from the lichens – vivid orange and lemon and ochre. They are tipped with glassy little petals of ice. Terry points out the pale lake in the distance. It lies at one end of the island, which is an oval shape, so the whole thing looks like a locket from the air.

'Now, this is what you've been waiting for!' she proclaims, pointing the other way.

Beside me, there's a long intake of breath from Mrs McCreedy. On the plain just below us are thousands and thousands of little figures like chessmen, some upright, some laid long-ways. A clamour of bird voices blows up to us on the wind. It's the Adélie penguin colony!

# 35

# Veronica

*Locket Island*

I MUST RATION my excitement or I shall give myself palpitations. For whilst this body stands, stares and leans heavily on a stick, this soul is dancing.

What an explosion of joy to be here once more, amongst my first and favourite penguins! I had never believed I would set foot on Locket Island again. My mind had filed my Antarctic adventures under 'past', a stash of memories to revisit from my fireside in the Ballahays snug, to dip into with nostalgia as my slippered feet rested, useless, on my footstool. Yet here I am, granted another chance to gather stunning, life-affirming experiences. Here I am, intermingling with Adélies! I must savour every moment.

I am older than last time, and closer to the final

curtain, and the coldness bites more than ever, yet hope clamours in my chest. Because now I know that, even though this must be my last hurrah in the Antarctic, my future will also be amongst penguins. True, they will not be free as these ones are, but I am determined they will be the happiest penguins ever to be found in captivity. And though I will leave my beloved home, I will still reside in my beloved Scotland.

Victory trills in my veins. I transfer my stick to Terry, asking her to hold it if she would be so kind, for a few minutes. I reach out my hands to my two walking companions, Eileen and Daisy, one on either side of me; something I have never done before.

'Let us go forth into the colony together,' I proclaim.

The three of us walk – a trifle unsteadily but with a dignity that becomes us – into the glorious, noisy, smelly penguin rabble.

Daisy has entrusted her phone to Patrick with strict directions, and he videos us as we step forward, a smiling threesome amongst five thousand feathered friends. The Adélies, one of the smaller species, barely come up to our knees, but they are fearless. Countless pairs of white-rimmed eyes gaze up at us from beaky faces as we pass. Some of the little fellows follow us a short way, all curiosity. Others are too busy bickering, flirting or egg-sitting to take much notice. At times we break our handhold to avoid stepping on guano, on the carefully constructed nests or on the penguins themselves, but then we join together again.

Daisy squeezes my hand repeatedly. 'Look, Veronica, look!' she calls, over and over. 'Look at that one now, scratching his chin with his foot. Look at that one, slipping over on the snow! Look at that one, kissing her husband!'

I enjoy the fact that she sees them as married.

Eileen is no less elated. They have both seen countless penguins by now, but this is the first time they have witnessed a colony in the snow. The first time, also, that they have seen penguins flop down on to their fronts and scoot along the ice, propelled by flippers and feet. What a comical, endearing sight this is. Daisy points to a line of penguins in the distance, sliding along like a row of oval beads drawn across a pale décolletage.

'I love them! I love them all!' she proclaims.

My heart is brimming over. I hope this excess emotion is not the precursor to some cardio-related health issue.

I try to take it in: the snow-laden slopes, the gleaming strata, the boisterous calling and brawling of the birds. Everything is the same and yet different. I once stood in this exact spot, haunted by my past yet, little by little, letting the joy of penguins penetrate my hard shell, bringing their unique brand of healing. And, of course, it was right here that I met Pip.

'They're totally beautiful, but they do all look the same as each other,' Daisy points out. 'How will we recognize Pip if we see him?'

Last time I set eyes on him was a couple of years ago, when he was a comical combination of chick and adult, with a little topknot of fluff on his head. But the photo of the grown-up Pip (taken by Terry and gifted by Sir Robert) hangs in my hallway, and I have looked at it every day since it came into my possession. I believe I would, by some spiritual, transcendent means, recognize him were he to waddle into my line of sight. Still, Daisy has a valid point.

'It will be easy,' I tell her. 'As you see, many of the penguins here have yellow flipper bands, printed with a number for identification. The scientists have been monitoring them for years.'

'I can't read the numbers very well from here, though,' Daisy responds, squinting.

'Yes, but Pip has an altogether different band. His is orange.'

'Oh, you did say that. I remember now.'

'Pip is not here at present, but not all the penguins are yet returned from overwintering on the sea ice. We shall see him soon.'

I summon him now, mentally. We have saved each other's lives, and if a bond can exist between human and bird (and I know from experience that it can), then this must be the strongest one. He will come. Surely, he will come?

The computer room is much in demand. Terry ('I just need to hop on there to email the AARC'), Dietrich ('some info for the penguinologists' worldwide network') and Mike ('lab results on bird faeces to add to the database') all take their turn. Then Daisy is desperate to write up and post her first Antarctic blog. Eileen wants to check the latest additions to the Operation PIP appeal following the ambassadorship ceremony, but says she will wait for me first.

Heart racing, I check my emails to see if there are any developments with the house sale or with Lochnamorghy. There aren't, particularly. The Ballahays survey is scheduled for later this week, Mr Wallace informs me. The Lochnamorghy agents confirm that my counter-bidder has reached his limit; my own offer has been accepted, providing all proceeds satisfactorily with the documentation once I am back. More interesting is an email from Sir Robert, from the Centaurus research station on the Antarctic mainland. I print it out so that I can peruse it at my leisure.

In my bedroom, I locate my glasses with remarkable promptitude.

*My dear Veronica* (he writes),

*I hope this finds you as fit as ever, and safely arrived on Locket Island. You will doubtless already have conquered the slopes and visited the Adélies. I bet you have been scanning their ranks for any sign of Pip* (how well he knows me!) *and I hope that you have found him.*

*Whilst the signal holds out, I must congratulate you, for now you are officially the first Penguin Ambassador! I have heard reports of your powerful speech and managed to access a few news articles when the internet has worked, and I am bursting with admiration. You are quite wonderful. I am greedy for an account of it all from your own lips.*

*The film crew and I are enjoying the yet colder climes and the sight of the Emperor penguins is truly inspiring. You will see for yourself very soon, and I cannot wait to welcome you here. If Daisy and Eileen are already amazed (I'm guessing that they are), they will be even more amazed when they get here. Your penguin namesakes are all doing well.*

*The film schedule is relentless as always, but as well as the Emperors we have captured some great footage*

*of albatrosses, Weddell seals and leopard seals. You will*
*see all these in a few days' time.*
   *With much affection until then,*
   *Your true friend,*
   *Robert. X*

I am on my second reading of the email when there is a tap at the door, and Eileen comes in beaming from ear to ear.

'You're not going to believe this, but hundreds – literally hundreds – more people have signed up and pledged money. We have £133,694! And there are so many comments from fans saying they loved your speech and they want to be like you when they're older.'

I let out a cry of flabbergasted triumph.

Eileen echoes me with her own crow of delight. 'The Falklands papers and radio have all run our mission as a main story. Some of them have centred on your speech, others on the incident with the sea lion. It's hit the UK papers, too. Mrs McCreedy, you are enormous!'

I presume she is speaking of my celebrity status rather than my physical dimensions.

She waves some sheets of paper in my face. I quickly skim through the articles. Several of them feature Daisy's picture of Eileen rushing to help as the sea lion rears over me. One even dubs her my saviour.

I smile.

'Eileen, you seem to have become somewhat enormous yourself.'

# Daisy's Penguin Blog

## LOCKET ISLAND LOVE

Ever since I've known Veronica, she's been going on and on about this place. And now, at last, I'm here.

Snow, soup and scientists!

And it's IMPOSSIBLE not to fall in love with the Adélie penguins. They're little but just so feisty. When they squabble they slap each other with their flippers. Some have eggs already, others are still nest-building. Of course, there aren't any trees here, so they can't use twigs. They collect pebbles with their beaks and make them into a circle on the ground. They're always naughtily pinching pebbles from each other's nests. It's pebble-mad!

It's the boy penguins who make the nests, trying to impress the girls by building the best and biggest ones. They even chat up the girl penguins by giving them a pebble, like it's a diamond or something. Romantic or what? Then they climb on top of each other to . . . Eileen won't let me say what they're doing but it makes me laugh because sometimes they can't balance and slide off sideways.

Adélies breed on land in the warmer months (= between now and February). In winter they're out at sea in the pack ice. Terry and Patrick say they can swim more than 1,200 km away from their breeding site.

We still haven't found Pip, the orphaned penguin who Veronica saved, but I expect he'll show up soon. I'm dying to meet him. Maybe he can send a postcard to Mac.

# 36

# Veronica

*Locket Island*

TIRED FEET. ACHING muscles. Creaking joints. Eighty-five miles completed. £143,000 raised, assuming we complete our task. This will contribute greatly to the repairing and running of Lochnamorghy. Having said that, it is nowhere near enough to buy the place, so it is just as well I have sold The Ballahays. My sacrifice has struck a chord with our supporters, but it still feels as if I have undergone major surgery; the removal of a vital organ, the amputation of a limb.

We need to keep plugging on, as it is already 24 October. One week left to cover fifteen miles, but in Antarctica everything is slower, colder and harder ... and it will soon become slower, colder and harder still. It is just as well all three of us are keen to visit the Adélies again

310

today. Terry and Patrick accompany us up the slope, the most gruelling slog for me. I notice, however, that Eileen walks sturdily, hardly panting at all. She is so much fitter than when we started back in Scotland.

This is Terry's allocated patch, so my grandson bids us au revoir and makes his way westward to his specific area.

Terry pulls some equipment from her rucksack.

'Fancy learning how to weigh penguins, Daisy?'

Need she ask?

Daisy is a fizzing firework of excitement. 'Yes, oh-my-God-yes!'

'You need to be super-calm or they'll get stressed,' Terry advises. 'I'd better do the penguin-grabbing; there's quite a knack to it and it is easy to get pecked.'

She deftly swoops on an unsuspecting penguin, and before it knows what has happened, it has been bundled into the weighing bag. Daisy listens attentively as she is shown how to take the reading. She is allowed to stroke the penguin very lightly and briefly whilst Terry holds its beak shut, then it is released once more. It scuttles off back into the crowd.

'It doesn't look too bothered, does it?' Eileen observes.

Terry smiles, proud of her little ones. 'No. Brave as lions, are Adélies.'

Once the obligatory photograph has been taken of us with the scales and the penguins, we must leave Terry to it, because walking is our business.

'Here, take this radio,' she says, handing it over. 'And please stay within sight.'

She trusts me very little because I went wandering off

into the snow here once before, with somewhat dire consequences. I gather also that Daisy's parents have made her vouch for our safety.

Dots of snow flitter and scurry around us as we walk. Speckles land on our hats and shoulders. The air blurs, the outline of the rocks softens. Whiteness brushes the penguins' darker plumage. The glacial slopes and peaks reach up and blend with the sky.

We scan the hordes of bustling figures. Many have yellow bands, but as yet there is no sign of an orange one. I happen to look at Eileen, who is uncharacteristically quiet, a strange solemn expression on her face.

Glad of stout boots, we trudge in a wide arc, watching many a scene of devotion between couples, and many a play-pecking game between juveniles.

'I can't see any orange bands, can you?' Daisy asks.

'You won't, dear,' Eileen replies very softly.

My heart plummets like a stone. Eileen knows something. Nosy as she is, she has doubtless been listening in to a conversation between the researchers.

Automatically my hand goes to my neck, seeking my locket. I pull it out from under my many layers of clothing, from its warm place against my heart, and I hold it in my gloved hands, a kind of prayer.

I attempt to modulate my voice but it comes out hard as a hacksaw. 'What do you mean?'

'Nothing, it's really nothing, Mrs McCreedy,' Eileen stammers. 'I just thought it unlikely you'd see Pip, what with there being so many penguins. There must be at least . . .' She casts her eyes over the penguins as if attempting to count them. 'Well, there are hundreds,

312

aren't there? Thousands. It would be like looking for a needle in a haystack, or a snowflake in a pillow factory . . . or a raisin in a . . . in a coalmine, or . . .'

She melts under my gaze. A flush of crimson rises up her throat and into her cheeks in spite of the cold. Her mouth carries on working even though the words have ceased.

An exchange passes between us by flicking our eyes towards Daisy, a tacit agreement that if there is something tragic to be revealed, it must not be revealed in front of her. Not at this juncture, anyway, when she is happy and we are so close to reaching our goal.

Eileen forces a smile. 'What am I prattling on about? I expect he's here somewhere. And just look at that pretty little penguin there with her tail all stuck out.'

The tactic has worked, and Daisy is distracted, focusing her phone on the preening penguin. Enough has passed between us, though, for me to realize that Pip must be dead.

Occasionally, in bad moments, I have feared this might be the case, but I never let myself believe it. Now the reality drains me of breath. A sickly coldness fills my chest. Once again I grasp for my locket, that contains so little and so much. Through thick gloves my fingertips lack the sensitivity to feel the smooth metal.

I glance down and let out a cry. The locket is gone; only two broken ends of fine silver chain remain, slithering through my fingers.

Eileen and Daisy have refocused their attention on me, faces full of alarm.

'My locket!' I gasp.

Desperate as I am, my stiff old body will not allow me to bend and scrutinize the proliferation of snow and pebbles underfoot.

'Oh, I'm so sorry, so sorry,' cries Eileen, all a-dither. 'Never mind, Mrs McCreedy. We'll find it in a jiffy. We will, won't we, Daisy?'

The two of them scamper about, checking the ground. 'Did you step forwards, or backwards at all? Was it just here . . . Or here?'

I do not know. My upset about Pip was so extreme I could have been rooted to the spot, or I could have staggered a few paces in any direction.

'Don't worry, we'll find it, Veronica,' Daisy asserts, all grown-up and businesslike. 'I'm good at this sort of thing. My mum always says I have eagle eyes and my dad says I have a supersonic radar inside me.'

She crawls along in the snow, heedless of the pink-and-grey sludge gathering on her trousers (which are waterproof and, I sincerely hope, guano-proof as well).

Eileen also lowers herself to ground level, searching, searching. I peruse the terrain as best I can, turning over pebbles with my stick. We are at it for a good half-hour.

We discuss radioing Terry and asking for her help. Her figure is easy to pick out since she is wearing a tangerine-coloured parka jacket, but she seems small on the other side of the colony and she looks busy with the penguins. I am reluctant to disturb her. I feel we have gone over the ground so many times it will be futile anyway.

After another ten minutes of searching, I come to the conclusion that my locket, like Pip, is gone for ever. My eyes are swilling now and hot tears drop from my cheeks, pitting the snow.

Daisy, charmingly, takes off her own locket – the one I gave her – and holds it out to me. 'Take mine, Veronica, please. I want you to have it.'

'No, Daisy. Thank you, thank you, sweet girl, but no. It isn't the locket itself that's important to me, but what's inside it.'

I think of the dear, dear human hairs that represent so much history, so much love . . . plus the one tiny tuft of fluff from a penguin chick. From Pip. My breath catches and a huge, unstoppable, unladylike sob blasts out of my throat.

Now Daisy starts bawling, too. We must be a pitiful sight, an ancient crone and a slip of a child crying together amongst the penguins. Eileen is apologizing as if her life depended on it, although none of this is her fault. She and Daisy are both covered in guano. I'd laugh if I didn't feel so very, very sad.

How cruel Fate is, not even to let me keep these tiny, personal comforts; these miniature threads that link me to my lost loved ones.

Around us, penguins continue picking up pebbles in their beaks to rearrange their nests. One very busy character waddles close to our feet. He pecks amongst stones with fervour, quite oblivious to the human grief that is taking place in his presence. Daisy watches him too, through her tears.

We see it at the same time and our cry shoots out into the air as if we are one.

'Look!'

At the nudging of a pebble, something has been dislodged; something shiny. It catches the light and, in the shadowy crevice, becomes a spot of sheer dazzle. It is an oval of silver, engraved with a V and curling vines. The penguin has uncovered my locket!

Daisy swoops down on it and delivers it into my hands with triumph, her tears vanishing as quickly as they'd come.

I receive the locket with relief so huge I am surprised it doesn't manifest itself as anything larger than a smile. 'Well, thank you, Daisy. And thank you, penguin.'

And thank you, Fate. Perhaps I did you a disservice.

I zip the locket into the inner pocket of my handbag. When I am back in Scotland I shall replace the chain with a much sturdier one.

It is not long before Terry joins us again to escort us back to the field centre. I wave Eileen and Daisy on ahead and accept Terry's arm.

I brace myself. I need to check that it is true.

'Pip is dead, isn't he?' I ask as we reach the crest. We look out over the view, over the locket-hole lake, over the undulating colony of Adélie penguins.

Terry bites her lip, turns a tremulous face towards me. 'I'm afraid so, Veronica. You knew we were tracking him. His device shows us that his body is stationary, deep down at the bottom of the sea. I thought there was a gleam of hope when it moved slightly, but it must have been just the tides sweeping it along the sea floor a little. He has not surfaced in days. I'm so very sorry.'

She is fighting back the emotion and I know that she feels

for Pip as I do. We stand together, facing the wind, trying to accept this small loss that means so much to us both.

'I want to hug you,' she whispers.

'Don't.'

I want to hug her, too, but if that happens the floodgates of grief will burst and neither of us will be able to hide the truth from Daisy.

'We mustn't tell Daisy about this.'

'Agreed,' she says.

Eileen and Daisy are just ahead of us, marching down the slope. I observe their back views with affection. They have been nothing like the hindrance I was expecting. On the contrary, they have both been a tremendous support, and I realize now that I could not have done this alone. I wonder how I ever even thought that was possible.

Terry, too, and Patrick, and Sir Robert, and the others we have met along the way. Cooperation is something I have never particularly experienced before, but now I see why it is so vital. The penguins have always understood this.

Over tea I sit through chit-chat from Dietrich about jazz music, a diatribe from Mike about the moral turpitudes of tourism, and an assortment of cheesy jokes from Patrick. Daisy also talks a lot, telling the scientists all about the penguin weighing and the locket episode. We have walked very little due to all the time spent searching for the locket. At least I have it in my possession again.

As soon as I can politely do so, I retire to the four walls of my bedroom, which provide no comfort but some much-needed privacy.

317

So Pip is gone.

I breathe.

Gently and with great reverence, I extract the locket from my handbag, click the catch so that it springs open. The contents pool into my palm. I gaze down at them and mourn quietly for the owners of each of these tiny samples, these beloved people whose absence has shaped my life, who are themselves so very long gone. The pain still sears and blisters, despite the disappearing decades. There is no expiry date on grief.

I coil the delicate hairs once more and replace them inside the locket. I turn my attention to the little tuft of fluff from a baby penguin. How soft it is, and how dear! Memories wash through me. Pip, miniature and bedraggled, left to die at the edge of the colony. Pip, poking his tiny head out from inside Terry's jacket. Pip gulping food from a syringe. Pip nestling into my turquoise cardigan in my open suitcase. Pip, stronger and feistier, toddling about the field centre, getting under our feet. Pip playing tug of war with Dietrich's scarf. Pip jumping on to the bed and arguing with an old lady who had given up on life, telling her it was worth living after all.

I had so hoped to see him again. I had been so sure that I would.

My throat burns. I gulp, and choke a little. I reprimand myself, tell myself he was only a penguin . . . but that argument is completely ineffectual.

My eyes screw shut, my fist tightens around that wispy feather. For a moment everything else in the world drops away. I give in to a bout of anguished sobbing, for, hard though my exterior may be, I know what it is to love – to

318

love wildly, fiercely and illogically. This is a cruel loss, so tiny yet so huge. Another loss. I will learn to accept it but I do not like it. I do not like it at all.

The pain comes in waves. I will allow myself a period of grief for Pip, for the change he wrought in me, for his short, incredibly sweet, mostly mysterious life. For everything he represented.

Time ticks by.

I rally a little.

Pip is dead, but his message of hope lives on, and the lesson that he and all the penguins have taught me: to be brave. To carry on, no matter what happens.

And that is exactly what I shall do.

# 37

# Veronica

*Centaurus research station, Antarctic mainland*

OUR STOP ON Locket Island lasted just three days. Now we have left Dietrich and Mike to their research and have travelled south again, via icebreaker and helicopter, to the eastern edge of the Antarctic Peninsula. It is wholly different to the Locket Island set-up. The new study centre, Centaurus (named after a constellation), stands on the sea ice and is a spidery structure made up of a series of pods on legs. Patrick informs us that the legs can be lengthened or shortened according to snow accumulation. Moreover, each pod can be towed to a new location when the seasons change and the building gets too close to the retreating edge of the ice shelf. The station includes an aircraft hangar, garages for snow vehicles, and several laboratories as well as living accommodation. It is buzzing with activity from some seventy scientists, technicians and other workers who assist in the daily running of the place.

The interior is well fitted out and comfortable, with even some luxuries such as a small cinema and a snooker table. Once again I have a bedroom to myself, and we are all treated like royalty. I suspect this might be something to do with a certain knight of the realm who is currently staying as well.

It was a touching reunion with Sir Robert Saddlebow. I shunned his embrace, fearing, as with Terry, that it might prompt in me an excessive outburst of emotion, but his quietly positive presence is a balm to my aching soul.

Today is 27 October, we are approaching the end of our walk and victory is within sight. I shall at last set eyes on that remotest and most impressive of all penguin species: the Emperor. In spite of all this – and a Herculean effort on my part – my former zest for Operation PIP seems to have deserted me. Where is that thrill I should be feeling? Gone, all gone.

We have completed many steps on our tour inside the building, but Eileen, Daisy and I must go and see the Emperors whilst the weather holds.

Our first sortie outside is on Ski-Doos. We are arranged in several vehicles, for Sir Robert and the film crew are also anxious not to miss any opportunity, and, of course, Patrick and Terry come too. Well muffled in our polar gear, we whistle across flat plains of snow strewn with icy monoliths. Some crouch low like humble cottages, others rise in elaborate facades, towers and castellations. The wind whips the snow into a fine mist, blurring their borders, transforming them to craggy ghosts. Daisy's pink scarf streams behind her. In the distance I can just make out a couple of dark beaky figures who trudge rhythmically towards a larger group.

We slide to a standstill and the engines give way to silence. No machines are permitted within a kilometre of the colony because the birds mustn't be disturbed by the noise. The last part must be trekked on foot, which suits our purposes well.

Stiff from the ride, I pull myself into action. The others cluster round.

'It's minus sixteen degrees C,' Patrick tells us helpfully. 'Nice and toasty.'

We struggle through knee-high snow, huddling in our gear, marvelling that we are finally here.

Sir Robert, always at my side, lifts an arm and points. 'There you are, Veronica.' His voice resonates with passion for his subject and I'm conscious of his warm, wonderfully soothing Scottish accent. 'There's the sight you were longing for when we chatted at the Cloverleaf in Edinburgh. The stuff of dreams.'

It is a group of three. The parents are stout, solid beings, even taller than I had imagined; colossal, as birds go. They arc over the chick, tummy to tummy, proud and protective. The chick reaches its head upwards. Flippers enfold, heads nuzzle, beaks touch. It is a scene of exquisite tenderness.

Eileen and Daisy have bunched around me now. The three of us look on, mesmerized.

And slowly the swirl of snowflakes clears, and reveals hundreds upon hundreds of similar families grouped behind them, smudges of grey, black, yellow and white blending into the whiter white. Tiny chicks peep out from brood pouches, insulated by their parents' padding. Toddlers waddle about in fuzzy fleeces, bedraggled wet fur on their nether regions, dragging tiny tails behind them. Adults look on or usher them forward. Every mother and father is swollen with pride, brimming with devotion; almost unbearable sweetness in the snow.

Daisy turns to Patrick. 'Can we find our own penguins? Is Veronica Penguin here, and Eileen Penguin and Daisy Penguin?'

'They're here somewhere, for sure,' Patrick assures her. 'Let me see.' He consults his gadget that can trace their exact whereabouts. 'OK, we need to bear right and walk a little further. Are you up to it, Granny?'

'Indeed I am.'

We progress further, step-by-step in the deep, wet whiteness.

And finally he indicates another tight group. Our three penguins, of course, look identical to all the others except that, as well as the trackers, they have colourful flipper tags to help them stand out. Veronica has a scarlet one, Eileen a mauve one, Daisy a pink one. Veronica Penguin stands tall and statuesque, wearing her red flipper band almost like . . . Well, almost like an ambassador's sash. Eileen is a little plumper and is pottering around absentmindedly, whilst Daisy is busy chasing a floating feather. I have to say, I am much enamoured with this soft, pudgy chick, her body a mass of fluff, her face white-cheeked, curious, bright-eyed. She looks squashier and cuddlier than any soft toy.

Daisy is understandably ecstatic. We pose for photographs with the penguins, and Miriam even sets up her tripod and takes some footage with the BBC equipment, under Sir Robert's instruction. 'We might be able to use it for the programme in some way, who knows?'

Sunlight threads through the clouds, highlighting the dips and dents in the surface of the snow, throwing dark shadows behind us. The blues become bluer, the whites whiter. Even with our sunglasses on, the dazzle is extreme. The penguins steam and glow.

Terry is now chatting with Eileen, whilst Patrick talks science with Sir Robert a little way ahead.

Antarctica, I recall, has a way of stripping back your shell and exposing the rawness underneath. For a single glance at Daisy tells me that something is going on. Her teeth are clenched, her face puckered up in agony. This is not homesickness, as I had presumed was her issue, but something else, something more akin to fear.

'What is it, dear girl? Tell me.' The words are a command now, not a request. 'How can I help you if I don't know what it is?'

She catches her breath, trying to hold it in, but it won't and can't stay inside her any longer. It blasts out into the frozen air on a jet of steam, a cry like the keening of a seagull.

'It's seeing all the families.'

I reach for her little hand. It clutches on to mine as if it will never, ever let go. Our skin cannot touch because of the chunky gloves, but I hope she can feel my aching fondness for her, my wish for her happiness, my desire to understand. This should be a joyous time for her. Not for me – not now – but surely for her?

'Mum and Dad don't love me any more.' The words are not uttered with a wail of despair but in a resigned voice, as if every emotion has ripped through her and left her with nothing left to feel. 'They only love Noah,' she adds, as if this is any explanation.

I stoop a little to look straight into her eyes, my knees and back protesting at the movement. The bevelled snow creaks as my weight shifts.

'How can you say that, Daisy? They adore you. They love you more than you could possibly conceive.'

How could they not?

But she, poor child, has latched on to the idea that they don't. A shiver runs through me. No wonder she's choked up at these scenes of penguin devotion.

Daisy starts listing things on the fingers of her free hand. 'They let me come away with you and Eileen; they didn't want me with them, you see. And they keep getting presents for Noah, really big ones, like the drum kit. And Mum went on that trip to Switzerland with Noah. She's never taken me anywhere.'

'But she did,' I argue. 'She took you to the Falklands last time!'

She stomps her feet with exasperation. 'Yes, but that was with the whole filming team and you and Sir Robert, and only because she thought she had to.'

I can see it might have appeared that way. I was very persuasive at the time, I seem to remember.

'And,' she continues, 'and they're tired of all the years they had to give me when I was ill, all the trips to hospital, all the home educating, all the crying in the night. They went off me then, but they *had* to look after me, didn't they, because I had cancer? Now they don't, and they just want to be with Noah. Noah Noah Noah.'

Her brother is a sweet little boy, but I have never noticed Gavin and Beth showing a particular favouritism towards him. Still, Daisy has a big imagination; no doubt something has been taken out of context or blown out of proportion.

Her eyes are fixed on a parent penguin bending low to nuzzle its child.

'I just want them to be proud of me,' she blurts, 'but I don't matter to them at all any more.'

Ah, so that is what lies behind her avid commitment. She desperately wants not only to save the penguins or to come on an incredible voyage, but to win her parents' attention.

'They *are* proud of you. So very, very proud,' I tell her firmly.

I am about to add more when she speaks again. 'And it's not just that.'

Her mouth moves but I can hear nothing except the roaring wind and the cries of penguins. 'Speak up, girl.'

Her brows knit furiously and she yells it out. 'Mum and Dad are splitting up.'

'No!' I exclaim.

From everything I've seen and heard, it seems impossible. I am flabbergasted . . . But one never truly knows what goes on in other people's relationships.

Daisy is nodding now, quite sure.

'They haven't told me but I know anyway. Because Dad is buying that place in Jedburgh and Mum is staying in Bolton and because of what Patrick said.'

I think back. I seem to remember something Patrick mentioned on Bolder Island, crammed into a car, and soon after that Daisy cried when we were viewing the King penguins.

My face is numb and my nose is beginning to run. It is too hard to have this conversation out here in the cold, with the wind biting into us.

'I'm sure that can't be right,' I declare, 'but I will most certainly find out.'

I can do this easily. Patrick and Gavin are very close friends, or 'best mates' or 'buddies' or engaged in a 'bromance', or whatever man-speak is for these close platonic relationships between males. I shall quiz Patrick once we are back in the warm. He will undoubtedly know what's going on.

# 38

# Veronica

*Centaurus research station, Antarctic mainland*

PATRICK PRESSES MUGS of tea into our hands. He is good at making tea, a fact for which I will never cease to be grateful. It is perhaps the most important requisite in a grandson.

'About Daisy,' he says.

Last night I took him aside and asked what he knew of his Bolton friends and their family circumstances. He said he'd check it out, but 'as far as I know, Gav and Beth are sound'.

Let's hope he can confirm it now.

He has summoned Eileen and me to a small, private lounge. We are both seated on neon-blue blocky arm-chairs, the sort that are almost impossible to get out of once you have sunk in. Patrick takes a wooden upright chair, turns it and sits on it the wrong way round with the back between his knees. Why he cannot sit on a chair forwards like a normal person I cannot comprehend, but there we are.

'So I messaged Gav,' he begins. 'And today I got a long email back from him and an even longer one from Beth. Then one from them both jointly. Explaining to me, so that I can talk to Daisy or tell you, whatever seems right. I thought I'd broach it with you first because you know her best.'

He pauses.

'Proceed, Patrick. We shall endeavour to break any news to her in the kindest and most suitable fashion.'

'Don't stress; you won't need to break anything. They've emailed her themselves, but it's best we all know what's going on.'

Eileen nods vigorously, and I see that her gossip antennae are out. It is forgivable, though. She cares for Daisy as much as I do.

Patrick blows on his tea then looks up. 'The fact is, Gav and Beth *have* been up against a few problems. Beth had a bad case of anxiety and, knackered from all the years caring for Daisy, she's had a near collapse herself. She had to go for a load of medical tests. She didn't let on to Gav, not wanting him to worry, but it turned out not to be anything too dire, thank God. She just needs to rest up. As for Gav, he was distracted, overworking with the bike business, trying to expand, trying to provide for his family, but that meant being away from them. The second bicycle shop in Jedburgh is no more than that. The flat above is somewhere they can stay occasionally, not a place for him to live away from Beth, which is what Daisy thought (especially when I mentioned he'd employed a guy to man the Bolton shop). He's been so wrapped up with it all, he didn't realize Beth was struggling. The two of them have worked through the issues now, though. And they're categorically staying together.'

Eileen interjects a 'Phew!'

Patrick continues. 'They're both besotted with Daisy, of course. But she's had a mountain of attention because of her illness, and because of you, Granny – and they knew her brother, Noah, must be feeling relatively neglected, which is why they've been lavishing him with treats. Which, of course, Daisy noticed. When they let her come on this trip she decided they must be trying to get rid of her (that's Daisy logic. Sounds like she didn't exactly give them much choice!). Anyhow, I'm sure they will have explained it to her just fine, but we're all here for her if she needs to talk it through, right?'

'Right,' says Eileen. 'I'm so glad Gav and Beth are staying together. It's important for the children ... and I know those two love each other, truly, madly, deeply. Not like Doug and me.'

We turn our eyes on her. Doug has not come up in conversation recently.

'Whatever do you mean, Eileen?'

For a split second I think she is going to cry, but she doesn't.

'Doug has been seeing another woman behind my back.'

The words have come out simply, without any hint of

330

accusation or acrimony. She produces a long sigh, pulls herself up, paces the length of the room. She is manifesting a strength and determination that I'm sure were never there before.

'You knew?' I ask, astounded.

She stops, frozen to the spot, and stares at me.

'You knew?' she echoes.

I'm flooded with a sudden and startling fondness for her. This stalwart woman who has turned up to clean The Ballahays and fetch and carry and organize my appointments and sort out recyclables from non-recyclables and countless other menial tasks over the years – she has always been there for me, yet I have scarcely noticed her.

It is time – it seems that time is overdue – for me to tell her what I saw that afternoon on my wet walk in Ayrshire, before all this began.

I reveal now how I witnessed her husband with the blonde (*peroxide* – that's the word) and deemed it unfitting to tell her but decided to take her out of the situation, hoping the rapscallion would grow to appreciate her.

She snatches a breath. 'Gosh, Mrs McCreedy. I don't know what to say. That's . . . That's kind. And thoughtful of you.' She sniffs. 'And there was I thinking you needed me so badly when you didn't actually need me at all.'

This is not turning out well. Her eyes are moistening. Yet the emotion seems to be more about *me* than about Doug.

'I *do* need you, Eileen,' I admit. 'I need you far more than I realized. And I need you now more than ever.' Not just for the physical assistance she offers, I realize, but for moral support, too.

'Well, that means a lot to me, Mrs McCreedy. I won't deny it.'

'But how come you already knew about your husband's infidelity?'

She swallows loudly. 'Oh, I've known ever since that day we saw the stag and I got soaked in the rain. The day there was the first viewing of The Ballahays. You remember I popped back home early to change out of my wet things? A car was driving off from our house just as I arrived. This brassy, skinny, tarty-looking blonde woman was behind the wheel, and she turned her head to stare at me as our cars passed. It was such a look: pity and spite and superiority, all mixed up. Doug was bundling the bed linen into the washing machine when I went in. I mean, when has he ever done that before? It wasn't hard to put two and two together, what with that funny smell, and the long hours he was spending at the oatcake factory and the way he kept checking out his muscles and wearing his nice shirt. It wasn't normal.

'I knew he was making a fool out of me. But I just felt he was right, because I *was* a fool, and how did I ever think he could love silly old Eileen anyway? And I thought, maybe he doesn't love me but at least we're *used* to each other and cosy together and I bet *she* wouldn't make him porridge every single morning and not mind the fact he sometimes wears the same underpants all week. She just wants him for one thing and one thing only. Well, maybe two things only. Maybe she wants his money, but she'll soon realize he doesn't have much of that, even if he does go and buy her expensive knick-knacks. That's never going to last, is it? And the other thing . . . well, I can't believe that was anything to write home about, either. And I thought, he'll come back to me and I'll be there waiting for him, I'll forgive him because that's the Christian thing to do . . . and I had no idea what else to do, anyway. That's what I was thinking.'

I am consumed with indignation at such topsy-turvy humility, but I hold back, for I have registered she is using the past tense.

'But that was a different Eileen,' she declares. 'That was before all the walking, before all the penguins, before I saved you from the sea lion, Mrs McCreedy, before Antarctica. Now I see that I should face up to what's happening, and if I want to keep my new self-respect then I need to set things straight with Doug. Change is coming, and it's a change I welcome. It'll be hard, I know that . . . but those Galápagos penguins have adapted to live in the extremely hot hotness and the Emperors have adapted to live in the extremely cold coldness, haven't they? If penguins can adapt such a humungous amount, then so can I.'

She plumps herself back into her chair.

Patrick has been squirming and scratching his head all this while. I, too, am stunned by this long speech.

Indeed, I am inclined to clap but I resist the temptation. I merely tell Eileen that she is quite right, that I agree with her entirely. I give her an encouraging pat on the shoulder.

I then assure her that she is welcome to stay with me at The Ballahays for however long she needs, to sort the situation out. As I say the words, I remember with a jolt that I have no right to make such an offer. Soon I must leave The Ballahays for ever.

Who knows where either of us will end up?

# Daisy's Penguin Blog

## BIG BUT FRAGILE

Yes, I do know how lucky I am to be here. Everyone's been telling me the whole time. It's really special to go to Antarctica. Really, REALLY special to see Emperors in the wild. And really, REALLY, REALLY special to stay at scientific research centres. Not many kids my age would have this opportunity etc. etc. blah blah blah . . .

And you can see from the cheesy-grin photos how happy I am!!

The Emperor chicks are 100 per cent adorable. The parents are handsome and ginormous.

Emperors must be called Emperors because they're incredibly powerful. As well as long-distance walkers, they're Olympic swimmers. They can dive deeper than any other bird and stay underwater for a whole 22 minutes.

Even though they're so huge, far bigger penguins once lived in the Antarctic. Fossils from near here reveal that 37 million years ago there were giant penguins – 2 metres high, way taller than me. Way taller than Patrick, even! I'm not sure I'd have liked to meet one of those!

You must read Terry's Penguin Blog (see link) because it's more scientific than mine, but in case you don't have time, here's the important bit: 'Our Emperor penguins are SEVERELY THREATENED and their populations are declining FAST. Overfishing means there's LESS FOOD for them to eat. And because they breed on ice, global warming means their BREEDING GROUND IS DISAPPEARING.'

It's hard enough for these penguins as it is. Not only do they have their massively long, freezing walk to do, but looking after the eggs and chicks is a real struggle. The mums and dads have to transfer the egg between them from one pair of feet to the other by shuffling around. If they drop the egg even for an instant, the baby inside will die; it's that cold. Also lots of chicks starve because the mum can't make the long trek back from the sea in time . . . or maybe she's died herself in the effort.

When all these penguins fight so, so hard for life, how can we even be thinking of killing 24 Scottish penguins?

Daisy Penguin is lucky to be alive. She still travels around on her parents' feet a lot, but sometimes, when they're at sea, she gets together with the other little ones in a group called a 'crèche'. She can't swim at the moment, but in December she'll have grown out of her baby fluff, have got herself some waterproof feathers and she'll take her first dip!

By then it will be midsummer here.

By then it will be Christmastime at home. We hope we'll be celebrating with Mac and his Lochnamorghy friends . . .

# 39

# Eileen

*Centaurus research station, Antarctic mainland*

I KEEP STUFFING it to the back of my mind, but it keeps sneaking back to the front. Especially now that I've voiced it out loud. I said some things, too, about change, which I didn't know I was going to say. They just came out. Funny how my mouth does that sometimes.

I spend the whole night thinking about it, what my mouth said and if that means I'm any closer to a decision. But I don't get any clarity, just a load of nasty images of that stick-insect blonde taking off her clothes in my bedroom and looking far sexier naked than I ever could. And of Doug . . . It brings me out in a cold sweat . . . I've never let myself picture any of it before, but suddenly there it is, playing out in front of me in technicolour . . .

My pillow is getting soggy. I get up and tiptoe around,

hunting in the cupboard for a fresh one, but I can't find any. I do notice a small, fluffy teddy bear who's sitting on the chest of drawers, for some reason. Maybe Patrick put it there for Daisy. It looks sympathetic, anyway. I grab it, take it back to bed with me and clutch it tight. I bury my face in its soft fur and let it absorb my wild, ugly sobbing.

Daisy's sleeping like a lamb in the other bed. I don't think she's heard a thing. She only stirs when my alarm goes off at 7.15 in the morning. Bless her, she must be exhausted with all that worry about her mum and dad, but hopefully she'll be all right now.

She skips to breakfast with her head held high, anyway. She's an amazing girl. At her age I wouldn't have managed anything like what she's managed. Not in my wildest dreams.

I'm flooded with that sicky feeling again; the feeling of not being good enough. It's always been there but I realize it's been getting out of hand recently. We have porridge for breakfast and even that makes me come over weepy. I don't think I'll be functioning very well today.

'For goodness' sake, stop dithering, Eileen. We have walking to do!'

'Of course we do, Mrs McCreedy,' I call back through the door. I'd only meant to pop back to the bedroom briefly but I seem to have gone into slow motion. I pull on my extra fleeces and boots and scarf and woolly hat (the one Keith gave me) then march out to the corridor. Everyone else is already gathered, ready for the next expedition.

Sir Robert and the BBC crew were due to film from the

air today but can't because the weather is doing the wrong things, so he comes with us again.

It's blustery and biting outside.

Daisy snuggles close to me as we whisk off in the Ski-Doos. There's no sun this morning, just powerful wind and snowflakes cascading down from the sky, whirling in our faces. The scientists keep radioing each other about 'conditions'. If it's this cold now, I can only imagine what it's like in winter.

The penguins are spread out like hundreds of skittles in a giant bowling alley. We stomp through the snow to find our three.

'There they are,' calls Terry. 'Oh, looks like Eileen is absent today.'

'Don't worry,' Patrick adds. 'She'll be busy out at sea, getting some food in.'

Of course, most of the parents are taking it in turns to get fish. I keep forgetting. All the same, I'm sad not to see Eileen Penguin. I hope she'll be back tomorrow.

Lots of parents are regurgitating into their babies' bills. Such long, strong beaks the mums and dads have. Veronica Penguin is standing staring into space. Daisy Penguin is scuttling around with some other chicks today, freckled with snow. They are unbelievably cute. I wouldn't mind cuddling one of them but it's not allowed.

'Look at that one,' Terry says, pointing to one that's diving into its mother's pouch head-first. The soles of tiny webbed feet disappear into the soft spongy feathers with a twist of grey fluff, then the tiny face pokes out from between the mum's feet. Daisy laughs.

We tramp along as best we can, but the wind is battering

us and getting stronger and stronger. The penguins hunch and huddle together. Mrs McCreedy totters wildly. She'd fall if Patrick wasn't gripping her arm so tightly on one side and Sir Robert on the other. Patrick looks at Terry with a face that's a question and Terry nods her answer.

'Right,' she says. 'Enough of this. For our own safety, we're going to have to take shelter.'

'Where?' I ask, looking around at the total lack of buildings.

'We'll have this up in a jiffy,' she answers, dragging a canvas bag from one of the Ski-Doos. The scientists act fast, unfolding it, hoisting it up and securing it against the gale with ropes and stakes.

'In you go,' calls Patrick, posting his grandmother into the tent.

We crawl inside after her. There's scarcely room for us and we're jam-packed, but I manage to put up the folding chair for Mrs McCreedy.

'Now we just have to sit tight until the squall is over,' Terry tells us.

So we do. We're so squished together it's almost snug.

Mrs McCreedy keeps looking at me. Not in the Eileen-do-this-Eileen-do-that way she sometimes does, but as if she's trying to work me out and is frankly a bit baffled. She's quiet. She's been down in the dumps ever since she found out Pip was dead, as if all her joy in the expedition has sapped away and she's just – literally – going through her paces.

I shouldn't have let that slip about Pip. My big mouth working overtime again. Maybe it's just as well she's had to concentrate on Daisy these last two days.

Daisy is grinning now, delighted with the adventure. She's perked up incredibly. She is so bouncy it's hard to keep her inside the tent. She keeps peering out of the crack in the flap.

'I want to see if any of the penguins are blowing about in the wind.'

'They'll be fine,' Patrick reassures her. 'They're totally used to it.'

A Thermos of mulligatawny soup is passed around. It's very welcome.

Daisy is full of questions. 'Terry, how do Emperors find their way all those miles across the ice in the solid dark of winter? How come they don't get lost?'

'That's a great question, and we don't really know the answer, Daisy. Some people think they navigate by the stars. Some people think they just have mysterious forces within themselves, a kind of inner satnav.'

'Birds are brilliant at that sort of thing,' Patrick says. 'Swifts migrate fourteen fricking thousand miles across the world back to the very same nook in the eaves of a cottage where they nested the year before. Homing pigeons are pretty cool that way, too.'

Sir Robert leans forward to tell Daisy a story. He's got such a knack of making people listen. 'A few years ago,' he begins, 'there was a kind old man who lived on an island off Brazil. And one day, on the beach, he discovered a Magellanic penguin who had swum too close to an oil spill. The poor bird was smothered in black, sticky oil all over his feathers, and couldn't move at all. The man took pity and spent hours cleaning off the penguin, then set him free. But that penguin, who lives way further south in Patagonia, knew his life had been saved. And he still regularly travels a whole two thousand miles back to the island just to visit the kind old man.'

Daisy's eyes are wide. 'Wow! Is that true?'

'Absolutely true.'

There's a gap in the conversation and we're all thinking our own thoughts. I am thinking about kind men. And unkind men. And thinking how strange it is that I told Mrs McCreedy and Patrick about Doug and the floozy. Even stranger to discover that Mrs McCreedy knew about his affair all along.

All through our trip I've been chatting with Doug on FaceTime as if he's the old Doug and I am the old Eileen, pretending to myself that everything's fine, because sometimes pretending is the only way to cope. I'm not sure I can pretend any longer, though. What on earth am I going to do?

The researchers are taking turns to check out the weather. They finally decide we can venture out and we crawl back into the scuffed snow. But we don't linger for long. Mrs M is shivering and, although she protests she is fine, we all know she's not. It's time to head back to base.

I'm getting used to those Ski-Doos now and am not so scared as I was to start with.

It's such a relief to get back to the warmth. In the bedroom at the research centre I update the logbook of our miles . . . we are at ninety-seven, so there are three more to go, which we'll have to do in the next two days. We've very nearly done it. I only wish Mrs McCreedy was happier about it. It's her grand scheme, after all, and it's a real shame she's lost her va-va-voom. Still, I expect she'll get it back once she's in charge of Lochnamorghy.

Next, I spend some time rummaging around my luggage and repacking my things. I won't be needing the swimming costume or T-shirt again, so they can go right to the bottom. And I'd like to make the most of the laundry facility here and get some smalls washed before the journey back to Scotland.

When I come back out into the lounge, I find the BBC crew chatting with Terry, Patrick and Daisy.

'Veronica's in the office, checking her emails,' Daisy tells me.

I had thought she was having a siesta. I should really make use of the office myself and see if there are any new sponsors for Operation PIP, but I'm aching with exhaustion.

Sir Robert pats the chair next to him and I feel honoured to go and sit there. We have a chat about seals, which is strangely soothing. He has just told me that the scientific name for seals is 'pinnipeds', when Mrs McCreedy marches into the room.

She eyes us all. Her face is like a thunderstorm. Her voice, when she speaks, is a harsh croak.

'I have an announcement to make.'

# 40

# Veronica

*Centaurus research station, Antarctic mainland*

THIS TIME I was not expecting anything much. However, an email from my agent, Mr Wallace, sprang up.

I ran through the sentences, failed to believe them, and read them again. Then I printed the message out, for my eyes sting if I look at a screen for too long and the letters were performing a slow waltz, making no sense. I adjusted my spectacles. The words still said the same.

> I regret to inform you that, following the survey, the buyer of The Ballahays has pulled out.

This in itself might not have been terrible news, as I was warming to him very little from what I knew of him. It would not be an exaggeration to say I have been fantasizing about giving him a sharp slap in the face. However, there was more.

The survey has unearthed not only the predictable problems with rotting beams and crumbling plaster, but an impediment huge enough to put off every potential buyer, to unequivocally block any sale and to render my home uninhabitable, even by me.

There is a structural problem: a colossal cavity under the house's foundations. It is partially filled with water and spells out subsidence and danger. It must have been there for years but, now that it has been discovered, it must be made safe immediately. My back room has been gradually sinking, without our noticing it. The kitchen is likely to follow.

The situation is not irremediable, but it will take a great deal of bolstering to shore the place up, a great deal of work by builders. And, of course, a very great deal of money.

We are talking hundreds of thousands of pounds. All my savings, and more.

I squeezed my eyes shut as the realization crept over me. The background throbbing of a distant generator seemed to grow louder, roaring through my head. How could I have thought The Ballahays was my strong fortress for so many years, whilst all the time it was liable to collapse at any minute? It is useless to me now.

I replied to the email immediately, punching the keys. I confirmed that my home is off the market until further notice.

No sooner had I done so than I was hit by another grim realization. Lochnamorghy.

To save it I am now reliant solely on our sponsorship

money. We have done well, but it is nowhere near enough. Even if it tripled in the next two days, it would be insufficient for me to buy the centre, let alone keep it running.

The truth sank into my heart like an icicle. Spitting bile at the cruel machinations of Fate, I jabbed out another email, to the agents of the sea life centre: *With regret and due to circumstances beyond my control, I must withdraw my offer.*

So as not to prolong the agony, I walk into the hall and announce the news to everyone at once. At least, I attempt to announce it, but I stumble over my words, curse myself for saying 'sustenance' instead of 'subsidence', march out of the room, fetch the bit of paper and simply read the email and my replies out to them.

Silence. Upturned faces filled with horror. I cannot bear to look at them, so I march straight out again.

Sir Robert follows me out. I pretend not to notice. His footsteps quicken behind me; he grasps my hand and forces me round, to face him.

'Veronica, listen!'

There is a crackling in my ears like a fire. I try to pull away, try not to listen, but his words filter through the noise and flames anyway.

'I am sorry, so very sorry about The Ballahays and what that means for your mission.'

'I do not want your pity.'

'Of course you don't but . . . I have been meaning to talk to you for so long. Trying to find the right moment, but there never seems to be the right moment, so I'm just going to say it now . . .'

345

'No!' I cry.

With a sharp twist, I wrest my hand free of his grasp, hissing at him like a goose.

I take refuge in my room, slamming the door shut behind me. I do not come out again, not even for supper.

I ignore the soft knock at my door and Terry's voice filtering through. 'It's me: Terry. Please let me in, Veronica. We need to talk. I really think it would help.'

I ignore the firmer knock from my grandson. 'Granny? We're all here for you. You should know that. Are you coming out for dinner? You should keep your strength up. Oh, come on, for Chrissake! No? Nothing doing? Oh well, have it your own way.'

I ignore the rhythmic *rat-tat-ta-tat* of Eileen's knock. 'Mrs McCreedy. Are you quite well? Is there anything I can bring you? Are we still going walking tomorrow? Only, it would be good to know.'

Daisy does not knock. She just yells through the wall. 'Remember the penguins!'

I am indeed remembering the penguins. Therein lies the problem. Is there any way I can possibly save them now?

No. Quite simply, no.

After night has fallen and everything has gone quiet, I stalk to the office again, a faint hope floundering that there might be some sort of news to redeem the situation. Another email has arrived, hot on the heels of the last. This time it's from Molly. She sounds upset. My competitor for the sea life centre has leapt straight in with a renewed offer, which has been accepted. The documents will be signed tomorrow.

No doubt the agents were wary of selling to a batty old woman anyway, and were just pleased that I have driven up the price somewhat.

Something inside my ribcage seems to collapse. Along with the fate of the sea life centre, the fate of its inhabitants is sealed. The date for the execution of twenty-four innocent penguins has now been brought forward and is set for 4 November. So soon! My companions and I will only just have set foot back in Scotland, and what a sad, sad welcome home that will be.

I spend the rest of the night warring with my bedclothes and forcing my brain down any channels of logic I can find, seeking some way we can save Lochnamorghy. However I look at it, we are doomed. Just when we were so close to achieving our goal and had gained so many supporters, too. Had the timing been different, it might have worked. If only we'd completed the walk a few months ago, we would have had time to garner more publicity and support; the funds could possibly have stretched enough to buy the sea life centre, anyway. I might then have somehow strung out my own money to pay for the Ballahays repairs. But even that would have been unlikely. I am not only financially ruined myself, but we have failed in everything we set out to do.

The next morning Eileen calls through the wall: 'Mrs McCreedy? Daisy and I are going to do our walk today anyway, if that's all right?'

She inserts a small pause which I do not fill. 'Only,' she continues, 'our time here is short and Daisy wants to see the Emperors again. She's keen to finish the hundred miles, so we'll keep track of the distance we cover.'

There is little point in this, but she is not going to stop pestering until she has had some sort of reply, so I give her a sharp 'As you wish' through the door.

'Are you sure you don't want to come, too? A bit of fresh air might do you good.'

'No.'

'No as in yes or no as in no?'

'No as in no, Eileen. I am not coming.'

The sounds of hustle and bustle and voices eventually fade. Everybody must have left for the day.

It seems Daisy has not yet realized that we have indeed failed in our mission. She will take it badly.

I feel responsible, as the one who introduced her to the idea of penguins in the first place, who fed her enthusiasm for them almost daily; who took her on her first penguin-spotting trip across the world and on this one; who introduced her to Mac. One moment I grieve for myself and The Ballahays, the next for the Lochnamorghy penguins. But most of all, I grieve for Daisy.

I hear voices again. I have not left my bedroom all day.

After much persuasion, I accept a baked potato but eat it alone in my room, loath to face anyone. But then Terry knocks and calls again. Reluctantly, I let her in. She perches on the edge of the bed and talks to me, telling me how much I have done to raise awareness of penguins and how important that is. How I should complete the hundred miles because the money raised might still go towards conservation projects that protect the environ-ment, saving the lives of many penguins.

'Not the Lochnamorghy penguins, though.'

'No, not those,' she acknowledges, 'but many others. Oh, Veronica, you haven't come this far only to come this far. Please keep going. We're all with you.'

The dear, kind girl – she is doing her utmost to make me feel better. It isn't working.


Patrick also comes in, and promises that he will visit the UK as soon as possible to help me tackle the issues with The Ballahays.

'It may not be all that bad, Granny. We'll get a second opinion, at least. We'll make plans slowly and wisely. I know that's not the normal Patrick approach, but I'm a hell of a lot better at sorting other peoples' lives than I am at my own. We'll work something out. Together.'

I look down at my bony, gnarled old hands. I try to say something but cannot trust my voice. In any case, there are no words.

Sir Robert, it seems, has decided to let me 'stew in my own juice', as my mother used to say. He will be exhausted from the day's filming, anyway.

Having brought me innumerable mugs of tea and foisted more food on me which I cannot eat, Terry and Patrick eventually leave me to rest. My bones ache. My head aches. My heart aches.

I am about to retire to bed when I catch sight of a square of white on the grey linoleum floor. A letter has been posted under my door.

# 41

# Veronica

*Dear, dear Veronica,*

*I can only guess how hard this must be for you. You have come so far and sacrificed so much. I am longing to help you with Operation PIP but it seems there is nothing I can do at this late stage. The Ballahays may yet be saved. Please hold on to this hope. You know that I and all your friends will support you every way we can.*

*This is a delicate time . . . but time is precious and I have let too much of it slip through my fingers. There is something I have been wanting to broach with you for months and it won't wait any longer. Forgive me for intruding on your thoughts now, but it is my hope that my request might bring you some comfort . . . Possibly even, after you have considered it for a while, some happiness.*

*Ever since we first met, I have felt a strange challenge in your presence. How can I describe it? It is almost as if you were daring me to love you but at the same time insisting that it was impossible. And, my goodness, love was the last thing on my mind. It seemed highly dangerous, especially where you were concerned. But how could I help myself? You shine with energy, with determination, with passion. You have a thirst for adventure and a fierce courage that leaves me in awe. You have been through terrible tragedies, and yet you find ways of turning everything to good. Such qualities are rare and precious. You are truly beautiful, inside and out. I think about you when I should be thinking about other things. You constantly surprise me. You make me a better man. I have loved you beyond belief these last two years and I will love you until my dying day.*

*I am not some green schoolboy blinded by infatuation and I'm aware you are not (quite) perfect, but who amongst us is? You know by now that I am far from it, but my hope is that you can put up with my moods, my tendency to overwork and to escape into nature when I cannot handle human issues. I question deeply if I deserve you, and I know that I do not; yet what a team you and I could be, Veronica! My life is insanely busy but over the last two years I have fought (mostly with the BBC) to ensure you are a part of it. How I would love you to be a much greater part. For as long as I can remember I have been wedded to my job, but you have opened up in me new wellsprings – longings to love you, to be loved by you, to be always at your side.*

*I want to wake every morning with you beside me. I want to look up from my breakfast coffee and see your dear face. I want always to talk with you, always to walk with you.*

*I would have declared all this long ago if I hadn't felt so stupid and inadequate. When we were in the Galápagos I clumsily asked you to come and live with me and hinted at marriage then, but it came out as a pathetic joke. No wonder you were angry.*

*So much has changed since then, but my heart has not changed. I ask you now, Veronica, will you consider taking one more great step? Will you marry me?*

*Forever yours,*
*Robert x*

# 42

# Veronica

*Dear Sir Robert,*
*I was astonished to receive your letter.*

*I am presuming this is not some kind of cruel prank and that your proposal is genuine?*

*If so, then I can only conclude that the extreme cold must have affected your brain. When you come to your senses again you will see that everything you've written is quite absurd.*

*With best regards,*
*Veronica*

# 43

# Veronica

'BEST REGARDS' ADMITTEDLY seems very formal for as good a friend as Sir Robert, but I am not going to spend hours agonizing about the wording. The intention is clear, and that is what matters.

I have delivered my message the same way he delivered his, by slipping it under his bedroom door.

I did not reread Sir Robert's missive. I have secreted it in the inside pocket of my suitcase, next to the lavender sachets. These days one rarely sees a letter that is so eloquent. These days one rarely sees a letter at all.

I was stunned to read his sentiments. Shocked. Dizzy. And for a moment, I will confess, those three pages of gallant handwriting did cheer me slightly. For a moment – a brief one – possibility trilled through my bloodstream.

For which person on earth does not long to be loved?

And who could be truer, kinder, more worthy than Sir

Robert? He whom I have admired since, years ago, I first set eyes on his face on the television screen as he expounded on the lifestyle of armadillos.

But we two are in the winter of our lives and can have few years left. It is useless to pretend otherwise. Flattered though I am, it is hard to believe this declaration was prompted by anything other than pity. I cannot boast the beauty for which I was once prized. Feminine wiles are no longer mine, and I possess neither that peachy complexion nor the sparkling vitality which should accompany romance. I am already growing deaf, slow and forgetful. Given the choice, I would conclude this long life with a triumphal flourish, but it is fast becoming apparent that that choice is not mine to make.

I have never been a fan of reality, for it is too unremittingly dark and bleak. I have chosen instead to see myself as a glorious heroine: strong, capable, indomitable. Now, much as I try to avoid it, reality is catching up with me. It descends like a black cloud.

Very little has ever scared me, and death itself holds no terrors. Yet I find myself, frankly, quite petrified at the prospect of sliding into a slow, ignominious decline. Sir Robert is several years younger than I. If, by any chance, he really did harbour fond feelings for me, how could I inflict upon him the grief of witnessing my disintegration? The thought of him seeing me so reduced is abhorrent. There is nothing in this world I should hate more.

Heart clogging with misery, I drag myself to the window, and draw back the curtain. More snow has fallen in the night. White wads are clinging to the pane.

Beyond, snow is stacked high on the roofs of the sheds and outbuildings, rumpled against their walls. The sky is hard, bare, bone-white.

I shudder. Today is the last day of October. The last day officially of our walk, and we have one single mile to complete. It will not be an easy mile.

Should we, in fact, bother with the mile at all?

Molly's news about Lochnamorghy has robbed me of all motivation, but everyone seems to think that the Operation PIP money we raise can be transferred to a different environmental cause.

Once more I have spent the whole night lamenting my losses. And the proposal from Sir Robert keeps haunting me, taunting me. I shake my head, trying to dispel the festering thoughts. The movement makes me reel and I sink back on to the bed.

I consider feigning illness to avoid the walk. I am in fact feeling distinctly under par. Pain inches up my vertebrae and stings the back of my eyes.

I suck in air, clutch at a last pale thread of hope. It may be that something ... something could have yet happened to redeem the penguins? A stay of execution by a kind benefactor, one of the wealthy cruise ship passengers who witnessed my Falklands speech?

I struggle up and make my way to the office. Breathless, I log on and bring up my emails once more. There is a new one.

*Dear Veronica,*
*I'm just writing to wish you good luck for your last day's walking.*

*I'm so very sorry you had to withdraw your offer. All the documents have been signed. Lochnamorghy now belongs to your competitor and there's nothing anyone can do for Mac and our other little guys. I know the money you've raised will go to a good cause anyway. Thank you so much for everything you've done to try to save us.*

*Warmest wishes,*
*Molly*

Poor Molly! She knew those twenty-four penguins better than anyone.

I shuffle back to my room.

At the door I am assailed by Daisy. Without any invitation she comes in and plomps herself beside me on my bed. Her mouth is downturned but her fists are clenched in determination.

'We have to finish the walk, Veronica. Remember the penguins.'

'I am remembering them, Daisy dear. But I fear we have done all we can.'

It is hard enough for me. How much harder it must be for her, a mere child who has not been toughened up by decades of disillusionment. I have no words of comfort to offer.

'Eileen thinks we should do the last mile,' she clamours. 'I think so, too. So many people are supporting us, all over the world.'

She still has not realized that this is indeed the end.

'We must accept our losses,' I tell her, my voice leaden.

'No. No, I'm not going to. We have to finish the walk, Veronica. Mac would want us to do it, even if . . .'

We both know how the sentence ends, although neither of us is prepared to complete it.

I summon up my last dregs of energy. With sorrow like a great yoke bearing down on me, I prepare for the last walk. I apply make-up – thick black on my eyebrows, deep rouge on my cheeks, bright scarlet on my lips; a bid to compensate for the faintness of my resolve.

Daisy and I proceed to the dining table, where miscellaneous scientists are gobbling down their full English breakfasts. Eileen fusses around me with a 'Mrs McCreedy this' and a 'Mrs McCreedy that', piling my plate high with sausages, toast and something that vaguely resembles scrambled eggs. I take a few mouthfuls but cannot manage more. My appetite has disappeared along with my dreams.

My eyes involuntarily flick across the room to Sir Robert, who is conversing with his filming posse. He registers my glance with a look of anguish. He walks towards me, uncertainty in every contour of his face.

I am in no mood for chatting, and he knows this. He pulls a seat close to me, perches on it, brushes my hand with his. I hope to God he is not going to say how sorry he is about The Ballahays, or Lochnamorghy, or press his romantic suit. I could not bear it.

I cannot, indeed, bear to look him in the eye. He informs me in a low voice that, seeing as time was lost in the blizzard the other day, he is required to fly over the land in the aircraft and do some filming from above for his BBC programme. There is no getting out of it.

'I was so hoping to do the final steps of your challenge with you, Veronica,' he adds miserably, 'but it wasn't meant to be.'

I manage a terse 'Never mind' before my mouth clamps shut again. In any case, it should be only Eileen, Daisy and myself who take the final steps together – we three who have made this long trek our binding commitment – with nobody else interfering. Not that it matters now.

It seems we are not to be left alone anyway, due to all the promises made to Daisy's parents. An argument is taking place between Terry and Patrick. As leader of the Locket Island project and a key researcher here, Terry feels she should escort Sir Robert and the documentary makers; she should be the one who points out the different areas of the colony, the route the Emperors took on their long march and the places where the ice has receded. But she also desperately wants to walk with us. Patrick is similarly divided.

They consult me on the matter, but I shrug my shoulders. It all seems so futile.

It is finally decided that Patrick will accompany us whilst Terry gets on with helping the BBC team. The latter all throw on their gear and take off together. The snow is so thick that two men have to lean heavily against the door of the study centre in order to open it. But the wind has dropped, they say. Soon after, I hear the noise of the Twin Otter aircraft lifting up and away.

My body is functioning at a particularly slow rate, and it takes me some time longer before I am ready. Patrick, Eileen and Daisy have all donned their many layers of outer clothing and mukluks way before I have managed the task.

Patrick ushers us on to the Ski-Doo and we set off for the colony once more. Not the triumphant trio I had envisaged, but a weary, doleful sample of humanity. We must be a sorry sight.

We are deposited in the same spot as before. It is apparently a good set-down point and a mile from the penguins via the easiest route. There is nothing easy about it, however.

The silence is profound, the coldness fierce. We are half swallowed up by the snow. It presses in on us, callous and clammy. Every step involves hauling a foot up, up, up, then planting it down deep again. It must be done with utmost care because I cannot see the hidden dips and dangers of the ground underneath. I feel my ankles might snap at any minute.

Patrick has brought a shovel with him. 'Tell you what. I can go a lot faster than you three. No offence, but I can. I'm used to it. But all this snowfall is only delaying you and making it fricking hard for you to get on. So what I'll do is I'll go on ahead and clear a track through it as I go. That way your walking will be easier. Don't worry, I won't go on too far, so you can just call if you need me.'

'Oh, you're such a good, kind lad,' Eileen exclaims.

He kicks and shovels the snow out of the way as he goes, and is soon some way ahead of us. We follow in the trench he has made, snow banked high on either side of us.

'Like following in the footsteps of good King Wenceslas, isn't it?' Eileen is doing her best to make it fun. She even warbles a few lines from the carol.

'Yes,' Daisy agrees and joins in shakily, also making an effort at cheeriness.

I remain silent, unable to dissemble.

The air tightens around us, hard and sour as disappointment. How can everything have turned out so terribly when we put in so much, when we gave it our all? I have always held that grit, determination (and medication) can get you anywhere. Failure, I believed, was impossible. How wrong I was. Just as I did when I was a young girl, I had got it into my head that I was invincible. Now it's plain that I am not. I have pushed and pushed, and I have pushed too far. Why didn't I recognize that failure is *always* a possibility, and in this particular venture was always, in truth, a probability.

No. I see I am like King Canute in the old stories, who wildly commanded the waves to stop, even as they greedily advanced up the beach to claim him.

I have unfairly dragged poor Eileen and Daisy into my preposterous scheme, too, making them rely on me, making them expect so much more than I could deliver. Why was I so damagingly ambitious? So unwilling to draw the line at a simple charity walk in Scotland? So unprepared for any small compromise that might have made success more likely?

I should have listened to Patrick. I belong in a care home. My life ought, by this time, to consist of television-watching with a circle of other oldies, slumped in an overheated beige lounge, playing bingo every Thursday and being brought mugs of dreadful tea made with teabags.

I begin to feel light-headed, but my heart is heavier than ever. I keep lifting my feet, putting one in front of the other. The ravaged snow creaks under my boots.

Fragments float on the air like ashes. I can hear my breath hissing; see it, too, fizzling out of me and into the atmosphere. It feels as if we have already walked miles this morning.

Cold prickles my cheeks, blades my skin, chills my marrow. I can no longer feel my limbs. My weight is so heavy on my stick I can almost sense it bending. Another step. And another.

I can't see anything around me any more, only murky glimpses of the future.

Mac and his friends will perish. Lochnamorghy will be demolished and replaced by concrete tower blocks. The Ballahays will doubtless be condemned, too, and may even have to be pulled down. And what will become of me, Veronica McCreedy? Sir Robert will shake his head sadly and say, 'I tried to help but she wouldn't have it. And alone she just wasn't enough.' Eileen will be shocked, at a loose end. She will go back to her vile husband and be enslaved to him for the rest of her days. Daisy will grow up bitter and disillusioned, never forgetting how she tried and failed to save twenty-four penguins and became attached to an old woman who let her down. Terry and Patrick will carry on with their scientific work, but for them it will be forever tainted by tragedy.

I let out a whimper, as if something inside me has died. Whatever made me think I could do it? Has there ever been anyone in the history of the world so puffed up with false self-belief? Now I see I count for very little. I am nothing more than an ancient husk of a woman, staggering through the snow, gasping for breath, failing more with every step. I have lost everything. I have disappointed those who put their trust in me. I am aware of them vaguely, the great mass of supporters, some from Scotland, many scattered throughout the world . . . And then there are Eileen and Daisy, who trudge on beside me, their forms becoming shadowy.

A wail of despair flings itself out from the depths of me. My legs buckle. The scenario feels strangely familiar.

I reach out for my two companions as I fall.

# 44

# Veronica

A TWISTED HEAP on the cold ground: me.

I allow myself to be hauled to my feet by Eileen and Daisy. I must make the effort. I must find it in me to go on, for their sakes. But I haven't the strength to take a single step further. It is as if the very blood in my veins has frozen.

'Shall we call Patrick?' Eileen asks, unaware of the gravity of the situation.

My grandson is ahead of us and I can just make him out, a tall figure shovelling madly. He has not seen my fall.

We cannot be far from the colony because I am aware of little shapes at the periphery of my vision, some zooming along horizontally, others waddling vertically. They are blurred, though, and my sight is further blocked by thick grains of snow heaped on my sunglasses.

'Look, Veronica!' Daisy's voice cuts through my faint-ness. 'It's an Adélie.'

I rub the snow away from my face. My eyes fix on a diminutive figure, closer than the others. It is waddling towards me, flippers stuck outwards, surrounded by brightness.

'Pip!'

The word shoots into the sky loudly, desperately. I cannot help it. This little one has reminded me so much and so suddenly of my dear Pip. Pip, who I had yearned to see again, who I had hoped to meet on Locket Island, but who is dead.

'Is it Pip?' asks Daisy.

Eileen's voice comes now. 'No, Daisy. It can't be, can it? He . . . lives on Locket Island, which is . . . well, a ter-ribly long way up north from here. It does look very like him, of course, but all the Adélies do look the same, don't they? All lovely, but very much the same. I mean, Terry and Patrick knew Pip extremely well, but even they could only tell him apart because of his unique orange flipper band, which . . . Oh . . . !'

Daisy gives a little shriek.

I sink to my knees once more, crippled by disbelief, ambushed by joy. The penguin, who – yes – is Pip, walks right into my open arms and lays his head against my old heart as if to say: 'I am here, Veronica. I have found you and you have found me, and everything is going to be all right.'

Of course, penguins always recognize the sound of their parents' calls, and I have just called him by name.

I sit there – a mishmash of bones and gristle and padded

Dynotherm fabrics and emotion – and a great guttural laugh erupts from my lungs. And doubtless it's against all the protocols of the scientific community but I am tightly hugging him. And for a moment I swing wildly into the past, to a time when I rocked my own darling baby in my arms. Then I swing back into the present and I know that this is not my child, far from it . . . but it *is* my own, long-lost penguin. My arms encircle the soft cylinder of his body, the wet feathers, the rubbery paddles of his feet. And his beak reaches up and touches my nose and his eyes look into mine. Now I am sobbing, sobbing into the great Antarctic wilderness; sobbing like a baby. My dearest, dearest Pip.

The voices of Daisy and Eileen are now raised, calling Patrick, and I lift my eyes briefly and register his face turned towards us and his figure pelting back down the track he's dug for our path.

Pip stretches out his flippers as if to show off the orangeness of his band.

Daisy is filming or taking photos or something. Eileen is making *oooh* and *aaah* noises. I am still sobbing and uttering the word 'Pip' again and again as if I am a speaking clock.

Patrick has arrived. He crouches low to look. Lets out a guffaw of delight and surprise.

'Christ-on-a-bike! It really is him. Well, little fella. We thought you were a goner! And there's me thinking those tracking devices were totally ungetoffable. Ditched yours and left it at the bottom of the sea, did you? Just as well you managed to keep on your armband. We knew some Adélies were moving south because of the changing

366

climate, but I never, never expected to find you here. I've always known birds have the most amazing inner radars but this is bloody fabulous. It's like you actually knew Granny was here, didn't you?'

'Of course he knew,' I say through my waterfall of tears. 'You knew, didn't you, Pip?'

My penguin looks up at me out of his white-rimmed eyes, with intelligence and curiosity and – call me ridiculous, but I'm sure it is there – love.

This is real. The snow is too wet, the ground too hard and Pip's little body too solid for this to be a dream. The story of the Patagonian penguin who still visits his rescuer in Brazil comes to my mind and I think: well, this does happen. And Pip, after all, sees me as his parent, for it is I who saved him and fed him and cared for him in his hour of need, and it is my voice that he recognizes.

I speak again, to assure him that it really is me. 'Pip, let me introduce you to my two dearest friends, Eileen and Daisy.'

'Pleased to meet you, Pip,' Eileen says, actually sticking out her hand as if she expects him to shake it. He doesn't shake it, but he does lever his head towards it and give it a gentle peck.

'We love you, Pip!' Daisy declares, over the moon to meet him, of course. He lets her stroke his gleaming chest feathers. He has not forgotten that our species were once his family.

'Not too much handling now, even with gloves on,' says Patrick. 'Rules is rules. Wild penguins is wild penguins, even if they *have* been brought up by humans.'

Then he laughs. 'My God, talking of "wild", Terry is going to go wild with joy.'

He reaches into his kitbag, takes out a new tracker and fixes it to Pip straight away. 'Don't want to lose you again, mate!'

'Are you going to stay down there all day, Mrs McCreedy?' Eileen asks.

In truth it is not 100 per cent comfortable. 'No. Help me up again, if you would be so kind. We have a little more walking to do.'

They haul me up again, and we set off towards the colony, verve and delight rekindled.

Pip walks with us.

Our long march is done. I am surprised and gladdened to see two familiar figures waiting for us at the colony. Sir Robert and Terry.

As we approach they come towards us with cautious smiles. 'Perfect conditions for filming today,' Terry explains, 'and we finished earlier than expected so managed to get away. We thought you'd be here by now and wanted to congratulate you on finishing your walk. Well done, well done, everyone!'

She wraps us in her warm hugs, which are most welcome in this searing cold.

Sir Robert kisses us all on both cheeks. Daisy stands on tiptoe to be kissed, understanding that stooping low is not good for old limbs. I am proud of Eileen, proud of Daisy and – yes – proud of myself. Pip's presence has lifted me enormously. He has been waddling alongside us, with typical penguin curiosity. No doubt he was on his way to the colony anyway, since Adélies get on very well with Emperors. And nobody can convince me otherwise: he knows me and wants to be with me.

Now Patrick points at him and says to Terry: 'Recognize anybody?'

She looks at Pip, performs what I believe is called a double-take, and gasps.

'Oh my God! PIP!'

She drops on to her knees, holding out her arms. Pip walks into them, just as he did with me. He knows her, too, I am sure of it.

The world has become very fuzzy due to my unfortunate eye condition and, much as I scrub at my cheeks, they seem to be wetter than ever. I catch a little sob coming from Eileen, and realize that, at this point, everyone else seems to be suffering from the eye condition, too.

Patrick is fumbling with a small flask.

'Champagne, anyone? There's just enough for a sip each, but more back at base. No posh glasses, I'm afraid – they wouldn't survive the cold.'

I accept the plastic champagne flute he holds out. We raise our glasses to Pip, to the Emperors and to each other. Then, hesitatingly, we also toast the Lochnamorghy penguins, wishing them a happy final few days of life.

'I am sorry,' I whisper across the world to them. 'We did our utmost.'

Sir Robert has somehow caught my words through his woolly hat and hood. 'Nobody could have done more,' he murmurs, his eyes fixed on mine. This time I hold his gaze for a moment.

'Photo shoot!' calls Daisy.

369

Phones are passed around and we pose with our plastic glasses aloft in different combinations with the penguins. Eileen takes out the folding chair and I lower my creaking body into it so that I am on the right level to pose with Pip. He stretches up and gives the glass a little peck, knocking it sideways, bringing us laughter. I manage to redeem a small amount of champagne.

I take a sip. The sensation is strange – freezing and vibrant – and with it comes an idea, a quick bolt of hope zizzing through me.

Eileen is stomping her feet. 'Brrr.'

Patrick is rummaging in his backpack again. 'OK, OK, that's enough of the cold stuff. Mugs! And a bit of warmth' – and he produces a Thermos. Thank goodness for his foresight, and for hot, gloopy tomato soup.

Sir Robert sidles up to me again. 'Are you all right, Veronica?' he whispers. 'I was worried earlier that you were putting on your brave face, but you seem so different now.'

'I *am* different, Sir Robert. I am indeed.'

# 45

# Veronica

I WAKE WITH a start. I reach for my watch, which is lying on the bedside table. It is 11.15 at night. Silence reigns in the building. Everyone has retired to bed because they all, myself included, believe in early mornings. In my dreams an image of digital numbers has been staring, blinking repetitively.

Alarmed, I struggle from my bed and reach for my pedometer.

It will only tell me of the day's walking, not the entirety of the month's distance. I try to think. Eileen, Daisy and I had an equal mileage two days ago . . . but I then missed a day's walking because I was so upset about the disaster of the Ballahays survey and losing Lochnamorghy. This can only mean that the others have completed their hundred miles but I have not. My own tally is a mere ninety-nine.

It is the last night of October, and time is out . . . Unless I can walk one mile in . . . what is now forty-two minutes. My head spins. A young person could do it easily, but could I?

The image of Pip, still imprinted on my heart, tells me I cannot give up now. I am so nearly there with it. I am the first Penguin Ambassador and I have vowed to complete this challenge; if it cannot save Mac and his friends, it will at least support penguin conservation.

And yes, cynics would say I should simply lie to the general public and pretend that I have walked the full distance, but I could never live with myself were I to take their money under false pretences.

In a mad flurry I throw on my warmest clothes and mukluks. I catapult out of my bedroom. I fiddle with my pedometer, squinting at it and ensuring it is set correctly, simultaneously pacing the corridor. A creak behind me tells me that another door has opened – one of the bedrooms. I turn and see Sir Robert, wrapped in a thick tartan dressing gown. He takes a step towards me.

'Where are you going, Veronica? Surely not out, not at this hour. You are in Antarctica, remember?'

He must think that the very last of my marbles has rolled away and been lost for ever. I attempt an explanation. 'Operation PIP,' I gasp, walking on the spot. 'There is another mile to do and I must do it by midnight. And, before you suggest it, I refuse to do it merely walking up and down the corridor.'

His eyes penetrate mine. He knows I will not stop, not at this stage.

'Well, I should like to walk with you, if I may? Would

you mind pacing around the sitting room a couple of times? I will be with you in two minutes.'

I do as I am told. To be honest, I am grateful for company on this last leg; and to be yet more honest, his is the company I crave. As I trek around the room I'm assailed by the strength of my own feelings, and I see how very much in denial of them I have been of late. The more I strive to banish them, the more they come hurtling back.

Sir Robert emerges very soon, clad in his winter warmers.

'Can I suggest that, yes, we go outside, but that we just walk around the periphery of the study centre? To go beyond would be risky and irresponsible, to say the least.'

He is quite right, of course.

'Ah, Sir Robert. The voice of reason.'

He smiles. 'Tough though we are, we're not highly trained in Antarctic survival. You may not be quite strong enough to carry me back to base if I happen to collapse.'

'Very well,' I reply.

The scientists keep the area around the building as free from snow as possible, so this seems a sensible plan.

Cold encircles us once more as we step outside. The night is wrapped in a shimmery shawl. A thousand stars have taken their places across the sky. They peep down on us like twinkling eyes; surprised, amused, goading us on.

A thick fleece of snow spreads, undulating, into the distance, finely sequinned in the silver light. A thinner tissue of fresh snow has gathered in the cleared pathway, but it is not sufficient to hinder our walk. I have my stick and Sir Robert's strong arm to support me on my other side. I am supporting him also.

We pace in silence for a while, covering the ground as quickly as we can. I skid slightly on some ice, uttering a sharp cry. Sir Robert tightens his hold and steadies me.

The silence resumes. The stars glimmer. With each footfall there is a soft crunch of snow.

'Veronica, may I ask you something?'

Despite the cold I feel warmth flooding into my heart.

If he proposes marriage again, I must refuse. The answer must categorically be no.

But at this moment, under those wickedly beautiful southern stars, I fear I may say yes.

It would be better, then, if he didn't ask.

'May I ask you something?' he repeats, thinking I haven't heard.

'Of course you may,' my voice answers without my permission.

Three more paces, then he speaks again. 'As you agreed earlier, you are different to the Veronica of twenty-four hours ago. Your spark seems to have come back.'

It is true. Despite the fact that everything else has gone awry, my inner spark, if I can claim to have one, is glowing brightly since my reunion with Pip.

'I am going to speak of this one last time,' Sir Robert declares. 'If it is painful to you, please tell me to stop . . .'

There is a pause here, and I should do that; I should tell him to stop . . . but I do not.

'I feel I didn't do you or myself justice in my letter,' he resumes, 'and I want to try again. And if I fail again, fail better. When I talk about wildlife I am competent with words, but when it comes to matters of the heart, my sentences tie themselves in terrible knots. I have tried to convey my feelings in writing, but there are some things our poxy vocabulary isn't wide or deep enough to express. On top of that, I can't let myself give up hope yet. I have read your answer over and over . . . and you did not actually say no.'

'Didn't I?' I reply with a sharp intake of breath. 'I thought I had made it perfectly clear.' That was uncivil of me. 'I am listening,' I add, still putting one foot carefully in front of the other.

'You must have known for ages how much I admire you. How much I always have done. How I adore you and love you, Veronica McCreedy.'

I drink up his words but at the same time I shake my head.

'Sir Robert, do not be so stupid.'

'Stupid? I think not. You . . . you didn't realize I had fallen for you? And there was me thinking it was written all over my face every time I looked at you.'

'No! It cannot be possible. How can you even entertain such an idea when I am always so cantankerous and crabby?'

'You have a forthright way about you, and that is one of the things I love. But it is your choices that reveal the true you. And your choices show you to be nothing short of extraordinary. In your world, possibilities become probabilities and probabilities become fact. And anything, literally anything, can happen. I want to be part of your world, Veronica McCreedy. You have lit me up with love – such a love – love like nothing I have ever known. And I so desperately want everything to be perfect for you. You are caring and courageous and nobody deserves happiness more than you. But all I have to offer is myself. I would get down on one knee but it would take a crane to get me up again, and we're in a hurry so I'd better not. And so, here goes. Once more I beg you: Veronica, will you marry me?'

I take another few paces, savouring the moment, listening to the echo of his words, feeling the contrast between the cold cut of the air and the warmth within that curls around my heart like a blanket.

Then I make myself say it. 'No, Sir Robert, I will not marry you.'

'You do not feel you could love me at all, then?'

. He sounds so crestfallen. His hold on my arm loosens a little. His feet are dragging.

'It isn't that,' I acknowledge. Why does this have to be so difficult?

'What is it, then?'

I owe him an explanation, but even that will be painful. I glance up at the stars, seeking inspiration. They look so near I could almost reach out and take one.

Another breath. Then, as if slowly carving up my own heart, I destroy all the magic of this moment. 'My personal dignity has always meant a lot to me, Sir Robert. If my physical functions deteriorate or my mental capacity should desert me . . . if am confined to a wheelchair . . . if I should become unable to use a fork or spell my own name . . .'

He finishes for me. 'You would not wish me to become your carer. Veronica, I have thought about it too, because at our age these things can happen. It would hurt, of course, to see you suffer in any way. But please know that my love is strong enough to withstand all of this, to endure no matter what happens.'

He talks of love so much. I stop walking for a moment and turn towards him, for I need to search his eyes. Even in the darkness I see the love right there; huge, fathomless, shining like the sea.

'Do you trust me on this?' he asks.

'I do,' I reply truthfully. Sir Robert does not lie. I should have given him more credit in the first place and never presumed his feeling was mere pity.

'Anyway,' he continues, 'it's just as likely I'll be the one who repeats myself endlessly and needs to be spoon-fed – who knows? The real question is this: do *you* care for *me* enough?'

'I do!' I cry, before I can stop myself.

At my answer, I sense a great gladdening going on right next to me. 'So – forgive me if I'm wrong,' he murmurs after another beat, and now his voice becomes louder, surer, 'but I thought you liked risk?'

'I do,' I protest.

Now I realize I have said 'I do' three times.

And, like the dawn, everything starts springing into focus. When you are depressed there are no answers; no good ones, anyway. There is only bleakness. But when something good happens – the sudden appearance of a much-loved penguin who you thought was dead, for example – a tide of possibilities comes flooding back.

If the remainder of my life is to contain any joy or significance, my dignity may just have to be sacrificed, my fear of decrepitude shunned. I shall take that risk, make that sacrifice; for at last I know it: my wish to be with Sir Robert is far, far greater than my fear.

Out of all the many risks I have taken, this is surely the biggest. I will be brave and I will trust ... in us. I will trust in love.

'I would very much like to walk by your side for a while longer,' I admit.

'Is that a yes?' he asks, breathless.

Dazzled, laughing with wonderment, I snatch my star. 'That is a yes, Sir Robert. I *shall* marry you.'

And then I feel it – what I have not felt for fifty years and what I have not felt with such soaring elation for a full seventy-five years: the touch of a man's lips on mine.

The moment lasts, so sweet – so unimaginably sweet – and his arms slip around me and I feel loved, madly and wholly loved at last.

'Incidentally, I love you too,' I confess. He lets out a cry, as if the joy is so huge it cannot be kept in.

And now my own emotion is causing me to hallucinate, for the sky is awash with dancing lights. I suck in deep breaths and blink several times, but they are still there, flickering, bending, fanning out in great waves of violet, green and gold.

'It's the Aurora Australis, the Southern Lights,' Sir Robert gasps.

We gaze and gaze. It seems that all the crazy, miraculous, wonderful things that have been hiding throughout my life now cannot contain themselves any longer; they are spilling out across the universe.

As the minutes slide towards midnight we carry on, talking about our love and much else besides. And as we talk we continue walking until our outsides are appallingly numb; but inside we are burning brighter than ever.

'Sir Robert?' I say as the lights fade and at last we step back into the warmth, my miles completed (slightly over, according to the pedometer).

'Do you think you could call me just Robert now?' he asks.

I consider. 'Oh no. I don't think so. Sir Robert,' I continue, 'there is something I'd like to ask you. This is not in any way a condition of our marriage, but it is a sort of proposal of my own.'

'Do you realize, Veronica, this is the first time you have ever asked me for anything?'

It is true.

'What a long way you've come,' he whispers. He smiles and kisses me again, lightly this time. 'Veronica, I would give you the Crown jewels if I could. But I doubt that's what you want.'

'No, that isn't what I want. It is just a small favour.'

'Name it,' he says.

# 46

# Veronica

WHAT SMILES MEET us when we break the news to our friends in the morning. What glowing congratulations! What cries of delight!

Eileen bursts into tears and I find myself wrapped in a damp, squashy hug.

'I can't help it, Mrs McCreedy! I have to, I'm just so happy for you. It's wonderful. Gosh! Just gosh. And double-gosh.'

Patrick is all agog, too. He prises Eileen off me so that he can embrace me tightly. 'This is well cool. Amazing. Nice one, Granny.'

Then Terry, taking her turn, cries, 'I've been hoping for this to happen for so long! You and Sir Robert are made for one another, and you deserve to be so happy. And I know you will be.' She adds, in a whisper that everyone can hear: 'What a catch, Veronica!'

Sir Robert is also receiving his share of hugs.

Daisy is beside herself with glee, pirouetting around us. 'Wow, I didn't think you could *do* marrying when you were so old.'

Eileen reprimands her. 'Don't be rude, Daisy. They are not old – well, not much . . . that is, I mean, age is only a matter of numbers. It's not a real thing, not if you're fit and well and can do things like long hikes in Antarctica. It's only in the mind, isn't it? And even if it wasn't, love is like a begonia . . . you never can predict when it's going to bloom. Or like a Hoover bag that might just suddenly explode at any time . . .'

Daisy hoots with laughter. 'You're saying love is like a HOOVER BAG, Eileen?'

Sir Robert smiles. 'Or like a fine Scotch whisky. It just gets better with age.'

We must inure ourselves to incredulity such as Daisy's. At her age, I, too, was baffled – disgusted, even – if ever I witnessed affection between two elderly people. Now I understand that this is the best and truest love, for it does not look with the eyes, but with the soul. It is not a physical compulsion; it is a deep inner connection. Just because our bodies are decayed, does it mean our hearts are decayed, too? No! Our hearts are grown huge.

We reveal our plans to the assembled company. We shall get married with all due pomp, circumstance and officialdom at some stage later in Scotland, but both my fiancé and I would like an immediate, informal ceremony whilst we are here in Antarctica. This is largely because we would love Pip to be present.

We cannot wear glad rags because warmth is of

paramount importance, but we don our mukluks, fleece jackets, hats and sundries and we are borne in the direction of the colony, this time in the snowmobile. In the milky promise of morning, we trek towards the Emperors one last time.

Sir Robert and I walk hand in hand. We are both a little weary, and our steps are slow. And we are aware of various issues, dark and menacing like the birds of prey that wheel above us. Life will never be free of such shadows. Yet for now we focus only on the good: each other's company and the prospect of the adventures together that still lie ahead.

Once again, we enter the enchanted world of penguins. Around us, stunning Emperors and Empresses stand like statues, slide on their bellies and waddle about in the snow. With Terry and Patrick's help, we quickly identify Veronica Penguin and Eileen Penguin. Crumbs of ice glint in their plumage, as if they are bedecked with jewels. Daisy Penguin rushes around them, bobbing her head up and down and twittering incessantly.

There is no sign of Pip, though. A couple of other Adélies scoot along the ice . . . but, no, they are not wearing orange flipper bands.

'Pip, Pip!' I call, hoping he might hear if he is anywhere in the vicinity, hoping he might recognize my voice.

We pick a place with a backdrop of sculpted ice, like a castle constructed from frosted glass and spun lace. We feel like a king and queen, with all our subjects gathered around; a motley assortment of humans jumping about to stay warm, but also a vast throng of courtiers arrayed in their liveries of silken black, grey, yellow and gold.

And suddenly, miraculously, Pip is amongst them, waddling to the front – a smaller, stumpier but most loyal and unique friend. And, once again, everything feels right.

'Now,' I say, turning to my husband-to-be.

We must be brief, because the icebreaker ship is already anchored not far away, and smaller boats are bobbing on the waves with provisions for the research centre. Sir Robert, Eileen, Daisy and I will shortly leave on the ship. With these singularly wonderful friends, I shall travel back through the Drake Passage to South America, across the land, sea and sky to Scotland. And, compared to the Veronica McCreedy who came here, I shall do it a wiser and a far happier woman.

Sir Robert cocoons my hands in his. We look into each other's eyes. My heart roars with joy because everything from now on will be shared with this dear, dear man.

'I hereby vow to marry you,' I proclaim, 'to love you for ever more, Sir Robert; to give to you all that I have and all that I am.'

'I hereby vow to marry you, Veronica, and to give you my all, and to love you for ever.'

We kiss tenderly to the sound of humans clapping, a wolf whistle that must have come from Patrick, and a cacophony of penguin squawks and trumpeting. In a moment there will be champagne in plastic glasses and there will be soup, for I spied Terry and my grandson stowing it away as we left. This is strange, as ceremonies go, but it is enough, for this cold, for this place, for now.

Except that Sir Robert gently tugs at my glove, pulls it off and slips a ring on to my finger.

It is simple but exquisitely beautiful; a single diamond flashing in a gold setting. On either side of the diamond, intricate patterns are etched into the metal. They are tiny penguins.

Sir Robert grins. 'Because penguins are for ever.'

The inclemency of the climate will not allow me to admire the ring for long, but there will be time for that. I pull my glove back on over it, feeling more deeply moved than I am prepared to admit. Indeed, my eyes are stinging profusely and I do not trust myself to speak at all.

Sir Robert's eyes are shining, too. The diamond, he informs me, is ethically sourced. He had the ring made months ago and has been carrying it around with him ever since, just in case.

When I look up again, I scan the penguins for the orange flipper band, for Pip, but he is nowhere to be seen. He must have waddled off, perhaps back to sea. I can't help wondering if he knew that this happy ceremony was also going to be the last time we would ever see each other, my dearest penguin and I. And that – for him, too – saying goodbye would simply be too painful.

I must not dwell on that. Against all the odds, I have been granted another chance to see him, and he has been here today, on this occasion that means so very much to me. I will not be cast down.

I send a quiet message out into the snow and wind and ice that I love him, and will never, never forget him.

# 47

# Eileen

*In transit*

IT WAS WONDERFUL seeing Mrs McCreedy and Sir Robert getting married – semi-married, I suppose. But it was awful saying goodbye to Pip. Wonderful that we've done all our hundred miles inside a month. But awful that we haven't saved Lochnamorghy in spite of it. Wonderful that we're going home. But awful that home isn't home any more, either for Mrs McCreedy or for me. She has the disaster of The Ballahays, and I have the disaster of Doug. What to do, what to do?

At least Daisy is happier about her family now. She's broken-hearted about Mac, though.

I am sick as a dog again during the Drake Passage, and that bit of the journey seems to go on for ever. The world and my insides crash around so much in opposite directions that I'm sure I'll never put all the pieces of me back together again.

I do eventually, though. Mrs M has been pretty much fine, just grumpy about the fact she couldn't 'perambulate along the deck' because she kept being thrown off balance. I think her new beau (haha, what fun to be calling Sir Robert Saddlebow that) was struck with seasickness, too, because I didn't see much of him.

Daisy wasn't as ill as last time, but has been hit by exhaustion. A girl her age does need routine and structure and her own family around, and all this excitement has maybe been too much for her. It certainly has been a month none of us will ever forget.

I am on deck, leaning on the ship's side and staring out to the miles and miles of ocean, when I suddenly realize I'm not alone. Mrs M is at my side, looking windswept and determined.

'Are you all right, Eileen?'

'Yes, Mrs McCreedy. I'm just having a think. Just trying to take it all in. There's such a lot to take in, isn't there?'

'There certainly is.'

'I do wish I was strong, like you, Mrs McCreedy.'

'Strong?' she mutters. 'Well, I must say, "strong" is open to interpretation. I used to believe it meant hardness, blocking off one's feelings, never sharing, never letting on, never crying. And I suspect you think strength means diving headlong into adventures. But real strength also means trusting. Trusting others, and trusting yourself, too. Allowing yourself to feel what you feel. Knowing that, although we cannot see it, there is more, much more, beyond.'

I nod wisely and turn my face back to the sea, but it still seems to be just full of questions; questions forever rolling in and out, backwards and forwards.

South America. We're stopping overnight in Ushuaia. We badly need to find our land legs.

Keith is here, waiting for us as we wobble off the ship, keen to help us with our luggage and anything else. It's just lovely to see him again. He is in a multicoloured bomber jacket and has a smart new haircut.

We have a nice dinner all together (king crab on the waterfront) and stroll back to the hotel. How strange it is not to be measuring every step!

Keith stops off for a drink in the bar, offering to buy a round, and I say yes please to a nightcap – perhaps a hot toddy (although I'd really prefer a Horlicks). But the others all say they need an early night and disappear quickly up to their rooms.

Keith and I are sitting there like a couple of lemons.

Keith says: 'It sounds as if you've had a (mostly) marvellous time. I hope you're proud of yourself, Eileen. You are the glue of this whole enterprise, I hope you realize?'

How funny he is. Me – the glue!

'I do feel proud, yes. Yes, I think I do. But, Keith, there's still so much to worry about. So much that's not settled or anywhere near right.'

'So I gather.' He pushes his hair back from his brow, frowning. 'Are you going to stay with Mrs McCreedy once she's moved in with her Robert?'

We've talked about this, of course. 'I'll help her out, for sure, wherever she ends up. We discussed it at Centaurus and she said: "I absolutely cannot manage without you, Eileen." Those were her exact words. So that's that. It's not so much a question of whether I stay with *her* as whether I stay with Doug.'

He blinks.

'You're thinking of leaving your husband?' he asks his beer. Only, he must really be asking me.

It's so hard. One day I think, well, of course I must leave Doug. Of course he is a selfish cad and not the man I fell in love with (or thought I did) all those years ago. He is no good for me and our marriage is a sham. But then I think, Eileen, what on earth are you going to do? Your whole life has circled around Mrs McCreedy and Doug, for decades and decades, and everything is going to be different in Mrs McCreedy-world, and if you lose Doug you'll have to build up some kind of new life for yourself out of nothing, nothing at all. And, if I'm quite honest, I'm knackered at even the thought of it. How can I, who haven't known anything else (except a month's walking and looking at penguins) – how can I manage? When I look ahead, all I see is a big black hole; a black hole that's threatening to swallow me up.

I try to explain this to Keith and he says that, although he's never been married, he gets what I mean. He, too, feels like he's looking into a void sometimes when he tries to imagine the future. After a little pause, he adds that it's exciting as well as scary, though. And he says, for what it's worth, he reckons I should leave Doug because he's clearly unworthy of me and you never know what's around the corner, do you?

Then I say 'Thank you,' and 'Thank you, Keith, that's helpful,' and 'I think I'll go to bed now.'

# 48

# Veronica

*Edinburgh*

I HAVE NEVER warmed to religion. There are good reasons for this. However, when I look back on my life, I sometimes wonder if there could be a guiding force after all, a benevolent being who has been keeping an eye on me all along; who sent me Eileen; who ensured I sought out my grandson; who steered me towards penguins; who gave me hope for the future embodied in the small personage of dear Daisy; who determined that I should meet Sir Robert.

I do not know. But I do know that life has regained its purpose. I am set on a clear path instead of wandering alone in the dark. I no longer spend my life looking back with bitterness and regret. I am striding forward, and I am doing so in the very best company.

I have learned a new lesson from the penguins. They have shown me that not everything can be achieved by a single individual, however tiresomely stubborn that individual may be. A great deal more can be achieved when we share. Together we are far, far stronger.

Eileen and I have been residing with Sir Robert in his Edinburgh abode for the last month. Our existence is somewhat cramped, for the house is not large. It is pleasant and sunny, though, with its high ceilings and south-facing balconette, although one must watch the three hazardously steep steps up to the front door. A selection of items from The Ballahays have been moved here whilst the builders are at work. Sir Robert is anxious that we should feel at home.

Eileen, who is in need of time to think, scuttles in and out; grateful, scatty, wavering about her own situation in regard to the despicable Doug. She occupies the spare room. There is only one. Which means it has been compulsory for me to share a bedroom with somebody else, a situation that has not arisen since the days of my late ex-husband, Hugh. I might add that sharing with Sir Robert is an altogether different and exponentially better experience.

We are not yet legally wed, but who am I, with my flawed past, to lay down rules in that department? We have, in any case, made vows in Antarctica amongst penguins, and if that is not a solemn oath, I don't know what is.

Our bond grows ever stronger, and daily we strive to understand one another better, sometimes using words, sometimes forgetting them, allowing each other mistakes.

I am learning to laugh at myself; a new and peculiarly agreeable sensation.

In many ways I feel like a teenager again. I had almost forgotten the sweetness of old-fashioned romance. So many playful little joys blossom daily. A smiling heart that I find carved in the butter pat as I am about to spread my toast. A red rose on the dressing table, lodged in the bristles of my hairbrush. A love letter discovered nestling inside my handbag when I am hunting for my powder compact. I think up ways of reciprocating. A forest of candles lit and soft orchestral music playing when Sir Robert arrives home. Chocolate penguins arranged beak-to-beak on his laptop. His favourite whisky. I have also been busy researching a more significant gift, something he has always wanted.

If anyone else knew of these amorous gestures between geriatrics, they might deride and scoff, but they do not know ... and even if they did, when have I ever cared about the opinion of others?

We each have our little ways. When I first came down to breakfast and discovered Sir Robert standing on one leg, I was somewhat startled.

'I do it every day when at home,' he informed me, 'whilst waiting for the kettle to boil. It is supposed to be very good for you, you know?'

'Indeed?' I asked, observing him wobble.

'Yes. When you attempt the one-leg balance, your brain recalibrates, forms new connections and strengthens the coordination between your ears, eyes, joints ... Falls are due to a lack of balance, you know. Have you ever seen me fall, Veronica?'

I had to admit, I had not.

'Well then, there you are. You should do it, too.'

He held out his hand to me. I accepted it, and raised one foot gingerly off the floor.

When Eileen entered the kitchen, she found us side by side, each standing on one leg on the herringbone tiles, with a look of utter concentration on our faces.

'Whoops, did I disturb something?'

She frets about coming across Sir Robert and I engaged in some sort of embarrassing entanglement. At the same time, I suspect she rather hopes she will.

Once I'd explained to her the health benefits of standing on one leg, she was fascinated.

'Let me try,' she said. Stretching out both arms to steady herself, she lifted one leg up.

'Look at us, like a trio of flamingos,' Sir Robert laughed.

With pleasure I recalled the flamingos we met in the Galápagos. I was unable to maintain the pose for long, though, and I was the first to topple and grab a chair. Sir Robert followed soon after. But Eileen ably remained one-legged for ages.

'It's my flat feet,' she said. 'I knew they had to be good for something.'

As well as a newly intimate personal relationship, Sir Robert and I are engaged in a budding professional relationship. Great plans are afoot, but I had not taken into account how extraordinarily busy he is with his conservation, charity and BBC work. Often he must be away. I have lost count of the number of meetings that we have held in the last few weeks, some in offices and some through the Skype oojamaflip and some weird contraption called Zoom. We sift through information, consult experts, discuss different eventualities. At times I feel quite addled with the labyrinth of decisions, but we remind each other that the only way forward is to take one step at a time. We shall get there.

I cannot say it is easy, though. Many are the times when I am close to cracking under the strain. Frequently this is due to the stupidity of the digital world, or to the stupidity of human beings and the progress-defying bureaucracy we have created. Sometimes I am so incensed I almost take my anger out on Sir Robert, or Eileen. Instead, I have been getting through my tea set collection, piece by piece. For the feelings of my loved ones are far more valuable than my teacups. With every new annoyance I have chosen a cup, a saucer, a jug or – when the frustration is particularly extreme – a teapot, and I have taken it to the concreted area behind the back wall of Sir Robert's house, and I have smashed it to smithereens. Afterwards I am able to proceed with my business with renewed equanimity.

If you are in possession of a short temper and a good selection of teacups, this is a therapy I would highly recommend.

Sir Robert owns an elderly maroon Volkswagen Golf, which he drives with speed and precision. One afternoon, at my request, he drives me to see the Lochnamorghy site. The sea life centre is no more. We peer through the barricades and 'Keep Out' notices. The property tycoon has already pulled down the penguins' home and it is a desultory sight indeed, full of rubble and crawling with builders and surveyors.

Memories haunt me. It was Daisy's insistence that first brought me here. This was where Eileen and I took her so that she could prove to her brother that penguins were to be found in Scotland. This was where her love of the birds was cemented. This was where we spent so many hours entranced by the antics of Mac, of Pablo, of Florence and the other twenty-one flippered residents, all now gone.

Just beyond that fence was where Mac seized my fallen glove. I recall so well his look of indignation when Molly strode in to reclaim it. What a mangled mess it was! But it was impossible not to forgive Mac. He stole all our hearts.

Penguins return to the same breeding grounds year after year, and I wonder – not for the first time – if they have some sense of home, as we do? If Mac would be upset if he could see the sad transformation of Lochnamorghy.

With Eileen's and Daisy's help, I would have managed to save this place, had it not been for Fate stepping in with the untimely news of the Ballahays crisis. But it was not to be.

However, I refuse to let Fate have everything its own way. The McCreedy way is better.

All that was required was a rethink and a little humility (a quality which is not, I now concede, so unattractive as it has always seemed). There is nothing shameful about asking for help. Pride can be useful, but sometimes it gets in the way. And what a uniquely wonderful ally I have in Sir Robert!

Next, he drives us to a much more pleasant destination: Edinburgh Zoo. The two of us visit often. It is important to maintain contact with the penguins.

Mac and his friends have resided here ever since we returned from our trip. It was all due to Sir Robert's influence. How he hated to use it, and how I hated to ask it of him, but compromise was called for in order to save a group of birds of whom we had become particularly fond. I mooted my idea the night of his proposal in Antarctica, and he promised he would try his best.

At first, Edinburgh Zoo protested they had no room whatsoever to accommodate twenty-four penguins. However, when Sir Robert pointed out that this was only temporary and mentioned, if they could oblige, that he would sing their praises during his next radio interview, they reconsidered. A couple of grumpy Komodo dragons were moved to one side and miraculously a penguin-appropriate space emerged.

Sir Robert and I were there to witness the move and ensure that the penguins' every need was catered for. So was Molly.

On emerging from their carriers, the penguins were keen to look around. A quick stretch, shake and run-around, and they seemed perfectly content. Mac immediately dived into his new pool, his yellow headdress streaming in the water, flippers angled like fins. Florence and the bevvy of African penguins waddled around, poking their beaks into everything.

'I've split up with Simon,' Molly announced as the last

penguin, a rather slow and startled-looking Pablo, was released into his new pen.

I had no idea who she was talking about. 'Simon?'

'Yes, Simon Tector. The guy who used to manage Lochnamorghy. I was going out with him. Not any more, though.'

She did not look remotely upset about this. Something tells me she never cared greatly for the man in the first place ... although, I must admit, the information she obtained from him has been most useful.

# 49

# Eileen

*Edinburgh and Kilmarnock*

TODAY, IN SIR Robert's kitchen, over tea and muffins, I had this conversation with Mrs McCreedy.

'Did you enjoy your time in Bolton, Eileen?'

'I did, Mrs McCreedy. And Daisy's family took me to see the new bicycle shop and flat in Jedburgh, too. There's still plenty to organize but it's going to be lovely. Daisy is quite taken with it. We had a long walk around Jedburgh as well.'

'The old Eileen would never have wanted a long walk!'

'Yes, but I like walking now. It was a good chance to chat with Daisy's parents, too. They are such a kind, caring family. It's funny, isn't it, when you go to different places and meet different people, how it makes you think different thoughts?'

'That is very true, Eileen.'

'I've been chatting a bit with Fiona from choir, too. She is so sensible.'

'And have you, by any chance, come to a decision about your future?'

'About me and Doug? Yes. And I'll tell you what, Mrs McCreedy. I've done a complete switch-round since October. Before, I wanted Doug to need me. I wanted to be enough for him. I wanted to be everything to him. But I clearly wasn't, was I? Now I look at it the opposite way. Do *I* need *him*? Is *he* enough for *me*? Is *he* everything to *me*? And you know what the answer is?'

She eyed me in that severe, no-nonsense way she's got. 'The answer to all of them is no, Eileen. Emphatically no.'

'Yes. I mean, no. I mean, you're right. But I needed to go all the way across the world with you and walk a hundred miles and see a tonne of penguins before I realized it. And I understand now that I haven't anywhere near reached my sell-by date. I'm only just beginning.'

'We both are,' said Mrs McCreedy.

I pop home to Kilmarnock occasionally when I need to fetch something of mine – the good frying pan or my knitting, for example. I don't exchange many words with Doug if he's there. It was always me that made the effort to keep conversation going, and now I don't any more and the house is filled with a strange silence. And tension.

Dougie-snuggles are a thing of the past. Staying in Edinburgh has made me see what a non-relationship I've had with Doug all these years. Mrs McCreedy and Sir

Robert are always eagerly engaged in discussions about clever things like the life cycle of the dragonfly and what makes the perfect voiceover and the ideal dimensions of a computer screen and how much expense is justifiable on wedding paraphernalia. And often they reach out and touch each other's fingers, and often they roar with laughter.

Being back home fills me with sad comparisons.

This morning I've arrived early. I'm holding two bowls of porridge. I made them out of habit, purely because that's what I've always done at home at this hour. Now I hear Doug yawning and his footsteps on the stairs, hear him opening the door, hear him thunk down in the chair. I turn, and there he is. Something grubby is caught in his stubble, and his shirt collar looks greasy. He has let himself go again, since the floozy stick insect left. Otherwise, he shows no signs of regret.

He doesn't say hello (that's apparently my job) but he's looking at the two bowls. I see the smugness in his face, the way he slouches at the table expecting me to hand one of them to him. Expecting me to smile and forgive. Expecting me to slip right back into the old habits. Good old Eileen, always reliable, always there to catch the pieces.

Without a word, I take the brimful salt pot and I tip the whole load over his porridge.

Not good old Eileen any more.

Bad, new Eileen!

I've imagined leaving him many times and it's always made me feel queasy in my tummy, worse than the Drake Passage.

The reality is quite different. I am not queasy at all. Actually, I feel pretty good.

I can't be bothered to eat my own porridge, even though I've sprinkled it with just the right amount of sugar. I grab my plastic dancing sunflower and put it under my arm. It switches itself on and waggles manically as I march out of the house.

I have no plans, not really. But I think, as a start, I'm going to trade in my old car and get myself a campervan.

Sir Robert pours us each a glass of mulled wine. He and Mrs McCreedy and I are huddled around a table in Thurlstone House, one of Mrs M's favourite Edinburgh restaurants. It's a posh one, and all decked out with holly, ivy and fairy lights. Judging by Mrs M's face, she's not in a Christmassy mood, though.

'News from Locket Island?' Sir Robert asks, seeing it too.

'Yes. An email.'

'Terry and Patrick?'

'They're well. Busy, as ever.'

I hardly dare ask, but I do. 'Pip?'

'They are still tracking him. He is safe and well, too, and has recently put in an appearance. They were kind enough to send a new photo.'

That's a relief.

'What's the trouble, then?' Sir Robert asks gently.

All her wrinkles cluster furiously on her forehead. 'Patrick writes that there has been a terrible crisis at the Centaurus centre. Due to the warming climate, the ice has receded far too fast this Antarctic summer. The centre itself was moved back safely, towed pod by pod to solid ground, and has been reassembled at a different site. The Emperor penguin colony had no such reprieve.'

'Oh no!' I cry, choking on my wine. What can have happened?

She doesn't keep us in suspense any longer. 'The parent penguins, as the ice cracked and broke, resumed foraging in the ocean, as is their wont. It was a different matter for the chicks. They had scarcely begun to fledge when the ground under their feet dissolved into the sea. Some were carried away on ice pans, to a death by starvation. Others will have drowned straight away. They had not yet learned to swim; their baby fluff became waterlogged and pulled them straight down into the icy water. Daisy Penguin was amongst the thousands of casualties.'

Sir Robert and I gape, horrified.

Mrs McCreedy continues. 'The scientists call it a breeding failure. I call it an unspeakable tragedy. When you think of all those miles the penguin parents trekked, the painstaking manoeuvre of eggs from brood pouch to brood pouch in freezing conditions, followed by all those months they suffered starvation, bone-chilling winds and total darkness . . . all of this to bring into the world these young ones, these dear, sweet fluffy babies . . . All for love. All lost.'

She pulls a hanky from her bag and dabs her eyes. I don't know what to say. It's too awful for words. We drink our mulled wine and eat our mince pies in stupefied silence. Then, slowly, conversation comes trickling back.

'It's so unfair,' I wail.

Sir Robert folds his napkin, and I don't think I've ever seen anyone fold their napkin with such sadness. 'You're not wrong, Eileen. It's unfair to the penguins, and it's unfair to a whole load of other creatures who have no chance of adapting fast enough to these climatic extremes. And it's unfair to the young people on this planet, too, like Daisy.'

Mrs McCreedy thrusts her hanky back in her bag and shuts it with a smart clopping noise. 'She will be utterly devastated.'

We discuss whether we should tell Daisy about the death of her namesake and all the others. In the end we decide we will break the news after Christmas. She is old enough to deal with the truth. She knows, and we know, that we are losing penguins too fast from this planet.

'How can they survive disasters like this,' I ask, 'when all their children are swept away? What on earth can we do?'

# 50

# Eileen

*On the road*
*Four months later*

DAISY ASKS THE very same question.

She is understandably distraught about the death of all those Emperor chicks. Thank goodness there is good news as well as the bad (she's looking forward to meeting Ginty) but I've been expecting a tantrum all the same. That's one of the reasons I've put off telling her for so long. It's a chilly April morning and I've come down to Jedburgh to collect her in my 'new' (eight years old, three owners but new to me) campervan. Daisy sits in the passenger seat beside me, eyes fixed to the front as we set off back north.

There's no tantrum. Instead she quietly weeps for those thousands of drowned pom-pom penguins.

How very grown-up she is becoming. Bigger, too. Soon she will be taller than me, the rate she is growing.

'Bad things happen if good people do nothing,' I say, quoting Mrs McCreedy. 'And if we all just do nothing . . .' I clear my throat. 'But if some of us do something, it might just help, don't you think?'

'So what *can* we do?' Daisy repeats, chewing her lip.

I am learning all sorts about wildlife these days, and I've done my best to memorize the points Sir Robert told me.

'Well, Daisy, you're very good already at litter-picking and recycling.'

'Oh yes, I know how important that is for wildlife.'

'So we should all avoid throwing things away if we can, and buy fewer things in the first place and find ways to mend things that are old or broken.'

This is met with an eye-roll. 'Don't patronize me, Eileen. I know all about that and I do it already.'

*Patronize.* My, what long words she is using! If we are not careful, we'll have another Mrs McCreedy on our hands. Slightly panicked, I start to rattle off the list of things Sir Robert mentioned about reducing carbon emissions: 'Check where your money's being invested. Insulate and draft-proof your house. Use a green energy supplier. Drive less . . .'

'Um, Eileen, I'm only eleven. I haven't got money or a house or a car or an energy supplier.'

'. . . Don't turn up your heating – put on another jumper instead. Switch things off when you're not using them. Protect green spaces. Plant trees. Cut down on your meat and dairy food – that's a biggie, Sir Robert says. Meat production creates tonnes of greenhouse gas, apparently. I've found a very nice veggie recipe for toad-in-the-hole, but I'm afraid I'm never going to warm to quinoa. *Or keen-wah*, or whatever it's called.'

'We sometimes have spinach and feta lasagne at home,' Daisy tells me. 'It's meat-free. And really yummy.'

'Another thing,' I add, remembering. 'It's best to choose nearby destinations for our holidays ...' She gives a guilty little cough here and crooks an eyebrow at me. I carry on. 'And when flying is unavoidable, pay a little extra for carbon offsetting. Mrs McCreedy and Sir Robert always do that, you know? And what was it now that he said was the most important thing? Let me think ...'

The fields and hills whizz by. We've reached the dual carriageway now. I drum my hands on the steering wheel whilst I'm trying to remember.

'Ah, that was it! Share! Share your passion with everyone. That way, caring for the world will gradually become the accepted norm, just as it should be. It takes hundreds of people to make change happen, so it's really important to put it out there that you care.'

Daisy stares out of the window, thinking hard. 'I could carry on writing my blogs, couldn't I?'

'That's a brilliant idea, Daisy. You do that. And while you're at it, you could let people know all about what Mrs McCreedy is doing.'

# 51

# Veronica

*The Ballahays*

'AFTER ALL,' I point out to Sir Robert, as we walk up the familiar road, 'there are many precedents for such things. That place in Somerset, for example. Or is it Wiltshire?' I rifle through my brain but it refuses to come up with the name of the park. 'With the lions,' I add, hoping he will catch on.

He is, thankfully, as attuned as ever to my way of thinking. And whilst many people would find it hard to resist a degree of snideness at my ineptitude, he continues as if I had said the name myself.

'Quite. Longleat Safari Park was initiated by a wealthy eccentric who had vision. It takes a great deal of vision to set up these things.'

'And, presumably, wealth and eccentricity. Both of which qualities I possess.'

'In abundance.' That perennial, famous twinkle is riding in his eyes.

I recall our conversation about it at the Centaurus research station in Antarctica; how I'd hinted that great things might be achieved if only we could pool our resources and add them to the money raised from Operation PIP.

It was the appearance of Pip himself on that near-disastrous day that first seeded the idea in my head. And it was shortly after Sir Robert's proposal that I recognized my new dream might just blossom into reality.

Life has become altogether a different creature since then; more complex, more stunning, more vivid. More wonderful in every way.

Ginty runs ahead of us, tail awhirl. She sniffs at something dark and turgid by the wayside then circles back to us. Sir Robert stops, picks up a stick and hurls it across the bracken. Ginty bounds after it, wildly happy, ears streaming in the wind. She has not quite grown into her big golden paws yet.

'She is perfect,' Sir Robert tells me, his eyes full of affection which is directed first at his new retriever-sheepdog conundrum and then at me.

'Nobody is perfect,' I reply. 'But she certainly merits admiration.'

My gift has been a resounding success. We named her Ginty after the island off Australia we visited last year, where, in addition to plenitudinous Little penguins, we were introduced to a couple of very sweet dogs. Precious memories indeed for us both, for it was on Ginty Island that Sir Robert and I first really got to know one another.

His argument about being absent too much to own a dog no longer stands. Sir Robert is nowhere near retiring (retirement is an untenable concept for him) and he will still be away filming several times a year, but now he has me and many others willing to dog-sit whenever this occurs. Besides, I decided a dog would forestall any laziness on our part, would make us get out every day, whatever the weather.

For we continue our habit of daily walking, and I believe it contributes much towards our general well-being. To walk is to think. To walk is to observe. To walk is to take in the wonders of this world. To walk is to preserve your health and longevity. To walk in the company of friends is to know happiness.

To walk with a dog adds an element of hilarity. We never know what Ginty will get up to next.

'Ginty! Ginty!' I call.

She lollops up and lays her stick at my feet. She looks at it lovingly then backs away with care and takes a quick glance up at me, willing me to throw it. Her disappointment when I get out the lead is palpable.

I apologize to her as I clip it to her collar.

'I'll take her,' Sir Robert offers. 'You need to hold on to your handbag. And litter tongs.'

We link our free arms and stride through the gates. My elegant oak 'The Ballahays' sign remains in place, but on the other side, in larger, brighter letters, hangs another sign which reads 'McCreedy Pip Penguin Centre', complete with opening times and ticket prices.

The name is one of the countless aspects that have

408

been discussed at length. I was in favour of making it the 'Saddlebow McCreedy Pip Penguin Centre', or some such combination, since my fiancé is now just as invested in the project as I am. But he would not have it. He is on the board of directors, and the trust is set up in his name as well as mine, along with Patrick's, Terry's and a few others, but he insists that, since this has been my home for so many decades, it should be my name only that adorns the gates.

We walk down the drive, Ginty straining at the lead. The garden, thanks to Mr Perkins's dedication, is as beautiful as ever. The lawn is mown; the early-flowering rhododendrons are a riot of magenta buds and blooms. The house, ahead of us, stands tall and proud, its mellow stonework dripping with wisteria.

Along with Molly's Ford Fiesta and Sir Robert's Volkswagen Golf, Eileen's campervan is parked beside the house. I consult my watch, for we were due to meet at three and it is still only ten minutes to. Having timed our walk to perfection, it is somewhat galling that they are so early. Still, I cannot conceal my pleasure at seeing the other two Mackateers, standing there in the porch, manically waving.

Daisy prances forward to greet us.

'It's so exciting!' she shouts as we embrace, making my hearing aid quiver. She receives her face-full of smelly dog tongue from Ginty with absolute delight. 'Oh, she's so beautiful!'

'Have you been here long?' I ask.

'Only about fifteen minutes, Mrs McCreedy,' Eileen answers, patting Ginty on the head. 'We made good time from Jedburgh. The kettle's on. I expect you'd like a nice cuppa and a ginger thin? Or perhaps a crumpet?'

'Oh no, *please*,' moans Daisy. 'Don't make me wait any longer! I'm dying to see them, but Eileen wouldn't let me until you were here.'

I turn to Sir Robert. 'Penguins first, tea after?'

'I don't think we have any choice in the matter.'

Together, the four of us proceed down the smart new steps that lead from the back room to the aquatic station.

Work is not yet finished, but the underground cavity has been shored up and is structurally stronger than ever it was. It has been used to accommodate the pool. A walkway passes beside the glass-tanked part so that avian underwater balletics can be observed. Black-and-white bodies glide and swoop gracefully through the water, as if for our benefit. Ginty observes them with her head tilted to one side, as fascinated as we are.

We follow the passage on as it slopes gently upwards. Sir Robert holds open the next door and we exit to the outside area that has been designated as the free-range penguin run. It features various huts and artificial burrows, another small pool and a striped penguin crossing (an idea adopted from Lochnamorghy). The wooden daytime cabin for penguin patrollers (re-employed from the Lochnamorghy staff) is almost finished.

Twenty-four penguins have moved in and now have a far bigger space than they had at either Lochnamorghy or Edinburgh Zoo. Their antics are as entertaining as ever. Some plop into the pool and engage in water sports. Some stand meditatively, inhaling the tang of salty Scottish air; some are busy preening. Some nestle against each other. Others squabble, flirt and explore the walkways.

'There he is, there he is!' calls Daisy.

Hoping, no doubt, for fish, Mac bobs his head and waddles towards us. Daisy crouches down. 'Oh, Mac, Mac, Mac!' she croons, joyously turning the monosyllable into a little tune.

We keep Ginty on a tight leash, but she seems to understand that these penguins are special. Her sheepdog instincts will hopefully make her easy to train, so she can become an extra protector for them and help us round them up when necessary. If the dogs of Ginty Island can do it, so can she.

Daisy is already deep in conversation with Mac, telling him that along with Tony in the Falklands and Pip in Antarctica and the Emperor penguins, Veronica and Eileen – and Daisy, the Emperor chick who is gone but definitely not forgotten – he is her very top favourite penguin ever.

She knows the rules, though, and does not touch him.

'Can we feed him?' she asks.

'Not quite yet,' I answer. 'Molly will let us know when it's time. She will be down in a minute.'

Molly was the first to move in, since the penguins needed an expert permanently on site to keep an eye on them. She was in need of a lodging anyway. She is installed in one of the upstairs bedrooms in the wing of the house that is now given over to staff and offices. Eileen will be moving in shortly, too. I am pleased the whole property has finally been put to good use, since the majority of the rooms have long stood empty. The remainder of The Ballahays is a comfortable space in which Sir Robert and I now live.

I realize that where human affection should have been, I have spent years stacking up artefacts and antiques; a plethora of self-indulgent but largely useless items which pleased my eye but not my heart. Most of these have now been auctioned off to raise money for the centre. However, I have retained three of my favourite tea sets because life is unequivocally better when one can drink Darjeeling from an elegant cup.

'It won't be long now until we open for tourists,' Eileen observes, rubbing her hands together with relish. She jumped at the chance to be receptionist and has already placed an unaccountably hideous plastic sunflower inside the cabin.

The idea of the general public worries me far more than the penguins, whose close proximity has ever brought me joy. But humans have their uses. The McCreedy Pip Penguin Centre will provide them with an entertaining, educational visit, which will ensure the future welfare of these twenty-four flippered residents. And they can help penguins in other ways, too.

Where my dining room used to be, a study centre has been set up. It includes computers that, with the touch of a key, bring to screen photos of penguins who live across the other side of the world, taken by Patrick's cameras and satellite imaging. Members of the public will be able to spend five minutes, an hour or as long as they like counting these penguins, thus contributing to the vital data that tells us about the penguins' environment in Antarctica, and indeed about climate change generally.

In addition, we have provided attractive cards for people to take home with them, printed with the link where these cameras can be found on their own computers. They may thus continue their useful penguin-counting whenever it suits them.

And, of course, if anyone is feeling particularly generous, they are able to adopt a penguin. Patrick and Terry are doing a grand job tagging more penguins than ever, allowing our customers in Scotland to name their penguins, and sending photos and updates of them.

I have, naturally, adopted Pip. Which does not alter anything materially, since I was already paying a monthly stipend towards the project and receiving updates. Pip, busy fishing and waddling in the snows of Antarctica, will doubtless never pause to think of me. But, my goodness, I shall be thinking of him. He will outlive me, of that I am certain.

Pablo may not, but he has already reached a ripe old age for a penguin. The octopus will also probably not last much longer. Nobody seemed to want him, so we took him on as well. He seems to have gone a funny colour and I just hope he was not too stressed by the change of habitation. The penguins have coped incredibly well. Mac is as cheeky as ever. I ensure that no fine pairs of gloves go near him.

To my shock and absolute delight, The Ballahays has become a vast community of penguins and people with links all over the world.

'Things could not be more different than they were just a few years ago,' I comment as I gaze around.

Sir Robert nods, his smile all-encompassing. 'Do you know, Veronica, Darwin said that it's not the strongest creatures who survive and thrive. Nor even the cleverest. The survivors are the ones who can adapt most quickly to change.'

Evidently, I am one such a creature.

# Daisy's Penguin Blog

THANKS FROM MAC

Just a quick one because I'm super-busy. I'll be starting
a new blog soon, which will be bursting with beautiful,
amazing wildlife and tips about how to protect it. But for
now I thought you'd like to see where Mac and his pals
have ended up (see photos).

Isn't it perfect? He is incredibly happy to be alive and
in a better home than ever.

He wants to say the most HUMUNGOUS HONK of a
thank-you to you all. And so do I.

# 52

# Veronica

*Ayrshire*
*June 2015*

PATRICK SITS NEXT to Keith. They seem to be competing for which of them can look most uncomfortable in a suit. Patrick has voiced his intention of visiting the UK more often, which is good news indeed. Keith has made it all the way here from the Falkland Islands. He purports it is solely to be present at the wedding, but I suspect there may also be other reasons. Eileen has promised to take him out in her campervan and show him the best of Ayrshire.

Gavin and Beth sit together, as do Mr and Mrs Perkins. Eileen's friend Fiona is behind them. The other seats are mainly occupied by my valued members of staff and Sir Robert's friends. The congregation is small. It is a private

415

affair, although we have decided to send photos to the press later. This is an unashamed publicity gimmick because the more visitors we get at the McCreedy Pip Penguin Centre in these early stages, the more likely it is to survive.

Sir Robert and I have specified no wedding gifts, just donations towards the Trust.

I am surrounded by bridesmaids. Terry, at first tickled when I asked her, then pulled a face.

'Does that mean I have to get all dolled up and wear a posh frock, Veronica?'

'Of course it fricking well does,' said Patrick.

Now that she has finally been coaxed into a satiny pale-gold number, a single rosebud peeping out from behind her ear, she is so stunning he cannot stop gawking at her. Molly also looks well in her matching gold. Daisy has elected to wear a flouncy pink creation that makes her look like the Sugar Plum Fairy. The quartet of brides-maids is completed, at her request, by her friend Aurora: she who can make a penguin from the cardboard cylinder inside a toilet roll. (She made one for me and presented it yesterday. It is utterly repugnant.)

Daisy's brother, Noah, is pageboy. Eileen, whose blush-ing cheeks match her outfit, is maid of honour and has the important duty of carrying my handbag.

She leans towards me. 'It's time,' she says in a hoarse whisper.

I cannot claim any beauty for myself these days, but I have chosen what I deem to be effective attire and am positively dripping in ivory silk and Victorian lace.

'I feel like a dinosaur in a doily,' I murmur.

'Don't say such things, Mrs McCreedy. You look wonderful, just wonderful. Like . . . like an empress.'

The bagpipes were perhaps an unwise choice for so small a chapel and at the first blast I nearly jump out of my skin. A hasty readjustment of my hearing aid and then I lead my troop up the aisle, accompanied by the stridently triumphant music.

Sir Robert's back view is dashing and dapper. His full white hair is neatly brushed, his jacket well tailored. His kilt hangs to just below his knees. As he turns, his face crinkles into a smile and his eyebrows flip aloft like a pair of dancing caterpillars.

I take my place at his side. How fine is his deep bass voice as we sing the hymns. How tender his glance as we listen to the reading from St Paul's letter to the Corinthians.

*Love is patient, love is kind. It does not envy, it does not boast, it is not proud. It does not dishonour others, it is not self-seeking, it is not easily angered, it keeps no record of wrongs. Love does not delight in evil but rejoices with the truth. It always protects, always trusts, always hopes, always perseveres.*

My eyelids twinge. I clear my throat clumsily. My hand opens out and reaches for Sir Robert's. Our two palms press, warm, wrinkled, as one.

Why, oh why, is there never a clean handkerchief when one needs it? I fear I am going to have to lean back and ask Eileen for my handbag.

I raise my eyes to meet Sir Robert's, register that his are

leaking tears, too. He whispers: 'I never thought I could . . . I never thought you would . . .'

He twizzles my engagement ring on my finger and the engraved miniature penguins catch the light. They seem to be forever marching on.

The first part of the ceremony completed, we leave the flinty, wind-worn chapel and take the seaside road, travelling in a variety of vehicles. Sir Robert drives me in the maroon Volkswagen, with Eileen and Daisy in the back.

Eileen shuffles in her seat behind me. 'Gosh, that was lovely. So, so lovely.'

'Eileen's crying!' Daisy chants.

'Only because it was so, so lovely,' Eileen repeats. 'And do you know, that was my very favourite hymn?'

She starts humming 'All Things Bright And Beautiful'.

'We aim to please,' chuckles my almost-husband, and only I know the magnitude of his own emotion.

We swish through the gates, alight and reassemble on the gravel driveway of The Ballahays. Sunlight splays across the lawn and a faint breeze ruffles the trees. A willow-woven archway stands at the end of the paved pathway. Together with Fiona, Eileen has festooned it with honeysuckle and roses.

At a signal from Sir Robert, Eileen and Keith slip away. They have been assigned a special duty. Whilst we are waiting for their return, a Rabbie Burns poem is read by Mr Perkins, then the piper plays again, then Eileen's choir sing an anthem, their voices fanning through the garden's tracery of gold and green. When the music hushes, a gentle squawking meets our ears.

And here they come, a gaggle of adorables. Mac leads

the gang with his yellow crest waving in the wind. Keith and Eileen shepherd them along the path with Ginty who, all paws, tail and tongue, is scarcely able to contain her excitement. Penguins all around us, Sir Robert and I process up to the archway, followed by our human companions.

As we arrive, I notice a little gold envelope tucked in behind one of the roses. I pull it out. The name on the front reads 'Veronica and Sir Robert' with today's date. I show Sir Robert, whose eyebrows ascend once more.

'We'd better open it.'

I do so. I am not wearing my glasses, but luckily the writing is large and rounded; a little splodgy.

*Dear Veronica and dear Sir Robert, my very dearest people-friends,*

*I wish I could be with you today, but it's too far to travel for a penguin, even a super-strong one like me. I know you have other penguins around, so that's good. They have a lot to thank you for. I want to say thank you, too, Veronica, for saving me when I was a baby and giving me a new life – one which I truly love. And I hope, for both of you, that in your own new life together you'll be as happy as I am.*

*I would regurgitate fish all over this postcard for you, but Daisy says you wouldn't like it, so I'm just sending love, flipper-hugs and a big, fishy beak-kiss,*

*Pip. X*

My eyes are misty again, but I catch a glance from Keith, who winks and points a finger at Daisy.

Daisy is sniggering. We will soon put a stop to that.

I swoop down on her, catch her tightly in my arms and plant a kiss on each of her sugar-plum cheeks. I let go faster than I'd intended, though, because there is a series of sharp tugs at the hem of my dress. Mac.

The photographer focuses in, capturing the moment, and I smile graciously. Then I gently extricate Mac because the Victorian lace cost a fortune.

The celebrant clears her throat. It is time for the vows. Surrounded by roses, friends and penguins, Sir Robert and I promise to have and to hold, for richer, for poorer, in sickness, in health, till death us do part.

'And I'm not planning on that last part happening any time soon,' I murmur as his lips touch mine.

We will take each day as it comes. Neither of us is a stranger to grief, but we are united and we are strong. Old age is remarkably edifying. Like wartime, it highlights the fragility of life, and its preciousness. Walk, for tomorrow you may be lame. Admire the flowers, for tomorrow you may be blind. Listen to the birds, for tomorrow you may be deaf. Hug those you love, for tomorrow they may be gone. So may you. It is more important to enjoy this moment than to worry about future ones or regret past ones.

And this particular moment is one that I hold very, very dear.

I glance down at Mac and his friends, some of whom are preening, some of whom are unceremoniously but happily defecating on the pristine lawn. They are living proof that one can be dependent and still perfectly content. Yet it is my hope that, like Her Majesty the Queen, I shall keep on working in the expectation of good health for many years to come. Indeed, I believe it will be so, for, as Sir Robert has pointed out, I am 'made of tough stuff'. I trust that the remainder of my life will be fruitful. And that I shall continue to serve worthily in my role as the very first Penguin Ambassador.

My legacy will live on. When Sir Robert and I are gone, the McCreedy Pip Penguin Centre will pass to Patrick and Terry who, after all, cannot stay in Antarctica for ever.

In the meantime, I shall, as Patrick would say, 'party hard'. And with Sir Robert, my penguin family, my lovely home and good-quality tea, how could I not be happy?

I kiss my new husband again amidst the cacophonous squawking.

Love is a shining landscape that Sir Robert and I will tread until the end of our days. We shall keep putting one foot in front of the other, and we shall do it together. Not forgetting, of course, the rest of my team: Eileen and Daisy. And the wider colony of which we are a part, wherever they may be: Mr and Mrs Perkins, Fiona, Molly and the clan of penguin patrollers here at The Ballahays; Daisy's family in Bolton and Jedburgh; Miriam and the others from the film crew as they tour around; José and Gabriela in the Galápagos, Keith in the Falklands, Dietrich and Mike on Locket Island, and, of course, my dear Patrick and Terry. Not forgetting every person who signed that petition and contributed what they could towards Operation PIP and the saving of twenty-four penguins. And every single person who makes some small gesture to help preserve our utterly incredible and wonderful planet.

This truth remains: just as each step, seemingly insignificant in itself, builds towards a journey of a hundred miles, so every little act of goodness plays its part in making the world a better place. Everything counts – every thought, every word, every small act of kindness. And every life counts, too. Even that of a penguin.

# Epilogue

Pip stands on an iceberg on the Weddell Sea. Beak pointed upwards, he gulps down his catch. He enjoys the sensation of fresh fish sliding down his gullet. He stretches his flippers and turns slowly to face the wind. An icy blast ruffles his feathers.

Pip has no idea that across the world humans are flying private jets, driving fast cars, burning vast amounts of fuel and doing a range of other things that threaten his life. He has no idea that programmes are broadcast about saving the planet; that politicians attend summits on climate change; that agreements are drawn up about the reduction of single-use plastics. Or that, heedless, a small girl on a beach is, at this moment, throwing away a crisp packet that will eventually kill one of his cousins.

He also has no notion that another girl has vowed to do everything she can to help penguins – perhaps even become the next Penguin Ambassador? Or that a middle-aged woman who is fond of knitting and humming is relishing her new position as a receptionist in a penguin centre in Ayrshire, Scotland.

Nor does he know that an older woman – one who once saved his life – is tirelessly campaigning for environmental issues. Or that she has now, at long last, found love.

Perhaps, though, Pip senses that there is more on this earth than he could ever possibly imagine . . . More than any of us could ever possibly imagine.

With a raucous cry, he arcs forward and plunges into the swirling waters.

# Acknowledgements

Thank you for picking up this book. Thank you especially to those of you who have accompanied Veronica from the very beginning, as she first travelled *Away with the Penguins*, who have joined her as she followed the *Call of the Penguins* and who have now *Gone with the Penguins* this one last time. I hope you've had fun. I know I have.

Just as a penguin can only survive in cahoots with other penguins, this book wouldn't exist without the skills and cooperation of a huge, vibrant, hard-working human colony.

So my deepest gratitude goes out to all of these:

Francesca Best, who has beautifully edited, gently guided and unstintingly supported me through the creation of five books. Lucky books, and lucky, lucky me!

Lara and Sarah, who have been such complete champions. Thank you both for listening and suggesting, for your endless patience through all my wobbles, for your expertise and your kindness.

Izzie, Sophie, Kate, Holly, Eleanor, and all those other brilliant people at Transworld who have helped in the development and distribution of this novel. My special thanks go to Irene for her totally gorgeous and striking cover illustration.

My agent Darley Anderson and his team, particularly Rebeka, Georgia, Mary, Francesca and Ilaria for the amazing foreign deals. With your help those penguins have reached many unexpected destinations around the globe and are now squawking in dozens of different languages. How can I ever thank you enough?

My dear fellow authors who have given me much-needed encouragement and provided lovely endorsements. I know how hard it is to find time to squeeze in one more read amongst all the writing pressures. Thank you, Trisha Ashley, Tracy Rees, Sam Tonge, Phaedra Patrick, Clare Pooley . . . and so many others. How proud you make me!

My Exmoor writing friends, Tracey Gemmell and Sarah Easter Collins, for all the chats and laughter at Writers' Corner in Periwinkle Tea Rooms, Selworthy. Also Paul, Dave and Meg for your tea and cakes, your cool giftshop full of hand-crafted goodies and your warm welcome.

The book-blogging community. I can't mention you all by name, but my goodness, your reviews make a world of difference and I never forget how much I owe you. Thank you.

Bookshops: Brendon Books in Taunton, Bookshop by the Blackdowns in Wellington, The Ivybridge Bookshop, Waterstones Yeovil, to name but a few! And all the libraries, too, especially my local Somerset libraries. Thank you for being such glorious treasure troves and for spreading the penguin positivity.

Last year, having written two books centred around penguins, I finally managed to see them in the wild myself (which was a whole different thing from visiting them in

Torquay!). My Falklands trip contributed massively to this novel and I want to thank the people who were a part of this: Petra, Carrot, Debbie and Bill, Adrian and Lisa on East Falkland (I didn't meet Lisa in person but sampled her delicious diddle-dee jam – and I hope she didn't mind that her copies of the books were rather sandy and penguin-pecked), Riki and Luis on Pebble Island and lovely Silke who toured with us there, Sue and David on Saunders Island, Sarah and Micky on Sea Lion Island (yes, I pinched the idea of the hat-stealing caracara from there), and Eileen Crofts, who arranged for me to stay in the beautiful Emperor suite. And a great big thank-you to Falkland Island Holidays. These were truly the experiences of a lifetime and I will treasure them always.

Noah Strycker, who has actually lived among penguins in Antarctica and who generously provided me with a mass of timely information about emperor colonies, research stations and Antarctic travel.

Ursula Franklin, my fabulous friend and travelling companion, whose own incredible 'Mission Penguin' is such an inspiration (check out Ursula's stunning book, everyone!). I doubt this trilogy of novels would have come into being without your powerful penguin commitment and I have no idea where I'd be without you. Thank you, thank you, thank you!

So many people have helped me with ideas, walks, talks, sympathy, empathy and non-writing creativity, which I absolutely need too. Thank you to my oh-so-vital musical friends: to Celia and Martin; to Ursula (again!), Monica, Marian and Sue; to Ian, Pauline and the Green Oak Barn gang; to my fellow 'harpies' and to all of In Ecclesia and other singing friends. Thank you to Gina, Elisabeth, Rosemary and Mark. And most of all, thank you to my dearest Jonathan and Purrsy for always being there for me, no matter what.

### Final Note about Penguins

The story of the Patagonian penguin who regularly travelled five thousand miles to visit his rescuer is absolutely true – proof, if any further proof is needed, of the amazingness of penguins. It seemed right to give Pip similar powers of love and gratitude and to end the trilogy on a note from him. Penguins are not just fluffy and cute. They are not just inspiring models of resilience and good cheer. They are also special in ways that are a complete mystery to us.

As I researched, I was shocked to discover the plight of penguins in Antarctica. Penguins are key indicators of climate change and when the ice melts they are the first to suffer. In recent years several entire Emperor colonies have been lost, and other species of penguin also teeter on the brink of extinction. Writing these books has heightened my awareness of the precariousness of this world and how each of our millions of tiny actions makes a difference. So I'm just going to put in a quick plea for our flippered friends. Do consider adopting a penguin, supporting a wildlife cause, or taking any other action you can. Eileen has a list of suggestions for lifestyle tweaks that will certainly help, Daisy is keen to take up the baton and Veronica will be proud of you – although she'd never say so out loud. As for Pip, he might just survive a while longer. I sincerely hope he will.

If you enjoyed *Gone with the Penguins*, don't miss
the first book in the series

Turn the page to read the first chapter . . .

# 1

# Veronica

*The Ballahays, Ayrshire, Scotland*
*May 2012*

I HAVE TOLD Eileen to get rid of all the mirrors. I used to like them but I certainly don't now. Mirrors are too honest. There is only so much truth a woman can take.

'Are you sure, Mrs McCreedy?' Her voice implies she knows my mind better than I do. She always does that. It is one of her innumerable annoying habits.

'Of course I'm sure!'

She clicks her tongue and tilts her head to one side so that her corkscrew curls brush against her shoulder. It's quite a manoeuvre when you consider the extraordinary width of her neck.

'Even the lovely one with the gilt edge, the one over the mantelpiece?'

'Yes, even that one,' I explain patiently.

'And all the bathroom mirrors too?'

'Especially those!' The bathroom is the last place I want to look at myself.

'Whatever you say.' This in a tone bordering on impertinence.

Eileen comes every day. Her main role is cleaning, but her domestic skills leave much to be desired. She seems to be labouring under the impression that I don't see dirt.

Eileen has a limited collection of facial expressions: cheerful, nosy, busy, nonplussed and vacant. Now she puts on her busy face. She bumbles around emitting a semi-musical noise like a bored bee, collecting the mirrors one at a time and stacking them in the hall. She is unable to close the doors behind her because her hands are full, so I follow in her wake, shutting them carefully. If there's one thing that I can't abide in life, it's a door left open.

I stroll into the larger of the two sitting rooms. There is now an unsightly dark rectangle on the wallpaper above the mantelpiece. I'll have to fill the space with something else. A nice oil painting with plenty of verdure, I think; maybe a Constable print. That would set off the Lincoln green of the velvet curtains. I should like a calming pastoral scene with hills and a lake. A swathe of landscape empty of human beings would be best.

'There we are, then, Mrs McCreedy. I think that's all of them.'

At least Eileen refrains from using my Christian name. Most young people these days seem to have abandoned Mr, Mrs and Miss, which, if you ask me, is a sad reflection on modern society. I addressed Eileen as Mrs

Thompson for the first six months she worked for me. I only stopped doing it because she begged me. ('Please call me Eileen, Mrs McCreedy. I would be so much happier if you would.' 'Well, please continue to call me Mrs McCreedy, Eileen,' I replied. 'I would be so much happier if you would.')

I like the house much better now that it's lost the appalling spectres of Veronica McCreedy taunting me from every corner.

Eileen puts her hands on her hips. 'Well, I'll be putting this lot away, then. I'll bung them in the back room, shall I? There's still some space in there.'

The back room is excessively dark and a little on the cold side, not really usable as a living space. The spiders think it belongs to them. Eileen, in her great wisdom, uses it as a depository for any item I desire to be rid of. She is a firm believer in hoarding everything 'just in case'.

She heaves the mirrors across the kitchen. I resist the urge to close the doors as she goes back and forth, knowing this will only make life more difficult for her. I console myself with the thought that they'll all be shut again soon.

She is back five minutes later. 'I hope you don't mind me asking, Mrs McCreedy, but I had to move this out of the way to fit the mirrors in. Do you know what it is, what's in it? Do you want it? I can always ask Doug to take it to the rubbish tip next time he goes.'

She dumps the old wooden box on the kitchen table and goggles at the rusty padlock.

I choose to ignore her questions and enquire instead, 'Who is this Doug?'

'You know. Doug. My husband.'

I'd forgotten she was married. I've never been introduced to the unfortunate man.

'Well, I shan't be requiring him to take any of my possessions to the rubbish tip in the near or indeed distant future,' I tell her. 'You can leave it on the table for the time being.'

She runs her finger along the top of the box, stroking a clean trail in the dust. Expression number two (nosy) has now established itself on her face. She leans in towards me conspiratorially. I lean backwards a little, having no desire whatsoever to conspire.

'I've tried the padlock to see if there might be something valuable inside,' she confesses, 'but it's stuck. You need to know the code if you want to open it.'

'I am well aware of that fact, Eileen.'

She clearly assumes I am as clueless about the contents as she is.

My skin crawls at the thought of Eileen looking inside. Other people meddling is the very reason I locked it all up in the first place. There is only one person who I will ever permit to see the contents of that box and that person is myself.

I am not ashamed. Oh no, never that. At least . . . But I absolutely refuse to be led down that path. There are things contained in that box that I have managed not to think about for decades. Now the mere sight of it provokes a distinct wobble in my knee joints. I sit down quickly. 'Eileen, would you be kind enough to put the kettle on?'

The clock strikes seven. Eileen has gone and I am alone in the house. Being alone is supposed to be an issue for

people such as me, but I have to say I find it deeply satisfying. Human company is necessary at times, I admit, but
it is almost always irksome in one way or another.

I am currently settled in the Queen Anne armchair by
the fire in the 'snug', my second and more intimate sitting
room. The fire isn't a real one with wood and coal, alas,
but an electric contraption with fake flames. I have had to
compromise on this, as with so much in life. It does at
least fulfil its primary requirement of producing heat.
Ayrshire is chilly, even in summer.

I switch on the television. A scraggy girl is on-screen.
She's screeching her head off, spiking her fingers in the air
and caterwauling, something about being titanium. I
hastily change channels. I flick through a quiz show, a
crime drama and an advertisement for cat food. When I
return to the original channel the girl is still caterwauling,
'I am titanium.' Somebody should tell her she isn't. She is
a silly, noisy, spoilt brat. What a relief when she finally
shuts her mouth.

At last it's time for *Earth Matters*, the only programme all week that is worth watching. Everything
else is sex, advertising, celebrities doing quizzes, celebrities trying to cook, celebrities on a desert island,
celebrities in a rainforest, celebrities interviewing other
celebrities, and a whole load of wannabes doing everything they can to become celebrities (with a spectacular
success rate in making fools of themselves). *Earth Matters* is a welcome respite, demonstrating as it does in
manifold ways how much more sensible animals are
than humans.

However, I am dismayed to find that the current series

of *Earth Matters* seems to have ended. In its place there's a programme called *The Plight of Penguins*. With a gleam of hope I observe that it is presented by Robert Saddlebow. That man demonstrates that it is occasionally possible to be a celebrity for the right reasons. Unlike the vast majority, he has actually done something. He has voyaged around the world campaigning and raising awareness of conservation issues for several decades. He is one of the few people for whom I feel a degree of admiration.

This evening Robert Saddlebow is relayed to my fireside all bundled up and hooded, in the midst of a white wasteland. A flurry of snowflakes whirls around his face. Behind him is a clump of dark shapes. The camera homes in and reveals them to be penguins, a seething great tribe of them. Some are huddled together, others sleeping on their bellies, others waddling round within the group, on missions of their own.

Mr Saddlebow informs me that there are eighteen species of penguin in the world (nineteen if you count White-flippered Little Blues as a separate species), many of which are endangered. During the filming of the programme, he says, he has developed a massive respect and admiration for these birds – for the race as a whole, for each species and for every individual penguin. They live in the harshest conditions on the planet and yet daily take on challenges with a gusto and spirit that would put many of us humans to shame. 'What a tragedy it would be if any one of these species was lost to the planet!' declares Robert Saddlebow, fixing his ice-blue eyes on me from the screen.

'A tragedy indeed!' I say back to him. If Robert Saddle-bow cares about penguins this much, then so do I.

He explains that each week he's going to pick a different penguin and show us the qualities that make the chosen species unique. This week features the Emperor penguins.

I am transfixed. Every year Emperor penguins walk some seventy miles across a desert of ice to reach their breeding ground. This is indeed a remarkable achievement, especially when you consider that travelling on foot isn't exactly their forte. They walk like Eileen, shuffling forward with a singular lack of grace. They look rather uncomfortable in their own skins. Yet their persistence is inspiring.

When the programme is finished, I pull myself out of the chair. I have to acknowledge this is not as difficult a task as it is for many others who have reached my mature years. I would even classify myself as sprightly. I am aware that this body cannot be wholly relied upon. In the past it was a faultless machine, but these days it has suffered losses in both elasticity and efficiency. I must be prepared for the fact that it might let me down at some point in the near future. Yet so far it has managed to keep going marvellously well. Eileen, with her habitual charm, often comments that I am 'as tough as old boots'. Every time she says this I'm tempted to reply, 'All the better to kick you with, my dear.' I repress the urge, though. One must always strive to avoid rudeness.

It is a quarter past eight. I make my way to the kitchen to get my evening cup of Darjeeling and a caramel wafer. My eye falls on the wooden box, still sitting unopened on the table. I consider twisting the combination on the pad-lock and taking a peek at what's inside. In an illogical, sadistic sort of way I'd like to. But no, that would be a foolish move. It would be like Pandora in the myth, let-ting loose a thousand demons. The box must absolutely go back to the spiders without my interference.

**Away with the Penguins** *is out now in paperback and ebook.*

Fiercely resilient and impeccably dressed, Veronica McCreedy has lived an incredible eighty-seven years. Most of them alone in her huge house by the sea.

But **Veronica** has recently discovered a late-life love for family and friendship, adventure and wildlife.

More specifically, a love for penguins!

And so, when she's invited to co-present a wildlife documentary, far away in the southern hemisphere, she jumps at the chance. Even though it will put her in the spotlight, just when she thought she would soon fade into the wings.

Perhaps it's never too late to shine . . .

'Funny, wise and touching. I loved it.'
**TRACY REES**

'Beautifully written by a born storyteller.'
**LORRAINE KELLY**

'The perfect fireside read. Hazel Prior's novels always make me smile.'
**TRISHA ASHLEY**

**Meet Ellie.** She's perfectly happy living her quiet life with her husband, Clive. Happy to wander the Exmoor countryside and write the occasional poem that nobody will read; happy to dream of all the things she hasn't yet managed to do.
Or is she?

**Meet Dan.** He thinks all he needs is the time and space to make harps in his isolated barn on Exmoor. He enjoys being on his own, far away from other people and – crucially – far away from any risk of surprises.

What Ellie and Dan don't know yet, is that a chance encounter is about to change all of this.

This book also contains a pheasant named Phineas . . .

'Uplifting and full of heart. Perfect for fans of *Eleanor Oliphant is Completely Fine*'
**JO THOMAS**

'A beautiful love song of a story, wonderfully told with a warm heart and much hope'
**PHAEDRA PATRICK**, author of
*The Library of Lost and Found*

*Down by the river, not everything is as it seems . . .*

Clever, nosy Phoebe Featherstone is unable to get out much, but she has a talent for uncovering her neighbours' secrets by examining the parcels delivered by her courier father, Al.

When they discover an abandoned baby otter on the riverbank, Phoebe must step out of her comfort zone – and she experiences an unexpected sense of happiness that she has not felt in a very long time. But now, further secrets are coming to light.

Phoebe soon realizes that something is amiss at the local otter sanctuary. She will need to overcome her own closely guarded issues and put all her sleuthing skills to good use if she wants to save the otters . . . and in the process, change her life for ever.

'A lovely holiday read . . . Packed full of humanity and otters!'
SALLY PAGE, bestselling author of *The Keeper of Stories*

'Uplifting, heartwarming and wonderful, an utterly charming story – I loved it! Another gorgeous book from Hazel Prior to lose yourself in!'
FAITH HOGAN, author of *The Ladies'*
*Midnight Swimming Club*

**HAZEL PRIOR** lives on Exmoor with her husband and a huge ginger cat. As well as writing, she works as a freelance harpist. Hazel is the author of *Ellie and the Harp-Maker*, the number one ebook and audio-book bestseller *Away with the Penguins* and its follow-up, *Call of the Penguins*. *Gone with the Penguins* is her fifth novel.

You can find Hazel on Twitter/X and Instagram @HazelPriorBooks

*Also by Hazel Prior*

Ellie and the Harp-Maker
Away with the Penguins
Call of the Penguins
Life and Otter Miracles